BITTER WATER

GORDON FERRIS

CORVUS

First published in Great Britain in 2012
by Corvus, an imprint of Atlantic Books Ltd.

9 8 7 6 5 4 3 2 1

A CIP catalogue record for this book is available from
the British Library.

ISBN: 978-0-85789-604-9 (Hardback)
ISBN: 978-0-85789-605-6 (Trade paperback)
ISBN: 978-0-85789-606-3 (eBook)

Printed in Great Britain by
TJ International Ltd, Padstow, Cornwall

Corvus
An imprint of Atlantic Books Ltd
Ormond House
26-27 Boswell Street
London WC1N 3JZ

www.corvus-books.co.uk

'Shall there be evil in a city, and the
Lord hath not done it?'

Amos 3:6

For Jenny Ferris
(1929–2011)

ONE

Bubonic plague starts with one flea bite. Spanish flu with one sneeze. Glasgow's outbreak of murder and mayhem began simply enough and, like a flea bite, hardly registered at the time. In a volatile city of hair-trigger egos one savage beating goes unnoticed, a single knife wound is nothing special. Fighting goes with the Celtic territory, runs with the Scottish grain, is indeed fuelled by the grain, distilled to 40 proof. These belligerent tendencies explain my countrymen's disproportionate occupation of war graves across the Empire.

So it's just as well Glasgow's a *northern* outpost of civilisation. The cold and damp keep tempers in check for much of the year. It's just too dispiriting to have a rammy in the rain. But even Glasgow knows the taste of summer. When the tarmac bubbles, and the tenement windows bounce back the light. When only the great green parks can absorb and dissipate the rays. When the women bare their legs and the men bow their bald pates to the frying sun. When lust boils up and tempers fray.

When suddenly, it's *bring out your dead . . .*

For the moment, in blithe ignorance, Glasgow was enjoying a hot July and I was enjoying Glasgow. It had been seven long years since I'd last stomped its checkerboard streets and bathed my ears in the tortured melodies of my countrymen. Six years of fighting across North Africa and Europe and one year trying to get over it.

What had I to show for it? They'd taken back the officer crowns and my life-and-death authority over a company of Seaforth Highlanders. A burden removed but my heart went with it. Now I queued with the housewives and the gap-toothed old fellas for a loaf of bread and a tin of Spam. I hated Spam. I had no more ration coupons than the wide-boy who'd spent the war dodging the call-up and pestering the lonely lassies. I had no wife to set my tea on the table or light the fire in the grate. I had no children to cuddle or skelp, read to or protect.

On the credit side, I had the clothes I stood up in – second-hand, having discarded my Burton's demob suit in the Firth of Clyde. Not a sartorial statement, merely a choice between wearing it or drowning. My officer's Omega had survived the dip as it had survived bombardments, desert dust and machine-gun vibrations. In a box in my digs, wrapped in a bit of velvet, lay the bronze stars of action in Africa, France and Germany. But they were common enough currency these days. Even the silver cross with its purple and white ribbon had little rarity value; not after Normandy.

I had a degree in languages; my French now sprinkled with the accents and oaths of the folk whose homes we razed in our liberation blitzkrieg; my German salted with the vocab-ulary of the tormented and the tormentors in the concentration camps I'd worked in after VE Day last year.

Outweighing all the negatives, I had a job. Not any old job. The job I was meant for after too many years of detours through academia and law enforcement. I was the newest and no doubt worst-paid journalist on the *Glasgow Gazette, the voice of the people, by the people, for the people.* Under-study and cup-bearer to Wullie McAllister, Chief Crime Reporter. The stories I'd fed him back in April about the wrongful hanging of my old pal Hugh Donovan had given him a spectacular series of scoops which had axed the inglo-rious careers of several prominent policemen. In return, when I came looking for a job on the *Gazette*, he'd opened

2

doors for me. Mostly saloon doors, but that was part and parcel of the job.

It was another man's death that called me to witness this morning. Big Eddie Paton, my editor, scuttled up to my desk in the far corner of the newsroom.

'Get your hat, Brodie. McAllister's no' around. They've found a body. *Foul play*. Go take a look and bring me back a' the details . . .'

Big Eddie rolled the words 'foul play' over his tongue as though he was savouring a single malt. I'd only been on the job a fortnight but I knew that when he said 'details' he meant as grisly as possible. Yet I liked Eddie. Beneath his rants and rages he was a newspaperman right down to the ink in his varicose veins. He could turn a run-of-the-mill tale of council overspend into a blood-boiling account of official corruption and incompetence.

The 'big' in front of Eddie was of course ironic. If you put a ruler alongside Big Eddie toe to top, you'd run out of Eddie about the 5' 2" mark. He earned his name from his girth. And his mouth. His office attire was braces, tartan waistcoat and armbands. He was fast on his feet and could materialise by your desk like a genie, fat hands tucked into his waistcoat pockets or fingering his pocket watch. Time was always running out for Eddie.

'How did you hear?'

Eddie tapped his pug nose. 'Ah'm surprised at you, Brodie. One of your ex-comrades tipped us the wink.'

In my time in the police I'd been aware of a cosy arrangement between a few of my fellow coppers and the press. For a couple of quid they'd make a call to an editor to leak some newsworthy bit of criminality, such as a prominent citizen being arrested for drunken or obscene behaviour. I'd tried to stamp it out, but now I was on the other side, my scruples seemed a wee bit quaint. It could be seen as a useful public service. Is that what six years of war does to you? You lose your moral footing?

I assumed Eddie's instruction about my hat was figurative. It was broiling outside. I'd have left my jacket too if I'd had more confidence in the office protocol for greeting the dead. I grabbed my notebook and a couple of sharp pencils and set off into the sweltering streets of Glasgow. I hopped on a tram on Union Street and got off down by the dockside at the Broomielaw. I walked past the shuttered faces of corrugated iron and wood till I spotted the police car parked askew outside a shattered goods shed. The warehouse had taken a pasting in the blitz of '41, and Glasgow weather and hooligans had been putting the boot in ever since. The big sliding door was jammed open with rust and distortion. There was a gap wide enough to slide through into a great echoing furnace. And there was a stench.

On the far side, in a shaft of sunlight slicing through the torn roof, stood a clutch of mourners. Two uniformed policemen and one civvie, presumably a detective, but all with their jackets over their arms and braces on show. They were gazing at a long pale lump that lay between their feet. They were arguing.

'Should we no' wait for the doctor, sir? And the forensics?' said a uniform. His pale young face and the sergeant's stripes on his jacket glowed white in the gloom.

The detective bristled. 'And what's that gonna tell us? That he's deid? Ah can see he's deid. Would you no' be deid if you'd had that done to you? Ah just want to know *who* he is!'

I walked nearer and could see the dilemma. It was a body all right. A man's. Podgy with skinny white legs. Shockingly naked apart from a pair of fouled pants. His mother would have ticked him off. His hands were tied behind him and his feet strapped together, with his own belt. But no matter where you looked, your eyes were always dragged back to the head. Or where the head should be. For the moment it was merely a presumption. It reminded me of a curious kid at the infirmary with its head stuck in a pot. To see if it would fit. But this very dead man-child had chosen a bucket. A grey knobbly bucket.

4

As I joined the crowd the officers turned their eyes to me. The impatient one snapped: 'Who the fuck are you?'

'Brodie. From the *Gazette*.' Our eyes met in a spark of mutual recognition. And dislike. His name would come to me.

'Brodie, is it? Aye well, here's something to wake up your readers, Brodie.'

'Who is it?' Then I realised what a stupid question that was. 'I mean any identification? Anyone reported missing?'

I cast my eyes around the shadows looking for a pile of clothes. There was just a shovel and a small mound of grey. The sergeant cut in: 'We're just waiting for the man wi' the X-ray machine to come by.'

That earned some guffaws. The detective tried to trump the witticism.

'Are you like this on Christmas Day, Brodie? Desperate to open your presents?'

Now I could see properly. The body wasn't *wearing* a bucket. He was wearing the contents of the bucket. I could also see the long rope trailing away from his ankle strap. I looked up. Sure enough there was a beam above us. I guessed this poor sod had been hung upside down by his ankles and then lowered until his head was fully in the bucket. Then they would have poured in the concrete. Whoever did it must have waited patiently until it set, and hauled the dead man up a couple of feet to get the bucket off. Prudence? Meanness – was it their only coal scuttle? Or to remove all evidence? Then why dump the shovel? Maybe it was as simple as wanting to leave as brutal a message as possible. This man had to be silenced and that's what they'd done. I shuddered at the horror of his last moments.

I glanced again at the detective: rheumy-eyed and mean-mouthed, long broken-veined nose. Hat pushed back on his head. The name came back. Sangster. Detective Inspector Walter Sangster. I'd run into Sangster before the war when I was a sergeant with the Tobago Street detectives. By reputation he was volatile, someone with a short temper and an even shorter concentration span. I had taken an instant dislike to him in '37 and found no reason to change my mind on renewing our acquaintance today.

Sangster turned to his fresh-faced sergeant, whose forehead was sheened in sweat. 'Get me something heavy.'

The sergeant flicked his head at his even younger constable. The lad handed his uniform jacket to his sergeant and set off into the piles of rubble. He eventually came back with a silly grin and a torn strip of steel girder.

Sangster sized it up. 'What are you waiting for, man? Hit it!'

The constable raised the girder in both hands and swung it at the dead man's thick head. A lump of concrete broke off. Encouraged, the young officer swung again and more cracks appeared.

'Go canny, now. Don't smash the face up or we're back to square one.'

The officer began delicately jabbing at his target using the steel like a spear. Suddenly the bucket-shaped lump broke in two. Too much sand in the mix. The constable used his boot to push aside the two halves of the concrete death mask and revealed the face itself. The tortured skin was bleached and burned by the lime. The nose and cheekbones were blue where the sadists had beaten him before drowning him in cement. His last moments had contorted his face in terror and anguish.

'Jesus Christ!'

'In the name of the wee man!'

'You ken who *that* is?'

I'd been otherwise engaged for the last seven years, so I asked the dumb question. 'Who?'

Sangster curled his lips. 'Ah thought you were a reporter? Do you no' recognise Councillor Alec Morton?'

I stared down at the man. He looked worse with a name. My spirit revolted at this latest addition to my mental gallery of violent deaths. Was there no end to it? Then, behind us, came steps and a familiar cigarette- and booze-roughened rasp.

'Did I hear you right, Chief Inspector?' he called out.

I turned to see Wullie McAllister, doyen of crime reporting at the *Gazette*, strolling towards us. He was able to pose his question despite the fag jammed in the corner of his mouth. He had his jacket slung over his shoulder and his sleeves rolled up. His thin scalp shone in the greasy light. The years of mutton pies and booze had not been kind, nor had his choice of profession. He would be lucky to draw his pension for a year beyond retirement. Glasgow statistics were against him, against all of us. Was he my ghost of years to come?

I assumed Wullie's query was aimed at Sangster. Seems Sangster had taken advantage of the war to get himself promoted.

Sangster turned to me. 'The organ grinder's arrived. You don't have to rack your brains coming up wi' penetrating questions any more, eh, Brodie?' The remark garnered some sycophantic chuckles from his cronies.

'Your sense of humour hasn't kept up with your promotions, Sangster.'

I had the satisfaction of wiping the grin off his sallow face.

Wullie got between us. 'I see you two are getting on like a hoose on fire.' Then he saw what – who – lay at our feet.

'Alas, pair Alec! I knew him, Brodie: a fellow of infinite jest, who liked his pint. That's an awfu' way to go.'

Wullie and I didn't stay long. No one knew anything. No one had any idea why Morton had been murdered, far less why it had been so brutal. Sangster had run out of sarcasm. We left them to ruminate and walked out into the blinding light.

'You knew Sangster, then?' he asked me.

'I knew *of* him. Saw him about. But never had the pleasure of working with him.'

'He's a hard bastard, but fairly clean. Relatively speaking, of course. Not the sharpest truncheon on the beat. More low cunning than great deductive brain. Watch your back, Brodie.'

TWO

Wullie let me try my hand at writing up the story. Though, truth to tell, apart from the gory details, all we had was speculation. The gore was enough for Big Eddie. Though many's the voter might have cursed their representative by inviting them to *go stick yer heid in a bucket*, it would still be a shock to read about the gruesome reality of it over the toast and jam in the morning. Next day I had the dubious delight of seeing my words – most of them, and not necessarily in the order I'd submitted – appearing in bold print on the front page of the *Gazette*. A fortnight on the job and making headlines. That's not to say Wullie was yet ready to share the credits with me. *Your time will come, Brodie, soon enough.*

As to the crime itself, the police remained at a loss, despite blustering statements from the Chief Constable's office. Alec Morton had gone missing the night before. His panicking wife had phoned in about eleven o'clock, long after the pubs had closed. The search had commenced properly this morning at first light, but it had been a bunch of wee boys playing in the ruins that had found the murdered councillor suspended from the beam. They'd gone screaming to their mammies, who'd raised the alarm. And someone within the central nick at Turnbull Street had passed the word to Big Eddie.

There were no obvious clues about Morton's private or public life that might have earned him such a miserable death. But Wullie seemed more than a little excited. I was beginning to find that murders always raised his pulse.

'Ah'm no' saying anything just for the moment, Brodie. But there's a smell here. A stink. Something big is under way and I will pursue it!

'Bigger than murder? What was Morton's role on the council?'

'*Finance*,' said Wullie, caressing the word like a pair of silk stockings. 'He was head of the Finance Committee.'

'How do we follow this up? Do you want me to have a go at the police? See if any of my old pals are around and want to talk?'

'Aye, you can do that, Brodie. But I think you and me need to interview a couple of Morton's fellow councillors. I'll set it up. It's time you got your hands dirty.'

I made a few calls to Central Division, where I assumed Sangster was based. But I ran into either a blank wall of ignorance or deliberate obtuseness. My name and my time on the force before the war meant nothing to anyone I talked to. Or maybe it did? Nobody wanted to comment on a hot potato like the savage murder of a prominent official. I got some mawkish guff from the Provost's office about it being a terrible tragedy and how Mr Morton was irreplaceable. But nothing that gave any insight into who or why.

I left the newsroom just after six. I had a clear evening, no plans or commitments, the sun was shining, and I felt I'd earned a pint. Or two. As I walked down the narrow slice of Mitchell Lane I became aware of footsteps quickly gaining on me. I glanced back. A tall gangling man was striding towards me. The gap was about twenty yards and closing. His head was up and he was staring straight at me, an intent look on his face, as though he held a knife and had just decided to use it. On me.

I walked another couple of steps, then stopped, turned and faced him full on. Automatically I found myself crouching slightly and moving on to the balls of my feet. The man came on, his face alight. When he was about ten feet away he

9

stopped dead and stared at me with blue unflinching eyes, the hue accentuated by the shock of red hair.

'Mr Brodie.' It wasn't a question. He knew who I was.

'What do you want?'

'Talk. I need to talk. I *have* to talk.'

There was the lilt of the North in his voice. A Highlander. And therefore referred to contemptuously by all we Lowlanders as a Teuchter. I once looked it up in the university library. Probably from the Gaelic: *peasant* or *drink*. It was in retaliation to Highlanders calling us Sassenachs, *Saxons*.

I sized him up and down. About my height but thin to the point of emaciation, though there was a hint of wiry strength. I thought I could take him. Unless he had that knife and knew how to use it. The face was all bones and angles, the eyes unslept and fevered. Despite the heat he wore leather gloves and a faded ex-army pullover. His trousers had perfect creases but they ran down into frayed cuffs. If this had been a dog I'd have diagnosed rabies. And run for my life.

'So, talk. What do you want?'

'Not here. I need help. We need help. We *must* have help.' His voice was rising.

'If it's money, I could give you a couple of bob.'

He shook his head. Annoyed. Affronted even. He took a deep breath. 'I read about you. You and your lawyer woman, Campbell. You tried to save your pal from a hanging.'

His words stung. It had been over three months ago, in all the papers, but people kept bringing it up. I'd been quietly pulling my life together in London, easing up on the booze, making some inroads into a new career as a freelance journalist when I was summoned north by advocate Samantha Campbell to try to save the life of a man on HMP Barlinnie's death row. Not just any man, my boyhood pal, Hugh Donovan. We failed. But Sam and I had the bitter satisfaction of proving they'd hanged an innocent man. The coppers had framed Hugh for murder. He'd died on the gallows because it was easier to blame him than do some proper police work.

'What about it?'

'I've got a pal. A good soldier. We served together. He's in trouble. Can. We. Talk?'

I had a choice. I could turn and walk away and have him jump me. Or I could knock him down and then run for it.

'Can we talk, *Major*?'

That got my attention. The press had mentioned my old army rank but only in passing. Someone had paid attention.

'Not here.' The smell of piss wafted at us down this dark tunnel between the lowering buildings.

He straightened. 'First pub? I'll buy.'

'OK, pal, here's how it works. You're going to stand there until I've walked ten paces, then you follow, keeping that distance. Fair?'

He nodded. 'Fair.'

I started to back away and when I was two or three steps distant I turned and walked on, trying not to run, trying not to squeeze my back muscles which were tensing in anticipation of the thrown blade. Or bullet. I counted to ten and heard him start. His pace matched mine and we emerged into Buchanan Street. I crossed over, sidestepping the buses, and slid into McCormick Lane. You're never more than a thrown bottle from a pub in Glasgow. It was a rough dive but this didn't feel like a social occasion. Besides, I still had my thirst. I pushed through the doors and went to the bar.

'Two pints of heavy please.'

I heard the door behind me swing and clunk into its frame. He materialised by my side.

'I will get these,' came the soft, correct lilt. A reminder of some of the men under me in the Seaforths. He was beside me, staring at the barman whose eyes flinched first. From the Highlander's worn clothes and wild manner I expected him to smell. Just another demobbed soldier prowling the dark lanes and sleeping rough. He didn't. A small personal triumph, at some cost, I imagine. He was freshly shaven, the nick on the jaw a recent encounter with a blade. Between gloved finger

11

and thumb he held out half a crown for inspection. The barman took it, hit the till and dropped the eight pence change back in the Highlander's still outstretched hand. He clenched his hand round the coins, opened it and counted the money. I almost said, I'll get them. But he'd forced this meeting.

I looked round the pub. Décor: functional brown. Sawdust: fresh. Clientele: seasoned drinkers and domino champions. Atmosphere: growing fug.

'Over there,' I said and nodded to a dark corner table. We sat. I supped my beer and took out my fags. 'You've bought yourself five minutes,' I said. 'Let's start with your name. You seem to know mine well enough.'

A twitch ran across his fleshy lips, as though he was stifling a grin.

'Call me Ishmael.'

I snorted. It was as good a *nom de guerre* as any, and showed some wit.

'Son of Abraham or hunter of whales?'

'We're all sons of Abraham,' he said with a serious shake of his head. 'It's my friend I want to talk about.'

'I'm listening, *Ishmael*.'

He began. 'One of my pals is in trouble. Johnson. He was caught stealing. He broke into one of those fine terraced places looking for money or something to sell and they set a bloody Alsatian on him. Ripped his arm and face and kept him there till the police came.'

I shrugged. 'Bad luck for your pal Johnson. But good luck for the owner of the house, I'd say.'

Ishmael's eyes tightened. The muscles on his jaw bulged. 'Aye, I suppose it is to you. But here's the thing. The man was starving. He fought for king and country and now he doesn't even have a roof over his head. Nor a penny in his pocket. Nor a bit of bread in his mouth.'

I felt a twinge of shame. It was an everyday story. Men like Ishmael and his pal Johnson helped win the war a year ago and came home to . . . nothing. No job. No family. No future. I'd been only a hair's breadth away.

'I'm sorry to hear that, but he broke the law.'

'That or starve!'

'We have soup kitchens! Others manage. It's rotten out there, but we need rules or it's chaos.'

His eyes grew cunning. 'Rules? Is that what *you* played by? If you'd followed the rules back in April would the police have been shown up for what they are? This city is corrupt.' He relished the word. 'The only way to get justice is to take it yourself.'

He had a point. And he didn't know the half of it.

'What do you want from me?'

'I want you to ask your fine lawyer lady friend if she'll defend Johnson. He's in Turnbull Street. He'll be in the Sheriff Court on Friday. He's facing years inside.'

'But he'll have a defence lawyer. The court will have appointed one if he's got no money.'

'Their man is a charlatan. He spent ten minutes with Johnson and the useless solicitor. As far as the advocate's concerned it's open and shut. He'll take his pieces of silver, say a few pious words and wave my friend farewell as they cart him off to Barlinnie. We need *help*!'

I thought about what he was asking me. Thought about Samantha Campbell. And wondered if she'd even take my call, far less take on a case for a mad stranger whose pal, by the sound of it, didn't stand a chance. Three months back, in the traumatic finale to our search for justice for Hugh Donovan, I thought Sam and I might – quite literally – sail off into the sunset together in our commandeered yacht. Sam's ill health threw a dose of cold common sense over me. Then, amidst the subsequent and seemingly endless police inquisitions and newspaper frenzy, we decided – well, *she* decided – we needed some distance and time apart to see how we felt. In short she threw me out. We hadn't spoken in a fortnight.

I studied his clenched jaw and his red eyes. 'Give me one good reason why I should.'

His voice dropped to whisper. 'Because you owe him.'

'I've never met the man!'

He sighed. 'He says he'd heard of you. He was at Saint-Valery. In your old division. But *he* was *taken*. Five years as a prisoner of war. He's served enough time, don't you think, *Major*?'

The name – Saint-Valery-en-Caux – punched me in the midriff. Ten thousand men of the 51st Highland Division, *my* division, were trapped in that pretty little fishing village just along from Dunkirk in 1940. A few of us slunk away and made it back to England to fight again. Most didn't.

'Which regiment?'

'Black Watch.'

Not mine, but still. 'Poor bastard.'

'Will you help?' he asked again, this time knowing the answer.

I found a box and dialled her number. It was now six thirty. She should be home. When I heard her voice, I pushed button A and the coins clattered in.

'Sam? It's Brodie. How are you?'

There was a brief lull, then: 'I thought you were in the huff with me.'

Just like a woman. 'Me? You were the one who flung me out!'

'You walked out, Brodie. By mutual agreement.'

'Sam, I'd love to debate this with you some other time, but I have a favour to ask you.'

'You want a bit of red-hot gossip from the courts? An inside track on my latest case? Or you've got a poke of chips in your pocket and nobody to share it with?'

'Samantha Campbell, will you just listen for a minute?'

'I'm all ears.'

I told her about Johnson and the plea from his mad pal. Her response was an echo of mine.

'Give me one good reason why I should, Brodie.'

It was unfair. I'd prepared my line. 'Because we didn't save Hugh.'

The pause went on for long seconds. 'That's playing dirty, Brodie.'

'I know.'

'Right. If I'm doing this, you're involved too. Meet me at Turnbull Street with this mad Highlander of yours tomorrow at ten. Tell him he needs to bring Johnson's solicitor with him. And any paperwork.'

'Thanks, Sam, I'll . . .' but the line was already dead and the tuppence change was clattering in the box. I hadn't told her the mad Highlander's name in case she thought the whole thing was a prank. A ploy to get to see her again. I wasn't that desperate.

I looked through the pane. No ploy. Ishmael was standing staring at me about three feet away. I nodded. His shoulders went down.

I got to Turnbull Street just before ten. I was jittery. This was likely to be a meeting full of undercurrents and strained emotions. And that was without the presence of the accused man.

The Highlander was already there and haranguing a sweating man in a three-piece suit, presumably the court-appointed solicitor. The cornered man was clutching a battered briefcase to his chest for protection against the Highlander's jabbing finger. I caught the tail end of a diatribe about the unfairness of the law. About how the rich could buy their justice and the poor got shafted. I had some sympathy with that view but confined myself to simple introductions. The solicitor – Carmichael – clutched my hand as if I were his long-lost brother.

I heard heels clicking towards us and turned in time to greet Sam striding forward, ready for battle. Grey suit, glistening white blouse, black briefcase swinging by her side. Her ash-blonde hair combed and clamped to her head like a helmet. She jammed her glasses further up her nose to properly line us up in her sights. From ten feet away she was the dashing, top-flight advocate, completely in control. Up close, as she did the rounds of handshaking, I could see the lines round the eyes. Her make-up was thicker than I recalled it, the cheekbones pronounced.

She got to me last and held my hand and eyes for a brief second longer than the others.

'Hello, Mr Brodie. I trust you're well?'

'I'm fine, thank you, Miss Campbell. Thank you for getting involved.'

'I'm not involved yet. Mr Johnson and Mr Carmichael need to appoint me. And I need to square it with the court-appointed advocate.'

The sweating solicitor jumped in. 'Oh, I'm sure that will be no problem, Miss Campbell. I had the honour of working with your father when he was Procurator Fiscal.'

'That was a while ago, Mr Carmichael.'

'Nigh on twenty years. I was—'

'This is all verra cosy. But my friend is in court in two days.'

Sam turned to the Highlander. Through her eyes I saw an unexploded bomb with a hair-trigger fuse.

'This is . . . *Ishmael*,' I said.

She blinked at me, but then smiled at him. 'Mr Ishmael, is it? I agree. Let's cut the pleasantries. If Mr Carmichael will allow me, we'll go and have a wee chat with your friend.'

She called me later at the newsroom and asked to meet me at George Square. It was past lunchtime and the secretaries and other office workers had reluctantly dragged themselves inside away from the blessed sunshine. We found a bench.

'It's good to see you, Sam. You're looking well.'

'Am I?' She took off her specs and rubbed at the bridge of her nose. 'God knows why.'

I studied her profile. In the harsh light, the dark shadows under the eyes were visible. The lines round the mouth sharper. She turned to me.

'What do you see, Brodie? An old woman, past her best?'

'It works for me, Sam,' I said gently. She turned her head away and slid her glasses back on.

'I'm just tired. Always tired these days, Brodie.'

'What you went through . . .'

'It's been three months! It's time I sorted myself out!'

I let her settle. 'What about Johnson?'

'He's for the high jump.'

'Tell me.'

'Caught *in flagrante*. Poor bugger is skin and bone. And stitches. That bloody Alsatian fair chewed him up.'

'Any previous?'

'No. First offence. Well, first time he's been caught.'

'So he might get off with six months?'

She shook her head. 'He killed the dog.'

'Self-defence, surely?'

'With a gun.'

'Idiot!'

'So he's on trial under Solemn Procedure in the Sheriff Court.'

'Remind me?'

'It's for serious offences. Jury and judge. He could get five years.'

'Ouch.'

'If he's lucky. The judge might want to kick it upstairs to the High Court to give him a longer sentence.'

'God, why? Don't tell me he raped the wife?'

'Not quite. But he chose the wrong house to break into.'

'Who's?'

'Mairi Baird's.'

I shrugged.

'Maiden name McCulloch. Sister of Malcolm McCulloch.'

'The Chief Constable? She wants his head.'

'On a silver platter. With an apple in the mouth.'

'Are you taking the case?'

'Are you always going to be my conscience, Brodie?'

'You don't need me. Not for that anyway.'

She turned and looked at me, and smiled for the first time since I saw her this morning. 'I told your pal, Ishmael, I'd have a go, even though it's not looking good. Is that his real name or is he just a Melville fan?'

'Could be both. How did he take it?'

'He didn't fall to his knees in gratitude. Just nodded, as though it was my duty. He seems to know about police work.'

'Did you tell him about the special circumstances?'

She sighed. 'I mentioned that emotions might be running high among the upper layers of Glasgow society.'

'And?'

'He had a wee fit. I was glad Carmichael was with me. I got a lecture and a bit of scripture thrown at me.'

'What bit?'

'The old "vengeance is mine, saith the Lord" stuff. I don't think your pal is a' there, as they say.'

'I think *I'd* better be there on Friday when the verdict comes through.'

'Can you bring a big stick?'

We parted; this time she reached up and held my shoulders and I bent to get a peck on the cheek. I smelled her hot skin beneath the smudge of her perfume. I wanted to take her in my arms and hold her and tell her it would get better. Tell her that the trauma would pass. But she'd have pushed me away and accused me of being patronising. When all it was was caring.

I got back to my desk just in time for Wullie McAllister to grab me.

'C'mon, Brodie. We've got a date.'

'Who with?'

'James Sheridan, esquire. Glasgow councillor and

Chairman of the Planning Committee. Oor Jimmie has graciously agreed to give us an interview about the vile murder of his pal, Councillor Alec Morton.'

THREE

As we walked towards George Square and the council offices, Wullie reminded me about *oor Jimmie,* Man of the People, sometime philanderer and rabble-rouser. Not that I needed much reminding. Sheridan was one of the larger-than-life characters that Glasgow throws up from time to time whether it needs one or not. Cometh the hour, cometh the fast-talking populist. I watched his rise before the war, continually surprised by voters' forbearance. They were smitten by his rhetoric and tolerant of his amorous escapades. *That's just oor Jimmie* was the forgiving response to the latest impropriety.

'You ken oor Jimmie has a certain reputation with the lasses?'

'Anything that had a skirt?'

'And watch your sporran if you're in the Gordon High-landers. The man was – is – a serial and indiscriminate shagger.' He made it sound biblical.

'What does his wife say?'

'Elsie Sheridan is as loyal as a collie dug. She's from the Gorbals. Jimmie was her escape route.'

It was coming back to me. Jimmie had the standard credentials for achieving high office and fame in the West of Scotland: a silver tongue, time served in the shipyards as a riveter and shop steward, and the backing of a left-wing 'workers' party. The Communists would do if you really wanted to brandish working-class credentials. Sheridan had all that and more; it was generally held that Jimmie had had his conscience and capacity for self-criticism thrown away with the afterbirth.

'Sheridan runs the Planning and Regeneration Committee. So Morton and him would have been hugger-mugger on the new big contracts. Morton had the money. Sheridan spent it. Oor Jimmie is the man who signs off everything and controls everything to do with what gets knocked doon, what gets built, where it gets built, and who wins the fat contracts to do it.'

'Corruption in high places?'

'No' very high, in fact. I've been getting hints for months that something was going on. This could be my finest hour, Brodie. Go oot with a bang, eh?'

The old devil was due for retirement in six months. A final scoop would set the seal on an illustrious career built on the great midden of crime and sleaze. And I would inherit his stained and greasy mantle. A fine prospect.

A flirty lady in high heels, tight skirt and low top showed us along the echoing corridors. She knocked on a door and we heard a 'come'.

She pushed open the door and said, 'The two gentlemen from the *Gazette*, Mr Sheridan. Would you be wanting some tea?'

'Aye, Nancy. With biscuits, eh? I think we can run to biscuits for these illustrious representatives of the Fourth Estate. Show the gentlemen in.'

Nancy pushed the door open and Wullie sidled in. I squeezed past Nancy and was given a big smile as I tried to avoid plunging my head into her proffered, scented bosom. Drawn in like a honey bee.

The man of the people was coming round from behind his huge wooden desk, his hand outstretched.

'Terrible times we live in, Wullie. Just terrible.'

'They are indeed, Jimmie.' They shook hands like blood

brothers. 'This is my number two, Douglas Brodie. He'll be taking over from me in due course. When I hang up my quill. I wanted him to meet you.'

'Mr Brodie, it's a pleasure. Though I could have wished we'd met in better circumstances.'

Apart from the Glasgow brogue, Jimmie Sheridan reminded me instantly of his namesake Cagney. Short but bouncy. The same quiff of hair and sharply drawn eyebrows. Thin lips and strong jaw line. Blue penetrating eyes that sized you up and said, *I'm maybe short but I could still steal your woman and bite your head off . . . don't cross me, pal.* The double-breasted suit was of far better cloth and cut than my own drab threads. 'Dapper' summed him up. 'Debonair' even. Close up, I could see the glory was fading, and that the hair was a shade too dark to be Jimmie's original. Nonetheless, I could see how he'd got into lady trouble so often.

Sheridan retired behind his desk and sat down. We took the seats in front of him. Sheridan suddenly seemed six inches taller. Cushion or high chair? I took out my notebook and pencil and hoped my struggling shorthand would cope.

'You must have been gie shocked, Jimmie?' asked Wullie.

'I tell you this, Ah broke doon. I'm not ashamed to say it. Ah just couldnae stop greeting. Alec and I go way back. Shop stewards thegither at Browns'.'

'We've heard nothing from the polis. Any word from your side about the investigation?'

'Nothing at a'. A complete shock. Like we've been hit by a thunderbolt.'

'Any ideas on why someone would do such a terrible thing?'

The answer was interrupted by a rattle of china. Nancy waltzed in with a tray bearing a small pile of biscuits, cups and a teapot, all nestling under her bosom to keep the tea warm. She made a fuss of pouring and handing the cups round, making sure we had a glimpse of cleavage and rear in the process. After she left, the conversation stayed stalled until her perfume dispersed and we regained our senses. Wullie was first to recover.

'I was asking if you had any ideas about *why*?'

Sheridan shook his head. 'Not a clue.'

'Anything in his personal life?'

Sheridan sat back and reached for his cigarettes. He visibly bristled. 'Like whit? Ah mean whit are you saying, Wullie? That he was up to something nefarious like gamblin' or some-thin'? That's no' Alec Morton.'

'I'm not making accusations, Jimmie. Just looking for a reason here. Somebody had it in for Morton. Unless you think it was mistaken identity? Or a random bout of sadism?'

'Ah can see that. It's just that Ah know Alec. He's as clean as a whistle.'

'He was chairman of the Finance Committee?'

'So what?'

'A lot of big deals going through his committee and yours.'

It was like a switch had been thrown. Sheridan burst into life.

'This city is in ruins. Folk are living in slums. Working people are living in squalor. It's not good enough. It is our duty to rebuild. Alec Morton and I saw it as our sacred duty to reclaim Glasgow for its citizens. Let Glasgow flourish!'

He all but climbed on to the desk as his voice and rhetoric went higher.

'Och, save us your soapbox, Jimmie. But you know as well as me that in the long history of public works in Scotland there are always folk out there with their hands oot. There are brown envelopes being slipped into back pockets. There are chancers who—'

'What are you saying, McAllister? What are you accusing Alec Morton of doing? The man is barely deid and already you're tarnishing his name! Muck-raking!'

I decided to halt the righteous rant.

'Wullie isn't accusing anyone of anything, Mr Sheridan. This is a terrible crime, and we're as much in the dark as you are. We're trying to find a motive, and either Mr Morton was cruelly murdered for personal reasons or for professional reasons. Perhaps he stood in the way of someone? Perhaps his very integrity, his unswerving sense of public duty was the reason he was murdered?'

Wullie was looking at me with raised eyebrows, Sheridan with suspicion. Then he started to nod.

'Aye, could be, could be. That would fit with Alec Morton. Is that what you'll write – Brodie, was it?'

'We'd like to. We just need your help. Let me ask a particular question.'

'Fire away.'

'What's the biggest project currently before your Planning Committee?'

The look of suspicion was back. 'Ah'm no' sure where you're going with this. But everybody kens we've got the Bruce plan under review.'

'I've been away, Mr Sheridan. The war and all that. Can you sum it up for me?'

'In a word, *visionary*! We're going to turn this city into a working man's paradise. We'll clear the tenement slums and build modern apartments. Like the French. They'll have inside toilets and bathrooms. Every one! There will be areas set aside for industry and business, and great parks for the workers. Regeneration, Brodie! That's what we're doing.'

I could see how he could sway the masses. But then so could Adolf.

'It sounds like a huge job, Mr Sheridan.'

'It's Jimmie.'

'A huge project, Jimmie. What will it cost?'

A crafty look flitted over his face. 'The budget isnae set yet. But in truth, Brodie, there is no choice. We have to do this. For the people!'

'Have you signed any of the contracts, yet, Jimmie?'

He drew himself up in his chair. 'Look, boys, this isnae the time to be talking about paperwork and such stuff. A man died yesterday. A good friend of mine. Ah don't feel like pursuing this line of questioning just at the moment. I'm sure you'll understand . . .'

Nancy was summoned and Wullie and I were given the sweetest bum's rush ever. Out on the pavement we looked at each other.

'Nice try, Brodie, but he was never going to tell us anything.'

'So why did we bother?'

'To let him know we're here, laddie. And to get a column out of it.'

'Do you want me to have a go?'

'No, no. This one's mine. I just wanted to give you a bit of exposure to our political classes. For future use.'

I glanced at Wullie. He'd said it lightly but I could see he'd smelt something big and wanted it for himself. Hard to blame him. I asked, 'And this Bruce plan? I'd heard the name. Saw something about it in the papers last year.'

'Robert Bruce, city engineer and master of works of this fair toon, came out with a plan last year. You'll have missed it, Brodie, being otherwise tied up gi'ing the Huns a bashing. In his dystopian vision, Bruce proposed to rip the guts out of the city centre and turn it into a wasteland of commerce. He wanted to knock down the likes of the School of Art, the City Chambers – maybe no' such a bad thing, as long as all the cooncillors are inside – and Central Station. In short, anything with style and grace had to go. And any citizens living in the centre to be cast into the wilderness of Castlemilk. Factories and office blocks to be installed in their place. Altars to Mammon.'

'I thought it had all been rejected.'

'It was. But Jimmie Sheridan's not the sort of man to take no for an answer, not when his livelihood's at stake. And I don't mean his council wage. Sheridan is going to push through Bruce's mad ideas by hook or by crook. Probably the latter.'

FOUR

I got to the imposing and colonnaded Sheriff Court in Brunswick Street just in time for Johnson's appearance. I took a pew at the back of the sparse public gallery. Ishmael was in the front row, gripping the wooden barrier. In front, to the right, in two tiered rows, were fifteen honest men and women, plucked from the streets to dispense justice to their fellow man.

The said man was brought in between two wardens. Ishmael sat up and almost rose to his feet. Johnson saw his pal and lifted his shoulders as if to say, *Here I am, what a carry-on.* His shirt was creased and dirty like his trousers. One arm was bandaged and in a sling. His face was stitched down one cheek. He had no belt so the trousers were falling from his bony hips. An air of defeat made his pale face sag. A wretch and a ruffian if ever you saw one. Guilty of something, surely.

Advocate Samantha Campbell was already in place next to the Procurator Fiscal's man. She stood up, looking distant and untouchable in her robes and wig. She nodded at Johnson, who tried a half-smile. Then the usher was calling order and the Sheriff was entering, in all his majesty. The whole court got to its feet, and the trial began.

The prosecutor had it easy and laid it on thick. Jobless ruffian . . . no fixed abode . . . raiding an honest citizen's house . . . brave dog killed defending its master . . . could have been its owner. The jury were loving this. It pandered to every one of their darkest prejudices and fears. There was nodding when he talked about sending a message . . . teaching this man a lesson . . . telling others that this is what they'd get. I swear he was looking for applause at the end of his attack.

Johnson made it simple for him. Though Sam had entered a plea of not guilty, Johnson was easily led into confessions, any one of which would get him sent on to the High Court for proper remedy. Mrs Baird, nee McCulloch, played her part as the honest and injured householder. She might as well have worn a veil and dressed in black. She dabbed a pure white hankie at her delicate wee nose to choke back the tears of remembered horror and terror. Mention was made of her relationship with the Chief Constable and a clear and sympathetic tsk tsk scampered round the court.

By the time she'd finished, the judge had already written his verdict and was reaching for the black cap. It was all over bar the jury vote. Then Sam had her go.

'Mr Johnson? In fact it was Sergeant Alan Johnson of the Black Watch, wasn't it?'

Johnson's back straightened. His head came up. 'It was, ma'am.'

'You were part of the valiant British Expeditionary Force that was captured in 1940 at Saint-Valery-en-Caux? The rest of the BEF got out at Dunkirk, but you and ten thousand other brave Scottish soldiers were taken into German prisoner-of-war camps for the duration?'

'Yes, ma'am. It wisnae oor fau't, ye ken. It was the French. They surrendered.'

I saw a rustle among the jury. Faces took on frowns. Bloody Frogs.

The prosecutor popped up. 'My lord, I'm sure we don't need a history lesson?'

Sam countered. 'This is pertinent, my lord, as to motivation.'

The Sheriff looked sceptical. 'See that it is, Miss Campbell.'

'Sergeant Johnson, you were liberated and flown home a year ago. What has happened to you since?'

Johnson looked distressed. 'Nothin'.'

'Nothing? Did you try to get a job?'

He snorted. 'Of course Ah did. Ah'm no' a sponger. But there was nothin'. The yards are no' up and running yet. Ah've been down to the brew a hunner times, so Ah have, looking for work.'

'Where do you live?'

'Here and there.'

'No home to come back to?'

He squared his shoulders. 'No, ma'am.'

'Why? You had a home before you joined up?'

'Aye, and a wife.'

'What happened, Sergeant Johnson?'

The prosecutor was back on his feet. 'With due respect, my lord, the defendant is no longer a sergeant.'

'I think we can extend the man some respect for his war service.'

Sam gave a little smile to the jury. 'Thank you, my lord. *Sergeant* Johnson . . .?'

'Ah came hame. She had a fancy man in ma place. And a wean.'

This time I heard intakes of breath and the word 'shame'.

'So you're living rough? Why did you break into this house?'

'Ah was hungry.'

'What were you trying to steal?'

'Food. Or if I couldnae find food, maybe something to flog for food.'

'Sergeant Johnson, why did the dog attack you?

His face screwed up. 'Ah suppose it was angry.'

'Why was it angry?'

His head dropped. 'Ah don't know,' he mumbled.

'Sergeant Johnson, why was the dog angry?'

There was a long pause, then his head came up. 'Ah stole its food.'

Hands were at mouths among the jury now. Sam pressed her advantage.

'But you shot the dog.'

'No really.'

'What do you mean, *not really*? Either you shot the dog or you didn't?'

'The gun. It was just a starting pistol. Nae bullets in it.'

'But the dog died?'

'It was an auld dug. A *fat* dug. Maybe it had a heart attack.'

A giggle broke out, from relief more than anything.

The jury was back in an hour. There was no way Johnson could be found innocent of the attempted burglary. But he won a 'not proven' on the armed burglary.

The Sheriff looked disappointed at not being able to send Johnson on to the High Court. But he knew the case didn't stack up high enough. He made the best of it: 'I sentence you, Alan Johnson, to five years at His Majesty's pleasure. Take him away.'

In front of me, Ishmael shot to his feet. 'Nooo! This is not justice! This cannot stand!'

Johnson swayed and called to his pal, 'I cannae dae this. I cannae face this again! I swear to God, I cannae take it! No' again!'

Hands dropped among the jury. They couldn't look at each other. One woman was in tears and shaking her head. The judge stood.

'Take him down, and clear the court! Any more outbreaks from you, sir, and you will be joining your friend here!' He aimed his finger directly at Ishmael. Ushers leaped in at the sound of raised voices. Two burly men pinioned Ishmael till the judge had left the court.

I got out as quickly as I could and into the corridor. I was just in time. Ishmael was being escorted past me in the clutch of the two big men. He was no longer struggling. His face was set. Tears were pouring down the bones and channels of his face. He caught sight of me and stopped. The ushers tugged at him but his wiry determination held them in check for long enough. His red eyes fixed on mine.

'It's the same crew, Brodie. The same dirty crew that did for *your* pal! The same rotten system. This is justice?' He spat on the flagstones. 'I'm damned if it is!'

'I'm sorry! It could have been worse.'

'How could it have been worse?' he spat. 'Five years? Five months will be enough to kill that man!' His voice dropped and he leaned towards me. 'A good man goes down. And all the time, the rapists and thieves, the gangsters and drug runners get away with it. It willnae do, Brodie. It willnae do. You of all folk must see that. So help me God, I will show this twice-damned city what true justice is!'

Me of all folk? Had the April newspapers painted me as some kind of flag-waver for the common man against an unfair justice system? I suppose so. But that was a one-off. There would be no more taking up of arms against a sea of troubles by yours truly.

As for Ishmael's oath, with hindsight it wasn't so much a warning as a prophecy. And in the event it didn't take five years or months. It took five days for retribution to begin.

FIVE

But first there came a more distant rumble of *national* retribution. The news started filtering through on Monday that a bomb had gone off in Jerusalem. By the afternoon the numbers of British dead were mounting. Some ninety staff of the British Mandate based in the King David Hotel died in the callous attack by Zionist terrorists. The *Gazette*'s front page was taken up for the rest of the week with photos and outrage.

It meant that the news about one man's death in Barlinnie Prison barely registered. Had we known what it heralded we might have given it more attention. The grapevine in the form of Big Eddie coughed up the news on Wednesday morning. Eddie crept up on me at my desk. There was none of his normal bounce. By Eddie's standards he was almost tentative.

'That fella that got sent down? The one your girlfriend defended?'

'She's not my girlfriend. Johnson? What about him?'

'Found dead in his cell this morning. Hanged.'

It shocked me like a cold shower. 'Shit!'

'Aye, it is. Suicide. Used a sheet from the top bunk.'

I shook my head. 'I never thought he meant it.'

'What?'

'That he couldn't face it. Couldn't face another prison.'

Eddie was watching my face. 'Do you want someone else to write it?'

'No. I owe him that.'

I wrote the story of how Sergeant Alan Johnson, formerly of the Black Watch, hanged himself in Barlinnie Prison just five days into his sentence. And how society had failed the man. How we'd demanded too much of him and those like him. Was that a personal plea? Then I called Sam. She'd already heard. Her voice was dull.

'I'm not covering myself in glory these days, am I, Brodie?'

'Sam, if it wasn't for you, he'd have got *ten* years! You were brilliant!'

'Five, ten? What does it matter? He went down. Now he's dead.'

We hung up, each in our way clinging to the rational argument that we'd done the best we could, but each troubled by guilt. We hadn't imagined he was serious. It was a lesson I was slow to learn; I'd forgotten about Ishmael's oath. The first hint came on the Sabbath.

It was work that got me up bright and early on this Sunday morning and out the door. Not for the kirk: God had mislaid me, or maybe it was the other way about. Anyway, we weren't on speaking terms. I was off to the hospital, as was my habit these past three weeks. It was McAllister's idea, a routine he'd followed for years and which had led to a number of roaring pieces in the *Gazette* on a Monday morning. Not that he was now having a lie-in. Wullie had his pick of hospitals and access to the sergeant's desk of most of the central nicks. Spoiled for choice.

I didn't mind on a morning like this. The day was crisp and sweetened by the westerly blowing up the Clyde. I left my digs in Dennistoun whistling 'Stardust'. Tommy Dorsey had just been belting it out on the wireless. I decided to walk along Duke Street and then up the hill to the infirmary. I was in shirtsleeves and feeling virtuous, my head as clear as the sky. Instead of the usual pain between the eyes and churning stomach – no wonder we called the beer *heavy* – I'd gone to the pictures with Morag Duffy, a lassie from the typing pool. Nothing serious, just a pleasant evening with a bonnie smiling girl with red curls and a cheeky swing of the hips. I'd walked Morag home, stolen a kiss or three in her tenement close and fallen into my own cold bed, alone and sober as a Salvation Army major. It did me good. I should do it more often. Except for the cold lone bed. And except for the teensiest tug of guilt, as though I was being unfaithful. Which was ridiculous given how things stood with Samantha Campbell.

I strode up the now familiar hospital steps and headed down the shining brown lino floors towards the accident ward.

As I pushed at the ward door, the Sister slid out from under her stone.

'*Mister* Brodie.'

'Good morning, Sister. A fine morning it is.'

She lifted her bosoms up and aimed them at me. 'And who are you visiting this morning, *Mister* Brodie?'

She'd made it clear last week that she didn't like her sanctified ward being cluttered up with riffraff like journalists. Unless of course they'd earned bed and nursing by dint of an injury, preferably serious. At the same time she was a staunch reader of the *Gazette* and as glad as the next to see the sins of her more wayward patients exposed. Salutary reminders of what happens when you fall from grace.

'Think of me as a church visitor, Sister. Bringing solace and comfort to the sick and injured.'

She crossed her beefy arms and gave me the look that said *If ever you find yourself in my clutches, laddie, I'll give you solace all right.*

'You might see what comfort you can bring to Mr Docherty. Bed three on the left. Though whether he deserves it, I'll leave to you to decide,' she said meaningfully and stood aside.

*

Jimmie Docherty wasn't expecting a visitor. His dented face – duelling scars from a hundred pub fights – screwed up at the sight of me sitting down on the chair by his bed. He would have pushed me away if he could. Indeed, with his heavy physique, flung me across the ward. But the job is that much harder when both arms are in stookie up to the shoulder.

'How's it going, Jimmie?'

His eyes scuttled around the room. 'Aye fine. As ye can see. Who's askin'?'

'Brodie. From the *Gazette*. I'm the crime reporter.'

'Crime? Whit's that to dae with me?' he growled.

I wished I had a pound of butter to see what would happen if I shoved it into his innocent big gub. It wouldn't so much melt as steam. From the look of him, Docherty had been inside Barlinnie more times than its governor.

'Jimmie, it's Sunday morning. After Saturday night. The big night out for hard men in Glasgow. They get drunk, they fight, they end up here, and I come along and get some material for the first edition of the *Glasgow Gazette* on Monday morning.' I took my pencil out and pointed at his plastered hands and arms. There wasn't an inch of skin showing from fingertip to shoulder. 'What happened?' I held the pencil poised above a clean page in my notebook.

'Ah'm no' a clype!'

'I'm not asking you to tell me *who* did it. I just want to know *how* you managed to break both arms. In several places. That takes talent. Or extreme carelessness.'

'Ah fell.'

'Where from? Ben Nevis?'

Jimmie stared at me for a while, his cogs grinding away. Then he embarrassed himself and me by letting his piggy eyes fill.

'There was two of the bastards. Ah admit Ah'd had a few. Saturday night as you say. And Ah was kinda stottin' doon the road when they jumped me. Twa big fellas. Big as me. Wan grabbed ma heid. The other tied a rope roon ma wrists, then flung the rope up ower a lamppost. They strung me up,

34

so they did. A drunk man. That's no fair, neither it is.' His eyes moistened again at this failure to play by the street rules.

I pointed at the arms, queasily reluctant now to know the details.

'So how . . .?'

'They had a crowbar, so they did. Ah was on ma tiptoes, ma airms up in the air. And then they started bashin' them. Great big swings. Ah tell you they made me yelp. Ah was greetin' Ah don't mind telling you. Ah might have had a skinfu' but they bastards fair sobered me up. Ah could hear the bones going, so help me God.'

There was a sucking in of teeth from the beds on either side. I felt my own arms wince in sympathy. I've seen bad things, heard terrible tales, but rarely such cold-blooded brutality. Except in the camps, of course.

'Good God, Jimmie! What did you do? Forget to buy your round?'

Jimmie was quiet for a bit. 'They kept saying this is what you get.'

'For what? Get for what?'

He spat it out. 'They said Ah was a collector. For a shark. And that this was to stop me collecting for a while. Anybody that can dae that to somebody else . . .' He shook his head.

'And were they right? You're a – *were* – a collector, Jimmie?'

'The judge didnae think so.'

'But you were accused?'

'There was nae proof. Naebody would talk.' Said with all the pride and arrogance of the professional muscle-man.

'You're a scary guy, Jimmie.'

It was hard to preen flat on your back with your arms plastered and hauled above your head but Docherty managed it fine. He lowered his voice.

'Look, pal, somebody has to do it. If you get a wee borrow, you have to pay it back. That's how it goes. But Ah'm sayin' nothin' else. In case it incriminalises me.' His face set in a stubborn scowl. 'Look, pal, dae me a favour, will ye? See that hankie on the table?' He pointed with his head. 'Could you see your way to . . .?'

His pinched and battered face was grubby with tears of self-pity. I picked up the hankie and dabbed at his cheeks and round his eyes. I even let him blow into it before piling it delicately back on the table. The things I do for a story.

'Would you recognise them again?'

'Naw. Balaclavas.'

'Local accents?'

'One was, but the other was a Teuchter.'

I stared at Docherty, my mouth suddenly dry in apprehension. *Call me Ishmael.* Surely not? I added some last notes to my pad and left him cursing his fate and the loss of honour between thugs and hoodlums.

I needed to think. I jumped on a tram outside the infirmary. We rattled and swayed down the quiet streets through the empty city centre. Everywhere was closed except the kirks and they didn't need my sceptical presence this morning. I got off at Jamaica Bridge and turned along by the river. It was bliss to walk in the sunshine down by the Clyde. Or it should have been. The path was deserted apart from a pair of old winos taking their own Sunday communion.

I searched my flexible conscience. I wasn't too upset at such barbaric come-uppance to a loan-shark enforcer. Docherty was the sort of guy who had no qualms about breaking someone's kneecap for missing a single payment of a debt at a scalding interest rate. He'd not be making any collection visits any time soon. Not unless he was wheeled round in a barrow.

But it might not have been the first such incident. There had been a late special from the *Daily Record* on Friday night which had some of the hallmarks of the attack on Docherty. It concerned a would-be razor king trying to emulate his pre-war legends by inflicting a small reign of terror in the Calton. It sound like the putative razor boss had been run over by a combine harvester, so extensive were the gashes in his own head. The story mentioned two men, in balaclavas.

36

I pushed the thought down but in a way it wasn't so strange. Summary justice was well understood and expected in the West of Scotland. There was an unwritten sliding scale for criminal offences which avoided paperwork and court time and all that pre-trial nail-biting for the accused. In the case of childhood misdemeanours these plenipotentiary powers were delegated to the nearest adult – family member or total stranger. Ring the door and run was a high-risk gamble if you were the fattest and slowest in a gang. Or pinching apples. A street urchin caught with his jumper stuffed with Granny Smiths in the vicinity of the mother tree could expect a cuff on the lug, especially from the owner of said apples. The urchin in question took it as a calculated risk in his line of business and made no objection other than to run greeting to his pals who'd evaded the fell and horny hand of justice. It would certainly not have crossed his or her mind to complain to his maw or paw, knowing with absolute certainty that it would simply earn him another skelp.

Glasgow constabulary had another level of powers alto-gether, which varied according to the individual polis and the criminal activity. The good citizens of Glasgow, and perhaps more crucially, the less good, had to take into account a particular officer's innate fondness for violence as well as his state of mind at the time of the encounter. Knowing for example that PC McBride had just come from another bust-up with his wife, or that the hound on which PC Fraser had wagered his pay packet had succumbed on the home stretch to the packet of Woodbine fed to it by a bribed handler, was essential to gauging the potential degree of physical assault. Villains caught *in flagrante* with the takings from a chip-shop raid knew that the arrest would earn them a severe trun-cheoning as a sort of pre-trial warm-up.

But this assault on Docherty – with a crowbar, for pity's sake – to discourage even the *intention* of criminal activity; well it just wisnae fitba'.

SIX

headed back through the deserted Sunday streets to the newspaper building. I pushed through the *Gazette*'s big doors and bounded up the three flights of stairs behind the splendidly tiled entrance hall. Outside the newsroom I stood for a moment to catch my breath and savour again the sweet notion that I'd at last found my place in the world. I heaved the door open and plunged into the smog, the clatter and ping of typewriters, the insistent phones and the shouted conversations. Even this half-shift was controlled bedlam, and I loved it. I'd been in the newsroom of the *London Bugle* a few times while I was freelancing down south after demob. But this was different. I belonged here. Not just as a full-time, salaried – though probationary – reporter, but in that ease and comfort that comes from operating in your natural habitat. Otters and brown water. Drunks and breweries.

The accent helped. The cut and thrust across the chaotic desks, the shouts and catcalls and patter, was in the tough nasalities of the West of Scotland. Entering the newsroom was like slipping into a hot bath: shocking at first but then utterly enveloping and cosy. In every sense they were speaking my language; or, to be truthful, the language of my boyhood. Though Big Eddie spoke a purple subset of it that would have brought a flush to the cheeks of a sergeant major. Not that Eddie had ever marched across a parade ground. He had enough health problems to get a regiment classed 4F. Between the fags, the booze and the stress it was a daily miracle to find him patrolling the newsroom spreading ash and anxiety in his path.

Assisting him was Sandy Logan, his whippet-thin sub-editor. Seeing the pair of them together was like looking in a fairground mirror. Sandy was nearly six foot with limbs the thickness of his fearsome blue pencils. He didn't say much. All his communicative energy poured out in a stream of corrections, admonitions and razor-sharp summations of some hack's garbled story. Sandy's editing eyes were all-seeing, all-knowing, pitiless. There were no split infinitives or dangling participles on Sandy's watch.

Sandy and Eddie inhabited tiny glass-fronted offices on either side of the corridor that led into the newsroom. Scylla and Charybdis. Reporters running late with a submission or with a nagging conscience about the provenance of a story had to steer past these twin hazards. Invariably the hapless hack would fall foul of one. Often both.

This fine Sunday morning I found Eddie in his den biting his nails and hiding behind mounds of old clippings and discarded drafts. Eddie kept his office like a crime scene. Smoke rose from several smouldering fag ends in an over-flowing ashtray.

The sub's office was empty, and out in the newsroom Wullie McAllister's desk was empty too. Either he'd already filed his copy from his morning meanderings or he was keeping it back for Monday. During the week Wullie would arrive mid morning, drink a cup or two of sugary tea and be back out the door in time for the pubs to open. Somehow – though it was still a mystery to me – a three-column article would appear in sharp prose that would hit the presses with scarcely a comma altered by Sandy. I could only aspire to such insouciance.

I scribbled out a rough draft of the story in pencil. I knew enough about Eddie's preferences to spare my gentle readers none of the details. There was a liking for blood with the morning porridge among the fair-minded citizens of Glasgow.

Reading of terrible things happening to other folk – especially *bad* folk – set them up for the day. It provided the juice in the conversation on the tram going to work; the spice in the gossip over the clothes line in the back close; the flavour in the first pint of heavy after work.

By midday I'd bashed out a fair copy of my article – in triplicate. I slid the top copy in through Eddie's window and a copy for Sandy to peruse on Monday, though it should have gone out by then. Eddie was doubling up as sub-editor on Sunday. I knew my piece was well enough written, but it didn't stop me feeling nervous. Eddie was almost as much a master of the blue pencil as Sandy, sometimes for the sake of it to show who was boss, but mostly because he'd edited more newspapers than got wrapped round fish suppers on a Saturday night across Scotland. Eddie had done Sandy's job for years before being promoted to editor.

He was at my desk almost before I got back to it. He passed me the scarred copy covered in his blue annotations and arrows. I glanced down and saw immediately how I could change it and why. Seems he loved the bit about crunching bones and wanted more. Eddie knew his audience. He leaned over and tapped the sheet.

'No' bad, Brodie. But no description of the nutters?'

'Balaclavas don't let in much daylight.'

He nodded and left me to rework it. His question had unsettled me for different reasons. I hadn't mentioned Ishmael and his vow. There was simply no proof. Glasgow was full of Highland accents. Docherty's beating was almost certainly the work of a rival shark. A turf battle.

By one o'clock I'd produced a draft Eddie was happy with. The pressure was off for Monday's edition. I had the rest of the day to myself and all of Monday morning to get something fresh on the stocks. For a reporter on the incident-strewn streets of Glasgow, surely a doddle.

*

The Docherty article went out on Monday and I had a pat on the back from Wullie McAllister himself over a pint or three that evening. I spent Tuesday and Wednesday stalking the parched pavements looking for trouble – though my aim was to report events, not provoke.

The sight of girls in summer frocks distracted me and I found myself detouring via George Square to remind myself how easily the skin of Glasgow secretaries took on a glow. There would be a run on Calamine lotion in Boots tonight. I couldn't get enough of the female form after years of being surrounded by shapeless males in khaki. Enforced abstinence gave every demobbed rake a licence to leer till we'd caught up on the lost time. I think the girls understood that. They might even have missed the attention.

I got back to the *Gazette* to cool off and eat my sandwich. But the room was like a furnace, even with all the windows open and a light breeze coming through. At least it dissipated the tobacco clouds. As I steered my way through the room I caught a hopeful look from wee Morag, the girl I'd taken out last weekend. I smiled and pressed on towards my sanctuary in the corner. I'd give her the nod later on for a drink after work.

I hung my sweat-damp jacket on my chair and slid in behind the desk. It was Spartan enough: front and centre an old Imperial with sticking keys; on the right a wooden tray with some draft articles and my early and as yet illegible efforts at shorthand. On the left sat an ashtray and a wood block with a spike skewering a small pile of letters. Underneath the desk was a single drawer with a few sheets of fresh foolscap, carbons, typewriter ribbons and a couple of chewed pencils left behind by a guy who never came back from the front. I hadn't the heart to throw them out.

A white envelope perched on the typewriter. It was stamped locally and addressed succinctly to 'Mr Brodie, Crime Column, The Glasgow Gazette'. Fan mail or barbs? I'd hardly been with the paper five minutes before the excitable readers of the back pages – *the voices of the people, by the people* – were unloading their views in a steady stream. Usually they were sounding off about the rise in violence and the fall in standards of civility. We were all away to hell in a hand basket and they needed to let me know they had no intention of going off gentle into that good night. There was even a sense that I was somehow to blame for delivering the message. Doubtless this envelope contained more such advice, but I was new and still keen, so I grabbed it, slid my knife under the join and sliced it open.

The message was in black ink in a fine sloping hand on lined paper. Here and there words were underlined or set in capitals. Sometimes both. Exclamation marks spluttered angrily across the page:

Dear Brodie,

Your story about Docherty was wrong. It wasn't random. He was chosen. Like the Calton razor king. Can't you see what's going on around you?

We are <u>tired</u> of ordinary folk being robbed and raped with impunity. We are <u>sick</u> of the rich getting away with murder. The POLICE are feckless and corrupt. Look at the ones you put on trial! The LAW protects the rich and hammers the poor!

We have had enough!!! This is a declaration to the people of Glasgow.

<u>*IT STOPS NOW!!!*</u>

<u>*We are taking it into our own hands.*</u> *Docherty wasn't the first. He won't be the last!!*

'. . . and they were judged every man according to their works.'

The Glasgow Marshals

The *Glasgow Marshals*? Someone had been reading too much Zane Gray. And the clinching sign of an over-excited brain: a quote, presumably from the Bible. It certainly fitted with Docherty's account of a punishment beating, and its thrust was consistent with Ishmael's vow about dispensing justice. But I told myself I was adding one and one and making three. I slid the letter and envelope into my desk drawer and headed for the door. I still needed something for next day's edition and a letter from a bampot wasn't yet a story, as Big Eddie would have delighted in pointing out.

On Thursday we slid into August and I wondered where the year was going and whether it would continue to be punctuated by hangovers. Throughout the week, I kept my eye on the rival papers. The mentions were building up. More injuries to bad people. Balaclavas seemed all the rage. They were edging out the Morton story in the absence of any new facts or leads about the brutal murder. But no one seemed to be making the link. Maybe there was none?

Friday morning found me gingerly picking my way over cobbles round the Gallowgate. The steaming piles of horse dung seemed as threatening as any minefield outside El Alamein. I was chasing a story about off-licence overpricing and the ensuing citizens' revolt. It was a patchy story, sparse on evidence but heavy on emotion. People take the price of drink seriously in that neck of the woods, especially on hot summer days. Some of the work-shy fancied a day out fishing in the Kelvin and had their minds set on chilling a couple of bottles of stout in the river, but the landlord's price hike had spoiled their wee picnic. A punch-up ensued. Windows got smashed. Heads got broken.

I thought I could squeeze a column out of it for the Monday edition to save coming in on Sunday. In the absence of anything more thrilling before the closing bell I headed back to the news desk to type it up.

This time Morag brought the envelope to my desk. She looked so big-eyed and smiling that it would have been churlish of me not to invite her to the dancing on Saturday. Our drink and cuddles on Wednesday had gone well. Maybe she was the one to fill those lonely nights? I hoped I could remember how to Lindy Hop – if that's what they were still doing at the Locarno.

I turned over the missive. I felt a chill run through me. This was no *billet doux*. Same envelope, same handwriting as the first one about Docherty. I opened it and read:

Dear Brodie,

I hope you're keeping count. Some have been found wanting and paid the penalty. Tell the others what to expect. Now you see how we deliver justice. No escape for the evil-doers!!! No legal tricks!!!

We bring justice by the people to the people who deserve it. Not like Johnson. You claim to be the voice of the people. Warn them that 'I . . . have the keys of hell and of death.' !!!

Tell them what you see on Sunday. Same time. Same place. Same vermin!!!

'. . . they also have erred through wine, and through strong drink are out of the way.'

The Glasgow Marshals.

Not like Johnson. The phrase reverberated across the page. Same foaming rage as the first letter and with a clear warning of impending violence of a tougher, scarier order altogether. They already had someone lined up for a pasting. It confirmed we had some evangelists on the loose with inflated ideas of their own rectitude and a taste for Old Testament justice. The sort of thing you'd expect from a son of Abraham.

SEVEN

I had the letter inside my jacket pocket on Sunday morning. Unlike a week ago, I was less jaunty climbing the hill to the infirmary. Morag and I had jived until my shirt was soaked and the very walls of the Locarno were running with the condensed breath of a thousand manic dancers. I'd known cooler nights in North Africa. She seemed to have inexhaustible energy: the transient gift of the young. The converse also being true: this morning my legs were feeling every one of their thirty-four years. I'd revived enough to see her home and participate in some sweaty entanglements in her close. But as well as finding myself too old for the jigging, it dawned on me that I was too old for close-quarter combat in a squalid entry. Next time I might just stick to the flicks. Hollywood has a job keeping up with demand in Glasgow. Or maybe take her to one of the comedy shows. I'd heard Alec Finlay was good.

Sitting in my vest and pants at three in the morning, that cut-your-wrists time after jolting awake from troubled sleep, I had come to the melancholy realisation that I was getting past it. I needed a wife. Someone to come home to and listen to my rants about my working day. To share a laugh with, listening to Tommy Handley and his ITMA pals on the wireless. Someone I could hand my wage-packet to and get pocket money for a pint and fags in return. To calm me in the night with soothing hands when the mortar shells came crashing through my dreams. I don't know what depressed me more:

realising I'd reached the pipe-and-slippers stage, or wanting it.

I limped along the dark brown corridors and pushed into the ward. The Sister just nodded. She looked weary too, sagging. Only her starched cap was stiff.

'Bed seven on the right. Gibson. The polis have already been,' she said and stood aside.

Her mood chilled me. How bad could this be? I walked on and into the ward. There were eight beds either side. All filled. A busy night in the emergency room. But what was special about bed seven? Then I saw him. He could have been stolen from the Egyptian collection at the Kelvingrove Museum. Only a strip over his eyes and mouth was uncovered. His shoulders and arms were swathed in bandages. I felt the gaze of the rest of the patients follow me as if they knew what the attraction was and were curious to see how I'd react. I got to his bedside. His eyes were closed.

'Hello? Mr Gibson?' I tried. 'Anybody in there?'

At first nothing, then his eyelids flickered and snapped open. He looked terrified. As much as you could judge from just two brown pools.

'Hello, Mr Gibson,' again. 'I'm from the *Gazette*. The name's Brodie. Can you talk? Can you tell me what happened?'

The man in the bandages turned his head away and then pulled back. I saw his eyes squint in pain. He flexed his lips and licked them.

'Fuck. Off.'

Which in the circumstances seemed fair comment.

'Look, I'm sorry, pal. I can see you're in a lot of pain. All I want is a couple of words about what happened last night. Did someone do this to you?'

His eyes glared at me. His lips curled. He cleared his throat. 'You might say that. You might well say that. Cunts!'

I took out my pad and pencil. Folk always felt obliged to help me fill the blank page. 'What did these – *folk* – do to you?

Beat you up? You were on your way home after shutting time, I expect . . .'

He was quiet for a bit, but then I could see him resolve something in his swaddled head.

'Aye. Doon by the Saltmarket. They were waiting for me. On a bomb site. They had a fire going. An auld oil drum. They asked me if I wanted a warm. I should have said no. I mean it was a hot night. But we a' like a fire. Like fucking moths. As it turns oot.'

'What happened?'

He paused. 'I thought they were wearing caps. But as I got close they pulled them doon. Balaclavas. They grabbed me. Christ, they were strong buggers! They didnae look it, but airms like pythons.'

'Then what?' In truth I wasn't sure I wanted to hear this.

'They roped me like a fuckin' steer. Like wan o' they cowboy pictures. I couldnae get up. One of them stuck a dirty rag in my mouth to shut me up. The other went across to the fire.'

I steeled myself and became aware that the ward was silent. The other fifteen beds were locked into this story.

'They had a tin on the fire. The wan that lifted it had to use a bit o' sacking. It was fu' and steaming.'

He was no longer looking at me. He was looking into the flames as someone brought a can of boiling . . .

I swallowed. 'What was in it? In the can?'

'Tar. Boiling fucking tar. He timmed it ower ma heid and all ower ma face and shoulders and airms and hands. I couldnae shout or greet or anything. Just rolled around while it burned ma skin off.'

The ward was squeezed dry with tension. He spoke again, quieter this time. 'They had a poke. A broon paper poke. He opened the top and timmed it ower me.'

'What?'

'Feathers. They turned me ower and ower to make sure I was covered. Then they took the rope off and left me.'

47

I felt the ward breathe out. A voice said, 'Jesus Christ.' There was a murmur of supporting oaths.

'Are you saying they tarred and feathered you?'

'Aye.'

A voice cut in from across the ward. 'Like the fucking Wild West!'

'Aye.'

'Did they say why?'

Gibson was quiet for a while.

'It's a' lies, so it is. Naw. I'm no' saying.'

He clammed up. I got up to go.

'Hie, pal. There's wan other thing.'

'What's that, Mr Gibson?'

He looked down the bedclothes. He moved his right hand. The bandages went all the way down and swathed his hands.

'They cut ma wee finger.' He said it with incredulity.

'Cut it?'

'Cut it *aff*. They cut aff ma pinkie wi' a cigar cutter. A momento they said.'

'Memento.'

'I just said that.'

On my way out of the ward I stopped at the Sister's desk.

'He wouldn't say why they attacked him. Did he tell you?'

She looked at me, then looked round her, checking no one was in earshot. 'He wouldnae say. But I heard one of the polis talking.'

'And?'

'They'd got him for rape a couple of weeks back. In drink, as usual.'

'He got off?'

'Aye. The lassie wouldnae talk. She was in the women's ward just the other side. In a terrible state.'

'Do you know why she didn't press charges? Was she scared?'

The Sister's face screwed up and I thought she was going to cry. 'It was his dochter.'

Sweet Jesus, where were you? You might be watching out for sparrows, but what about wee girls? I shook my head and walked away. Then I remembered something else.

'Gibson said they cut off his finger, his pinkie. With a cigar cutter?'

'Aye. The same as yon bruiser, last week.'

'Docherty! The one who got his arms broken? He never said.'

'He didnae know at first. What with all the pain and the stookie down to his fingers.'

'God almighty!'

'The good Lord had nothing to do with it, I hope, Mr Brodie.'

EIGHT

I'd already filed a piece on the great off-licence siege for the Monday edition. Tuesday too was covered; in the absence of any new leads on Alec Morton, Wullie had bashed out an article on the resurgence of the drug problem. It doesn't take long for organised crime to spot a gap and fill it. A new supply route had been set up, or the old one reopened under new management. It meant I could sit on the two letters and the Gibson piece until I'd done more research. Not to mention talking things over with Wullie on Monday night.

First, I put Elspeth Macpherson on the scent. Elspeth was the *Gazette*'s literary critic and by default the resident researcher and all-round fount of wisdom. Elspeth hid her first-class honours in Classics from Edinburgh behind a curtain of frizzy blonde hair, glasses and an aura of aloofness. Even Big Eddie was wary enough of her to avoid swearing in her presence. Mostly. Elspeth saw me as a kindred spirit. Though my own degree was a mere 2.1 in Modern Languages, it put us in a different educational league from just about everyone else on the *Gazette*. Reporters and editors came up the hard way from tea-making to typesetting. Sandy Logan was a self-taught master sub-editor. The basics of grammar had been hammered into him at primary school in Govan, but the rest came from thirty years of understudying his predecessor, and having for his pillow *Fowler's Dictionary of Modern English Usage*.

It had been a long while since I'd been able to discuss Camus or Kafka with anyone else without sounding like a pretentious swot. But at the same time I knew Elspeth had the edge on me with her well-hidden photographic memory. A rare bird was our Elspeth.

It took her five minutes.

'The first is easy: "and they were judged every man according to their works." It's from Revelations 20, verse 13. The second: "they also have erred through wine, and through strong drink are out of the way", took a bit longer. It's from Isaiah 28 verse 7.'

'How did you find it, Elspeth? A concordance?' I asked looking for the reference book.

She swung her hair behind her neck. 'Strong's? He's good, but I prefer my own research and cross-references. Besides, I knew straight away it was either in Leviticus or Isaiah. It has their style.'

'Style?'

'The original Greek. As different as Graham Greene and John Buchan. The English translations in the St James are good but they lose some of the tone.'

'Right. Thanks.' I backed away, feeling I'd just been with the Oracle of Delphi.

I scribbled some notes for the Gibson attack, referring to the two letters and linking it with last week's piece on Docherty. But I didn't run it past Eddie, not till I'd seen McAllister. I finally left the office an hour after the pubs were open. I found oor Wullie in his usual place in the high-backed corner seat of Ross's. He'd never formally annexed it with a personalised brass plaque, but he was as firmly in possession of it as any habitué of a kirk pew. It was in the order of things. Similarly, it was apparently my round. Cup-bearer indeed.

I was standing at the bar waiting for the barrel to be changed. Two old boozers were clinging to the brass rail next to me, ruminating.

'If the polis cannae catch them, then Ah don't care wha gi'es them a skelp.'

'But you cannae have folk taking the law into their ain hands. Where will it a' end?'

'Why no'? It's what Sillitoe's Cossacks did afore the war. That sorted oot the Billy Boys. But things have slipped back. Ah don't care wha does it, or how, if it gets thae scum aff the street . . .'

It was as if they were heralds for the letter-writer, the self-styled Marshals. Things were moving fast. The old boys rabbited on in this vein for a while, intimating that there was a new sheriff in town, a hard man, a crazy man, a potential folk hero of our times. Somewhere between Rob Roy McGregor and a Texas Ranger. I almost leaned over and said I might have met the man in question, and he was not the full shilling. Finally their conversation returned to the well-worn speculation that Celtic's new goalie was a Protestant plant.

I looked across the fug-filled room to the table where my drinking pal was waiting, still thirsty after three pints of heavy and chasers. The belching roll-up jammed in the corner of his mouth scored a yellow streak in his grey moustache. McAllister was checking the racing pages of a rival, more sports-inclined rag. This was my king-maker, the man who was handing over his life's work to me. As he kept telling me . . .

'You've earned it, Brodie. I was gonna insist on them making a funeral pyre of my desk with a copy of every edition I featured in. Me laid out on top with a pint in one hand and a copy of the *Gazette* in the other as the flames licked my arse. But, what the hell. The show goes on. We are the voice of the people, the scourge of the villains. My work must continue.'

He'd finish his rhetoric with the passing of an imaginary torch to me and a far-off look in his smoke-red eyes. This self-promoting funeral oratory happened when he was in his cups and feeling the weight of ages pressing on his furrowed forehead. In other words, most nights. The more he lauded me, the more I felt like handing back the torch and accompanying laurel leaf and catching the first train back to the anonymity of London. Did I want to end up like him? On the other hand there were enough attractions. The job itself. Being with my 'ain folk'. Being able to keep an eye on my mother. The West of Scotland weather? Hardly; this spell was a freak. Or just Samantha Campbell. Sam . . .

'Half a crown.'

I was torn from my reverie of blonde hair and lie-detecting eyes by the arrival of my pints. I slid the half-dollar on to the sweating counter, scooped up my drinks and change and slopped back to the table. McAllister pushed the empties aside to make room. I put the two glasses down in the puddle.

'You were in a dwam up at the bar. Thinking about that bint of yours?'

'Two things, Wullie. She's not a bint, and she's not mine.'

'Aw right, that burd you did the Sir Galahad thing for.'

I sighed. 'Sam. Samantha Campbell. She's not a *burd*. She's an advocate. A top lawyer. Her dad was Procurator Fiscal.'

'Aye, aye, her. Still shagging her?' The old devil cackled. There was no sensible answer to that, though the word *still* was severely redundant.

I nodded my head backwards. 'Wullie, see that pair at the bar? The old yins blethering away? They were talking about some bloke who's making life difficult for our criminal readership. It fits with a daft couple of letters I got last week claiming they're taking the law into their own hands. And I've seen proof up at the Royal these past two Sundays.'

Ace reporter William McAllister squinted through his own smoke signals. 'We're in a pub. It's past seven o'clock. Folk talk shite. But funnily enough, it's no' the first time *I've* heard something this past week. Just a wee word here and there. Facts, however – in which we alone deal, Brodie, we recorders of mankind's sins – facts are thin on the ground. My own wee gang of helpers – ye ken I have sources' – he touched his nose – 'have been intimating that folk are getting hurt out there. More than usual. The word I'm getting is that the treatment

53

is being dished out to known desperadoes. But nobody's been putting two and two thegither and making five. So far, it's being put down to the work of a fellow villain, shark or all-round general miscreant. In such circumstances nobody cares, except the wans getting the hiding, of course. And their mammies, I suppose.'

'Any mention of a gang calling themselves the Glasgow Marshals?'

'The whit? Roy Rogers has a lot to answer for. Show me the letters.'

He read the notes slowly, once, twice, and handed them back to me. He sucked on his fag, then his pint, and sat back.

'It's yours if you want it.'

'It's sort of already mine, Wullie. I think I know who's doing this. Or at least I know the leader.' I told him the story of Ishmael.

He squinted at me. 'You've got a rare talent for finding trouble, Brodie. Was it like this when you were in the polis?'

'These letters, this warning. You're saying we should take it seriously? And that I should run with it?'

'Aye. There's something going on. Could be big. And you've got an inside track by the sound of it. You've nothing to lose by following it up. Except a lie-in on Sunday.'

'What are you up to that you can be so magnanimous? A new angle on Morton's murder?'

'I've a couple of leads.' He tapped the side of his empty glass to signify it was none of my business. This was his scoop and he wasn't about to share it. 'Same again, laddie?'

NINE

Next morning, ignoring the pain between my eyes, I presented the letters to Big Eddie. I didn't mention my suspicions who was behind it. Lack of proof still kept me back, but also a daft reluctance to betray the Highlander a second time. It was suspect logic, but Eddie was getting enough material for a story as it is.

Eddie eyed me up. 'Next time you get an effin' written confession from a nutter you bring it straight to me. Is this for real?'

'That's why I ran it past McAllister. He thinks there's something in it. Especially after they followed through with their threat.'

I told him about the retribution dished out on Gibson but didn't mention the loss of his wee finger, or that he shared the mutilation with Docherty. It was partly my police training kicking in. I was reluctant to make the whole story public. *Always keep something back when talking to the press* had been the advice of Duncan Todd ten years ago. You never know when it'll come in handy. Even though I now *was* the press, it seemed as if I couldn't quite shake the habit.

Besides, it wasn't as though we didn't have enough macabre details to titillate the unhealthy appetites of the *Gazette* readers. Or editors. By the end, Eddie was shaking his head with disapproval and rubbing his hands with glee.

'Terrible, terrible. Write it up, Brodie, write it up.'

'Can we say anything about the rape charge?'

'*Alleged*. That'll keep us clean. The dirty bastard deserves a' he gets.'

'So who's side are we taking? The law or the Marshals?'

'It's a good question, Brodie. Let's play both sides for a while.'

'Terrible punishment but terrible *alleged* crime?'

'You're fair getting the hang o' this. You've got the instincts of a newspaperman. You just need to learn how to write like one. Cut oot the big words and tell the story.'

'How about inviting the loonies who did it to give up their evil ways?'

'Christ, we don't want them to stop now, Brodie! This is effin' gold!'

He saw my look.

'I mean of course we want them to stop. This is pure vigilantism – is that a word, Brodie? You've got the Latin. But maybe not quite yet. It's not as if they don't deserve it. I mean . . .'

I was in a similar quandary. My police training told me everything the Marshals were doing was plain wrong. My heart applauded.

'I know what you mean, Eddie. But we don't have any cast-iron proof that the likes of Docherty or Gibson earned their punishments. Even if they did, and even if we're secretly pleased at their come-uppance, we surely can't *publicly* condone eejits going round maiming folk until they see the light?'

'No, no. You're right, of course. It's our duty to take the high moral ground.' He dropped his voice. 'So that we can shout *gardyloo* and chuck things doon on Labour about the crime rate rising since they got in.'

'Is that relevant? Is it even true?'

'The truth is what the readers think it is. They think the politicians are useless. No point getting them confused.'

'What about the police? Should we be chastising them for failing to nick the baddies or stop the vigilantes?' It was as if I'd insulted his mother.

'Do you have any idea how much shit hit the fan back in April with your last set of calumnies about our boys in blue?'

'They weren't calumnies! They were the truth. Chief Superintendent Muncie and pals were guilty as sin. In cahoots with the Slattery gang. Protection rackets, drug-running, prostitutes. Not to mention Gerrit Slattery's taste for buggering and murdering wee boys. You name it. I just helped Wullie expose them.'

'Well, for your information, Mr Ace Reporter Brodie, I had everyone from the Chief Constable himself down to the traffic polis at George Square shouting at me for dragging their good name through the mud. Do I make myself clear, Brodie?'

He had. Crystal. I left his fuming presence, shoved a new sheaf of foolscap and carbon in my Imperial and bashed out a draft column which omitted mention of the finger-nabbing or any link to an angry Teuchter.

As it was, it made a good spread on the inside back page. A bit of conspiracy theory gets lapped up by the readership. I had the crime columns to myself as McAllister was digging away at the Morton murder and council contract corruption and hadn't yet got anything to show for it. Or not that he was telling me.

Throughout the week other papers failed to catch up. None of them referred to any letters *they'd* received. Why was I being singled out? And no one mentioned missing fingers. I needed some corroboration of my own theories. I decided to take a leaf out of McAllister's notepad and get myself some helpers, as he put it. All I had was a false name for the Teuchter, and I hadn't a clue where to find him.

I already had a list of contacts, but they were long shots. I was casting back at least seven years to my days on the force dealing with shady characters working the wrong side of the line. A lot can happen to such folk in seven years. Mortality levels were high in the badlands: those that had lived by the razor had probably died by it by now. Others would be taking their ease at His Majesty's pleasure. Conceivably a few might have gone straight, only to be buried a hero in some corner of a foreign field that is forever Scotland.

I'd also had solid citizens in my network. But that didn't mean they were trained SOE agents. Just folk wanting to do their bit in the hope that they could keep the barbarians at the gate till they'd had their tea. Or plain old nosy parkers. They kept their eyes and ears open and gave me snippets of information that I pieced together into a map of comings and goings in the principality of the Eastern Division. Shop-keepers and publicans, newspaper-sellers and street sweeps, tram conductors and school janitors. Everyone who met the great Glasgow public on a daily basis. It was amazing just how much they observed and just how much they enjoyed gossiping about it. But I thought I should start with someone nearer the action. I made a call.

Duncan Todd had risen fast to detective sergeant in Glasgow's Marine Division before the war. Then his career had stalled. I met him in '35 when I was a green officer at detective training school and he was a lecturer. He was sharp, funny and keen as a Mountie to get his man. Destined for the top. He only faced two barriers: being a Catholic and having an aversion to joining the Masons. Either one was a career-limiting handicap anywhere in the West of Scotland. Duncan took this anti-Freemason stance not simply because he'd have been excommunicated on the spot, but because he despised all the rituals and job stitch-ups. We were of the same naive persuasion, he and I, that talent would out, regardless of whether you could do funny handshakes or not. We were wrong.

I'd phoned him back in April from London to get the scuttlebutt on the trial of Hugh Donovan. He'd sounded weary then. He'd been transferred to Central Division – HQ – in Turnbull Street and been buried away in some dark corner and forgotten about.

We met down by the Clyde in the Victoria Bar. A place of

mean measures and mean habits. He looked wearier than ever. He was still in Turnbull Street and still a sergeant. We eyed each other up speculatively across our pints. I wondered if he was viewing me as pityingly as I was him.

His hair was still thick but grey as fag ash. It matched his complexion. Lines ran down the side of his nose and past his mouth. His eyes were lustreless and heavy. Nicotine stained the fingers on both hands. Ambidextrous.

'You're lookin' well, Brodie.'

'So are you, Duncan.'

'You're a liar. But that's OK. I see masel' in the mirror each morning. Though I don't need a reflection to tell me I'm knackered. I'm just hoping to get oot wi' ma pension before they find me collapsed in ma harness and have tae shoot me.'

'It's surely no' that bad, Dunc.' But I could see it was. 'Though it's a shame Sillitoe's gone.'

'You're right there, Brodie. Chief Constable Sir Percy Sillitoe, blessed boss of these streets, was a fixer. We could dae with another like him. We've lost ground since he left. It's just a pity he didnae get rid of that shite Muncie before he went. You did us all a favour there.'

Chief Superintendent George Muncie had been the prime malignancy behind the framing of my pal Hugh. Muncie was currently being held in solitary at Duke Street – for his own safety – while awaiting a trial date. I hoped he was enjoying his new perspective on the application of the law.

'Did I? I suppose so. He was rotten and he'd infected others on the force. But I wish . . .'

'That he'd been better? That he'd had a finer set of morals than a rabid dug? Don't we all. By the way, there was another wee bonus from your work.'

'Promotions all round?'

'Aye, but not for me. No, when you put the searchlight on the Slattery gang and they vanished, the drug trade in this fair metropolis halved overnight.'

'Delighted to hear it, Dunc.' I bit my tongue to avoid

confessing how much of a hand I'd had in the Slatterys' vanishing act. Or how permanent a disappearance it was. Duncan might – if he was still as bloody-minded and scrupulous as always – have to arrest me.

'But of course it's starting up again. Somebody new.'

'Like targets at a fun fair. Knock 'em down and they pop up again.'

'Why don't you come back, Brodie? We could do with you. You were a major in the Seaforths? Good going, pal. You'd come straight in as an inspector.'

I'd thought of it. Especially as I'd nearly frittered away my demob gratuity. But I'd done my bit for king and country. No more uniforms. I wanted a quiet life. So what was I doing here?

'I was always out of step with the force. You know that. And do you really think they'd welcome me back with open arms after what I've put them through?'

'I suppose not. Anyway, you're here about possible vigilante attacks?'

'I've got two letters and two attacks. That and pub gossip.'

'Well, we've got a couple of possible cases that might fit. And if we add yours in, it could be something. Saying that, and far be it from me to condone it, but you have to admit it's quicker than due process.'

'If you get the right man.'

'There's that. But it's maybe better than no' getting anybody at all.'

'It's that bad, Duncan?'

'Maybe I'm jaundiced. Maybe it's the war. Everybody's tired. Nobody cares.'

'That's what these guys said in their letters. You're not moonlighting, are you?' I was only half joking.

He sighed. 'It's the last scruple I've got, Brodie. It's why I've never got past sergeant. That and being a dirty papist.' He pulled himself upright. 'Can I see them?'

I handed over the warnings about Docherty and Gibson. He read them twice and whistled.

'A bampot. A *religious* bampot. I wonder when we'll get the first body?'

I nodded. 'That's what I'm waiting for. It's funny how moral certainty leads to intolerance.'

'Then dictatorship.'

'Hitler.'

'The Pope.'

We laughed and for the first time I saw something of the old Duncan Todd in front of me.

'How can I help, Brodie?'

'I need to build a picture of what's going on. I need to know who's getting hurt and where. And how do they choose who gets the hiding?'

'They could follow our Black Marias on ony Saturday night. Pick out the plums.'

'And who's "they", Dunc? Who's doing this? You've heard they're wearing balaclavas?'

'Aye. I heard that from one of the fellas we picked up. Broken kneecaps. A bookie's runner that didnae run fast enough.'

I decided to be open with Duncan. 'I might have met the man who started this. The man who wrote the letters. But I don't have proof.'

'Do you now? Tell all!'

I told him, and gave him Ishmael's description. I also mentioned the mutilated fingers.

'You're right to keep the finger thing back, Brodie. Could be useful. But you say we might be looking for a red-haired Teuchter? In this city, where half the polis fit that description?'

I sighed. 'Exactly. It's why I've not written about it yet.'

'Well, it's a start, I suppose.'

We finished our pints. I got up to go. 'By the by, Duncan, there was another bloke I was trying to get hold of. Another of your former pupils.'

He grinned. 'Let me guess. Another troublemaker like you, Brodie?'

I shrugged in wounded agreement. 'McRae. Danny McRae. Any word?'

Duncan's brow furrowed. 'Last I heard he didnae make it back. Was hijacked by the SOE and got lost in France.'

'No. He made it back all right. At least as far as London. He was in all the papers down there earlier this year.'

'Good God! What for?'

'This and that. Murder and such stuff.'

'Christ! What happened?'

'A set-up. His old boss in the SOE did for him. Slaughtered a girl in France and five prostitutes in London and framed Danny for the lot of them. But Danny turned the tables. After nearly killing a corrupt inspector from the Yard.'

'What *is* it with you pair and senior coppers?' Duncan shook his head. 'Did you get in touch?'

I sighed. 'No. I was, shall we say, otherwise engaged. Me and Johnnie Walker got too close. Let me know if he turns up, will you?

'Sure thing, Brodie. Re-form the old team, eh?'

TEN

I left Duncan topped up with another pint and headed on over Victoria Bridge into Laurieston and the Gorbals. I could have reached my destination in a few minutes, but decided to take the long way round to stretch my legs. I passed a phone box and wondered how Sam was bearing up. I hadn't spoken to her since we'd heard about Johnson's death. I pushed my pennies in and dialled Sam's home number, not expecting to get her in on a weekday.

'Hello?' Her voice was faint and dull, as though she'd just got up. I pressed button A and the money clattered in.

'Sam? It's Brodie. How are you getting on?'

She coughed. 'Fine, fine. I just haven't spoken to anyone today. It's nice to hear from you.'

'You're not trying to say you missed me?'

'Don't fish, Brodie. What are you up to? Other than spreading morbid tales of blood and anarchy.'

'You saw my story this week?'

'You're like a big trouble magnet, Brodie.'

'You have it wrong, Sam. I'm only reporting it, not causing it.'

'Hmmm. I wish I could believe that. Is this a social call or have you another lost soul to save?'

'You're a hard woman, Samantha Campbell. I was just phoning to see if you were alive and kicking. The bruises on my ear suggest you're just fine.'

'Well, that's nice of you, Brodie. I'm touched.'

'There is one thing . . .'

I heard her sigh and pictured her eyebrows going up. 'Oh aye?'

'Fancy the pictures?'

There was a long silence. 'Hello? Sam? You still there?'

'I was just getting the paper. Tomorrow night? Curzon in Sauchiehall Street? See you at the door at seven o'clock.'

'That's just . . . great. What's on?'

'The main picture's *Brief Encounter*.'

The phone went dead.

I slung my jacket over my shoulder, lit a cigarette and tried to saunter down the dusty street like Jimmy Stewart not giving a damn about a broad.

The Gorbals was steaming. The smells from back-street middens funnelled through the closes and merged with aromas of fresh horse pish from the coal and fish carts. Kids were everywhere doing mysterious kids' things now the schools were out. But among them were the sure signs of deprivation: one with callipers on her legs from polio; several with the rounded skinny legs of rickets; bare feet, ragged shorts and patched dresses. I'd seen weans in better health in the bombed-out cities of the Third Reich. It was hard to see who'd won. But at least these wee ruffians seemed happy. If it weren't for the likelihood of catching something, you'd hug them all.

As I walked I was reminded again that the Gorbals is a hotchpotch of enclaves. The area is bursting at the seams with refugees from Ireland, the Highlands, Russia, Lithuania, Poland, Italy and Asia. Life must have been pretty tough to seek haven in this cold wet fastness so far to the north of anywhere. It meant that there were pocket nations throughout the district, each with its own language and customs. All they lacked were flags and customs posts. You could hear Irish-Gaelic and Polish, Scots-Yiddish and Gorbals-Italian in a twenty-minute stroll across Hutcheson-town.

I'd had enough sightseeing in the heat. I turned round and headed back towards Laurieston and the Jewish quarter – hardly a *schtetl*, but certainly a concentration of things Jewish – centred on their Great Synagogue in South Portland Street. As far as I know, Scotland is the only country in the world not to have expelled or murdered its Jews. Maybe it's because we share a taste for diasporas. And outlooks. There's something very Scottish in the Jewish view that good times won't last and you'd better not get happy thinking they will. Same applies to our self-wounding sense of humour. Not to mention our reputed interest in money. But I'd like to think it's because we're also a broadly tolerant mob, accepting of strangers from any quarter: Ireland, the Highlands and, if pushed, England.

I recall back in '33 signing the petition that resulted in the council boycotting German goods in protest at their anti-Semitism. Much good it did the poor buggers. Of course it's not all altruistic; I'm convinced there's a master plan to improve Scottish cooking. It's hard to imagine life without Italian chippies and ice-cream vans and I have high hopes for curry and noodles. As for the tooth-dissolving treats from Glickman's in the Gallowgate . . .

The shop was still there, thank God, or whoever was currently looking after this lost tribe of Israel. It wasn't any god I'd obey. If you asked me, it was time they traded in their Old Testament guy for someone with a little less rancour in his heart for his followers.

The sign still read 'Isaac Feldmann, Tailor and Fancy Linens' in English and Yiddish above the shop. Two large windows either side of a central door. The window displays were unchanged in the years I'd been away. Sombre brown curtains starting halfway up and falling to the foot. Above the curtain, in the left window, the torso and head of a male mannequin stared blindly out towards me. On the right, a female gazed coquettishly at the male. It made me smile to see the dummies dressed in the latest style – of the twenties. I liked tradition.

I walked over and pushed through the door. The bell tinkled twice. It was dim and cosy, just as I recalled. Even the dust looked the same depth. Same long counter inset with a long brass ruler. The torso of a dressmaker's dummy on a base. Shelf upon shelf of bolts of cloth. I waited for the bell to summon assistance, and then I called out: 'Hello?'

I heard a grumbling in the back and through the faded curtain came a man wearing a tan apron, a corner of which he was using to clean a pair of thick specs. He was more stooped and greyer, but recognisable.

'Shalom, Isaac. How's business?'

'Shalom. Ach, mustn't grumble. Holding body and soul together but it's the cost of everything. *Mein Gott*, this government wants its pound of flesh.' Then he put on his glasses and squinted at me against the light pouring in through the windows from the sun-drenched street. 'I know that voice. Come here, man. Let me see you.'

I walked forward so the light was on me and let him inspect me.

'Sergeant Douglas Brodie? *Bist du es? Ist es wirklich wahr? Gott sei Dank!*' He smiled and stretched his hands out. I took them both. The fingers were long and cool: piano-playing hands, or scissor-wielding.

I'd known Isaac and his growing family since my university days, wandering around Glasgow. He helped me buff up my German, though my language professor was often pained to hear a Munich accent or the odd Yiddish phrase.

I continued in German. 'It's really me, Isaac. It seems we've both been spared. How is Hannah?'

His face creased and his fingers gripped mine harder. The words choked in his throat. 'Ach, Douglas, she has passed on without me. Three years ago. TB it was. I kept saying, but she wouldn't see the hospital. Then it was too late.' He turned from me and I saw his hands go up to his eyes.

'Isaac, I'm so sorry. Hannah was a fine woman. She was kind to me.'

Hannah Feldman took in strays. She could see into hearts. She made tea and stuffed her guests with home-made pastries until she'd wrought her soothing magic on the spirit. I'd walk away from the shop, well fed – body and soul – ready to face the madding crowd again. It was hard to accept such solace had been removed from the world.

Isaac turned back to me. 'It doesn't get better, Douglas. They say it does. But it doesn't. A man just has to endure until it's his time. Then I will join her.' He nodded his head in certainty.

'Well, for my sake, Isaac, I hope that day is not soon.'

'As God wills, Douglas. Come, tell me your news. We have – what is it? – six, seven? Seven long years to catch up. That will take at least two pots.' He began to head for the back shop.

'What about your customers?'

'Ach, what customers?'

We sat sipping sugar-thickened black coffee in front of the tall window that looked out on the small back yard. The room could have been conjured from my memory apart from the absence of the smell of lavender and the wearer herself. Our words were cushioned and softened amidst the ceiling-high bales. He told me of his grown-up children, one in medicine and one in teaching, and of their move to the smarter parts of the city with their own expanding families. He told me why he still worked on, unable to leave the shop and the home that Hannah and he had set up. But how he enjoyed the ceremony of Friday nights at his daughter's home and the grandchildren.

I told him my news. It wasn't a fair trade: his domestic joys for my horrors. For I told him a little of my war and what I'd found in the summer of 1945 after the fighting was over. My knowledge of German earned me a transfer to mop-up duties interrogating the camp commandants and SS officers rounded up near Bremen. But what I told him wasn't news to Isaac. He'd heard what they'd done to his people. He was following the Nuremberg trials. He'd lost family around Munich. Dachau was just up the road.

I tried to soften the imagery but he'd have none of it. He burned to know details. It was almost as though the tables had been turned, that I was the one being interrogated in gentle clipped German. It churned up the monstrous images that I kept firmly under lock and key. But at the end of it, as we stared into our cups, I knew it had been cathartic for him and me. There was no one else I could have told the tale to in the language of the nightmares that still rocked my sleep.

Finally we dragged ourselves back to the present.

'So, I should call you Major Brodie now. I'm not surprised. And you're a reporter. A wordsmith. Also not a surprise. It's what you should have done. And I think there's more in you to come, Douglas. Stories. Tales of love and action. Truths told within a story. Hannah always said so.'

'I hope she was right. She usually was. But tell me, Isaac, what do you know of these rumours about people taking the law into their own hands? Of punishment squads?'

'Yes, yes. It's the talk of the community.'

'It's happening *within* your community?'

'No. Not among us. But we have Gentile friends and customers. They have first-hand knowledge. I tell you this, Douglas, some of us are happy about it. If the police won't deal with it, then the citizens must, is what some say.'

'Where is the law then, Isaac? Where are the rules that we live by? Where is the city?'

'Where was the law on *Kristallnacht*? Where was the law in Belsen? If a tyrant rises up and lays down new laws that give power to one group over another, is that a law to be followed? Or if the laws themselves are good and fair but are not enforced, then the powerful fill the vacuum for their own ends. So what should a citizen do?'

I had no answer, or none that I could support with good arguments. I left more troubled than when I arrived, though glad to pick up the links of an old friendship. Isaac promised to call me at the *Gazette* if he had solid news and firm sightings of the work of these self-appointed lawmen.

ELEVEN

I had a restless sleep and it wasn't just the hot night or the shouting match in the flat below. The tenement block where I rented digs looked solid enough from the outside but the builders had stinted on the walls and ceilings. I sat at my open window in the dark, nursing a cigarette and praying for some cool breeze to ruffle the air. Below me was a torn square of tarmac enclosed by the straggling backs of other tenements. Unsparing moonlight exposed our poverty.

It wasn't the first sleepless night since demob last November but it was the first in a while when I was reluctant to close my eyes. I missed my command but it had left seeping sores in my mind. It wasn't that I expected ghouls or incoming shells, though they often figured in my dreams. Sometimes it would be me running and getting nowhere, sometimes being pressed and surrounded by great boulders. Forces I could do nothing to surmount. One of the variations on helplessness that left me drained and depressed.

It didn't take a student of Freud or a fairground gypsy stirring tea leaves to fathom out what it meant. Most of us get through our days, our lives, pretending we're in control of events. Not far beneath this veneer we know it's shit. Too many times in the past few years I'd had my nose rubbed in my own insignificance, my own non-mastery of my fate. For my sanity's sake I usually managed to paper over it and convince myself and others that I'm a free man with a free spirit. I knew tonight I wasn't going to fool anyone, especially not me. Whisky wouldn't help.

To add to it, the rowing began down below. I lay on my clammy sheets and listened to the pattern of tears and anger. I wanted to tell them not to waste their breath, that whatever was eating them didn't count for much. That what mattered was having someone else in your life to share a sunrise or a memory with. That what mattered was not being alone. But why would they listen to *me*?

I woke, groggy and hot, and wishing for a cool bath to soak away the sweat and fog in my brain. I made do with a flannel and cold water from the sink. I masked a pot of tea and looked round my domain in the harsh daylight. It didn't take me long. One room with a hole-in-the-wall bed, the sheets perfectly folded for inspection. A metal grate and two gas rings, a sink, a coal hole and a rickety table and one wooden chair. Gas lights, one with a broken mantle. Two strips of lino that didn't meet and were riddled with holes. A wardrobe surely salvaged from the Clydebank blitz topped by my empty suitcase.

This wouldn't do. I was going to make a success of my job at the *Gazette* and get myself a decent place in the West End, that blessed land created in the last century by the mercantile class who wanted to be dishing out smog rather than receiving it from the prevailing westerlies. An *apartment*, as they were now calling them, maybe with two rooms, and even my own bathroom with a toilet and bath. A man must dream.

It was barely seven and already heating up outside. I left my hat and jacket behind and set out into the morning with a new determination to at least live for the day. I got to the newsroom and belted out five hundred words on the anecdotes I'd picked up on yesterday and spent the rest of the day renewing acquaintances or striking old ones off my list if they'd gone to ground. In whatever sense.

*

By the time I was in the evening queue outside the Curzon I was regretting suggesting the pictures. It was a pint I needed. Or two. Sam arrived on the dot of seven looking well scrubbed and remarkably cool. She wore a white blouse and grey skirt and a neat little grey cap at a jaunty perch on her short blonde hair. She looked thinner, and as she leaned close for a peck on the cheek, I saw the dark eyes under the make-up. I smelled peppermint on her warm breath, and the faint tang of the classy perfume she sometimes wore.

'You look fine, Sam.'

'Death warmed up. But you look worse, Brodie. Been burning the candle both ends? You won't keep up with McAllister. Or is it some young thing you're seeing? It can fair drain a man.'

'I'm sure it's the heat. Look, how much do you really want to see this flick? You know it's going to drift along for a bit then end badly for everybody. The title says it all. Unrequited love.'

'You sound like an expert.'

'I need a drink.'

Her face tightened. I saw a flash of – what? Panic? – in her expression.

'I really don't. Do you mind? I hear it's good.'

As she was talking she was digging out her specs from her bag. She popped them on and drew a halt to the discussion.

We watched it. Towards the end she dabbed her eyes. I blew my nose. We stood outside in the twilight.

'Told you so,' I said.

'Och, I knew that's how it'd end too.'

'Not where I grew up.'

'Oh?'

'Too civilised. They never even got into bed.'

Sam coloured. 'It's about morals, standards. How people handle themselves when they're torn between loyalty and desire.'

'Among the middle classes, maybe. Not round here.' The

street was teeming with laughing shop girls and their beaus, teasing and tantalising in their unashamed celebration of being young and lusty.

'At least they gave it a try. The important thing is having a go, Brodie.'

It had been a double feature and it was too late now for a drink. The pubs were shutting. It meant we didn't talk about Johnson and I didn't raise the small matters of Ishmael, revenge and the Glasgow Marshals. I hailed a cab and waved her off, wondering how and whether I should have a go. And at what.

So far, I'd had two clear signs of vigilantes at work: Docherty and Gibson's punishments, both substantiated by letter. I'd also had hints of wider, targeted violence from Duncan Todd and Isaac. There were other potential examples in other newspapers. But I needed to bring it all together to see the extent, to understand the pattern. Like standing back from an Impressionist in the Kelvingrove Art Gallery.

Over the next couple of days I went to the Mitchell library and read back issues of our competitors covering the past couple of months before and since the Johnson trial: The Glasgow Herald, The Scotsman, The Times, the Daily Record. A story here, an anecdote there; taken separately, nothing unusual. Nobody connecting the incidents. No other paper reported receiving a warning letter. Maybe I was reading too much into it, like Gypsy Jean's tea leaves.

I tuned my ears to conversations: old women passing the time of day in the post office queue, gossiping in the butcher's or hanging out the tenement windows in the summer warmth; men making casual observations over a pint in between the more serious contemplation of Hibs' chances in the Cup and the prospects of petrol coming off rationing any time this side of the last trump. Scatterings and eddies of something different happening, something possibly momentous.

I got hold of a sixpenny street map of Glasgow and put a number on places where incidents had been reported. Separately I kept descriptions of the incidents. In particular I noted down any criminal accusation made against the victim either from a newspaper or bit of street gossip. I began trying to trace the people. I started with the Glasgow Royal and the Western Infirmary. The ward matrons were quick to get over their qualms about revealing ward gossip.

'We've had four now, to my knowledge. Three lost a finger as well as what else got done to them. More tea, Mr Brodie?' She aimed her pot at me.

'Thank you, Matron. It's very good of you to take the time.' I held out my cup for a second. I'd caught this tiny wee field marshal of the nursing profession just as she was going off duty at the Royal.

'Ah'm no saying anything, mind, but every one of them deserved what they got. If you believe the stories.' She began counting. 'Number one was into drugs; selling them to weans, so he wis. We had to pump his stomach oot – filled with his ain medicine. Number two was a pimp always beating up his lassies. They carved out his trade on his forehead. The third one drowned his ain wife, they said, but they couldnae prove it. He got fished oot the Clyde wi' weights tied round him. Only just in time. The last yin. Oh dear . . .'

'Was it that bad, Matron?'

'Naw. It was really funny. You shouldnae laugh, neither you should. This fella had been fiddling the wages of the workers down at the yards. They found him tied to a lamppost in his bare bum.'

I laughed. 'Is there a photo?'

'That wisnae it. They'd got hold of one o' they rivets from the shipyards. A thing about nine inches long with a cap. A wide cap.' Her face filled with proper matronly rectitude. 'They had to—'

'Don't tell me!'

*

Where I uncovered a name and address I went and knocked on the door. The first was a double bus ride away in Partick. It was a leafy street of semi-detached villas. Why should that be an unlikely setting for a victim of vigilantes? I walked up to the door and pressed the bell. Finally a woman answered. Middle-aged, hair in curlers, wary-eyed.

'Sorry to bother you, Mrs Stephens. My name is Brodie. I'm from the *Gazette*. Can I—'

'No, you can't!' She slammed the door.

I waited a minute, then rang again.

She came back out. This time she was weeping. 'We don't want to talk about it. It's all too, too horrible.'

A man appeared behind her. 'I'm not running away. Is this what you wanted to see?'

He was a lank-haired man with a barrel chest. He pushed back his forelock. The weals and scar tissue stood out red against his pale skin. The letter T glowed in jagged letters across his forehead.

'They called me a thief! But *they* robbed *me*!'

'How much did they take?'

'Does it matter?'

'Possibly.'

'Five or six pounds. They were good enough to leave me the taxi fare to the infirmary.' The sarcasm dripped from his lips.

'Last question, Mr Stephens. I understand your company went bust. A hundred men laid off without a penny. But all the bosses walked off with fat pensions and bonuses. Do you think that's what they meant about thieving?'

'Ridiculous! We did everything by the book! And you can stick that in your rag of a paper! Now clear off before we call the police.'

I tracked down another name to a pawnbroker in the East End. The shop was dark and jammed with glass cases overflowing with baubles. People's precious knick-knacks.

'How can I help, sir?' The man stood behind his counter with his hands behind his back.

'Mr Gillespie? I'm from the *Gazette*. I hear you had some trouble.'

'Trouble? Is this what you mean?' He brought his hands round and held them out to me. His fingers were claws drawing the eye to the perfect raw circle at the centre of each palm. A scorch mark.

'What happened?'

He nodded upwards at set of three balls, a miniature sign of his profession hanging above his head.

'They dragged me roon the back. I've a wee kitchen there wi' a gas stove. They heated them up. They made me haud two o' them.' His face creased in horror. 'It was the smell that was the worst.' His eyes lost focus and I thought for a moment he would faint. 'I can still smell it.' Then he staggered and came to. 'Sorry, pal. Sorry. It was just a couple of weeks back. Ah still . . . '

'It's OK, Mr Gillespie. Did they say anything?'

He drooped with weariness. 'Oh aye. They said it was for playing wi' the weights. That I was fiddling.'

'And were you, Mr Gillespie?'

'Who disnae? It's the only way to make ony money these days.'

'Did they take anything?'

'A few quid. Funny that. I had a fair amount in the till but they just took about a fiver's worth.'

I could only trace or interview ten of the nineteen on my list. Even fewer were prepared to talk about what had happened. Embarrassed? But a picture was emerging. A pattern of people being attacked, mainly in the scruffier parts of the city. No surprises in that. But these weren't random. Nor were they happening just after the pubs closed on a Saturday. Nor because Rangers lost at home, or an Orange March had got out of hand. They seemed to be targeted on known bad boys.

This made the attacks popular – unless of course you were on the receiving end. In the earlier attacks no one was robbed. Later, money was being taken. But they weren't cleaning out their victims.

Someone was bypassing the tiresome bureaucracy of the courts and ministering punishment to the wayward. Just like the good old days when criminals and fornicators were branded with hot irons, these self-appointed judges, jury and executioners were leaving an indelible reminder of wickedness chastised. Some were being scarred. Some losing the end joint of the pinkie. With a cigar cutter. Neat job. I wondered if the mad cigar men kept them as souvenirs? Cannibal chiefs in grass skirts sporting a string of dried digits round their necks?

My doubts about the threats and portents in the Marshals' letters shaded into certainty. The timing fitted with Ishmael being at the heart of it. The big story started unfolding after Johnson's trial. Then it accelerated following his suicide. Doubling up like an epidemic stirring. I could plead being the new boy for not reporting it sooner. Or not wanting to set the hounds after Ishmael without real proof; not to mention my guilt about Johnson. Alternatively, I'd ignored the signs because I wanted to. Bad guys were getting what was coming to them for a change. What was happening was too near my own cavalier sense of morality for comfort. In the opaque glasshouse of my soul, I wasn't about to start throwing stones at anyone.

On Friday I took my street map, my interview notes and my deductions to Eddie. But I was worried. Once we gave publicity to an outbreak of vigilante acts, I could picture light bulbs going off in a thousand dumb heads across Glasgow: *Oh, that's a good idea.* Before you know it, everybody would be at it. I could at least play down the finger-snipping and the face-marking. We'd then stand a chance of sifting the general score-settling from the specific acts of the Marshals.

I was thinking more as a copper than a reporter, but that's what you get when you jump careers.

'Fuck me, Brodie! This is big! You think there's more to come?'

'It's likely, Eddie. I've identified nineteen cases that fit this profile.' I showed him my list. 'The guys who wrote these letters aren't seeing things through normal eyes. They're on a mission. I don't know if I'll be the recipient of the next letter but I'm sure there will be one.'

'Brodie, it had effin' better be you. This is the sort of thing that the public loves. A story they can follow every day. Like a Jane cartoon. It's what sells!'

As I was talking through the material with Eddie, a theory presented itself. I should have spotted it sooner. I could have done the further research of this lead myself but why pass up an opportunity? I found myself seeking a second opinion – a legal opinion – late on Friday night.

TWELVE

That evening I made beer patterns on the pub's table to explain my findings to Wullie. I got his breezy agreement that we had a big story. Almost as big as the one he himself claimed to be unravelling about the savage death of Alec Morton. Not that he was ready to share the details yet . . .

Come closing time, Wullie and I fell out of Ross's, did the usual hand-clasping brothers-in-ink vows, and stumbled on our separate ways. Creature of habit that I am, the siren smell of battered cod, deep fried in beef dripping, dragged me into the nearby Tallies. I asked for double salt and vinegar and shied off into the night clutching my hot poke, burning my fingers with every chip and sucking them for relief and for savour.

With an imp in charge of my brain I found myself steering a path directly away from my tenement flat in Dennistoun. Like a faulty homing pigeon I ploughed my way along Sauchiehall Street, on up the hill to the rarefied heights of the terraces of Kelvingrove Park. I took a final flight of stone stairs up on to a sweep of grand grey sandstone townhouses. I started counting them off until I was outside my target. There was a light on at the upstairs window. I wondered whether to try a halloo or hurl a chip at the window. I chose discretion.

I used the big brass knocker to echo my presence through the hallway. The echo died. A couple of lines from 'Tam o'

Shanter' came to mind: 'Where sits our sulky sullen dame . . . Nursing her wrath to keep her warm.' There was a long still spell. I swayed and reached for the knocker again, but just then I heard light feet descending the stairs and marching towards the door. Bolts were drawn and Tam's nemesis stood there with arms folded. She cocked her head to one side.

'It's Friday night. The pubs have closed. Sweet Romeo calls.'

I stuck out the remnants of my fish supper. 'Want a chip?' I smiled encouragingly.

Sam Campbell looked at me in that way of hers. A parent permanently disappointed in her wayward offspring. She shook her head. 'No,' she sighed. 'Come in, Brodie, and leave your poke outside. I don't want the stink through the house.'

'Fussy now, are we?' I nevertheless carefully tucked the newspaper round the smelly repast and laid it gently on the step. For later. Just in case my visit was curtailed. 'There was a time . . .'

'. . . for everything under the heavens. Even fish suppers. I know, I know. I'll make tea. Shut the door.'

I followed her downstairs. Soon the bellyful of starch and fat in a lake of sweet milky tea did its trick and I began to sober up fast at Sam's kitchen table. I began to notice things about her. The red eyes. The paler-than-usual face. Chain-smoking. In turn, she eyed me warily across her own cup until she saw something approaching lucidity in my expression.

'So, an early wake-up call, Brodie?'

'Sorry, sorry, Sam. I didn't mean to . . .'

'You never do, Brodie.'

'I just miss . . .' – I fought back the word *you* – '. . . talking to you.'

Her face softened into the gentle shape that I'd once – just once – seen beside me on a pillow. Then it tightened again.

'You're drunk. Don't start.'

I reined in the maudlin outburst before it got me thrown out. I never managed to hit the right tone with women. There was something about what I said or how I said it that made them wary. It had been a close-run thing with me and Samantha Campbell. Sam of the dirty blonde hair and freckles. My partner in the failed attempt to save Hugh Donovan from a hanging. My brave sidekick as we tracked down the real culprits: the Slattery gang aided by corrupt police and forsworn priests.

In so many ways, we'd failed to take at the flood this particular tide in the affairs of men – and women. Afterwards I told myself that Sam and I could still take up with each other romantically and properly. That we could still avoid the shallows and the miseries. But in the immediate aftermath of the murder and the newspaper frenzy, there had been too much between us and yet not enough. Contact stopped. Friday nights excepted, of course.

'Was there a particular topic? Or did you just have random blethering in mind?' she was asking me, not unkindly.

'Do you read the *Gazette*?'

'When I want the gossip.' There was mischief in her reddened eyes.

'I wasn't fishing . . .'

'Brodie, of *course* I read your wee column. I'm really pleased for you.'

I looked at her warily, searching for any hint of irony and finding none. She pushed her hair back behind her ears. I noticed her nails were bitten and ragged, not like the short, neat grooming when I first met her. I noticed, too, the dark rings under her sharp blue eyes. I'd also spotted a couple of empties under the sink.

'OK, you'll maybe have seen my article the other day about the guy—'

'The tar and feathering! God almighty, that must have hurt.'

'And the week before that I wrote about a fella who'd had his arms broken in umpteen places by an iron bar?'

She nodded and grimaced. 'Connected?'

I told her about the knife scars and the letters.

'Sam, this all started after Alan Johnson's trial. It spread like chickenpox following his suicide.'

Her hand clasped her mouth. 'Ishmael!'

'I'm sure of it.'

We gazed at each other for a bit.

She said, 'So, Ishmael and a pal?'

'A lot more than one pal. Unless they've got bikes. These boys have been busy. I've identified seventeen similar cases. Nineteen including Docherty and Gibson.'

'If it is him, how does he choose them?'

'From the courts.'

'You mean they're punishing convicted criminals?'

'I mean they're punishing folk who *weren't* convicted. Acquittals. The ones who *should* have been. The ones that got off.'

'Thanks to lawyers like me, you mean!'

'Sam. Samantha, I didn't come here to accuse you. Or your fellow advocates. If there's not enough evidence to convict, then your job is to get your client off.'

She was mollified. 'You want me to do some checking?'

I smiled and pulled out a scruffy piece of paper with nineteen names on it. She grabbed it. She scanned it quickly then pushed it back. 'None I recognise.'

There was relief in her voice. She meant *none of mine*.

She stood up. 'This needs something stronger. Come on.' She led the way up the stairs and into the hall, then on up a further flight to the drawing room. She left the room for a bit then came back with a writing pad under one arm and carrying two crystal tumblers and a bottle of something pale and wonderful. She saw me looking askance.

'Or have you had enough for one night?'

I glanced at my watch. 'It's a new day. In fact it's a Saturday. We're on holiday.'

She went over to the gramophone. She lifted the lid and selected a record. She wound up the handle and placed the needle on the vinyl. The sound of Peggy Lee filled the room:

'. . . Jack of all trades, master of none,
And isn't it a shame,
I'm so sure that you'd be good for me
If only you'd play my game . . .'

I wondered if it was deliberate. What was Sam's game? Did she even know herself? She came back to the table and splashed some golden fluid in both glasses.

'You can stop here the night. What's left of it. But don't get any ideas, Brodie. Your old room, OK? It might be dusty. Everything's locked up . . . '

I smiled. '*Sláinte*, Sam. To my old room, dusty or not.'

'Cheers, Brodie. Now give me the list. Then you can tell me all the gossip about this job of yours . . . '

I woke Saturday morning unsure of where I was or who I was. Or whose head I'd borrowed. Sam was nursing a tea when I got down to the kitchen. I guess neither of us was a pretty sight.

'I should have brought two fish suppers. To soak it up.'

'You're the snake in the garden, Brodie.'

'You brought the apple.'

'Don't get at me.'

'I need some fresh air.'

'Fancy a swim?'

'What? Where?'

'The Western Baths Club. Just over the back of the park. Off the Byres Road. As a woman, I'm only an associate member but I can take a guest. The Bathsmaster is a Campbell. My folks got me in years ago. I should use it more often. More than once a year.'

Suddenly the thought of sliding into a cool body of water seemed exactly what my hot brain needed. To feel weightless. To float on my back and let all the cares drift away from me. To let the cool water soak into my skin and rehydrate my poor innards.

'I don't have a cossie.'

'They provide them. Red for a boy. Black for us girls.'

'Lead me to it.'

She did. It was bliss. I'd seen the building years ago and admired its Athenian red sandstone colonnades. We walked into an imposing tiled hall with a double-sided staircase winding away from the front door. Sam asked for the Baths-master, her namesake Robert Campbell. An upright man in his late years appeared with a smile.

'Miss Campbell, how nice to see you. But it's not ladies' day.'

'I know, Robert. But I'd like to introduce Major Douglas Brodie. The major would like to join the club. Do you have a vacancy for a war hero?'

'I'm sure we do, Miss Campbell. Welcome to our club, Major.'

I nodded with all the dignity expected of a decorated veteran.

'We'll need another seconder, but I'm sure that's no bother, and in the meantime, we can provide temporary membership for a month while we check out references and do all the paperwork.'

The Bathsmaster personally went off to get a pair of trunks and towel. I turned to Sam.

'References?'

'They just want to know if you've got a job, Brodie, and haven't got a criminal record. You don't, do you?'

'Thanks for the unquestioning belief in me, Sam. Can I afford this?'

'It's only five guineas. Can you afford not to? You're drinking too much.'

'*I* am . . .!'

Robert appeared and I was left to stifle my protests. Besides, she was right.

Sam left me to it and I took my first glorious dip in the great vaulted chamber. The dangling trapezes and hoops over the pool were a bit too much *mens sana in corpore sano* for my liking, but the swimming itself was bliss.

That night I met Morag for a drink and a long walk by the river. I suddenly felt confused holding hands with this nubile wee lassie and stealing kisses like a spotty youth.

'How old are you, Morag?'

'Ah'm nineteen. Twenty next month.'

Oh, God. 'Do you know how old I am?'

'It disnae matter. You're a nice bloke. An officer in the army. And you write great. A' the girls fancy you. A' that stuff about the Slattery gang . . .'

Just what my ego needed: hero worship by a teenager. We kissed and cuddled on a bench, but I could swear there were a pair of shrewd blue eyes watching every move. Appraising. Mocking.

The swimming club was closed on Sunday or I'd have gone back for more. Carving steady lengths gives a man time to think. Time to weigh the attractions of a bouncy wee redhead versus a hard-shelled blonde.

Instead I woke early in my hot bed and replayed in my head the image of a pool that was so far removed from the pea-green experience of my youth. No dive-bombing, towel-flicking hooligans. Just cool clear water and two other men swimming lanes and wishing me good morning. I had a month to sort out my priorities before facing the sharp financial choice: fags and booze versus watery bliss and exercise. I knew what I *needed* to do. What I ought to do. But whether or not a daily swim would clear my thoughts about women was another matter. Besides, I had the morning planned. I'd decided to skip my Sunday morning hospital round in favour of a duty visit to Kilmarnock. I'd promised my mother I'd go to the kirk with her. I caught an early train and met her outside the big wooden door of St Andrew's. She was beaming and wanting to show me off. We did the rounds of her pals who all scrutinised me for signs of sin and degeneracy. That's what Glasgow does for you. It's in the water. I wished I still had my major's uniform to give them something more positive to crow over. But at demob we'd had to hand back our khaki in exchange for a pinstripe from Burton's. A poor trade.

Still, the columns of the church didn't tremble as I entered, and the words of the hymns didn't stick in my throat. It was a long hot service. All I was aware of was the dust drifting through the sunlit shafts from the stained-glass windows. I was a boy again in my Boys' Brigade uniform, bowed over my bible, looking reverential, but in truth reading dirty bits from the Song of Solomon.

We walked home to Bonnyton and ate the potted herring and boiled tatties she'd saved. As a Sunday treat she fried up a slice of clootie dumpling. We had it with cream from the top of the bottle. While she was in the scullery I left her two ten-bob notes under the clock on her mantelpiece. I gave her a kiss and headed back to Glasgow on the late-afternoon train.

THIRTEEN

I was outside the front door of the Western Baths Club as it opened first thing Monday morning. Two other men were hovering with rolled-up towels for an early-morning treat. We nodded to each other and wished each other a good morning in that focused way of men about to go over the top. An hour later I came out starving, but convinced that there were no problems that couldn't be solved by thirty laps of a tiled pond.

The sense of well-being sustained me right up to the moment I found two blue uniforms waiting for me as I walked into the newsroom. They were in Eddie's office and were surely suffocating from the smoke. I tried to sneak past but that's why Eddie's office is positioned where it is. His door bounced open and a gust of foul air blasted out, followed by Big Eddie himself.

'*Mister* Brodie! Just the man. Come right in.'

I squeezed into the already jammed room. Eddie climbed back behind his paper fortifications and faced the two policemen sitting in cramped chairs opposite. They hadn't got up as I entered. I stood with my back against the wall and weighed up the boys in blue. The last time we'd met had been over the injured body of Alec Morton. One was the baby-faced sergeant, clasping his old-style pointy helmet in his lap as though hiding an erection. A copper's notebook lay open in front of him. The other was Chief Inspector Walter Sangster in full dress uniform. To impress me? His flat cap with the

Sillitoe check round its circumference was perched on a wobbly pile of Eddie's documents. He held both of the letters in his gloved hand.

I nodded at them. 'Chief Inspector Sangster, nice to see you again.'

'*Detective* Chief Inspector Sangster, *Mister* Brodie.'

'*Mazel tov*. What can I do for you, gentlemen?' I wondered if Duncan reported to him? And why hadn't he brought Todd along?

Sangster eyed me up and down. 'It seems you have a talent for attracting bother, Brodie.'

If anyone else told me that, I might start to believe it. I raised an eyebrow and waited.

'What's your connection with these vigilantes?' he asked.

'They commit crimes. I report them.'

His thin mouth tightened. 'I mean why are they writing to you, *personally*, Brodie?'

I noted we'd dropped the *Mister* pretty fast. 'I get fan mail. Maybe he likes my column.' Out of the corner of my eye I noticed warning frowns from my boss. I ignored him. 'What exactly are you insinuating, Sangster? That I'm somehow in cahoots with these characters?'

His sergeant – still unidentified apart from the number 71 on his shoulder – stuttered into life with a high voice. 'They haven't written to any other paper. Isn't that a bit strange?'

'Maybe they want the publicity? It was the *Gazette* that exploded the Donovan case. You'll recall? The innocent man you got hanged?'

Sangster coloured and took a deep breath to release the apoplexy that was threatening to melt his handful of brain cells. He raised his hand to stop his sergeant saying any more.

'An unfortunate business, Brodie, no doubt. Bad apples. But here' – he waved the letters – 'we've got a group of men on the rampage, taking the law into their own hands, and we need to know all we can about them.'

'Everything we know, you know. It's all in the paper.' Except for the *nom de guerre* of the leader and reference to missing fingertips.

'So you say, Brodie. But I can read between the lines.' He waved the letters at me.

'Ah, that would be the invisible ink.'

'Don't be funny, Brodie.'

'And what are you finding between the lines?'

'I'm finding that you're in correspondence with men who claim to have carried out at least two major acts of grievous bodily harm. I even saw for myself the extent of the burns on this poor fellow . . .?'

'Gibson, sir,' said the sergeant.

'Aye, him. This could make you an accessory after the fact, Brodie, if you're holding anything back.'

'Oh spare me, Sangster. I'm a reporter. I'm doing my job. Isn't that right, Mr Paton?'

'Eh? Oh, aye, right enough.'

'Who's this man Johnson then?'

'You've a short memory. Just another innocent man hanged in Barlinnie. This time by his own hand. Remember the case of Sergeant Alan Johnson? Three weeks ago? Sent down for five for upsetting the Chief Constable's sister?'

Sangster's mouth screwed up. He let his bird-of-prey look flick between Eddie and me as if wondering which one to pounce on first. Suddenly he was on his feet. 'I'm keeping these.'

'Certainly, certainly,' said Eddie, leaping to his own feet and knocking over the pile of papers with the chief inspector's hat. Sangster's minion grappled around on the floor to retrieve his boss's headgear while Eddie spluttered apologies. I tried not to laugh. Sangster finally eased out of the door murmuring not very veiled threats about the consequences of failing to report crimes or withholding information about crimes about to be committed.

I turned to Eddie. 'You were very cooperative.'

'Fuck me, Brodie, what was I to do? I had to hand over the letters.'

'They like throwing their weight about. We need to stand up to them.'

'Oh aye, it's OK for you to talk, Brodie. But it's my ba's that get kicked first. Besides, we have a useful relationship with the polis. Something we have to cultivate.'

He even winked at me.

FOURTEEN

Sam called me back on Tuesday morning and we met for a drink after work in Sloan's off Argyll Street. It was her suggestion, and it was, by a long way, more salubrious than any of the bars I frequented with my partner in crime-reporting. Polished wood panelling and tiled floors, etched glass divides and glittering lighting. We met in the lounge bar below the smart restaurant. I promised myself a meal there when my pay packet caught up with my aspirations. Maybe I needed a second job? A paper round, perhaps.

I rose from my seat as she appeared. She looked every inch the professional lawyer. Hair sleek and trimmed, make-up accentuating her eyes behind the inquisitorial glasses. She wore a dark blue business ensemble that would have got nodding approval from the fustiest judge. My shiny second-hand suit felt dowdy by comparison. Under her arm she'd tucked a slim black briefcase. To an onlooker it could have been a meeting between a top lawyer and her down-at-heel client. The only giveaway was her nails; still near the quick but filed instead of savaged.

I smiled. 'We should do this more often.'

'Let's see how this one goes,' she said, smacking me into place. Coolness personified. I still didn't know how it had come out this way between us. Not after what we'd been through together. Not after – well, not to put too modest a point on it – I'd saved her skinny backside. Within a few days of getting her back to her grand house in Kelvingrove, and making her endless cups of tea, she'd asked me to leave. *Need some time; it's not about you, Brodie; just want some peace for a while; think things through; try to forget, etc. etc.* Admittedly Sam had been chloroformed, abducted, beaten up and generally badly treated by a psychopathic child abuser, but I thought our shared horrors would have brought us together. Women are unfathomable. But, still, she was here.

We bantered for a bit while drinks were brought. Sam had a sherry; I had a lemonade. She looked at me and my drink sceptically, then drew out a foolscap jotter from her briefcase. She laid it down between us, sideways to us both. It had a list of the names I'd given her. Against each, in her elegant writing, were three columns. She reached over and pointed with her fountain pen.

'These are the dates in the last two months when these men came before the court. These are the offences they were accused of. These are the verdicts.'

All of the nineteen names had court dates and accusations against them. Sixteen were found not guilty. Three, not proven. The two I'd taken grapes to at Glasgow Infirmary had been found not guilty a month ago.

I whistled. 'Are these details available to the public?'

'At the court offices.'

'But none of yours?'

She flushed, the freckles round her nose fading into the pink. 'No. I've not ... I've not been that busy lately. Been having some time off. But to tell the truth, none of mine was found innocent.'

I leaned over to her and put my hand out to hers. She drew it back as though I was a fully charged lighting rod.

'Sam, you've had a rough time. Take it easy.'

Her eyes glistened. 'Damn it, Brodie. It's been four months! It's stupid!'

'It's not.'

'Look at *you*! Not a care. A new job. Everything going for you. And I'm glad. I mean it.'

I took out my cigarettes, gave her one and lit them both. It steadied us both. I shook my head.

'You were right at the weekend, Sam. I'm drinking too much. Hardly surprising, working alongside Wullie McAllister.' I pointed at the untouched lemonade. I grinned and got a small smile in return. 'The booze helps me sleep. Sometimes. The stuff I dream about!'

'Good! No, I'm sorry. I mean it's good that you're not immune. That you feel . . . something.'

I lowered my voice and leaned closer to avoid being overheard. 'It's not guilt though.' I wanted her to understand. 'Maybe war blunts the conscience. All I know is that Gerrit Slattery was going to kill you. And me.' I didn't mention the other blood on my hands. Sam knew there had been violence at Dermot Slattery's farm in Fermanagh but I'd never told her the details, and she'd never asked.

'Like this lot?' She tapped the paper in front of her.

I sighed. 'That's the thing, isn't it? Who am I to talk?'

Her mouth turned up. 'You should be in the clear. Ishmael's work is cold and calculating. Premeditated. Whatever happened between you and Gerrit was self-defence. I'm worse than you. I wanted those scum dead. What they did to those wee boys . . .'

'And you, Sam. And you.'

I had stomach-churning picture of her pale face with far-off eyes, lying in the bottom of a boat as she was carried away from me. The same image must have passed through her mind. Her eyes filled. She waved her hand.

'He didn't rape me. I'm not dead. I just wish I could get on. I'm sure I'm already getting a reputation; if you want to get a conviction, pray that Sam Campbell is the defence lawyer. I'm getting fewer instructions from Glasgow solicitors. My stable in Edinburgh has been dropping hints that maybe it's time to close this particular outpost. Bring me into the fold. Keep an eye on me, more like.'

The prospect of her moving to Edinburgh seemed like a terrible idea. 'Rubbish, Sam. Do you have anyone to talk to about it? A doctor?'

'And say what? My doctor said it was nerves. He gave me some pills. They made me throw up.'

'Friends?' She'd mentioned girlfriends before.

'Oh, I've had them all round. Maggie Dalrymple, Moira Rankin. The gossips. Sorry, that's not fair. They're old pals and they've been kind. Moira even stayed a couple of nights to make sure I didn't swallow my whole prescription at once. That, and nosiness. Wanting to know all about Douglas Brodie, scourge of gangsters and corrupt cops.' She gazed at me with a furious intensity, as if daring me to laugh.

'They say talking helps.'

She shook her head. 'Not when you can't discuss it all. Not when there are some things that can't be said.'

I wondered how much she did know, or guess? She suddenly stubbed her fag out and took a couple of deep breaths. She took off her glasses, rubbed the bridge of her nose and focused her limpid blue eyes on me again.

'Brodie, how're your digs?'

I blinked at the change in topic. 'They're fine. I mean the landlady gives me a hard time about taking my turn cleaning the stairs. And the gas meter eats shillings. But it's fine.'

I didn't tell her it was a top-floor hovel up a spiral of worn concrete steps and falling plaster. That I looked out on a barren back close with a midden heap in one corner. That the ground-floor houses seemed to be occupied by a large number of over-made-up lassies who had visitors at all times of day and night.

'Because if you needed . . . I mean if you ever had to . . .'

'Sam, what are you saying? Spit it out.'

She pushed back from the table, eyes blazing. 'My house is so bloody big and so bloody quiet and so bloody empty it's driving me bloody crazy and I can't talk to anyone else about what happened and I hate drinking alone . . .' She stopped, took a deep breath, then, 'Do you want your old room back?'

I hid the smile that threatened to split my face. 'Well, I'd need to give notice. And I couldn't afford to pay much . . .'

'Don't you play hard to get with me, Douglas Brodie! Unless you've got a rich benefactor who's putting you up at the Ritz, this is a great offer. Hand over your ration card and two pounds a week and it's a deal. I'll feed us. I might even get a woman in to clean for us, like I used to. The place is like a tip. We split the whisky. Not that we're going to be drinking much.' She stared contemptuously at my glass.

'How could I refuse?'

I hadn't had such an offer since basic training when my sergeant major asked me if I'd mind terribly much doing a further twice round the assault course with full pack for failing to get back from two days' leave on time. Irresistible. Except of course for one thing: wee Morag. What was I going to do about her? Sneak her back to my bedroom past my new landlady? Why not? It wasn't as if the landlady in question was offering me anything other than a roof over my head.

'Sod you, Brodie, if you don't want to . . .'

'Sam, Sam, nothing would give me greater pleasure. Would this weekend do? I won't need a van for the flitting. Nor even a barra'. Why are you crying?'

'I'm not.' She dabbed at her eyes, sniffed and pointed at the list of names. 'Good. That's settled. So what are we going to do now, Sherlock?'

I liked the use of *we*. 'See Big Eddie.'

FIFTEEN

I found Eddie in his den behind his ransacked desk.

'Murder and havoc, Brodie! Don't you enter these sacred portals unless you have a tale of gore and outrageous effing depravity.'

'I've got an angle, Eddie. On this vigilante case.'

'Spit it oot.'

I told him about the match between the victim list and the acquittals without mentioning Sam's role; she didn't want any limelight.

'. . . and I'd like to put a column out that shows this connection.'

'Bloody brilliant, Brodie! I can see how you did well in the polis!'

'I'll write it up. I also want to make sure we're the only paper he talks to.'

'He?'

'He or they. But as far as I can tell, no other paper's getting those charming epistles. We want to keep it that way.'

'How?'

'I'd like to offer them a chance to go into print themselves. Make a personal appeal inviting them to write a letter to the *Gazette* agreeing to give up their evil ways.'

'You think they will?' Eddie looked disappointed.

'Not a chance. But that's not the point. They've twice contacted us. We should respond directly. Make this a dialogue. They're looking for publicity and we can control it.

I'm also scared that unless someone reins them in, people will die.'

I watched his face. His eyes scuttled round his office, then: 'Ah've had nothing from McAllister for days. We'll do yours as an editorial. Write it. Show me.' He yanked out his watch. 'Two hours. Go.'

It took me an hour. It was already in my head. But it was as though someone else was writing it. Amanuensis or mild schizophrenia? The dark side of me kept asking why I was trying to put a stop to an effective, if irregular form of crime reduction. But the saner part had control of the typewriter. After a sharp and educational encounter with Sandy's blue pencil, this was what went to press on Wednesday:

VIGILANTES STALK GLASGOW COURTS

Today, the *Gazette* can reveal that self-appointed law enforcers are prowling the Scottish Courts of Justice. Where these malcontents disagree with not-guilty verdicts, they take the law into their own hands and administer brutal punishment to innocent people. For let there be no doubt. In the eyes of the law, if a man has been found innocent then he is innocent. No one standing outside the law has the right or authority to overturn a legal judgment, far less inflict illegal chastisement. That is the slippery slope to barbarism.

Brilliant detective work by the *Gazette*'s Special Crime Reporter reveals a pattern of mal intent. In the past two months nineteen men were charged with crimes ranging from rape to grievous bodily harm. In each case the defendants were duly tried and found innocent or the case was not proven. It is not this paper's job to question the judgment of the courts. And it is certainly not the job of any amateur and wholly unauthorised private citizen. Yet every one of these nineteen innocent men has since suffered cruel punishment by self-appointed vigilantes.

Over the last two weeks the *Gazette* has received anonymous letters threatening action of this kind. We assume
the letter-writers are the perpetrators of these vile acts.
We call on these disaffected citizens to cease their illegal
activities. There is no place in a civilised society for taking
the law into private hands. All men are equal before the
law and the law must be allowed to carry out its duties
impartially and by careful sifting of the evidence.

The *Gazette* makes a public offer to these vigilantes.
Write to us again, but this time renouncing violence. We
will publish your letter in full . . .

There then followed the list of names of the men who'd
been found innocent in law but had nevertheless been cruelly
chastised by person or persons unknown. I had little hope of
getting a reasoned response from these letter-writing
maniacs, far less a full *mea culpa*, but it might get some sort
of reaction.

That evening I sat in Sam's library sipping some ruthlessly
diluted whisky and reviewing the column with her. In
advance of flitting in at the weekend I'd gone round to talk
about her contribution to the revelations. We had the Home
Service on in the background. I placed the paper down on the
side table between us.

'I have to confess to feeling a wee bit hypocritical about
this.'

Sam peered over her glasses and picked up the paper. 'That
conscience again, Brodie?'

'Last vestiges.'

'Tosh. *You* were rescuing a damsel in distress. This is
different. Ishmael and his gang' – she stabbed at the paper –
'are sadistic loonies. When I met him he was already burning
with righteous certainty. I wouldn't be surprised if he thought
he had a direct line to God. It's the sort of thinking that got
old dears burnt at the stake for keeping cats.'

'That's why we're trying to get a stronger line to him. It's only a matter of time before someone dies.'

'You think he'd go that far?'

'Why not? All it takes is for someone accused of murder to get off, and these loonies, as you call them, will don the black bonnet. They've already shown a penchant for playing with rope.'

Sam shivered. 'But why would they give up just because the *Gazette* asked them to? Aren't they more likely to feel vindicated with all this publicity? He's probably lapping this up.'

'Loving it. What really worries me is that the great Glasgow public are beginning to see the Marshals as heroes. Stand at any bar in the city and you'll hear them referred to in the same rank as a Scotland captain after a win against the auld enemy. The simple fact is that there's something appealing to Joe Public about bypassing the long-drawn-out legal machinations, especially if they think it came up with the wrong result in their opinion, and giving the baddies a good hiding.'

Sam nodded. 'Even worse if the message gets out and crime starts to drop.'

'Exactly what's giving me qualms. There are nineteen men here' – now I pointed at the paper – 'who're so incapacitated that even if they had evil written through their bones like Rothesay rock, there's bugger all they could do about it for a while.'

I got up and retrieved the bottle and topped us both up to a level above homeopathic.

'I'll do four more laps in the morning.'

Sam studied me over her specs. Then we sat silently, sipping away, thinking about the consequences of the vigilante action. Knowing that taking the law into your own hands was wrong. Unless it seemed to be the better option.

SIXTEEN

There are pivotal moments in your life, usually when you don't realise it. A small change that leads to a bigger shift that causes a seismic upheaval. The Big Signalman throws a lever and switches the points. Suddenly you're on a completely different track, picking up speed, destination unknown.

On Saturday morning I went for a glorious wake-up swim. Then I went back to my squalid flat and packed my entire belongings in my one case, wrapped my set of sheets, pillow and towels – a Co-op special offer – in brown paper and string, and left my digs without a backward glance. I'd paid up to the end of the following week. One pound 15 shillings down the drain but I didn't regret a farthing. The harridan who owned the entire close sent her factor to try to strong-arm me into paying a month in lieu of the short notice. When I pointed out that my job at the *Glasgow Gazette* meant I could turn the spotlight on any criminal activity I liked, including tax-dodging, rent-overcharging and running a bawdy house, the factor grabbed the week's rent and ran for it.

I had no idea where Sam Campbell and I were going on a personal basis – nowhere probably. Maybe I had to accept that I just wasn't her type? – but I felt happy at the prospect of being around her. Our exchanges were a bit too sharp for comfort at times, but that's what you get when you befriend an educated woman of independent mind and means. I had no sense from her that this arrangement was anything other than sharing a bottle, some painful memories and a big empty house. There was certainly no prospect – she'd made it plain – of sharing her bed. Which kept bringing me back to Morag Duffy. She was in so many ways the opposite of Sam: light, frothy, fun and street-smart, as opposed to serious, challenging and intellectual-smart. If I boiled it down to basic chemistry and the even more basic chances of uninhibited sex, the choice was easy. But what would we talk about afterwards?

Leaving aside all thoughts carnal, there was the not inconsiderable bonus of swapping a dive for the run of an elegant house where my bedroom would be bigger than the entire single-end I was leaving. There was also the sheer hedonistic prospect of a toilet and bath to myself instead of sharing the stairheid lavvy and – in the days before joining the Western – paying for a slipper bath once a week at the municipal pool. These pluses more than compensated for anything as transitory as unrequited lust. I supposed.

It might also keep me out of the pub a bit. If I could afford my share of the whisky bill. Wullie would be disappointed.

I took the cross-city trams and deposited myself like a war evacuee at her door. All I lacked was a label round my neck. *Needs regular feeding and occasional Scotch. Ignore bouts of maudlin sentimentality.*

Sam opened the door and cocked her head to one side. She crossed her arms. 'I must be daft.' Only a slight lift of the corners of her eyes gave her away.

'Changed your mind?'

'Several times, Brodie. Several times. Come in. You know where your room is.'

It felt like coming home. High ceilings. Tasteful striped wallpaper and stucco coving. Big window looking out on the tiny back garden and the cobbled street that ran behind all the big townhouses in the terrace to provide access for tradesmen. Despite herself, Sam had even put a wee bunch of cheery marigolds in a vase on the sideboard. I put my case down on the carpet, feeling an untoward and no doubt unwarranted sense of peace.

I found Sam downstairs in the kitchen. Two cups of tea were laid out. Best china. She poured, and pushed across a set of keys. She smiled.

'I was ungracious at the door, Brodie. You know what I'm like. Welcome back.'

I smiled back. 'As you noticed, I didn't need much persuasion.' I dug in my jacket pocket and placed my ration card on the table together with two one-pound notes. 'Are you sure this is enough?'

'Booze separate. And another thing: I have certain standards in this house.'

I wondered what was coming and whether I'd switched one dragon landlady for another.

'That's your only suit, I suppose? Shirts? Collars?'

I flushed. 'I'm saving for a trip to the Co-op.'

'Good. But before you do, I want you to take a look in my dad's wardrobe. I'm finally having a clearout. Before anything goes to the church jumble sale, rummage through it. The suits are a bit on the old-fashioned side, but good cloth. And I had them all cleaned before I put them away. Don't know why I kept them really . . .'

I'd borrowed a good tweed suit of her father's before, having carelessly discarded my own in the Firth of Clyde. It was either maintain sartorial standards or drown. But I'd given it back when I bought the second-hand outfit I was wearing. I was touched and mildly embarrassed. I found myself jabbering.

'Sam, you're too kind. That's amazingly good of you. I can't thank you enough.'

'Wheesht. You'll be doing me a favour. The waists were a bit loose, I recall? Can you get them taken in? What are you smiling about?'

'I know just the man.'

'Oh, and for future reference the guns are locked away again. Not that you'll ever need to know that, will you? Your pen now being mightier than any sword?'

It was a pity. The other thing worth lusting after in this house was the matched pair of Dickson shotguns left by her dad. Scots-made killing machines of rare and exquisite beauty and balance. Their trademark round action gave a silk-smooth opening. And efficient; spent cartridges automatically eject when the gun is broken, saving crucial time on reloading.

'That's right. I'm an office boy now, Sam. Determined to lead a quiet and saintly life from here on. But remind me to have a look at your dad's ammunition. I had no problems with it – as you know. But we should check for moisture and rust. Maybe we can bag a few grouse sometime?'

I said it facetiously but she looked at me queerly and then finally said, 'Maybe we could at that, Brodie. I have a standing invitation to shoot at the estate of an old friend of my dad's. Up by Aberfoyle.'

Of course she did. We left it at that. I wasn't sure if that had constituted a date or just a pleasantry, but I fancied the idea of me in my tweeds stalking across the heather with Sam beside me carrying a silver whisky flask and spare shells. Such a dreamer. But it would be nice to overlay the last memory I had of crawling through gorse with a gun. My old outfit, the Seaforths, trained at Spean Bridge after we re-formed the regiment from the remnants of the British Expeditionary Force. We were wet for a fortnight, living in dripping tents, wearing sodden clothes, squelching through peat bogs. At first we had to stick heather fronds in our helmets and uniform as camouflage. But by the time we were dragged from the swamp our own personal moorland had taken root on us. We were at one with nature. It would have been perfect training for invading Holland, say. So our first posting was North Africa.

*

The second shift of track occurred later that afternoon. I'd agreed to meet Wullie at the Highland Light Infantry memorial in Kelvingrove Park. Though it was a fine day for strolling in the fresh air, I hadn't ever imagined doing so with Wullie McAllister. His invite to meet at the weekend so far from his saloon-bar haunts had been mysterious and out of character. Admittedly the pubs were closed in the afternoon but he'd have been able to raid an off licence to bridge the gap. I hadn't seen him for a few days and the invite had come by phone to the newsroom.

'Brodie? It's Wullie. I could do with a wee chat. What are you doing Saturday afternoon?'

'I'm flitting in the morning but free later. What's up?'

'I cannae just say. I'll explain the morn.' He told me where and when and hung up before I could ask anything else.

SEVENTEEN

I got to the HLI memorial and studied the soldier in his pith helmet and puttees. He sat awkwardly but realistically on a high rock, scouting for Boers. Given the choice of wars, I'd take his over mine. North Africa had been desert hot, and, later, it always seemed to be raining in France, except when it snowed in the Ardennes. There was no sign of Wullie. I walked a little past the memorial and saw him slouched over the parapet of the Prince of Wales Bridge.

He saw me coming, pushed himself up and with a nod of his head invited me to walk with him. Apart from the habitual fag dangling from his lip he looked different. Smarter, almost dashing. It wasn't just that he was in pale slacks and short sleeves. He seemed looser limbed, younger, as though he was wearing weekend skin. We started heading towards the Stewart Fountain.

'Fine day,' I said.

'It is that. Sorry for a' the mystery, Brodie.'

'Am I in bother, Wullie? Are you trying to break it to me gently that I'm getting my books?'

'Nut at a'. You're doing fine, so you are. Big Eddie's in awe of a' that education of yours. Not to mention the war-hero bit while he was sat on his fat arse. And Sandy says you have a nice style on the page. He says he hardly has to change a word.'

'I'd hate to see his blue pencil in full flow.'

'Trust me, Brodie, when you take over my desk, he'll hardly notice I've gone.'

'Don't be daft, Wullie . . .'

'Wheesht. Look, I wanted to meet you away from the office and away from the pub because wa's still have ears.'

I looked at him, wondering if he'd sneaked in a couple of wee goldies at lunchtime.

'Sounds big. What are you up to?'

'A breakthrough on the Morton murder. Beginning to hit the high notes in my swan song. Let's sit here.' He chose an isolated bench off the main path under the shade of a thick chestnut. He quickly and effortlessly rolled his own and lit up. I tugged on a Senior Service and waited.

'I'm no' going to tell you everything just yet. Partly because I still don't have all the facts.' He took a meaningful drag on his cigarette. 'Partly because it's *need to know.*'

'Christ, Wullie, have you been conscripted into the SOE? I thought they'd been disbanded.'

'That's the other thing. I didnae think you'd believe me.'

'I'm unshockable. Fire away.'

'You'll recall Sheridan mentioning the Bruce report?'

'The plan to knock down Glasgow and rebuild it out in the Campsies? A new Jerusalem? Where Rangers and Celtic fans will lie down together in brotherly love amidst green pastures . . .'

'Aye, aye, the very man. A heidcase. But the worst kind. A heidcase with a vision. The fact is, something's got to be done. The city's bursting. Have you smelt the Saltmarket in this heat? Even if Bruce's plans don't get totally accepted there's going to be upheaval. Hale streets torn down. Thoosands of new houses built. And where there's big change there's big money . . .'

He took a deep pull on his fag and spun it into the under-growth. Then, there, in the sunny park, surrounded by folk going about their Saturday business, laughing and joking, or just lying soaking up the sunshine, Wullie told me a tale of thieves and robber barons . . .

*

Glasgow corporation, like every big city after the war, had decided to renew itself. Whether like Coventry they were starting with a clean sheet thanks to Goering's Baedeker raids, or like Glasgow where decades of overcrowding had led to the worst slums in Europe, the city fathers were dreaming grandiose dreams. They'd heard the French had style and wanted to pay homage to Le Corbusier here in the North. They'd create an urban paradise where carefree citizens could promenade down leafy boulevards, where rickets and TB were banished. Where the gangs would lay down their razors and take up harp lessons. And where all would be happy, healthy and wise. All thanks to town planning. Tom Johnston, Secretary of State for Scotland – Churchill's 'King of Scotland' – had commissioned the Clyde Valley Regional Plan, a visionary masterpiece and, like enough, a recipe for chaos and profligacy.

The trouble is that in many a Glaswegian's veins runs the blood of an entrepreneur. Stand in a pub for longer than five minutes and strangers will sidle up with offers to sell you anything from dirty postcards to the bloody head of a freshly rustled sheep. At the other end of the scale the city has more than its fair share of dynasties built on the shipyards and the railways. Men who'd made fortunes in the colonies buying and selling tobacco, spices and slaves. These were gentlemen of acumen, risk-taking and guile. Or, as we ordinary mortals knew it, men on the make. The Depression and the two World Wars had put a lid on opportunities for advancing their fortunes unless they'd been able to turn over their steelworks to ammunition factories. And the luckier ones who had now needed to turn their shell-case production lines into prefab or tramcar manufacturing.

So the prospect of being in on the ground floor of the rebuilding of an entire city centre was a mouth-watering opportunity. A bonanza for anyone in the building and finance businesses. If you could round up an army of Irish labourers, they'd be kept busy for a decade. If you owned a concrete factory, you should be cornering the market in sand and gravel. A lorry contractor? You had a one-way bet on ordering as many new trucks as could fit on an assembly line. Roll up, roll up for a once-in-a-century chance to triple your money.

There would be contracts going out to tender and the winners' rewards would make Croesus look like a bum. And who would be dispensing such largesse? A bunch of low-grade, low-paid politicians on Glasgow City Council.

It was almost taken for granted that City Hall was infected by corruption. That even the most pious and high-minded servant of the public just needed a few sniffs of the tainted air in the grand corridors to be smitten by a severe bout of avarice, the only known palliative being the discreetly palmed brown envelope.

It also seemed to be a fact of human nature that the louder a man flaunted his working-class credentials and the more strident his opposition to the dark forces of capitalism, the more suspect he was. His interpretation of the socialist ideal of wealth redistribution was filling his own pockets first. It was a perfect alliance of interests: politicians with power and industrialists with spare capacity, all in support of worthy objectives sanctioned by the new Labour Government. Everyone a winner.

'You think Morton was on the make? Or getting in the road of someone who was?'

'One of the two, that's for sure.'

'If I could be devil's advocate, does it really matter who fills their pockets? I mean, if the job has to be done, does it matter who does it?'

It was as though I'd punched him. He twisted round on the seat and with blazing eyes began a finger-pointing exposition.

'It matters to the poor bastards whose communities are going to get a worse kicking than Clydebank in the blitz. Because you can bet your granny's best silk drawers that corners will be cut, expediency will reign, tin shacks will rise fifty storeys tall with the sole aim of making as much stinking profit as possible. Councillors willnae take decisions that will materially improve the lot of the ordinary working man. Not if the councillor's wife wants a hoose wi' a view at Helensburgh instead of a tenement in Partick. Not if a big developer can provide said councillor with said hoose in return for the councillor swinging a vote to buy a shitty swamp in Timbuctoo aff the developer in order to house the Glasgow dispossessed. The forces of greed being unleashed will leave this brave metropolis a gutted shell. Its outcast citizens will be left wailing in the hills. It will be like the Clearances in reverse!'

A woman in a pram veered away from us, thinking we were a pair of alkies.

'Good God, Wullie, we're only talking about moving to Easterhouse! I had no idea you were such a socialist.'

He sat back, surprised by his own outburst. 'Aye, well, ye ken noo.'

'So, what's the story? What have you found?'

He paused to roll another fag. 'I've got a man in the council offices. He's given me some names. He's handed over some documents. There are nefarious deals in the offing. If I can expose them, the council will implode and half the developers in Scotland will be basking in a cell at the Bar L. But I still don't have a cast-iron case. I'm close. I just need the final stuff that ties a certain councillor with certain big men in the building game.'

'Sheridan?'

He put a finger to his lips. 'Wheesht.'

'What do you want me to do? How can I help?'

'You saw what happened to pair Alec Morton?'

I nodded.

'Just watch my back, Brodie. And if anything happens, go see my brother Stewart.'

I studied McAllister. He was clearly torn between filling me in fully and hogging the story to himself. His last big scoop. But he wasn't a dramatist. Morton had died in agony.

'You're six months off retirement, Wullie. Is a last front-pager worth it?'

He looked at me as though I was daft. 'If not, what's the point?'

'At least get the police in?'

'Ah've no hard proof yet. We're dealing with big names here and unproven accusations. The polis would make a mess of it and the sky would fall in on me with nothing to show for it.'

I argued with him for a while but it was pointless. And on a glorious summer day surrounded by folk in their shirt-sleeves and light frocks, it was hard to believe anything too bad could happen. I left McAllister sitting in the sun gazing into his future. I hoped he'd have one.

EIGHTEEN

By Sunday evening, the weather was breaking at last. The first spots stirred up the dust and then the deluge made rivers of the gutters. The rain drummed on the roofs and the city exhaled in relief.

On the sodden Monday morning I borrowed Sam's car to take the heavy pile of her father's suits into Isaac's shop. I left him smoothing and admiring this material treasure-trove. I'd barely parked near the *Gazette* and reached my desk when I got the call that put Wullie's fears in perspective. It was a response to my revelations about how the Marshals selected their victims. A call from Sam. From the infirmary.

I ran out of the *Gazette* offices and found the car. By the time I'd cranked the engine into life my back was soaked. I scudded through a deluge that was driving weeks of dirt down the steep city hills. I flung myself up the stairs into the hospital and down the brown lobbies. I found Sam in the accident ward.

I stood panting and dripping beside her. 'Who is it?'

'Davie Allardyce. He's an advocate pal of mine. A different stable but, like me, based in Glasgow rather than Edinburgh. His wife's with him. Let's see how he is.'

She walked towards a curtained enclosure. She stuck her head in, and then signalled to me. I followed her into the partitioned area. A red-eyed woman sat by the bed. She was holding the hand of a man lying flat out under a sheet. His head was heavily bandaged. A drip ran into his arm. His eyes were closed. The woman looked up. Her eyes were full of fear.

'He hasnae said a word, Samantha.'

'They'll have sedated him, Maisie. Don't you worry. I've told him often enough he's got a thick skull. He'll be fine. This is Douglas Brodie. He worked with me earlier this year on the Donovan case.'

She nodded at me. 'I remember.'

'Now he's a reporter with the *Gazette*.'

'The one who spotted what these madmen were up to?' Did I see blame in her eyes?

'That's right, Mrs Allardyce. What happened to your husband?'

She gulped and looked down at her man. 'We were just sitting having breakfast this morning. Davie, the girls and me. Shona and Leslie are twins. Aged four. There was a knock at the door. It was only half past eight. When I went to see who it was, two men bashed past me, shouting: "Where is he? Where is he?" They had hoods on. Balaclavas, I suppose. Davie came out to ask what all the noise was and they hit him. They just smashed him on the head.' She stopped and broke into tears.

Sam went round and held her.

'Sorry, sorry . . .'

'Wheesht. Take your time, Maisie. Has someone got the girls?'

'Aye. My mum came round.'

'Mrs Allardyce, you say they smashed him on the head?' I asked.

'With an *iron bar*. They both had iron bars! One of them hit him on the head and then when he was down, hit him again across his poor wee face. The other gave him a whack on his body and then his legs. They were trying to do something to his hand when I flew at them. I was screaming and kicking at them. They just laughed and said it's what you get for defending vermin. Then the girls came out and *they* started screaming. They were greeting and Davie was just lying there, a' covered in blood and groaning. Then the pair of them just up and walked out. Casual as you like.'

Maisie was shaking in Sam's arms. 'He didnae do anything. He was a good man. Why did they pick on him?'

Sam looked up at me and held my gaze. My fault?

'Did they say anything else, Mrs Allardyce?'

'It was something like, *someone who sins before his maker . . . and the hands of his physician . . .* I'm not sure. What does it mean? Davie's not a sinner. He's a good man. He's a good man!'

Sam and I walked out of the hospital together.

'*Will* he be fine, Sam? Did you speak to the doctor?'

'It's touch and go. They split his skull open. They had to remove some of the bone.'

'Shit.'

'You're right there, Brodie. *Shit!*'

'At least his brave wee wife saved his fingers.'

'I'm glad you didn't tell her. She's in enough of a state.'

'I assume he was one of the defence lawyers?'

'He got two of the men on your list off. It's a high price to pay for doing your job.'

I didn't say it, couldn't say it, but she said it for me.

'Just as well all my clients have been getting banged up, eh, Brodie? At least I can tell them I've saved them a kicking. And me, I suppose.'

I didn't try to soft soap her. Anything I said would get me in trouble.

We walked on for a while before I asked the next obvious question: 'Did my article provoke this?'

'Who knows? Maisie was right. They're madmen. There's no point applying reason or logic to their actions.'

I drove Sam home and garaged the car. I took a tram back to the newsroom and gave Elspeth the gist of the quote flung at

Maisie Allardyce. I could see her brain whirring through her mental archives.

'Interesting, Brodie. It's from Ecclesiasticus. Chapter 38, I think.'

'Ecclesiastes?'

'No. Ecclesiast*icus*. Or Sirach. You'll find it in the Catholic bibles. The Douay. Ecclesiasticus is one of the so-called Apocrypha. One of the books that didn't make it into the latter-day Protestant versions of the King James'.'

'No wonder we have arguments in the West of Scotland. We don't even have the same handbook. How does the quote go?'

She turned her eyes up, presumably seeing the words on the ceiling. '"He that sinneth before his Maker, let him fall into the hand of the physician."'

'They certainly made that happen.' I explained the source of the quote. 'But it's a wee bit obscure, is it not?'

'I think your man just likes showing off. Intoning a few words from the bible lets your conscience away with murder.'

'No bodies yet, Elspeth. Not yet.'

I turned in a short article about this latest escalation in lawlessness and it appeared on Tuesday with heavy headlines: 'LAWYER IN COMA'. And sub-heads: 'Vigilantes Strike at Heart of Justice System'.

Sam was keeping me up to date with Davie Allardyce's progress. It wasn't good. The poor man remained in a critical condition, his predicament causing uproar in all the papers. It seemed to be one thing for those narrowly acquitted of a crime to get their comeuppance by illegal means. But attacking the man who got them off went beyond even the elastic moral code of the man on the Glasgow tramcar. I was certainly off the fence. Any guilt I had felt about Ishmael and his pal Johnson had been washed away with the rain. Same with my ambivalent and tacit support of rough justice. The whole point of the blundering legal system was its checks and balances. No one was checking the Marshals.

Then we really found ourselves in Wonderland. I met Sam on Tuesday evening at the hospital to see how Davie was getting on. There was no change. But at least he wasn't worse. They'd drained some blood from his skull, which seemed to have eased the pressure, but he hadn't regained consciousness. Sam and I were sitting over a fag in the waiting room.

'The world's gone mad, Brodie.'

'I know that. Any particular aspect?'

'I have a case just now. A man caught stealing some booze from Whyte and Mackay where he works.'

'They all do that. The odd bottle in their pocket. A perk of the job.'

'This was ten barrels and involved a horse and cart.'

'That would have been some party.'

'I was pretty sure I'd be able to get him off on a technicality.'

'Like he was just borrowing them for safe keeping?'

'Never mind, Brodie! That's not the point. Anyway, he told me today that he didn't want to get off. He was ready to do some time.'

'To avoid an encounter with the Marshals? God help us!'

On Wednesday came a rather more direct response to my revelatory article and challenge. It came to the newsroom by second post. It wasn't the reply I'd expected.

Major Brodie,

Now we know who you are and what you did! Your secrets are out. It's time to choose sides.

'Out of thine own mouth will I judge thee.'

Come alone to the Horseshoe, Drury Street, tonight, Wednesday, six o'clock. Don't even think about involving the police. We'll know if you do.

The Glasgow Marshals

Ishmael was breaking cover. *Major* Brodie. *Now we know what you did.* The words ran through me like a blade. It flung

115

up all my guilt, all my fears that one day I'd feel the heavy hand of the law on my shoulder with a personal invitation to appear in the dock to account for my sins. But was he bluffing? How could anyone know *all* the details? Only Sam knew about the fight with Gerrit on the boat, though not the precise outcome, and she was hardly going to talk. The other deaths took place in the remote backwoods of Northern Ireland. But all those kirk sermons must have had more impact than I thought. Thanks, Dad.

My first instinct was to ignore the letter and hope it would just all fade away. Who did they think they were anyway? Who would listen to a bunch of malcontents and criminals? On the other hand, maybe I ought at least to find out what they knew. What *Ishmael* knew. For I was certain it was Ishmael who was summoning me to another tête-à-tête in a pub. His choice of a meeting place was low threat. A public space. What harm could befall me?

NINETEEN

He'd chosen well. Six o'clock on any night of the week, any pub in Glasgow is heaving. The Horseshoe in particular. It's a secular cathedral whose centrepiece is a massive circular altar of polished wood and brass. Growing from the bar is a fence of wood panels which swivel and provide intimate enclosures for two men, head to head, to gossip and slander with impunity. I pushed open the swing doors and walked into a mass confessional. Sinners circled the bar. The priests behind it dished up pies, pints and homilies. Unholy communion.

I stood at the door, looking around for his red hair, his mad eyes. The words he'd written scuttled round my brain: *Major Brodie . . . your secrets are out.* It wasn't my war record he was referring to. That was public knowledge; it had been in the papers back in April. Besides, I had nothing to hide and everything to be proud of. You don't earn a battlefield commission with the 51st Highland Division for nothing. But how much did he know about the Slatterys – or guess? Until four months ago they were the most feared gang bosses in Glasgow. Then they disappeared and their gang melted away. Not that they were missed, unless you were a drug addict or a client of their red-light establishments.

It's time to choose sides. In that, they were wrong. I was on my own side. Always had been.

At least there was safety in numbers in this Wednesday night mêlée. Drinkers stood three deep round the bar and every table was covered by elbows, pints and dominoes. Despite the height of the ceiling, the pall of smoke had already reached the level of a gas attack on the Somme. The noise was a crescendo, like a mini-Hampden roar. Flat caps mixed with city trilbies, Clydeside nasals with Hillhead vowels.

I stood nursing a pint until seven o'clock. I hung round the bar area as if I'd been stood up, which indeed I had. I wasn't conscious of anyone eyeing me over but in that scrum, who could tell? Maybe he just changed his mind. Maybe they were off duffing up some poor bastard who'd failed their probity test. I slid the last mouthful down and headed back to Sam's.

It was still a good feeling to insert your own key in a fine big portal and not have to share an entry. I called a cheery halloo in the hall and parked my hat on the coat-stand. I could see a light on downstairs under the kitchen door and headed down, wondering if I should have stopped off at the Tallies and brought supper back with me.

The smell should have warned me. I was too late. I pushed open the door and saw Sam sitting at the table facing me. Her hands were flat on the table. Her eyes were strained and her lips pursed. Her face white.

I glanced at the crack where the door hinged. I hit the door with my shoulder. It bounced. I heard a grunt and jumped into the room aiming to follow up my assault on the man behind the door with a good punch to the face, and then as many kicks to the head as it would take before it came off. As I twirled round with my right arm shaping a fist I felt a sharp point crush into my neck.

'Stop it, Brodie, or she's dead!'

I froze. Not just because of the gun in my neck but because if there was one man behind the door and one holding the pistol on me, a third man could be waiting to put a bullet in Sam. Anyway there's no saying where and how a bullet will ricochet. I raised my hands and stood back to see my attackers. The one who'd come up behind me held a revolver steady in both hands. He wore a dark green balaclava, but I knew him well enough. Knew his Highland lilt and his wild pale eyes.

The door eased back and his pal stepped out, rubbing his shoulder. He was in matching headgear and also levelled a revolver at me, either a Webley like Sam's dad or the Enfield copycat. Not that it mattered. At this range a .38 lead slug from the latter would have the same bone-smashing impact as a .455. Both men wore thick brown sweaters that flapped on their spare frames. A sour unwashed smell hung in the air. There was no third man. But they didn't need any help. They looked grubby, but alert and competent. Their steady, gloved hands had held guns before. Ex-forces. But who wasn't?

'Sam, are you OK?' I asked.

'You didn't warn me you were expecting the infamous Glasgow Marshals for tea, Brodie.' Her voice was brave, but higher than normal.

'They weren't invited. Were you, *Ishmael*?' I walked backwards very slowly round the table until I was beside Sam. They kept their guns trained on me all the way. I put my hand on her shoulder. She was trembling. I squeezed gently.

'Verra touching,' he said, pulling back his woollen mask. The eyes were still mad and intense, but they were framed in dark pools. Stubble lined his twitching jaw.

'It's you I want to touch,' I said.

'Brave words, Brodie, when you know you don't have a chance to do anything about it.'

'Put the gun down and we'll see.'

'Enough, the pair of you,' demanded Sam. 'What do you want, Ishmael, if that's your real name?'

'It'll do. Your lodger here has caused us a wee bit of bother. We wanted a word with him.' The Teuchter motioned to his pal and they both sat down facing us with the guns pointing at our chests. I pulled up a chair alongside Sam and sat down.

'I thought we had a date at the Horseshoe?'

'Too busy. Too loud.' He waved his gun nonchalantly at me. I shut up and waited. I pressed Sam's thigh under the table. It was shaking.

'Well?' she asked.

'We're upset. Your boyfriend here exposed our selection process.'

'You didn't have to take it out on David Allardyce!' said Sam.

'A simple but effective way of discouraging smart alec lawyers. Always looking for loopholes, you and your kind.'

'Everyone's entitled to proper defence. Like your pal Johnson. I got his sentence reduced, remember?'

'They still put him away! The man died because of you and your kind!'

'*You'll* maybe be glad of us. If Davie dies, you're on a murder charge!'

The men looked at each other. I cut in.

'What do you want?'

'More cooperation. From the *Gazette*. We don't like being lectured.'

'*We* don't cooperate with thugs.'

Ishmael sighed. 'Neither do we. We stop them.'

'Who gave you the job?'

'Situation vacant. We took it. The police were doing bugger all. Things were falling apart.'

'And the centre couldn't hold?'

Ishmael smiled. 'Exactly, Brodie, exactly. ' He capped my quotation:

'*Mere anarchy is loosed upon the world,*
The blood-dimmed tide is loosed, and everywhere
The ceremony of innocence is drowned.'

'Do you only communicate in quotes? But Yeats goes on to say "the worst are full of passionate intensity." Is that you, my fine fellow, with your big gun, your trite quotes from the Bible and your liking for exclamation marks?'

I felt Sam's hand grip me under the table. She obviously didn't want me to go on goading him. It was hard. I was furious at being set up like this. Even more furious that these clowns had broken into Sam's house. Threatened her. Any sympathy I might have had for their stance had evaporated.

He shook his head. 'Someone needs to care enough to *do* something, Brodie. You of all folk should understand that, surely?'

Sam squeezed my leg again.

He went on, 'That's right. We know all about the Slatterys. The top gang leaders in Glasgow tangled with Major Douglas Brodie, formerly of the Seaforths, and boom, they're gone. Vanished. You got rid of them, didn't you, Brodie?'

'They left,' I said.

'They left all right. This world. Tell him.'

Ishmael turned to his so far silent sidekick. His buddy stiffened, as though he'd just received an order. When his broad Northern Irish accent started up I knew what was coming.

'Ah'm jist back from visiting the folks in Enniskillen. Ah've got a friend who knows someone who knows what happened down by, in Lisnaskea. Knows the weeping widow of Dermot Slattery.'

He raised a gloved hand, pointed at the table with his index finger and started to pound out the list. 'Three men gunned down, three burials. A trail of blood to Arran. Another two men seriously wounded. Gerrit Slattery missing in action, presumed dead. *Four* men dead at your hand. Yer a feckin' murder machine, *Major* Brodie.'

'You can't count. You're forgetting the priest the Slatterys hanged and the mother and four children *they* murdered. Not to mention five other kids abused and slaughtered for kicks. What – do – you – want?'

Ishmael replied, 'I see you don't deny it. We understand

you. They deserved their punishment. You're one of us, Brodie. Join us. Help the cause.'

'I'm nobody's man except my own. And I don't like causes. The last guy with a cause died in his bunker after wrecking Europe. What's your excuse for beating up folk and robbing them?'

'It's not robbing. Call it a fine. We have to eat. Or do you want us to steal dog food like poor bloody Johnson?'

'Bullshit. You're enjoying this. You're not punishing people, you're torturing them.'

The raging blue eyes hardened. 'And what's five years' hard labour in Barlinnie?'

'It's called the law. Someone breaks society's rules and gets society's punishment.'

Ishmael shrugged. 'Sounds like what I do – what *you* did – right enough.'

'The difference is a fair trial based on evidence.' I told them off one by one, on my fingers: 'Procurator Fiscal, defence counsel, fifteen-man jury, judge, executioner. You've stolen *all* the jobs. You're just another egomaniac with a gun and a side-line in sadism. There's a man in a coma in hospital right now just for doing his job!'

The maniac's mouth tightened, then he forced a grin. 'That's where you can help, Brodie. If you won't play an active part, you can provide the balance. You can send out a message to all those flouting the law. It's verra simple. Mend your ways or feel my wrath.'

'Whose? Yours or the Lord's? Or are they synonymous in your mind?'

'Hold your blasphemous tongue!' He slapped the table and took a deep breath. 'You've got a rare wit on you, Brodie. It will get you killed one day.'

'Do I take it that I can tell my editor you won't be repenting of your ways?'

'Only the sinners out there need repent. That's what I want to see in your paper. Is that clear?'

I shrugged. 'It's not up to me. I'm only the reporter.'

'Like it or not, you're one of us, Brodie. I'm relying on you. If we can't, the police will have to re-open their files on the Slattery boys.'

'You're blackmailers too, then?'

'Call it civic duty.'

'Using the law when it suits you?'

'Any weapon that comes to hand.'

With that he got up and motioned to his pal. They both slid their guns inside their waistbands, pulled their jumpers down over them and walked casually out of the door. Ishmael turned.

'We're the same, Brodie. It's time you admitted it to yourself. This was a warning. Your one and only.'

We waited till they'd clumped up the stairs and heard the front door open and close before breaking loose. Sam fell against me, shaking. I felt her hot tears on my shirt and held her close and stroked her hair, but only for a moment. She shoved herself back from me and stared at me with maddened eyes. She punched the table. Sheer raw anger was pulsing through her.

'Bastards! Bloody bastards!'

'I'm sorry, Sam. I'm so sorry.' I thought *I* was angry.

'How do you do it, Brodie! How do you attract them!' They weren't really questions.

'Are you throwing me out again, Sam?'

'You'd better tell me the full story about the Slatterys. If that pair have the details, it's best I do too. In case anybody asks.'

It made sense. I told her about tracking Dermot Slattery down to his farm in the Fermanagh countryside. How it was kill or be killed when I confronted his two bodyguards. And the hound. But I hadn't shot Dermot; he'd rammed his own stone gatepost trying to get away. He'd died with a steering column in his chest. She knew about Arran. She was there when I attacked the house. I'd wounded the two men who'd been guarding her captor, Dermot's younger, psychotic brother Gerrit. As far as I knew the two thugs had survived – more's the pity – albeit with some scorch marks from hot shrapnel. She knew I'd fought Gerrit on the boat, and that Gerrit hadn't made it back to landfall.

'For six years I learned to get my shot in first. Do you think I handed back the reflex with the uniform?'

She studied my face for a while, then said, 'What do *you* think? You were a policeman.'

'And you're a lawyer, sitting on the fence.'

'I'm on your side. But the law is blind.'

'And deaf and dumb. You think I've got a problem, though, don't you?'

'Depends on witnesses. You said only old Mrs Slattery could testify, but it's easy to buy some others. How would you view it, wearing a blue uniform?' she persisted.

'I'd have needed proof of any criminal activity. Proof of deaths. Proof that I was there. It's a long way to—'

'—Tipperary?'

'Might as well be. Enniskillen. The bad lands of the IRA. '

'So, you should relax.'

'I should, shouldn't I. Why can't I?'

'Conscience?' She kicked back the chair, got up and went to the sink. She slapped water on her face and dried away the tears. She put the kettle on, clattered the crockery and spoons for a bit, then reached inside a cupboard and pulled out a tin. Something rattled.

'Should we call the police about our uninvited guests?' I asked.

'Probably,' she said and flung something bright at me. I caught it. It was a key. 'In the meantime, you know where the gun cupboard is.'

TWENTY

'This is great stuff, Brodie. A scoop! "Gazette reporter held hostage at gunpoint".' Eddie wrote the banner headlines in the air in front of his desk. 'We'll do a front page. All the trimmings. Your personal account, of course. Some added words from me about putting our reporters' lives on the line for the sake of the truth. Maybe a photo of your sobbing girl-friend . . .'

'Stop, stop. Not a chance, Eddie. For one thing she's not my girlfriend and for another she's been through enough without having her face plastered over the *Gazette*. She's an advocate, remember. She needs anonymity!'

'OK, OK. But that's an effin' great angle.' He poked the scrap of paper. 'Just one thing. What were they talking about: "Your secrets are out"?'

'It was just a diversion. To make me take the bait for the meeting at the pub. Raking over the Slattery stuff.' I changed the topic. 'What about making his point? Why not send out a warning to the public: "repent your sins or face the mad High-lander"?'

'We could.'

'But?'

'We're not the effin' mouthpiece of a pair of bampots trying to put the fear of God into our readership!'

'I thought we were? Fear and anger sells newsprint, you said.'

'It does. But I'm buggered if we're gonna jump to the crack o' his whip.'

It was good of Eddie to be brave for both of us.

Eddie enthused on, 'So our line is the bampot one. These are nutters who need to be opposed. We have a justice system. It's not perfect but it's the effin' bedrock of our civilisation. No one gets to play God except God.'

Eddie was now leaning across the slew of papers on his desk, jabbing his finger at me. 'We're on the side of the law. We reject, utterly, demands by gun-waving eejits! Write it!'

I did. But without mentioning the Marshals' attempt at blackmailing me. On balance, they'd have a job proving my bloody deeds and I was willing to call their bluff. For one thing, why would the police listen to a bunch of homeless ruffians?

Sandy polished the piece – as in eviscerated and rewrote – and here's what went out on Friday morning as an editorial:

GAZETTE REPORTER CONFRONTS HOSTAGE GANG

Gallant *Gazette* reporter Douglas Brodie was taken hostage yesterday by the self-appointed Glasgow Marshals in retaliation for the stance your paper is taking in upholding the law.

I then gave a colourful report of the so-called hostage event before concluding with:

There is no room in a civilised society for egomaniacs who want to impose their rule on others. These men are not heroes. They are not Robin Hood's merry men. They are dangerous crackpots who see themselves above the law and above society. This newspaper for one will give no platform to madmen intent on undermining the very foundations of liberty and justice. We fought and beat Hitler. We will not kowtow to yet another jumped-up petty dictator.

We say to the men in masks in the language of their

own epistles: 'Vengeance is mine; I will repay, saith the Lord.' And again: 'Repent ye: for the kingdom of heaven is at hand.'

It hit the Friday morning editions in a big, front-page splash under inch-high capitals. On my way to my desk across the newsroom, I got nods and smiles, even the odd V for Victory sign. I had about half an hour of enjoying the rosy glow before Morag came over to my desk looking troubled. Which troubled me. We'd had a walk and a drink last night but I didn't recall upsetting her. I told her about my flit but not about Sam.

'It's the phone, Douglas. A man wants you. He sounded really angry.'

I walked over to the group of secretaries and took the handset.

'Brodie here.'

'You bloody hypocrite, Brodie! You can sit there and make accusations about *us*! While your own hands are reeking!'

'I didn't put a gun to the head of an innocent woman!'

'. . . and to compare me with Hitler!'

'I don't know you any better to judge. I don't even know your real name. But you seem to be living in some sort of fairy story!'

'You think I'm mad, don't you, Brodie? You think you're dealing with an eejit. That I don't count!'

'Here's what I think. I think if you ever point a gun at me or mine again, I will shoot you down like the mad dog you are!' I realised I was shouting. The rest of the newsroom had gone quiet. Morag and her fellow secretaries were sitting stunned around me. Eddie was marching towards me.

The line had gone quiet, then, 'You've had your one warning, Brodie. "We have made a covenant with death and with hell are we at agreement"!'

'Oh, spare me your sanctimonious Bible-thumping!'

The line went dead. Big Eddie was staring at me wide-eyed. A long column of ash tumbled from the fag in his mouth and left a trail down his waistcoat. The whole newsroom was transfixed like refugees from Madame Tussaud's. A lone phone was ringing. I gave the handset back to Morag. She looked scared; not for me, of me. I turned to Eddie. I flicked the ash from his front.

'I think we've just lost a reader.'

I worked with Sandy to prepare Monday's front page. It would save us both coming in on Sunday. We'd follow up our hostage edition with a report on the vigilantes' reaction. This time we could include his quote in full. The moment he'd hung up I'd jotted down in my improving shorthand every word he'd said before I forgot them. It took Elspeth no time to find the reference. 'It comes from Isaiah, chapter 28, verse 15: "Because ye have said, We have made a covenant with death, and with hell are we at agreement; when the overflowing scourge shall pass through, it shall not come unto us: for we have made lies our refuge, and under falsehood have we hid ourselves."'

'He's a big fan of Isaiah, then.'

She shoved her blonde mop back. 'Isaiah was one of the early prophets. Eighth century BC. A bit of a rebel too, speaking out against the aristocracy on behalf of the people. A sort of early shop steward.'

'So our man likes the comparison?'

Elspeth looked at me gravely over her glasses. 'It's in the nature of fanatics. They're selective in their reading. And their quoting.'

'Thanks, Elspeth.' I left her to return to her well-thumbed copy of the Mahabharata. In the original Sanskrit.

TWENTY-ONE

On Saturday morning after my swim, Sam and I checked her house from top to bottom. We found they'd got in through a second-storey window, having climbed off the roof of the outhouse. We went round locking windows and empty rooms.

After breakfast I freed up her father's guns and checked the ammunition. I sat at the kitchen table with the Dixon shotguns laid out like salmon, glinting blue and grey against the leather table cover. I set up my cleaning brushes and cloths and took up the first weapon, cradling it in my arms. Sam sat watching me, supping two-handed at her tea. 'You love them, don't you?'

'That's a funny thing to say. They're just guns.' But she could see I was lying. And I'd be lying to myself if I ignored the thrill I got from handling them.

'It's how my dad looked. The way he touched them. Like babies.'

Now I really was embarrassed. 'They just need cleaning.'

'So does the porridge pot.'

'All right, I admit it. They are the most beautiful weapons I've ever held.'

'It's OK, Brodie. I understand. I'm glad. Give me the other one.'

I stood and handed it to her. She took it, broke it, clicked it shut and aimed down the sights at the kitchen door. She looked handy.

'My dad taught me. Before the war when we used to go to Arrochar. He showed me. There's a couple of old whisky barrels full of buckshot lying by the shoreline. I had bruises for a month.' She rubbed her right shoulder. 'Then I learned how to take the recoil. Mum hated them. Hated me learning to use them.' She shrugged. 'But it was fun and it was something to share with him. I once took a deer.' She frowned at the memory.

'Like my father and me. But fish, not monarchs of the glen. You should have seen the flies he made.'

For a moment Sam and I smiled at each other and shared the smiles with the younger Samantha Campbell and Douglas Brodie. Until the phone went. Sam went upstairs into the hall and took it. I heard her voice start formal then soften. She came back down. Her face was fixed.

'It's for you, Douglas. It's your mum.'

I was on my feet. 'Is she . . .?'

'She's fine. She wants a word.'

I'd given her Sam's phone number when I moved back in. I never expected her to use it. For her phones were transitory mediums compared with a well-crafted letter that could be reread. She had a point.

'Mum, are you OK?'

'Yes, of course, Douglas. What a nice young woman. Does she live in the close too?' Her voice was loud, almost shouting. It was a long way to Glasgow.

'Sort of. Why are you calling, Mum? Are you sure you're all right?'

'It's nothing to worry about. I just thought you should know.'

'Know what? What's happened?'

'A man came by yesterday afternoon. Said he knew you. An army connection. Said to pass on his regards.'

There was something in her voice that put me on guard.

'Oh aye. What was his name?'

'He said his name was Lord. He didn't give his first name.

He was asking after you. I gave him a cup of tea. And a bit of shortbread; he was that thin. A red-haired man. Well spoken. Inverness by the sound of him.'

I could feel the blood congealing in my veins. I found my voice. I tried to keep it level.

'It was good of him to drop by. But why did you call me about him? It's lovely to hear you, but you usually avoid the phone like the plague.'

'Well, I didn't want to worry you. It's just you'd never mentioned him before. And . . .'

'And? What is it, Mum?' I held my breath.

'He quoted from the Scriptures. Wait, I wrote it down after. Wait till I get my specs. It was Isaiah 28, verse 15. I looked it up. It's not very nice. Did I do wrong letting him in, Douglas? I'm a wee bit feart.'

I nearly crushed the handset. 'Everything's all right. Don't you worry. In fact I was planning to come by later this week. Why don't I pop in this morning?

'Oh, no, Douglas, you don't have to fuss. Really, there's no need.' But there was. Her relief was audible. 'But it would be lovely to see you. It always is. I'll make some tattie scones.'

I hung up. 'You baaastaaard!' My cry went echoing round the hall and down the stairwell. Sam ran out and when I'd stopped punching the wall I explained what my mother had said.

Within ten minutes Sam and I were in her garage and I was cranking the Riley. It took three good turns before the engine coughed and spluttered. I nearly broke my wrist as it kicked back each time. On the third go, Sam, behind the wheel, heard the spark ignite and pumped fuel into the engine. It caught, and coughed, and roared, and Sam slid across the seat for me to take over. Soon we were trundling across Jamaica Bridge and on to the Kilmarnock road.

I gunned the Kestrel's twin cam as we charged across the Fenwick Moors. The morning clouds were lifting and the green hills stretched away either side. Here and there red barns dotted the Ayrshire countryside. In the distance to our right the hump of Arran loomed in and out of the mists. I could have enjoyed the run if it weren't for the rage and worry.

By the time I'd steered through Kilmarnock and up to Bonnyton, the sun was steaming the damp patches off the tarmac. We came to a halt in front of the line of grey tenements. They seemed to be sagging in the heat, dissolving back to their constituent cement and sand. I looked round at the broken concrete in front of the tenements, at the scrubby patches of green glinting through the mouths of the entries. The back yards were already flapping with filled clothes lines. A different world from Kelvingrove and its blond sandstone terraces perched proudly above the city and the park. It was only then that I realised what I'd done.

'Sam, look, you don't have to come in. Sorry, I wasn't thinking . . .' I trailed away.

She cocked her head at me. 'Ashamed of me, Brodie?'

'Of course not. It's just . . . well, I've never explained . . . I mean my mum . . .'

Sam was smiling at my consternation.

'Relax, Brodie. There's nothing to explain. Just tell her the truth. I'll try not to let the side down.'

I examined her fine fair features and her questioning blue eyes, and wondered exactly which bit of the truth I was supposed to tell. 'You're my landlady? That we sometimes work together? That I helped you with Hugh? That one night we shared a bed? That sort of truth?'

She paused. 'That sort. But maybe not the bed bit. Come on, Brodie. Your mum needs to see her wee boy.' With that, Sam opened her door and stepped out.

I should have known better. Instead of an awkward *what am I doing here, what is she doing here with my wee boy* stilted conversation between Sam and my mother, they were nattering away like long-lost cousins over two pots of tea. They sat either side of the blackened iron fireplace in the two winged chairs that had come into the world long before I did. I took the battered pouffe in the middle and let them get on with it. Sam seemed oblivious to the smallness and darkness of the room and scullery, and the hole-in-the-wall bed masked by a floral curtain. My mother's white head had been bobbing away in agreement to Sam's comments on the plans for the new National Health Service. Then I realised they were talking about me.

'He's really no bother.'

'He got tidier after he joined the army.'

'They should all have to do it.'

'Without the shooting, though.'

That seemed to be my cue. 'Mum, about this man, this Mr Lord.'

'Ah'm sorry, son, if it upset you. I hope I haven't done anything wrong?'

'It's not you, it's him. I don't think you're in any danger but I think he was trying to get a message to me.'

'Oh my goodness. Who is he?'

I swithered about telling her the truth, about frightening her all the more.

'Have you been reading about the so-called vigilantes in Glasgow?' She nodded. 'Well, I think he's the leader. He broke into Samantha's house three nights back and tried to get me to write something in the *Gazette*. We didn't and now he's unhappy.'

'Well, he won't be getting any more shortbread from me in future, that's for sure.'

'Mrs Brodie, Douglas and I were worried about you. Would you like a wee holiday in Glasgow? I've got a big place. You could have your own room.'

I stared at Sam. She stared back as if to say, *Well, what exactly were we planning to do here; just send your mum into a panic and tell her not to open her door to strange men?*

'No, no, lassie. I'm fine. But it's awfu' kind of you. I've got plenty of good neighbours around. Pit men. Big strong fellas.'

'But not during the day. Sam's right, Mum.'

'Sam?'

'Samantha. She's right. Just for a few days. Till we know what this Highlander is up to. You've always liked a trip to Glasgow. I'll take you to tea at Miss Cranston's.'

She went quiet. Glory be. She was actually considering Sam's offer. Was she so worried? As far as I knew, my mother hadn't stayed away from home since my father died, fifteen years ago. They sometimes recounted their honeymoon adventure: a stolen night or two in digs in Blackpool before the war – the first one – but that was it.

'Go on, Mrs Brodie. It'll be fun.'

Mum's face softened. Was that what it took? Fun? My mother wanted some fun? Her face suddenly dissolved.

'I cannae. I just cannae.'

'Why not, Mrs Brodie?'

'I don't have a case. I've no' much to put in it, mind. But I don't have one.'

'What do you put your messages in, Mrs Brodie?'

'If I can call you Samantha, you're to call me Agnes. Och, it's just an old shopping bag. What would that look like going into a grand hoose like yours?'

'Agnes, that would be absolutely fine. You just need a bag to keep your stuff together. We've got the car outside.'

'A car!'

I gazed in wonder at this transaction. My mother, who never went further than the local shops, was bustling about like a girl, eyes sparkling, as she put together her two bits of clothes; basically a change of blouse and underthings and her Sunday skirt and coat. Sam bustled with her to share the excitement, and to assure her she didn't need towels or bed linen. Mum rolled up a couple of rashers of bacon and some butter in case they went off, double-wrapped them in brown paper and put them in her bag.

With a final check of the windows and a turn of the big key in the lock, we left the close. The telepathy that operates in the tenements ensured that at least three of Mum's white-haired pals materialised to cluck her on her way. The big car parked outside was the draw. Only the factor arrived by car. The fluid lines of the Riley had already attracted some admiring neighbours. Mrs Cuthbertson said she'd take Mum's turn on the stairs in case she was gone longer than two days. There was a brief debate about who sat in the front seat; Sam won and insisted Mum join me up front, then we were off, with much waving to the crowd, like royalty.

As I headed up the Glasgow Road and across the moors, I saw her face was flushed.

'Am I going too fast, Mum?'

'Not at all, Douglas. Not at all.'

I caught Sam's face in my rear mirror. She stuck out her tongue at me.

TWENTY-TWO

Sunday was spent settling my mother in. It didn't take long to hang up her few things and position her soap and flannel in the spare bathroom. At first I noticed her going round touching things, sliding her hand down the polished wood bannister of the deep stairwell, feeling the good cloth of the curtains. She didn't say much and I could see her adjusting, measuring her own home against this spacious mansion. But there came a moment over her second cup of tea when I saw her face settle and her shoulders relax. My mother had never judged another's worth by their finery or fanciness. By the time we'd had an afternoon's good walk in the park, and listened to the wireless together in the evening, she was at home.

Next morning I came down to the kitchen for an early cup of tea before my swim, but not early enough. Sam and my mother were scrubbed and fully dressed and sitting at the breakfast table nursing their own cups. They looked up conspiratorially as I came in.

'Morning, Douglas. I was just saying how lucky you are to be here.'

'I am. *You* are. We have a generous landlady.'

'Who's being paid to have company. Everyone wins,' Sam said. 'Douglas, we've been talking. I'm calling the police in. This has got completely out of hand.'

'You think? But what do you expect them to do? Apart from driving you daft with stupid questions.'

'I know,' she sighed. 'But it just looks gie strange for an advocate not to call the police when there's a crime. As though I didn't believe in them. That's how the vigilantes started. And your old pals are still in the huff that we didn't call them when the Marshals broke in and waved guns at us. They didn't take kindly to hearing about it first in the *Gazette*.'

'You're right. When you speak to them, could you ask them to call Kilmarnock nick and get a bobby to keep an eye on Bonnyton?'

'And here. We could do with a nice young officer or two patrolling outside.'

I nodded. 'I'd better get going. I have a column to write. What will you two be doing?'

'I've got a case today. Agnes says she want to see a court in action.'

'You'll be bored, Mum.'

'I certainly won't. It's a *fraud* case!' Her eyes were shining.

'Alleged fraud, Agnes. Alleged.'

It turned out that we didn't need to go looking for the police. Waiting for me in Eddie's office were the boys in blue. They didn't look happy. Sangster was in civvies this time, having brandished his rank at me before. But Sergeant 71 was in his hot tunic, buttoned to the throat. He was waving the latest vigilante letter at me in accusation. He was excited. Or maybe suffering heat exhaustion.

'The last time we were here, Brodie, you denied having any links with these . . . hoodlums. We want to know why he wrote . . .' He peered at the letter, '"<u>Major</u> Brodie? Now we know who you are and what you did. Your secrets are out. It's time to choose sides."'

I looked at Big Eddie. He shrugged in embarrassment.

Sergeant 71 continued, 'What *did* you do, *Mister* Brodie? What are these secrets?'

'Look, do you have a name or are you just a number?'

His virgin cheeks adopted deeper points of red. 'Murdoch.'

'Sergeant Murdoch, we're dealing with nutters here, I think you'll agree. Why should I know what their ravings are about?' I took out a cigarette, lit it and added to the fug.

'And whose side *have* you chosen?' he persisted.

He was a dogged little choirboy, but I had to admit he was asking the right questions. He was getting approving nods from Sangster. I went on the attack.

'Truth? Maybe these guys hoped I'd be a megaphone for their mad ideas. I'm good at publicising evil deeds by corrupt coppers!'

Sangster coloured. His neck went pink. 'The point is, Brodie, you seem to be a bit too involved. Mr Paton here tells us that you're even phoning them. You've got us wondering whether this hostage stunt really happened or . . .'

'Or what, Sangster?'

'Or whether you've gone over to the other side!'

'Have you been at the sherry this early in the day, Sangster? Do you really think I made up a story about them breaking into my home and holding my landlady and me at gunpoint?'

'But why did they? Your article doesn't say why. Just some guff about them wanting you to write nice stories about them.'

'Why? Other than being mad bastards? All right, all right. We exposed their method for victim selection. That pissed them off. To make amends – in their twisted little minds – they demanded that the *Gazette* send a message to the good folk of Glasgow. That sins would be punished, even if the law decided otherwise.'

'You said they had guns?' The sergeant was wrestling with his hat and his notebook to scribble down my answers. This was better than traffic duties.

'Handguns. Looked like Army-issue revolvers.'

'Dressed?'

'Pullovers. Probably Army surplus. And balaclavas.'

'So you didn't see their faces?'

'No, but I can tell you one was a blue-eyed Highland Scot, the other Irish, northern Irish. The Highlander was the boss.'

I didn't name Ishmael. It wasn't his real name and his red hair and pale face could be seen on any street corner. I put them right on the phone contact – that they had phoned *me* – when we didn't write what they wanted.

'There's another thing . . .' I told them about the visit of the Highlander to my mother. That we now had her safely installed in Kelvingrove Park. This got them more agitated. I was able to say that Sam was calling the police this morning to report it.

'If it's the same man, according to my mother he had red hair and blue eyes.' I thought this showed how open and cooperative I could be.

'Address?' asked the sergeant.

'Whose? My mother's or mine?'

'Your digs. Landlady's name.'

I told them.

Sangster perked up. 'Campbell? Samantha Campbell, you said?'

I smiled. I hadn't put Sam's name in the article. 'The very one. Advocate Campbell. She defended Hugh Donovan.' I left the thought hanging in the air and watched its implications seep under the thin skin of Sangster.

TWENTY-THREE

When I got to my desk there was another message, a small one, not threatening in any way. It was in Morag's neat hand. A man – one of my old contacts – had returned my call. Bless her, she'd even signed off with a couple of kisses. The caller was an altogether nicer bloke than the bolshie boss of the vigilantes. It raised my mood. I decided that instead of phoning back I could use the fresh air. I strode off in the direction of the East End.

In a dusty street scarred with bomb-damaged tenements a small parade of shops huddled together. It included one of the chippies I used to frequent, being scarcely five minutes' walk from Tobago Street nick. They were just clearing the decks in advance of the lunchtime trade.

'We're no' actually open yet,' said a wee dark-haired lassie. She was burling a mop around the floor like a dance partner at the Cameo.

'I'm after Aldo. You look like one of his.'

'Ah'm his dochter. Who's asking?'

'Douglas Brodie. I used to be a policeman round these parts. Before the war. Aldo's an old pal.'

She sized me up and down using the same dark lustrous eyes as her parents. She turned and walked to the door behind the counter. 'Faither! There's somebody here fur ye. Says he used to be a pal o' yours? A polisman?' Said with incredulity as if she couldn't credit the juxtaposition of 'pal' and 'polis'.

There was a grumbling reply from within, then a figure emerged drying his hands on his apron. The apron looked more strained than ever round his comfortable girth. Aldo was a great one for testing his wares; to keep the quality up, he said. His black waxed moustache turned up in a great Neapolitan smile.

'You've met my youngest and bonniest, Brodie? *Bella* Sophia. She has her mother's looks, you can see.'

'Faither!'

'Sophia took your phone call the other day. Sophia, why you no' get Mr Brodie and me a nice cup of coffee. Brodie, come, sit, tell me some good news.'

'Aldo, the good news is we're both still here and you have a fine daughter.'

'So right, my friend, so right. And we have our freedom, and Hitler and that strutting Roman *maiale* – pig – are both dead.' He spat figuratively on his newly mopped floor.

A thought struck me. 'Freedom? Aldo, were you . . .'

He sighed. 'Interned? Shut away from my family and friends? Yes, Brodie. I had a little holiday on the Isle of Man. And before that, the locals here smashed all the windows. A little taste of Fascism. Or maybe they no' like my black pudding suppers. It was . . . how you say, educational.'

'I'm sorry, Aldo. It was . . .'

'Wheesht. It is done. Forgotten. Now, you wanted to talk 'bout this vigilante thing? OK, but before we get into all that, tell me what you've been up to.'

I told him, though I didn't tell him that the last Italians I'd encountered had been shooting at me. I gave him my potted war story, filling it with enough anecdote to make it sound like a great adventure. One I wouldn't have missed for anything. Truth to tell, I wouldn't. No one admits to having *enjoyed* the war, but there were moments – rare enough for sure – when I felt shot through with a kind of exaltation. When all the training kicked in and all the hard-won experience could be drawn down. When attacking a fortified enemy position seemed the most natural thing in the world and that no bullet had my name on it. I didn't say much about the bulk of my time broiling in the desert sun or freezing in a French bog, waiting for the off, sometimes bored, usually terrified.

When I explained about my new job, he leaned in.

'Yes! I saw you in all the papers back in April.' He pointed to the big pile of newsprint on his counter ready to receive his miraculous fish suppers and tattie fritters and soak away the hot dripping and vinegar. 'I no' realise then it was my Brodie! Now you write in the *Gazette*. You are famous, no?'

'Infamous, possibly. But I'd like to get better known for my writing. I'd like to get a name as a reporter. Not for *being* the story. The one I'm working on now is—'

'Ha! Your message is about these men who are. . . *prendendo la legge nelle loro proprie mani*. How do you say?'

'Taking the law into their own hands? It's getting worse, Aldo. I still don't know who they are, but I've found out how they chose their victims.'

'Oh, but that is how I can help. You called the right man, my friend. It's no' true.'

'What do you mean, it's not true? They've been watching the court results and attacking anyone who gets off.'

'Then maybe they found a new way.'

'You what?'

Aldo was a great dramatist. He took his time lighting a cigarette and thanking his blushing *bella* Sophia for the coffee and taking a sip.

'*Si. La scrittura è sulla parete.*' He pretended to wield a pen in the air.

'The writing is on the wall? What the hell does that mean, Aldo?'

'It does not *mean* anything. It is a statement of fact. Look across the road. The bomb site. Can you see the chalk on the wall of the building?'

I stood and peered over the curtain. A huge gap had been torn in a row of tenements by a bomb. There were words scrawled on the dark wallpaper of the former sitting room. It was too far away to make out. 'What does it say?'

'It is an invitation. It was put up a few days ago. They want people to contact them if they know someone is bad. If they have done a bad thing and need punishing.'

'Christ! I'll be right back.'

I ran over the road and read it for myself. I wrote it down in my notepad.

Do you know a thief, a rapist, a bully, a wife-beater? Has someone done wrong but not been punished? We will help. Leave their name and address, and details of their crime, at Café Ritz. We will give you justice.
Bringing justice to the streets of Glasgow.
The Glasgow Marshals

It sounded like an advert for a removal company. Which in a sense they were, I suppose. I looked across the road at the Café Ritz. Aldo was peering through the window with a big smile on his face. He shrugged. I went back over the road and we sat down again. This time he laid two envelopes in front of me. I gazed at them, then at Aldo, stupefied at the range of possibilities.

'Aldo, please tell me it's not you.' For a daft moment I thought he'd been harbouring ill feelings against us for being interned.

'No, no, no. I am not a violent man. I am only the temporary post office.'

'What?'

'That's what they say to me.'

'Who?'

'The two men who came in. They asked me to collect their envelopes and give them to them when they come by.'

'Did they explain what they were up to?'

'*Si, si*. It's OK. In Napoli, this is familiar. The Cosa Nostra looked after such things.'

'Are they paying you?'

'A little. For my trouble. One shilling for one envelope. These two came in yesterday.' He touched the envelopes. 'So I called you.'

'Can you describe the men?'

Aldo sucked his teeth and played with his moustache. 'It's not easy. They wear caps pulled down. And scarves pulled up. I don't try to see better. Sometimes it is good not to see too much.'

I was scribbling it all down. 'Height, accent? Were they local?'

'The leader one was tall, like you, Brodie. But skinny. His friend was not so big. They were hard men, I thought. Like Mafiosi in Napoli. They were men with *uno scopo, un obiettivo.*'

'A purpose. A goal?'

He nodded.

'What did they sound like? Were they local men?

Aldo shook his head. 'No. I can tell. I have heard others talk this way. We have all accents round here. One is Irish. The other is from the north.'

'Highlands?'

'*Si.* I think so.'

'When will they come to collect these?'

He shrugged. 'Sometime. Soon. They did not say exactly. They say they are watching.'

'Can I open them?' I picked the scruffy envelopes up and eased back the gummed edges.

The first note was in a good hand but bad English:

Bert Sloan, 43 Brandon Street.
    He steals meet from the market and sells it. Got aff wi it at the court, but everybody kens. Its no that I mind a bit of helping yersel. Everybudy is on the black. Its jist the meet is mingin.

I tried not to laugh. As a summary of everything that was wrong in Britain today, it was hard to beat.

The second was no laughing matter:

Jenny MacIntosh, 22 Lambert Street.
Crime – abortionist.
'Life for life.' Exodus 21:23.

I folded the notes and put them back in the envelopes. What should I do? Confiscate them and stop two punishments? Leave them with Aldo and let things unfold – because who was I to interfere? Should I hang around for the next few days to try to catch this pair in the act? And then what? Confront them and get a knife for my troubles? Phone Duncan Todd and line up a police squad to nab them? I reminded myself I was still trying to stay on the outside of events, observing not participating. It didn't come naturally. I just needed practice. It would make a good story but the last thing I wanted was to bring retribution down on Aldo either from the cops or the vigilantes.

As if reading my thoughts, Aldo asked, 'I hope this is no trouble for me?'

That made my mind up. This was going in the paper but with all details of place and names omitted. It was a reporter's privilege, was it not, to claim source confidentiality? Or was that something from a movie with Cary Grant?

'Aldo, I won't say where I got this information and I won't try to interfere with these guys who want you to be a post office. OK?'

He breathed out. 'OK. I trust you, Brodie. Will this make you famous?'

'Fame? I'm all for the quiet life, Aldo. I just want to keep my job.' I smiled. 'This helps. Thank you, Aldo.'

*

The tram back to the centre passed the end of Lambert Street and I found myself wondering and worrying about Jenny MacIntosh. Should I warn her about the vicious clype who'd reported her or of the possible retribution coming her way? For one second I had a glimpse into how a god must feel a million times a day. Assuming he was bothered one way or the other. The phrase *back-street abortion* brought out strong feelings in some folk. I was in two minds. Was it better to force a fourteen-year-old lassie to have her life ruined by an unwanted child or to be given another chance? Some families quietly enfolded the girl to their collective bosom, and the baby became her sister. Others cast mother and child out on the street. Much depended on the motives and skills of the wee 'auntie' practising her trade. There was a kind of female masonic order about it – secret rituals and black arts – beyond the ken of men. Maybe it was no business of mine. I was only a reporter.

TWENTY-FOUR

I had to admit, Ishmael and his gang had moved fast. I'd no sooner exposed his modus operandi for victim selection using the court reports than he'd added a whole new dimension to the game. He'd clearly decided the city was full of sinners who'd been getting away with it for too long, and was determined that his brand of Old Testament justice should catch them up.

I also needed to stop thinking about *him*. As in one man. I was more and more certain that Ishmael had put together a team of like-minded souls. A posse, I suppose. His punishment rate seemed to be creeping up week by week. I wondered which other cafés, pubs and corner stores were participating in his 'hunt the sinner' campaign.

I soon had confirmation of how fast things were spreading. Back at the *Gazette* I took calls from both Duncan Todd and Isaac within the space of three hours.

Duncan first. 'I thought you should know, Brodie, one of my snitches tells me these independent lawmen of yours are getting nominations direct from the public-minded citizens of Trongate.'

'They're not *my* lawmen, Duncan. I'm above the battle.'

'Oh aye. That sounds like you.'

'Be that as it may. How are they doing it? I've just seen an operation over at Gallowgate. Instructions chalked on the wall. Details of transgressions to be left in an envelope at a local café. Name, address and alleged crime.'

'Same here. But they're touting for business by word of mouth at the local. You know how fast the grapevine is. Shagged at teatime, shamed by breakfast. They're passing the word to drop nominations into the Scotia on Stockwell. Then someone picks it up . . .'

'. . . and justice is dished out.'

'Exactly. There's only been one so far. A known wife-beater. Broken arms, nose, and teeth. Between you and me, he was due it. A big bullying bastard. Wish I'd seen it.'

'Don't sound so wistful, Dunc. The next one could be innocent.'

'Oh, I know. But it's the same gang a' right. They'd cut off his pinkie. You still not mentioning it in the paper?'

'It's not consistent. But mainly I'm now minded to say nothing in public.'

I could almost see Duncan nodding. 'Differentiates them. We don't want copycats. Ah've not made a thing of it either.'

'So what are you going to do about it in Central, Duncan? Are you and Sangster talking?'

'He gets his boy to talk to me.'

'Murdoch? Sergeant 71?'

'That's him. An arse-licker. Anyroad, I've put two o' my guys in plain clothes in the Scotia. No shortage of volunteers. I might do a stint myself. We'll cover it for a few days and see what happens.'

'Sounds like fun. Call me if you catch them, Duncan. I'd like a quiet word with their boss. Alone.'

'Your uninvited guests? I read that too. I'll bear it in mind, Brodie.'

Then Isaac. 'Douglas? I may have something for you.'

'Let me guess. You've been asked to gather some envelopes?'

He switched to German. 'Ach no. Not me. But the bagel shop in Portland Street. You know what's going on?'

'The vigilantes are inviting the public to tell them who to punish. They're using pubs and cafés to collect targets. And now a *bagel* shop? At least they're not anti-Semitic.'

'Small comfort. The word went round the synagogue on Friday like a comet. Everybody was talking about it.'

'Are any of them tempted to clype on their neighbours?'

'Oh, everyone says no. They all say it's immoral. But, Douglas, I tell you, some of our people are a little more, how you say, old book than others. An eye for an eye, you know? I fear it will be used to get even. False accusations.'

I thought again about the woman named in the envelope handed in to Aldo. I *should* have confiscated it. There was still time.

'Isaac, it's what I fear too. Spread the word round your people. The police know about this. They will come down like a ton of bricks on anyone setting up someone else for punishment.'

'I will, Douglas, I will. But they can do this anonymously . . .'

I phoned Aldo's café. I was too late. A man had picked up the envelopes an hour ago. I grabbed my jacket and ran for the door with no clear idea of what I was going to do when I got to Lambert Street. Maybe just warn her. Maybe take her to hospital.

I jumped off the tram at the end of the street. It was a nondescript row of blackened terraces. Number 22 had three rows of windows, implying anywhere from two to three houses on each level. Maybe six to eight flats in all. I walked into the entry. It was cooler and dark. The smell of poverty stung my nostrils. There were two front doors facing each other in the entry and a spiral stair winding up from the end. The back green was framed at the end of the entry. Burnt grass and drooping grey sheets on the clothes line.

I peered at the names on each door. Anderson and Murray. No MacIntosh. I started up the concrete stairway. Behind me I heard a door open. It was the Anderson door.

'If you're looking for yon wee whore she's on the tap flair!'

I turned and stepped down into the entry. A sour-faced old woman clung to her door. Her hair was matted and grey, her eyes cloudy and spiteful.

'I've got a message for Mrs MacIntosh. That's all.'

'Oh, aye? A message, is it? You'll have got some lassie in trouble and noo you're trying to sort it, ur ye? Well, it's a scandal so it is. The polis should be telt.'

'Mrs Anderson, is it? We've never met but you're quick to judge. In fact you're wrong about me. I'm not – as you seem to think – some sort of customer. But I do have a message. Top floor, you say?'

My smart accent stilled her. She stood silently giving me the evil eye, sure I was lying. I turned and walked up to the third floor and found the door. I knocked. Eventually I heard locks going and the door swung open. It opened a crack, on a chain.

'Who is it? Whit do ye want?'

'Mrs MacIntosh? I need to warn you.'

'Whit aboot? You the polis?'

'No. Look, do you want Dracula's auntie down the stairs to hear this?'

The door closed. The chain rattled and the door opened wider again. A soft-eyed granny stood there, looking as innocent as a buttercup.

'Are you Mrs Jenny MacIntosh?'

She looked me over. 'You'd better come in.'

The flat had two rooms, one a busy kitchen cum living room cum bedroom, the other closed. She led me to a seat by the dead fireplace. There was no sign of wealth. Whatever she did it wasn't for the money, or maybe the mattress was lumpy.

'Have you a lassie in trouble? It's no' like the man to come.'

'No, Mrs MacIntosh. It's not me or a lass that's in trouble. It's you.'

Her face buckled. 'So you *are* the polis.'

'No, I'm not. Look, let me spit it out. There's been an accusation that you perform abortions.' I raised my hand to stop her. 'Don't say anything. I don't even need to know if it's true or not. It's just that someone has accused you—'

'It'll be that auld besom doon below. Jeannie Anderson.'

150

'Well, whoever it is has given your name to someone else. There's a strong chance that someone will come here and . . .'

'And what? Wave a bible at me? Tell me I'm going to hell?' A firmness had entered her voice. A wary intelligence focused her eyes. 'I've heard it all, Mr . . .'

'Brodie. I'm with the *Gazette*. But I'm not going to write this up. I'm not going to make you a story.'

'Then why are you here, Mr Brodie? What do you care?'

I stared at the floor. It was a good question. 'I'm not sure. There're usually two sides. I'm not a judge. But there's some out there who think they are.'

'What am I to do? Hide in the coal hole?' She nodded at the wooden box built into the side of the range.

'I don't know, Mrs MacIntosh. Can you stay with friends for a while? Family?'

'It's that bad, is it?'

'The folk who've been given your name have been doling out pastings to folk they think have done something. I saw the message left for them.'

'When? How long have I got?' She said it calmly, as though she'd been expecting it.

'I don't know. This was yesterday. They move fast.'

She nodded. 'I've nowhere to go. I'm no' running. I'll manage fine here.' There was a defiance in her face that brooked no discussion.

She saw me to the door. I stopped and turned. 'Could I ask something?'

The resignation was back in her face. 'You want to know why.'

'You've no reason to tell me.'

'I ken. But you've done a decent thing. I had a dochter. She went to . . . somebody. She died through there.' She indicated the door to the spare room. 'It's always the lasses, isn't it? It's always gontae happen. I used to be a nurse. It disnae take much to ease ma conscience.'

She closed the door and I went downstairs. The old harridan was waiting.

'Did you get what ye were after? A' fixed, are ye?'

I stopped and faced her. 'Do you go to the kirk?'

She stepped back and folded her arms. 'Of course!'

I nodded. 'I thought so.' I walked out of the entry.

'Whit do ye mean by that? Whit do you mean, ya cheeky nyaff! Who do you think you are?' she shouted after me, till I was well down the road.

TWENTY-FIVE

Throughout the last days of August, violence in the tarnished name of justice went up a gear. During the first full week of my mother's stay in Sam's house, there were daily examples of punishments: splintered shins for pimps, forced overdoses of their own wares for drug dealers. I was glad to have Mum safe under our roof, where I could see her. Especially when – as expected – the first fatality was announced in the form of a surprising phone call from McAllister. For a normally loquacious man, he could sometimes be too terse for comfort. But it wasn't the demise of Davie Allardyce; Sam got word from his wife that he was out of the coma. Whether he ever got all his faculties back remained to be seen.

It happened at the beginning of September, in the second week of cosy family breakfasts; Sam, Agnes and me. It was taking some getting used to. I wondered how long this could go on. It seemed a bit unfair on Sam to have all these Brodie squatters in her nice home. Mother was looking well ensconced, as though she'd always lived in a four-storey, four-bedroom Georgian townhouse in the best part of Glasgow. But the pair seemed to have worked out a routine of sorts. Sam would sometimes work from home on a case, and have companionable breaks during the day with my mother. Or if Sam was in court, Mother would sit in the gallery absorbed in the machinations of justice. I asked her at least not to take her knitting. Too *tricoteuse* by far. Or if Sam went alone to her office she'd come home to find fireplace brasses burnished like the sun.

It was cramping my style, but it was saving me a fortune in whisky. There was even the strong suspicion that Sam was using my mother as a shield against our own negligible will power. Tea had displaced Teacher's and I'm sure we were both the better for it. I was even bowing out after a mere couple of pints with McAllister, much to his scathing amusement. Somehow rolling home fu' was not an option if you were going home to your mother.

I took refuge each morning before breakfast in the swimming pool under the high arched roof of the Western Baths Club. There was nothing fancy like the wave-making machine my mum told me about in the new Kilmarnock public baths. Only the dangling hoops and trapeze over the simple rectangle of water. The first impact seemed like diving into the North Sea. Then my skin adjusted and it felt like cool silk. The physical afterglow was worth the torture of a dawn start and a cold immersion. I had a good front crawl thanks to my father, and each day I added a couple more lengths to my routine.

My love life – such as it was – had hit the buffers. Morag had started going round in the huff once I told her I'd moved in with another woman. And then installed my mother as well.

'It would be nice to meet your mum, Douglas.'

'It's all a bit delicate, Morag. And my landlady . . .'

'Aye and what *about* this woman? Why did she want you to come and live wi' her?'

It was a good question. Saying Sam was lonely was only going to add to the suspicions of a young woman brim full of lusty hormones and marriage inclinations.

'We worked together on the Donovan case back in April. It's a kind of professional arrangement.'

'Oh aye, I ken what a professional arrangement looks like!'

I decided to give my mother till Friday. I'd check with the

Kilmarnock police station and also the neighbours. If there were no menacing signs I'd take her back home. I didn't want her to get above herself.

We were buttering toast together round the cosy kitchen table when the phone went.

'I'll get it.' I went into the hall and picked up the phone. 'Hello?'

I listened as the coins clanked into the phone box at the other end.

'Brodie? It's Wullie. They've killed a poof.'

'What?' I crammed the phone tighter to my ear, not sure I'd heard McAllister right.

'A poof. We've found a body. It's one of yours.'

'Wait, wait. One of mine? What do you mean, one of mine? And how do you know it was a poof? I mean they don't look any different.'

'Naw, naw. I ken that. This was a *known* poofter. Besides . . .'

'Besides what, Wullie?'

'It's what he's wearing.'

'Where is he?'

'Do you ken the Monkey Club? A drinking den off Bath Street. Get here quick. Before the polis.'

I ducked the questions from the kitchen. How would I have explained it to my mother? I grabbed a piece of toast, my hat and coat, and was out splashing down the Great Western Road in a typical September monsoon before my brain began properly to sift what McAllister had told me: . . . *we've found a body . . . get here quick . . . before the polis. . . one of yours.*

I grabbed the pole of a tram as it trundled away from the stop and sat upstairs shaking water from my hat.

Homosexuals live in a parallel universe to me, their lifestyle a puzzle. They confound the whole notion of Darwinian selection. I'd read enough Classics at Glasgow University to know it was a commonplace among toga-wearers. In Sparta it seemed compulsory but it didn't make them a bunch of limp-wristed jessies in the gory pass of Thermopylae. Was it simply a personal choice, then? Did you wake up one day and think today's the day I fancy a bit of sodomy? Surely not. Surely there would need to be some insistent need, an insatiable itch?

As an NCO and then an officer in a company of rough tough soldiers, you were well aware that one or two of the boys were, shall we say, a bit more aesthetically inclined than the others. The men knew it too. There was always talk among the troops in my unit about a particular bugger who was unsafe to share a foxhole with. But as long as the kilt-lifting wasn't blatant or got in the way of the primary purpose of the regiment – killing the enemy – it wasn't something we dwelt on.

I first became aware that there were different persuasions when I was a schoolboy. There was the odd flasher stationed in the public loos near the Cross in Kilmarnock, waving his sausage at giggling schoolboys. Then there was the Boys' Brigade captain at summer camp who slipped his hand up my shorts. He was clearly disappointed by what he found there as he never tried it again. At university, among the *jeunesse dorée* there was the odd flamboyant creature, with fluttering scarf and eyelashes, but I always assumed it was just an act to get himself noticed.

And of course during my time with Eastern Division there were odd incidents reported of perverse acts and molestation in the Buchanan Street toilets and on Glasgow Green and Kelvingrove Park. They always struck me as triumphs of lust over the Scottish climate.

My attitude was of mild squeamishness if forced to contemplate the physical acts, but as long as the queer brigade left me alone, I was largely indifferent. On the whole, their twilight world passed me by.

The same couldn't be said about one or two of my pals down the years. Their response to homosexuals ranged from fear to fury, as though it was catching as well as illegal. This attitude applied to some of the more dogmatic of the Glasgow gangs. The slightest hint of divergence from the narrow path of boy shags girl among, say, the Norman Conks, was summarily dealt with. Indeed, so violent was their rejection and ejection of wayward sexuality I sometimes wondered if they were protesting too much.

Which of course makes me wonder what was going on in the minds of the Nazi top brass with their propensity for lumping homosexuals in with Jews and Gypsies as fodder for their Final Solution. And when it came down to it, anything and anyone banned by the Third Reich had me on their side: books, Jews or poofs.

The club was down Sauchiehall Lane, the rambling tradesman's alley that runs for a mile between its broader namesake and Bath Street. The club had been a drinking den back in the thirties and lived up to the image of such establishments: a plunging flight of stairs to a subterranean metal door with an anonymous face plate and a buzzer. There was no indication of purpose. The door was open. I pushed at it.

'Wullie, are you there?'

'Come ben, Brodie.'

I walked forward through a gloomy tunnel. The ripe smell of years of fags and booze wafted at me. I pushed through another door and into a cavern. It was starkly lit and filled with tables covered by upturned chairs. A bar ran across one side. Wullie was standing behind it, smoking. He had a glass of whisky in his hand. Another man, his back to me and his wide buttocks overflowing a bar stool, lay across the counter. His head was in his arms. He was sobbing, his head and shoulders rippling and lifting like a sounding whale.

Wullie nodded a greeting to me. 'We've got maybe five minutes. The polis are on their way. In there.' He jerked his head towards the toilet door. 'Ah hope you're no' squeamish, Brodie.'

TWENTY-SIX

I walked to the toilet and pushed the door open. Inside, on the floor, lay a man. He was motionless, on his back, his face in a rictus of pain. His mouth was frozen wide in a scream. Mascara was smeared round his bulging eyes. Ripe red lipstick smudged his thin face. He was wearing a bra, a garter belt and torn stockings. Otherwise he was naked.

His hands were lashed in front of him at the wrist. He was grasping his genitals. Blood flowed from the junction of his thighs. Flowed from around the protruding pole of a floor brush. The brush-head lay obscenely between his knees.

I gagged, swallowed and walked over to look down on him. He didn't look better close up. But I could now see the blond wig which pooled round his head. He also had a piece of paper stuffed in his mouth. But his face was unmarked. I looked closely at the bound hands. No fingers missing. The smell was overwhelming. I didn't envy the police doctor. I went back into the bar. Wullie had a second glass on the counter and was filling it. He pushed it towards me. I took it and gulped down half the contents. It stung but it couldn't cauterise the wound in my mind's eye.

'Who's he?' I asked indicating the sobbing fat man.

'Bertie. Dead man's boyfriend. He manages this place. Came in this morning to get the bar cleaned and found our friend, Connie, next door.'

'Connie?'

'Conrad Jamieson. Bar tender and singer. Better behind the bar.'

There was a great whoosh and the chief mourner sat up, eyes streaming. 'That's no' true! Connie was a marvel! He was gonna make it big! And now, look at him!' He burst into tears and flung himself back on the counter.

I drank the rest of my Scotch. 'Why did you say this was one of mine? He's had a terrible time but all his fingers are accounted for. No letters carved on his face.'

'Did you look at the paper in his mouth?'

'No. Someone clyping to the Marshals? You read it?'

He nodded.

'So, are you writing this up, or am I?' I asked.

'It's your story. That's why I called you.'

I dug out my notebook. 'I'm not so sure. Tell me what you know.'

There was little to tell. Connie and Bertie ran a private drinking den that catered for the more exotic end of the broad spectrum of sexuality. We used to shut clubs like this down before the war then decided they at least kept the weirdos off the street. They were harmless except to each other. And it made it easier to keep track of them. During the war, homo-sexuality seemed the least of anyone's worries and the club had flourished. Connie had been left – as usual, apparently – to lock up, sometime in the wee small hours. He should have been safely home tucked up with Bertie by two or three o'clock. Instead, Bertie had found him cold and dead when he came in an hour ago. Bertie phoned Wullie first rather than the coppers. He thought he'd get more sympathy from a reporter.

'When did you phone the police?'

'About quarter of an hour ago now. After I called you.'

I turned and walked back into the toilet. I took out my hankie. I bent over Connie and tugged at the slip of paper using the corner of my hankie. I opened it up. It was as McAllister had suggested:

Conrad Jamieson, the Monkey Club.
He's a dirty homo. He buggers wee boys.
He needs putting down! Like the rest of them. Filth!

Still avoiding touching the slip with my bare hands –
though the chances of a fingerprint on the soggy paper were
slim – I stuffed it back in Connie's mouth. He didn't seem to
mind. I'd just got back to the bar when there was the sound
of a crashing door and heavy feet. Wullie turned to me.

'That'll be the milkman then.'

The inner door burst open and Detective Chief Inspector
Sangster erupted into the bar, closely followed by the rosy-
cheeked Sergeant Murdoch.

'What the fuck is going on, Brodie? What are *you* doing
here?'

Wullie cut across Sangster's burning-eyed inquisition.
'Walter, Walter. Chief Inspector. *I* called you. Bertie here
called *me*. He's feart of the polis. Brodie and I are here to take
notes.' *And keep an eye on you, Mr Polis.*

Sangster opened his mouth, shut it, fired his venomous
glance at all three of us, then: 'The message we got was that
you'd found a body. Where?'

McAllister pointed at the toilet. Sangster and Murdoch
hustled over and through the toilet door. There was a brief
pause.

'Fuck! Christ almighty!'

Murdoch backed out and turned to show an ashen face. His
eyes were wild. He stared at us as though we were strangers
and stumbled out of the door. We heard the outside metal door
clang followed by the sound of the dry boke.

Sangster walked slowly out of the toilet, his face set. Beside
me, Wullie poured another glass and pushed it over. Without
a word, Sangster picked it up and drained it. He stood leaning
against the counter for a moment waiting for the fire to hit
his stomach. His voice was quiet: 'Will one of you tell me what
the fuck is going on?'

McAllister told him. Bertie corroborated it between sobs. Wullie mentioned he'd seen a bit of paper in Connie's mouth; had the chief inspector looked at it?

Sangster sighed. He turned and went back into the toilet. He came out holding the much-inspected scrap of paper in a pair of tweezers. He placed it on the bar and carefully opened it. I was close enough to read it again. Sangster didn't try to shield it. He turned to me.

'Is this what you're writing about, Brodie?' His voice was still low key. The anger had gone out of it. Weariness had taken over.

I chose to stifle my doubts. 'It's like the public's being invited to take out contracts,' I said. 'Remember before the war, Sangster? Glasgow had a rotten reputation. But it was all run of the mill: domestic assaults, illicit stills in a wash-house, gang fights on the Green with axes and razors. Brainless violence. Over in New York, they were having shootouts with the Feds, Tommy-gun massacres on St Valentine's Day, Prohibition and Humphrey Bogart.'

'He was in the movies,' said Sangster. 'He wisnae real.'

'Picky, picky. I'm just saying it was a wee bit more professional over there.'

'Professional? What the hell are you talking about, Brodie?' Sangster helped himself to another shot of whisky.

'Organised crime. Glasgow criminals couldn't organise salt and vinegar on a fish supper. If a New York gang wanted rid of someone, they did it professionally. They commissioned an independent hit man from Murder Incorporated to do the dirty work. Contract killers.'

'That's what this is?' Sangster nodded to the toilet.

'Sort of. For Murder Incorporated, read the self-appointed Glasgow Marshals. For the commissioners, read the great Glasgow public. Though the Marshals are happy to do it for free. Fed up with a noisy neighbour? Disagree with someone's morals? Drop us a note and we'll take care of it. Free revenge. That's an offer you can't refuse.'

Murdoch came back in, looking grey. He stood, holding his helmet, sweat beading his brow, looking at the three of us. Bertie didn't count.

'For fuck's sake, Murdoch, tak' a drink and pu' yersel' thegither,' said his boss.

Wullie and I left them to it, and walked to a tram shelter together.

'A bad business, Wullie.'

'It is that. There'll be mair, I expect.'

'It doesn't fit though. The calling card of the Marshals is the finger snip or the face carving.'

'Maybe they thought they'd leave a bigger mark. Get more attention.'

'Could be. But the other difference is that the others were criminals or bad folk in some way. What did Connie do?'

Wullie considered me from the side of his eyes. 'Besides being a poof?'

We walked on for a bit in silence.

'How's the Morton murder going? Anything new?' I asked.

'Connections. Making connections. More papers. Contract copies in fact. Stewart has them in safe keeping. If anything happens ... Look, you'd better get going, Brodie. File that story before anyone else gets it.'

I watched him walk off into the gloomy morning. 'Scoop' McAllister still keeping the story tight to his chest. I wanted to say he was being melodramatic. But after what we'd just seen?

TWENTY-SEVEN

I headed into the *Gazette* to write it up. I didn't know where to start. It seemed too ugly a scene to commit to paper and serve up to the masses. Folk would be reading it through their fingers if I spelled out the details. Old ladies would be fainting into their porridge. Yet it was the details that mattered. The fact that Connie – Conrad – was killed solely because he was a homosexual. The way he'd died. How he'd been dressed. Where he'd been killed. The scrap of paper stuffed in his lipsticked mouth by a hysteric with a prissy view of others' behaviour. Condemning him to die just for being different.

And who was to blame? The Marshals, presumably. It fitted with their new pattern of victim selection, and it was the escalation that both Duncan Todd and I expected. Given the biblical righteousness of the Marshals' warning letters, it was in keeping for the Holy Willies of this world to want to kill someone whose sex life was different to theirs. Who *had* a sex life. As Wullie suggested, the absence of their now familiar and bloody signatures could simply indicate an escalation in violence. And a further departure from sanity.

I tried to sneak through the newsroom to my desk for a bit of quiet contemplation of how to frame my story but Eddie was soon on the scent. His colour rose as I told him the details.

'Fuck me! This is front page, Brodie. We'll get a late edition out. Scoop the *Record* and the *Scotsman*! Don't sit there talking, get on with it!'

I flipped the back of my hands at him to shoo him away and began hitting the keys.

A man died today. He was murdered by the vigilante gang who call themselves the Marshals. His crime? There was no crime. A man died today because of what he was, not for what he'd done.

Conrad Jamieson – Connie to his pals – was brutally murdered in a private drinking den called the Monkey Club. It's not the sort of place you would go for a quiet pint after a football match. The Monkey Club clientele have different standards to you and me. They have different tastes. They keep their interests and allegiances to themselves. They don't, as far as this reporter knows, harm others or try to recruit anyone to their choice of lifestyle.

A man died today because he was a homosexual. You may not like the fact that such people exist. You may not want to mix with them or even share a room with them. But that doesn't mean that they should be tortured and murdered. Oscar Wilde was one of our greatest poets and wits. He was also a homosexual. Should he too have been murdered out of hand? The law is clear. Sodomy is illegal. But it is not a capital offence. And, God help us, never will be.

A man died today. He was a singer. He had a lover. He wore women's clothes. Do these things add up to punishable crimes, far less crimes punishable by death?

These cowboys who style themselves 'Marshals' have gone too far. As we always knew they would. If you set barbarism in motion you need strong reins to keep the madness in check.

A man died today. Another will die tomorrow. And tomorrow and tomorrow while this ignominious crew of anarchists are allowed to walk the streets. We urge all our readers to reject the invitations for petty revenge that are being scrawled on our city walls. Such actions are not only cowardly, they make the citizen who nominates someone for punishment an accessory to crime.

A man died today and the accessory to such a crime will surely share a scaffold with the perpetrators.

'You're bloody joking, Brodie! Who do ye think you are? Tommy Handley? We cannae print this! It makes the *Gazette* sound like we support bum boys!'

'We support the rule of law, Eddie. That's all. If we don't put a stop to this it will become an epidemic!'

Eddie was pacing up and down by my desk. Sandy stood like an exclamation mark in front of me waiting for Eddie to come to a halt. I could see other journalists had paused to listen. In fact I'd noticed an all-round difference in attitude in the newsroom following my telephone shouting match with the Marshals and their attack on Sam and me. A wariness, as if they had a dangerous animal in their midst and had to be nice to it in case it bit.

'We are the people's paper, Brodie. I know the people. They don't like this . . . this behaviour.'

'Which behaviour? Being a poof or being a murderer?'

'It's what they do to weans. Our readers wouldnae thole that sort of caper.'

'For God's sake, Eddie! Just because a man prefers buggery to shagging doesn't mean he's a child abuser!'

That brought a hush right across the newsroom. I could see Morag's mouth falling open. I lowered my voice and stood up to get closer to Eddie.

'They're different things, Eddie. In all my time with the Glasgow polis ninety-nine times out of a hundred the kiddies who were abused were wee lassies and their abusers were Uncle John or Cousin Jimmie.'

By this point Eddie and I were nose to nose. Or to be precise, chin to top of head. Both our faces were flushed. The newsroom was agog. Eddie grabbed the draft from my hand and stormed off. He shouted to Sandy to follow him and they closeted themselves in Eddie's office. His room quickly filled with smog. I waited, trying to read the smoke signals. Half an hour later, Eddie stuck his head out and waved at me to join them. I walked over, wondering if I was about to have my short career as a journalist nipped in the bud.

'Brodie, if I lose my job with this, you're coming with me! Get back to your desk and do another draft. This time, I want detail. You're an effin' reporter, are you not? Well, where's the stuff about what he was wearing? Where's the description of this gorilla club?'

'Monkey Club.'

'Eh, aye. Exactly. This effin' Monkey Club. Where's the bit about the *Gazette* being the first on the spot. Before the bloody polis!'

I looked at the subie. He just raised his eyebrows. 'What are you waiting for, Brodie?'

I took the crumpled page, now punctuated with ash, blue pencil and teacup rings, and headed back to my typewriter. This was going to get some attention from our readership.

Behind me, in one of Eddie's Parthian farewells, came, 'And don't mention Oscar effin' Wilde!'

When I got into the *Gazette* early next morning, the phones were ringing off the hook. We'd got a reaction all right. The girls were jotting down the comments and adding them to sheets on their desks. There would be an editorial review later. I didn't try to sneak a look at what people were saying. I wasn't sure I wanted to hear.

I'd been at my desk for only twenty minutes when I noticed a lull in the voices of the girls taking the calls. They had all paused, looking at Morag. She was standing up, holding a phone against her soft round breast so that the mouthpiece was covered. Lucky phone. She was pointing at me, then at the phone.

I walked across. She said something to the caller, then mouthed, 'It's him,' to me. I seemed to have struck a nerve. I recognised the voice but before I could say more than my name he hushed me with instructions. He wanted to meet. Right now. Alone.

'Why the hell should I?'

'It's about the murder. Call it a scoop.'

'Why don't you drop me a note?'

'Face to face. We didn't do it!' There was urgency, tension in his voice.

'You stood me up before.'

'No tricks this time.'

I hung up. Morag was looking at me with her big eyes full of concern. Eddie was chewing on a fag by my elbow.

'It's a personal invitation to meet Mr Balaclava.'

'Great! Where? We'll get the polis.'

I shook my head. 'Don't follow me, Eddie.'

I walked out in the silence. It wasn't bravado. It was curiosity. If Ishmael wanted to kill me he wouldn't give me a warning wrapped up in a personal invitation. I hoped.

TWENTY-EIGHT

I worry about people. Not all of them. Just the ones standing by themselves at the edge of railway platforms or sitting on a wall over water. We're each alone, and inside our heads are worlds with only one inhabitant. Some of the worlds are vague and woolly. Some are bright and joyous with hope. Some are dark and distorted. It's the denizens of those warped worlds I worry about. In relation to me.

He'd told me to come to the bridge above the subway station at Kelvinbridge. Someone would meet me. If I'd been coming from Sam's it would have been a short and pleasant walk through the park. From the *Gazette*, I caught the inner circle line at Buchanan Street and travelled the three brief stops anticlockwise to Kelvinbridge. Even if I'd wanted to, I'd had no time to arrange any welcoming party. I emerged from the subway into the grey mid morning. It was cool and threatening to rain. I came out on the south side of the bridge and saw a man on the far pavement near the middle, about twenty yards along from me.

He was leaning on the parapet, gazing into the 200-foot depths below. The Kelvin itself flowed brown and sluggish far beneath. He wore a trilby not a balaclava, and a trench coat belted tight.

He turned as he felt my stare. He would have heard each train come and go and would be checking each time. He was expecting me. I crossed directly over the road and started walking towards him. He kept his face in shadow but I could tell from his stance and his hunched shoulders it wasn't Ishmael. Nor was it the bog Irish who'd denounced me at Sam's. Which meant there were at least three of them. As I got near he looked up and down the road. He flicked his fag into the air. I saw it glow as it fluttered into the depths. He nodded once at me and then turned and walked away. I followed about twenty paces behind as he walked into the park along Kelvin Way. From time to time he glanced about him and behind, but kept up an easy rhythm. We dropped down and down past the great dark bulk of the art gallery, into the run of streets around Kelvinhaugh.

The tenement blocks mingled with factories and open ground where the bombs had hit. We came to an office block built in sandstone. Part of its wing had been sliced off by the Luftwaffe. The rest seemed deserted. All the windows were still blacked out a year after the final whistle. We came to a big metal door. He hammered twice. I saw a blackout curtain twitch, then the door creaked open. My new pal stepped up and, halfway in, beckoned me with a jerk of his head.

It felt like a really stupid thing to follow him into the black interior. But I'd come this far. I stepped into the dark. Suddenly the door was slammed shut behind me with a great crash, and a torch blazed into my face.

'Alone?' It was addressed to the man I'd followed. He stood to the left of the man holding the torch.

'Aye. Naebody ahint. As far's I could see.'

The torch dropped from my face and on to the floor. 'Walk this way, Brodie.' It was said in a Highland accent.

We went through a further two doors into a well-lit, cavernous space. There were a dozen or so desks and chairs scattered around near the walls. Three men were draped over the furniture. Incongruously, each wore a balaclava. That made a squad of five counting the man I'd followed and Ishmael with the torch. The man I'd tailed sauntered over to join them. With his back to me, he took off his coat and hat and donned the standard headgear. Now, of the four in woolly helmets, two were in shirtsleeves, open-necked shirts and braces. Two wore brown pullovers. But regardless of what they were wearing, it might as well have been full khaki. I'd seen similar tableaux in every battleground where men were stood easy. This was a bunch of ex-soldiers. All the hooded eyes were on me.

Two held shotguns. The other two had revolvers stuffed in their belts. The torch-bearer shut it off and turned to me. Ishmael's great sculpted forehead and cheekbones faced me. His red hair was close-cropped, his face newly shaven, giving the pale skin a ghastly pallor. He grinned and showed ragged teeth.

'Welcome to our wee den, Brodie.'

I walked forward and stopped four feet away from him.

'How did you know I wasn't going to arrive with three Black Marias?' I asked.

'An officer and a gentleman?' he sneered.

I closed the gap with one step and punched him right in his smirking mouth. He went down and I stood over him.

'*Retired* officer. And never a gentleman. That's for scaring my mother, you prick!'

Around me four men jumped off tables and streamed towards me. At least they didn't open up with their shotguns and pistols. Arms pinned me roughly and threw me back against the nearest wall. One put my head in a vice of muscled arm. Ishmael scrambled to his feet, wiping his bloody mouth. He pulled a hankie out of his pocket and held it to his torn lips.

'You bastard, Brodie!' His words were thick and muffled.

An enthusiastic follower tried to wrestle me to the ground. I managed to break his grip and smashed my forehead into his face. He went down, but others jumped me and we fell over a chair in a jumble of legs and arms and twisting bodies.

'Stop it! Enough! Let him up!' Ishmael was waving his hankie like a white flag. 'I've no time for this, Brodie. We need to talk.'

I got to my feet, my limbs shaking from the burst of action. I was panting.

'Shame. I don't. I just want to hit you again.'

I saw him consciously steady himself. He could have had two of his cronies hold me while he punched my head in. He chose not to. Which took some self-control.

'Do you want the truth or not?' he asked.

'*Your* truth? Why should I believe a psychopath?'

His blue eyes blazed. 'That's what I'm trying to tell you!' He stopped to spit out some blood and dab his mouth. 'We didna kill the queer. It wasn't us.'

'So where does your flexible morality stop? Tarring and feathering? Frightening old women?'

He shook his head and took some deep breaths. 'We're not murderers. "Thou shalt not kill." Not unless it's warranted. Not unless a man gets off with murder and should have hanged.'

'Oh, I see. That's a nice distinction. I lost a friend on the gallows because at least eight jurors decided he was guilty. Turns out they were wrong, but at least he had a sporting chance. What right has one man – what right has one loony, and I do mean *you*, to take a life-or-death decision? Some kind of sign from your jealous god?'

'You've got a blasphemous mouth, Brodie!'

'"Vengeance is mine," says *your* Lord. Which of us is really committing the blasphemy? And before we go any further, who the hell are you, *Ishmael*?'

By now colour was flooding back into his bony face. As much anger as reaction to being felled.

'You don't need to know that, *Major* Brodie. But I know you. You, with your medals and your battlefield promotions. Fields of glory, right enough.'

'How do you know all this? And why does it seem to bother you?'

I saw his eyes flicker and wondered what was going on.

'All you need to know is that the Marshals didn't kill this queer you've written such a fine eulogy for.'

'For God's sake, listen to yourself, man! You sound like a bunch of wee boys playing cowboys and Indians. The *Glasgow Marshals*! We used to have names for our gang too. When we were about eight.'

'Sneer away, Brodie. But don't underestimate the power of a name. Ask the people. They know who we are now.'

'And they think you murder homosexuals.'

'We didn't, I tell you!'

'Prove it.'

'I can hardly provide proof of something we *didn't* do. I need you to tell your readers.'

'Need? You don't like bad publicity? You don't strike me as a sensitive wee flower.'

'We're doing the right thing. We don't want it tarnished.'

I laughed. 'Tarnished? It's a bit late for that, Marshal Earp. If that's all you wanted to say, I'll be on my way.' I turned and started to head for the door.

'Brodie! We didna kill the boy!'

I stopped and turned. 'Yes, you did. One way or the other, you killed Connie Jamieson. You started this madness. You set a bandwagon going. A green light to all heidcases to have a go. Give it up, man, before anyone else dies.'

'Tell me this, Brodie! Was the dead man marked in any way? For instance, did he have all his fingers?'

I stared at him. He looked embarrassed. As he should. Mutilation crosses the line, even if you think you're doing God's work.

'Other than a broom handle stuck up his arse? If you're trying to say the murder didn't have your calling cards all over it, you're wrong.' I flung the words at him. 'The written accusation. The sadistic violence. The biblical intolerance prescribed by a bunch of desert nomads four thousand years ago!'

His shoulders slumped. He turned to his men. He nodded. For a split second I thought I was going to die. I tensed. One of the four men stood forward. Ishmael said, 'Tell him.'

The man was awkward, head down, but then he pulled up his mask to reveal the lower half of his face, his nose and mouth.

'I'm a poof. OK?' It was brave and defiant, and I believed him instantly.

I turned to Ishmael. 'I thought your God didn't like homosexuals?'

'It's an abomination. A sin. But if a man's strong enough he can change. With help. With my help.' His eyes burned with certainty.

I turned to the man. His face was red, his mouth tight. He nodded. It wasn't a clincher. And there was no way of proving that one of his men was homosexual. But it was just such a bizarre thing to do that I'd been convinced. It might still not prove their innocence, but it went a long way. I came back to Ishmael. He and I stood facing each other like gunslingers. Around me the four men on his team stood quietly waiting for orders. I hoped he wasn't going to tell them to break out the iron bars. There was a long pause. I nodded. His eyes flickered at his men. I turned and walked away. No one stopped me. I got to the door and stepped out into drizzle and walked back through the park.

Ishmael left me troubled. There was something different in his look. I couldn't pin it down. It wasn't regret, more a wistfulness. As though he wanted to say more, to explain himself. But that's how the obsessed worked; always trying to convince you, to turn your mind, to make you part of their belief system. And there was the undercurrent: the references to my army career. It seemed to fester with him, as though our paths had crossed and I'd somehow slighted him. Had we met? Had he been in the army and been passed over?

Whatever it was, I didn't have time or inclination to psychoanalyse him. I was just glad to have had the chance to hit him.

TWENTY-NINE

got back to the newsroom and found it in pandemonium. Big Eddie was waiting to pounce. He saw the signs of my brief struggle: tie askew, lump on my forehead, nursing my bruised knuckles.

'Christ, what happened, Brodie? Did you have a fight? Did you meet him? What did he say? Who is he? Why are they doing it? What's our story?'

'Eddie, Eddie, give me a chance to get my coat off. What's going on?

All around was a hubbub of shouts and girls scurrying about. Eddie grabbed my arm.

'Keep it on! You need to get back out there. There've been two more murders. Homos again. Down at Glasgow Green. In the Winter Gardens. McAllister phoned it in but he's tied up. But tell me first what happened with you. Did they hit you? What—'

'OK, OK. Just listen.' I gave him a speeded-up version of my encounter with the leader of the vigilantes. Eddie's excitement was making him hop up and down as though he needed the toilet.

'You were taken to their den and took the lot o' them on? Single-handed? That's brilliant, Brodie. We'll get the polis round and raid them. A good siege and a shoot-out! Oh, I can see it now . . .'

'You don't think they'll still be there, do you?'

His face dropped, but then brightened again. 'You actually

hit the boss? We can use that. Oh, we can use that.' He did his headline in the air thing: '"Fearless *Gazette* reporter battles with murderer"! No! "... with gangster leader"! I love it, Brodie. Tell me more!'

'I'm not sure he did it, Eddie. I don't think he murdered Connie.'

'What? Of course he did! You read the note in the poofter's mouth. He was set up for a killing by these bloody Marshals. It all fits. You don't really believe that one o' them is a queer? That's a try-on. And it proves nothing. Actually, maybe you should stay and write it up. No, no, we need you over at the Green. Oh fuck. It's all too much.'

'Eddie, I've given you the outline. Why don't you and Sandy scribble something down and I'll go off and find out more about these other killings. Then I'll come back and we'll piece it together.'

'Right, right, Brodie. Good thinking. Off you go.'

I got the details from Morag between her pleas to bathe my fevered brow and bandage my hand. I stopped her fussing and ran down the stairs. These new killings made no sense. Either that, or I'd handed back my ability to read character with my major's crowns. I thought of the expression on the Highlander's face and couldn't imagine how he could stand there and lie about Connie and two new murders. On the other hand, maybe I hadn't met enough maniacs to judge.

It was pouring now and I wished I'd grabbed an umbrella. I pulled my hat down and tugged my mac tighter and splashed through the Trongate, along London Road and into the Green at the McLennan Arch. I could see a black squad car in front of the People's Palace and a couple of black figures at the rear outside the great glass canopy of the Winter Gardens.

I trudged round to the side door of the conservatory. It was barred by two policeman in dripping waterproofs. Just inside I could see several police huddled together.

'Hello, Constable, I'm from the *Gazette*. Can I speak to the officer in charge?'

'I'm afraid not, sir. I have strict instructions.'

Just then I saw one of the men inside look up. He saw me. Duncan Todd waved and came to the door.

'It's all right, officer. Let him in. You're drookit, Brodie. Come in before you catch your death. We've got enough bodies as it is.'

'Don't tell me Sangster's recognised your talents?'

'As if. He's been summoned to the Chief Constable. These vigilantes are beginning to piss everybody off. Right to the top. I was the nearest on duty who knew anything about this . . . this madness.'

I walked into the tropics. Great palm trees reached to the glass roof. Cheese plants and tropical ferns crowded together in green profusion. The air was warm and heavy. It made you want to throw all your clothes off and run down to the nearest jungle pool beach and frolic in the warm water. But six policemen would have disapproved.

'Over here, Brodie. Another one of yours. Or rather, two.'

I shook my hat and squelched after him. 'I wish folk would stop referring to them as mine, Duncan.'

'Yours or no', brace yersel'.'

The other officers were standing or moving about in a wide circle near a clump of greenery. They were working carefully, trying not to disturb the scene too much, but already the ground was flattened. As I drew near I saw a small pool, about fifteen feet across, but I had no inclination now to jump in. The water was green with algae, punctuated with patches of red scum. Besides, it was already occupied. Two bodies languished by the edge where they'd been dragged. There were footprints round them and the ground was freshly damp. Both sets of eyes were staring up at the tree canopy, seemingly terrified by what they'd seen there. Both were naked, their hands bound in front of them, groping fruitlessly at their crotches. Their mouths were open but stuffed, as

176

though they'd been caught halfway through their tea. Blood oozed from their lips and down their chins.

'Fuck.'

'Fuck indeed, Brodie.'

'This is maybe a stupid question, but how did they die, Duncan?'

'No' stupid at a'. We're not sure if they died from drowning, bleeding to death, choking, or maybe sheer bloody shock. Poor bastards.'

'I was told they were queers. Is that right? How do we know?'

'Ah could say something flippant and disgusting like they died as they lived, wi' their mouths fu'. But . . . Constable!' A uniformed officer came over. 'Show Mister Brodie exhibit A.'

The constable dug in his breast pocket and produced an envelope. He carefully opened it and pulled out a half sheet of paper. He handed it to Duncan who handed it to me. It read:

To the Glasgow Marshals
There's a gang of filthy homos on the Green every night
after ten. Doing it right there ahint the Winter Gardens.
Next to the weans' play park. This is a God-fearing city,
not Sodom and Gomorrah! It's just wicked and must be
stopped. Root them out!
_   A concerned citizen._

'Seems like whoever did it took the advice to root them out a wee bit too literally. Any other evidence?'

'Like alphabets on their foreheads? Fingers missing? And that's no' what's in their gubs. Constable, any sign of other wounds?'

'No, sir.'

Duncan handed back the piece of paper to his officer and turned back to me.

'You said "whoever did it". Interesting choice of words,

Brodie. Does that mean you don't blame the Marshals or you're just keeping an open mind? Which of course we all are.'

'I met their leader this morning.'

'For a wee coffee at Miss Cranston's? That must have been nice. Walk over here.'

He led me away from the greenery back towards the People's Palace part of the building. We sat at a table in the echoing café. We broke out the fags. I wished they had a drink licence.

'Tell me more,' he asked.

I described the meeting, including hitting Ishmael, including one of the men's claim to be queer, including my unease about Ishmael's interest in my war experience.

'I didnae ken there were that many nancy boys in the world. As far as this guy Ishmael's concerned, maybe he's just jealous, Brodie? He'd have found out easy enough from all the stuff in the papers back in April about you and the Slatterys.'

'You're right. I'm being paranoiac. The main thing is his claim about not killing Connie, the queer I wrote about yesterday. How it didn't fit with their nasty habits.'

'Clipping fingers? Doodling on their brows?'

'Aye. But that's no proof the Marshals *didn't*. But if they didn't do it, they were probably up to something criminal at the time and could hardly use that as an alibi. And unless I'm going soft, there was no indication in Ishmael's face that there was more blood on his hands for this pair. But he might be an awfully good liar. Or a psychopath. He's certainly *no' a' there*. Thinks he's doing God's work. You know the kind.'

'Aye. Ah sure do.' He shook his head. 'Look, Ah think you're right not to broadcast the exact details of the Marshals' brutality. Go on leaving it vague. It might just be useful.'

'Come in handy, you mean?'

'I do the jokes, Brodie. But you'd better tell me where you met them this morning. Worth a wee shufti.'

We promised to keep in touch and I set off back to the *Gazette* to distil a column or two of elegant prose from a deepening and widening circle of bloody chaos. As I walked I wondered why I was feeling so down. Then I recognised the emotion: regret. I wanted it to be me leading the investigation back there, not writing about it. Just nostalgia, I suppose. That life was behind me. But through it all, I kept asking myself, if the Marshals didn't do it, who was killing queers across Glasgow? Why? And who would be next?

THIRTY

Eddie decided to spread the two news stories across two days' editions.

'Nae use squandering all your ammo in one go, Brodie. You should ken that.' He mimicked holding a machine gun and spraying the newsroom. Nobody ducked.

We ran the double murders first, on Wednesday, under the sombre banner: 'Death in the Winter Gardens'. At Sandy's urging I began the story in dramatic style:

In its time, Glasgow Green has been the dumb witness to many perverted acts. But surely none more so than the brutal maiming and murder of two alleged homosexuals last night. Their bodies were discovered in the Winter Gardens in a macabre ritual killing . . .

'Are you sure. Sandy? It sounds like an Agatha Christie.'

'Exactly! Bread and circuses, Brodie. Bread and circuses.'

'But this time we can't put all the gruesome details in, surely? There'll be an outcry.'

'Never underestimate our readers' capacity to lap up pain, Brodie. As long as it's happening to somebody else. But I agree we'd better choose our words carefully. You'll need to find a gentler way of saying that they'd been found with their cocks in their mouths.'

'Dismembered appendages?'

'Aye, that'll do nicely.'

'I was joking . . .'

'Maybe you're right. Too many syllables. You'll think of something.' He turned to leave. I poised my fingers over the keys and made a mental note to bring in my Thesaurus.

Sandy pirouetted back. 'Oh, Brodie. Just a wee thing. And no' really important. Do you happen to ken if it was their ane – *appendages*? I mean, no, of course. How would you? Not unless they were different, you ken, colours . . .'

I stared at his retreating back wondering if I'd made another wrong choice of career.

I rolled the foolscap and carbons through the Imperial. Of course by running the two pieces in this order, it meant that I wasn't yet mentioning my meeting with the Marshals. Which in turn meant not raising any doubt about the Marshals' guilt, at least of these killings. And there *was* doubt, at least in my own mind. But as Eddie pointed out, that's not what the public wanted to hear. And why would you believe that madmen would have such a fine and unwavering moral compass as to stop at finger removal? Eddie was also of the opinion that the Marshal who'd confessed to being homosexual was lying.

'There's no' that many about, Brodie. Too big an effin' coincidence for my liking.'

We could have run with an evening edition, a special, but we decided to keep up the daily momentum and save it for Thursday. Eddie even talked about running a Saturday paper to keep the story simmering over the weekend, but the overtime would have cost too much. All the rival papers had a front page on the twin killings. Some of the headlines made ours look like a kirk magazine. 'Slaughter of the Queers', ran one. 'Homos Hacked to Death', ran another. All of them blamed the Marshals.

It was certainly selling newsprint. The corner boys were hoarse, and the *Gazette*'s directors were purring, we heard, but demanding ever more eye-popping scoops. Eddie was wandering around dispensing unremitting zeal and excitement. Summer had returned and the newsroom was sweltering again. It was wearing. Only McAllister was conspicuous by his absence. Until he suddenly popped up just before noon. He came to my corner.

'Let me buy you a beer, Brodie. We need to have words.'

As we emerged into the warm September sun I naturally turned towards Ross's, McAllister's usual haunt. Wullie grabbed my arm and we set off in the opposite direction. We cut across West Nile Street, ploughed up Blythswood Hill, and stood panting on West George Street. We looked back down at the undulating criss-cross of Georgian streets. I pulled out my hankie and wiped my brow.

'I didn't have you down as a mountaineer, Wullie.'

'We could do wi' some o' they wee tram cars they have in San Francisco,' he gasped. 'Come on. We're earning that pint.'

We struck west again along Bath Street. Along the way we talked about the vigilante story and how it was unfolding, but Wullie refused to be drawn on his own investigations into the Morton murder. The matter had sunk from the public mind except for the odd newspaper castigation of the police for making zero progress. The *Record* had an interview with poor Mrs Morton. She seemed in a daze, uncomprehending and bereft. Wullie himself had written nothing lately about the murder. I assumed he wanted to fill me in on the latest.

We pressed on downhill, past the New Mitchell library, then down a side street. Halfway along was an unprepossessing pub: the Sodger's Lament, with a badly painted picture of a tartan-clad warrior lying, dying, on some distant battlefield. He was clutching a thistle in his pale hand to hammer home the point that this was a *Scottish* soldier. As if the spelling wasn't enough.

'This looks fun, Wullie.'

'It's quiet. That's the main thing. And the beer's no' wattered.'

We pushed inside. Coming in from the sun, we felt we'd entered a coal hole. As my eyes adjusted I could make out a big man standing behind the bar, smoking. He nodded at Wullie. 'Usual?'

'Make it two, Alec. We're through here.' He walked to the left of the bar and pushed through into the saloon. It was only big enough for two small tables. Six drinkers would crowd it. The walls were brown, the ceiling brown, the fading photos of shipyards were brown. A brown study. Two pints of heavy materialised. We sat. Wullie did his usual sleight of hand and a roll-up appeared. We supped our beer, lit up and then he started.

'I've had a breakthrough, Brodie.'

I nodded and waited.

Wullie now had names. Names of big-time developers operating as a cartel to corner the market in development sites and building contracts. The name of a senior councillor who was acting as the conduit for dirty money. It was his job to sprinkle cash among his fellow flexible officials. Fairy dust to grease the passage of certain proposals and specific contracts.

'No guesses who the councillor is . . .' Wullie raised his nico-tine-stained finger to his nicotine-stained mouth. He pulled out his notebook, opened it and showed me the name he'd written. _James Sheridan_. It was underlined.

'What's your proof?'

'Mind I said his long-suffering wife, Elsie, was loyalty incarnate? Well, even she's had enough. Three weeks back, just after we had our wee talk with him and they'd found Morton with his head in cement, our man set up a wee nest for himself with some floozy from Edinburgh. Installed her in a nice flat in Hyndland where she can flaunt her Athenian airs and graces.'

'And you're hearing this from Elsie Sheridan?'

'The fury of a woman scorned.' Wullie shook his head. 'I've met her once now. This'll be the second.'

'What! You mean she's coming here? Does she know I'll be here? Why do you want me involved?'

'Yes and yes. And I want you to listen in, take notes, and to be another link in this story. As I said before. Just in case.'

'In case . . .?'

'A link gets broken. And here she is.'

THIRTY-ONE

A tiny woman stood in the now opened doorway. She was wearing a headscarf and a buttoned raincoat despite how warm it was outside. Her eyes were darting between McAllister and me. We got to our feet.

'Hello, Elsie. Come ben. Take a seat. This is Douglas Brodie. He answers to Brodie.'

'Hello, Mrs Sheridan.'

'Ah'm Elsie, jist Elsie.'

'What'll you have, Elsie?' asked Wullie.

'Port and lemon.'

Her voice was like sand running off velvet, rough but enticing. The product of a lifetime of marinating her tonsils in fortified wine and fags. She sat down opposite me and took off her scarf. She didn't look around so I assumed this was where she'd met McAllister before. Not that there was much to see. Elsie herself looked to be in her late forties. Pretty dark eyes, and hair now a denser black than the original. Plucked and redrawn black curves over her eyes. Sweet bow mouth and perky nose. Heavy make-up just about hiding crows' feet. I realised I'd seen her photo alongside her man. Her *former* man, by the sound of it.

She took off her coat and sat down again in a summer frock of pink and red roses. Her too-strong perfume quickly filled the tiny space. Wullie stepped back from the counter and plonked down a glass. She took a swig, delved in her handbag for cigarettes and I lit her.

'Thanks for coming Elsie,' he said.

'It's a' right. It needs dain'.'

Her accent was local. Deeper and more nasal than her petite form and gamine face suggested. Hedy Lamarr plays Glesga fishwife.

'Why don't we start with you telling Brodie here what you telt me last time?'

Elsie polished off her drink and indicated her vocal cords required more lubrication. Wullie got her another. Then she seemed ready.

'Whit's gontae happen? You'se gontae put a' this in the paper?'

Wullie responded. 'Eventually, Elsie. But the only bit that we'll be putting in to begin with is about Jimmie's new-found wealth. I know you've got other information which will come out in due course. But we need more hard evidence otherwise they'll sue my erse off.'

'We wouldnae want that, Wullie, would we? Ye need yer erse. Somewhere to hing yer legs frae.' Her cackle would have emptied the Citizen's Theatre. Elsie had a sense of humour. I supposed she'd needed it.

I asked her, 'So tell us about Jimmie going up in the world. You told Wullie that he's come into money. Do you know where he got it?'

'Aye, I ken fine. He's been wining and dining wi' some big spenders for months. Rogano's, can you believe it? Never took me.'

'And who are these big spenders?' I asked.

'Wait, Elsie. Don't say it out loud. Just write it down here.' McAllister placed his pad in front of her and gave her his pencil.'

In a slow, schoolgirl hand, as though she was being tested, and with tongue sticking out, Elsie wrote three names: *Kenneth Rankin, Tom Fowler* and *Colin Maxwell*. She didn't have to spell out any more. These names were synonymous with some of the biggest deals in Glasgow's history. Big men.

Each reputed to be worth millions. Rankin had made it in the shipyards and then the ammunition factories. Fowler's wealth was in shipping. He was said to have tripled the already sizeable fortune handed down by his granddaddy from the slave trade. Maxwell was said to own half of the West End and a fair chunk of land east of Loch Lomond in the Forest of Ard. Rich company for a jumped-up Glasgow councillor to keep.

'This is all suspicious stuff, Elsie, but circumstantial,' I said. Her eyebrows went up.

Wullie interpreted. 'What Brodie is saying is, so what? You cannae hang a man for having expensive friends. Even in Glasgow.'

'Oh, Ah ken that. But after these nichts oot, Jimmie – when he was still wi' me – would come rolling hame, fu' as a monkey with French brandy and tell me how clever he was. How he'd be showing a' the doubters. How he was gontae come out on top.'

'But again, Elsie, it's only your word against his. I assume there was no one there to witness what he said? Other than you?' I asked.

'Naw.'

'So we've no proof. No hard evidence?'

'I suppose.' There was silence for a bit. 'Except for the flat, the car and the suits, you mean?'

I looked at Wullie. He raised his eyebrow. 'Right, Elsie. Why don't you tell us all about Jimmie's good fortune.'

'Ah'll tell ye first about his *bad* fortune. I mean, that man was always broke. Never a farthing to his bloody name. Ah had to keep working at the hairdresser's to keep him in white shirts for his politicking. Ah kept the bank account and the cheque book. Ah kept the savings book. You don't live wi' a man for twenty-five years without kenning his worth. An' his was zero.'

'Until recently . . .' Wullie suggested.

She nodded. 'About a year back. Roon about the time there

was a' this talk about knocking doon Glasgow and rebuilding it in the Campsies. Or wherever. It was wee things. New socks.'

'Socks?' I asked.

'Ah've been darning his bloody socks a' ma days. There's mair darn than sock noo. So you notice a new pair. Then there was the new suit. And a few ties. *Another* suit. No' just any suit. You could tell the quality. Quite the spiv getting. He said it was paid for by the Cooncil. For keeping up appearances. That everybody was getting an allowance. But Ah never saw ony other cooncillor wearing onythin' other than the shiny auld suits they'd hud for the last twenty years.'

I'm not one for coincidence, but it was worth a try. 'Elsie, do you know where he got his new suits?'

'Aye. Ah checked the label. Yon fancy Jew tailor in the Gorbals. Only the best for oor Jimmie, noo.'

'Isaac Feldmann?'

'Aye, him.' Her glass had emptied again. Wullie refilled it. Thirsty work, betrayal.

'Then there was the other woman, Elsie?' he asked.

'The whore, ye mean. She micht have come from Edinburgh, but ye ken a whore when ye see wan. Jist makes her a high-class whore. Supposed to be his secretary or campaign manager or some such guff. Jimmie was drooling. Next thing, he's aff and set up a wee love nest in the West End. Jist about a month ago.'

'After his pal Alec Morton was murdered?'

'It was like Jimmie got a burr up his bum.'

'The flat, was it rented?' I asked.

'Bought. I mean *bought*! Paid for outright. Ye hear everything at the hairdresser's. It's a wee place, Glasgow.'

'It could be her money?'

'Aye, that's what Ah thocht to begin with. But the word Ah got back from certain enquiries—'

McAllister butted in. 'Elsie hired a private investigator.'

'Word was that she was being kept by a fancy man in Edinburgh but his money ran oot. And so did she. A' she had to her name when she got aff the train at Buchanan Street was a pair o' high heels and a coney stole. Nae need for drawers,' she sneered.

It was a powerful picture. Wullie and I tried not to look at each other.

'An' then there's the car.'

'Jimmie's got a car?'

'Brand new Morris Eight. Toad of Toad Hall, he is. Flaunting his motor and his whore. Living it up at parties in his fancy hoose. Is that enough hard proof, then?'

Wullie and I smiled.

When Elsie had left us, we sat with our notebooks in front of us, supping at our pints, and staring at each other.

'Jimmie got spooked by Morton's murder?' I asked.

'So he decided to live life to the limit while he could, you mean? Either that or he was given the choice of being bought off or wearing a concrete hat.'

'Some choice.'

'What do you think, Brodie? Have we got a case?'

'We've got innuendo, circumstantial evidence, and a bitter wife. In themselves they hardly add up to a conviction. But if you can find out who paid for all the trappings of his new-found wealth you're well on your way.'

Wullie nodded.

I continued, 'It certainly adds up to a story. And if you wanted to run it now, you could pose the questions about Jimmie Sheridan's sudden good fortune, and see what he says.'

'That's what I thought. We've got enough incontestable facts. *He* has to explain himself. Or sue. I'll pen something, then stand back while Jimmie starts screaming blue murder about slanderous allegations from the right-wing press.'

'Are we right-wing? I thought we were the people's voice.'

'We're whichever wing our upset accuser isnae.'

'So, will you run it?'

'It's short of what I wanted, Brodie. I was hoping for a foot-high pile of signed documents and independent testimonials that would stand in a court of law. I've got some paperwork but not solid enough. This new-found wealth angle could be a dead end. There's the risk it might get everybody het up, but the wheeler-dealers would just close ranks. Pu' up the drawbridge. These boys are no' stupid. They know how to perform dirty work. Any paper trail would soon be up in smoke. And every stinking pound note that bought Sheridan will have been laundered through umpteen holding companies in Scotland and abroad. Keep mind, the likes of Fowler made his money in the Bahamas. They know how to make money disappear over there. If so, end of career-capping story for yours truly.'

'But?'

'But, fuck it. I've had enough sitting around wi' my thumb up ma erse, waiting for a breakthrough. I've been close enough lately but, well, let's say it didn't work out. It's time to assemble the hot lead, and ink up the rollers. To publish, and get right royally screwed. But at least we'll get a reaction.'

THIRTY-TWO

Wullie's forecast was spot on. Eddie ran with the story on Thursday under the provocative:

COUNCILLOR SETS UP LOVE NEST

Councillor James Sheridan is alleged to have purchased an expensive Georgian apartment in the fashionable West End and installed an Edinburgh socialite as his hostess. According to neighbours, the elegant blonde has been holding parties at the address and has been seen coming and going in a brand-new car driven by Mr Sheridan. The *Gazette* asks, 'Where did "oor Jimmie" get the funds? And what does his long-suffering wife Elsie think?'

Wullie's report was brilliantly shaped and worded to appeal to every base instinct of Glasgow gossips. In other words, some 90 per cent of the citizenry. He gave Elsie the wounded-wife treatment, dabbing her eyes as she told her tale of betrayal and hurt. She appeared to have had a quick dose of elocution lessons too:

'I have stood by Jimmie through thick and thin, but I have finally had enough. This is not the man I married. If he comes to his senses, I will of course consider taking him back. But my heart is broken, and it may be too late to save our marriage . . .'

She was then quoted as saying:

'What I don't understand is where Jimmie got the money. The Edinburgh woman arrived in Glasgow without a penny to her name. And I know that Jimmie's pay as a councillor is barely enough to keep him in clean handkerchiefs, far less the new suits he's been wearing. I do hope that he hasn't done anything wrong.'

According to Wullie, she broke down in sobs at this stage, but then pulled herself together to deliver the *coo de grass*.

'Jimmie's always been a man of great integrity, fighting for the common man. But it's so easy to be tempted, isn't it? Fancy restaurants and nice clothes, flashy new car. Even a nice wee house. I refuse to think the worst. I'm sure there is a perfectly good explanation for Jimmie's sudden prosperity. Perhaps he won the pools? I only wish I had been able to enjoy it with him after all the years of scrimping and saving while he pursued his career in public office . . .'

The wickedly provocative piece was supported by an editorial of more sober style, but still posing the questions about Jimmie Sheridan's morals and newly improved finances. The word *alleged* featured throughout but it was well understood that it was one of those words that were invisible to the readership at large; unless of course you were the allegee's lawyer.

They had to do another print run to meet demand. I heard the big lorries pounding out of the basement late morning. All round the city, the newsboys were engaged in a city-wide opera, chanting: '*Councillor's love nest! Read all about it! Love rat under suspicion!*'

I went home at six and found my mother sitting on the stairs waiting for me like a child.

'Douglas, this will never do.'

I panicked. 'I'm sorry, Mum, what have I done?'

'It's not you. It's me. I've overstayed my welcome here. My hoose will be thick in stoor. All the sheets I put out to dry will have been taken in by Maggie Cuthbertson and will be murder to iron. And I've been eating this poor lassie out of house and home.'

I didn't point out that a sparrow could out-eat her any day of the week. 'Have you fallen out with Samantha?'

A voice called from down in the kitchen. 'Not a bit, Brodie. Your mum just wants home. I've tried to talk her out of it.'

My mum stood up. 'I'm ashamed of mysel'. It's just been that lovely being here. In all of this.' She waved her hand round the roomy hall with the sweep of stairs up and down. It could have swallowed her house ten times over. 'We all need a purpose. And mine is to mind my own hoose. You must take me back in the morning, Douglas.'

It was her usual telepathy at work. She'd pre-empted my suggestion about returning to Bonnyton.

'Now I'm going to pack. We can get going first thing.' She turned and walked up the stair to her room, leaving me staring down at Sam framed in the kitchen door. Sam smiled and shrugged.

I could have argued with Mum about the packing. That it would take no time at all to get ready in the morning; there was no train to catch; and it wasn't such a lot to pack. But it was her way; just as she always made up my dad's lunch for him the night before his early shift, and laid out his clothes. But, she would argue, she was going home with more than she came, her shabby message bag augmented by an old but good holdall filled with cast-offs from Sam and Sam's own mother. Doubtless – knowing Sam – there would be bacon slices wrapped up to replace Mum's meagre contribution. I think Sam was going to miss having her around.

*

My mum went off to bed so as to be up early. Sam and I sat sipping a nightcap and chortling over the day's *Gazette* columns.

'I love the bit about a "man of integrity" and the juxtaposition with Elsie's wistful comment about wanting to enjoy his sudden good fortune. Perfect!'

'Wullie's cheek was gowping with his tongue stuck in it all day.'

'But you said Elsie mentioned names? Jimmie's paymasters?'

'Doubtless. But we can't say them out loud. Not without a law suit.'

'You'd better tell me,' she said with something that looked like foreboding.

'Kenneth Rankin, Tom Fowler and Colin Maxwell.'

She took off her glasses and began cleaning them.

'You know them, Sam?'

'Of course. If you move in certain circles, like my parents did, you know them all. But in particular I know Kenny Rankin and Colin Maxwell and his son Charlie. Though I'm not surprised at Tommy Fowler being in there with them. A thieves' kitchen right enough. Corporate thieves, but thieves all right. It's a thin line between entrepreneur and shyster.'

'What do you know of them?'

'Hang on.' We were sitting comfortably in the drawing room, either side of the big oak fireplace. The grate was dark and still, waiting for the autumn evenings to cool. She got up and walked over to the mantelpiece. A number of cards were stuck either side of a loud gold and black clock. Invitation cards. She picked up a handful and started shuffling them. She discarded most in the fireplace for kindling. She kept one and put the others back.

'My social life has stalled lately, Brodie, but I'm not forgotten. Not quite. I still get invitations. Take a look.' She gave me a stamped and addressed RSVP envelope and a

white card edged with gold and engraved with fine lettering.
The card said:

Sir Kenneth and Lady Rankin
request the pleasure of the company of
Miss Samantha Campbell, LL B Hons,
at the grand re-opening of
the Rankin Wing of the Kelvingrove Art Gallery
on Saturday 14 September 1946.

Cocktails at 7 p.m. followed by a private tour
of the Art Gallery.

Evening Dress RSVP
Decorations Gideon Caldwell
Private secretary to Sir Kenneth Rankin

Of course I sometimes forgot that Sam and her parents had moved in such rarefied circles. It seems she still did. And why not? Daughter of a prominent Procurator Fiscal, and high-profile advocate in her own right, Samatha Campbell, LL B Hons, would be on everyone's list for major events. She was reading my mind.

'It's a wee social group in Glasgow. I went to school with Moira Rankin, Sir Kenny's second wife. Moira finally snared money. And a title. I didn't talk to her for ages after Kenny divorced his first wife for her. *O tempora! O mores!* We're pals again, sort of. She was one of the first to visit me after all the hoo-hah in the papers about Hugh and the Slattery boys. Probably just nosy. Anyway, we rebuilt bridges. I don't know Tommy Fowler so well. He's usually away sunning himself in the Caribbean. Still plays at running a plantation, I hear. But I know the Maxwells. We used to go shooting on Colin Maxwell's estate. I'm surprised old Colin's still in the game. I'd heard he was in decline since his wife Clarinda passed away. If there is a Maxwell involved it's more likely to be Charlie.' There was an edge to her words.

'You don't like Charlie?'

'A pompous ass. And one I've suffered most of my life.' She looked as if she was about to say more but held her tongue. She took back the invitation. 'I've been a recluse lately. But it's not too late to start moving in the right circles again. What do you think, Brodie?'

'What will you do? Just go up to Rankin and ask him if he's a corrupt businessman who's been buying off councillors?'

'Not me, Brodie. *Us.*'

THIRTY-THREE

am ignored my look of panic and went on, 'But I suggest you find a subtler way of asking him. Or possibly *them*. The chances are that all the great and good – and not so good – will be there. Including Maxwell senior and junior, and Fowler. It's how they operate. All stroking each other and outdoing each other in public declarations of citizenship.'

'But I'm not invited.' I was aghast at the idea. I'd done enough socialising among such groupings in my university days.

'I'm inviting you. They're not going to bar you if I'm on your arm. I've got time to RSVP saying I'll be escorted by Major Douglas Brodie, late of the Seaforth Highlanders. '

'It says Evening Dress.' My dread was growing.

'Regimental mess kit?'

'We didn't have much use for number 10s in Normandy. And I sold my subaltern mess kit years ago. Not that it would fit me.'

'Shame. I bet you looked great in a kilt.'

'I'll have you know I did. And you should have seen these twinkling feet.' I smiled at the memory of a mess night in a freezing cold castle in Kent in the winter before D-Day. The officers of the 2nd and 4th Battalions of the Seaforths, in full Highland dress, dancing over swords to the sound of five regimental pipers. The whisky helped.

'You'll at least have decorations? I assume they gave you a couple. You were in long enough. You haven't sold them?'

'Things aren't that bad.' Though it had been close.

'Fine. Are those suits ready from your tailor pal? I've got one more up the stairs. Dad's dinner jacket will look terrific, Brodie.'

'It's a week on Saturday, Sam!' I pointed at the card.

'I thought your man needed the business? He'll have your new suit ready in a trice.'

Next morning I borrowed the car and piled Mum's bags in the back along with the dinner suit. I turned away as Sam and Mum embraced and said goodbye on the steps. I blinked back an unaccountable set of emotions and didn't speak until we were over the Jamaica Bridge.

'A nice lassie, Douglas.'

'She's kind.'

'She likes you.'

'Does she?'

'You can be as dense as your faither.'

'I know, Mum.'

I got her in and set her bags down. Neither of us commented on how small and dark it was compared to what she'd left. Besides, it was her home. She was glad to be back. Neighbours were already queuing up for tea and debriefing. I left her to it, promising to bring Sam to see her again.

I drove back to the Gorbals. The bell tinkled in Isaac's shop as I pushed in. He emerged, stooped, from the back room.

'Douglas, you are just in time. Everything is done.' He went into the back again and returned, laden. He put the clothes down on the counter. 'Let me tell you, this is good cloth. They will last you for years. I've had them steamed and pressed. You will cut a dash.'

'That's wonderful, Isaac, but I have another favour.' I laid out the shiny black suit.

Isaac smoothed out the double breasted jacket, then the trousers with their smart piping. 'Lovely, lovely. The seat is a

198

little shiny but I can bring up the cloth. You are moving up in the world, Douglas?'

'I'm being dragged up, Isaac. My landlady – Samantha Campbell – wants an escort to a big fling a week on Saturday. Can you do it?'

'Same as before? Trousers up a little, waist in a little, jacket sleeves?'

'I'm most grateful. And there's someone else I need to talk about. Someone else who's been moving up in the world.'

Isaac was nodding. 'I saw the paper. I know what you're going to ask me. Mr James Sheridan, no?'

'New suits?'

'For a while last year he was one of my only customers. I made three for him. The last I fitted this January. All the finest cloth. One with matching waistcoat. He came by last month and ordered two more in different cloths. He said he wanted the best. I said you've come to the right shop.'

'How did he pay, Isaac? Cash or cheque? I assume he *has* paid?'

He was shaking his head. 'I suppose I won't be completing the new orders now. The first ones were paid for all right, Douglas. But not by Mr Sheridan. Wait, I have it here.'

Isaac ducked below the counter and pulled out a fat ledger. He opened it and worked down the pages of beautiful German script. I'd seen ledgers like it in the camps, but they had a very different purpose.

'Ach yes, here. I had to send the bill to Mr Andrew Cunningham. A cheque came back by return. It was a good cheque. No problem. Covered my heating bills this winter.'

I was disappointed. I'd never heard of Cunningham. 'Do you know him? This man who promptly paid up?'

'No. But I know the address. It's the offices in the city of Sir Colin Maxwell.'

I spent another half-hour at Isaac's trying on my haul. He was right. It was all good cloth, from heavy tweeds that would see me through a damp day in the heather or repel barbed wire, to smart lounge suits that would have the maître d' at the Ritz bowing and scraping. I stood in the last of Sam's father's suits – a lightweight blue wool – and glanced at the discarded Co-op rig I'd come in wearing. Isaac was nodding and smiling.

'I'll keep this one on, Isaac. And I won't be needing that rag. Can you give it away?'

'With pleasure, sir.'

I paid him a ridiculously small amount for his labours and marched off into the warm morning, feeling transformed. Isaac would have the other suits sent round to Sam's. The dinner jacket would be ready for the gallery opening and I would have purchased a new pair of shoes to live up to this new image.

Which reminded me; I needed more money. The *Gazette* was paying me a pittance as Wullie's understudy, though promises had been made about a salary hike to a fiver per week if I proved worthy of filling his down-at-heel shoes. In the meantime, my demob gratuity had all but run out and I was struggling to keep up with the swimming-club membership and day-to-day living. I was a poor man living in a palace. It rankled. Maybe the fags would have to go. Maybe I could start writing some articles and get them published?

THIRTY-FOUR

All the following week, between us, McAllister and I were selling newspapers like free mutton pies at Hampden. People couldn't wait to get their hands on them. I told Wullie about my impending rendezvous with his prime suspects and promised him, under pain of excommunication from Ross's, that I'd tell him everything I learned. City Hall corruption was his story and I was merely contributing to it. Wullie was mollified and suggested he might give me a mention in passing.

As McAllister's headlines about Jimmie Sheridan fell from the public's immediate attention I provided new grist to the gossip mills with a column about my encounter with the Marshals, the Glasgow vigilantes.

The police were helping the sales by making a big production of the murder inquiries and linking them to the vigilante activities. Spokesmen from the Chief Constable's office were being quoted in all the papers: *no stone left unturned . . . escalation of violence . . . eradicate this criminal gang who have taken the law into their own hands . . .*

I almost felt sorry for the Marshals, if they were indeed innocent of the murders. I called Duncan to check our stance again.

'Duncan, I know we want to avoid mentioning the severed pinkies in the paper, but it sounds like you and Sangster are only focusing on the Marshals for the murders.'

'Sangster just disnae believe anyone else is involved. His brain can't imagine two sets of bampots causing mayhem in his patch. He's absolutely clear that you should not mention the pinkies or try to suggest there's another outfit at work.'

In the meantime, the punishments went on. Either Ishmael had been recruiting again, or, as I'd feared, Glasgow was littering copycats. I had a call that Cowcaddens was erupting. I grabbed one of our photographers and we shot round in a taxi. We found a mob, lead by wifies in headscarves and pinnies, clearing out a vipers' nest of drug dealers. We cheered them on as they surrounded the dingy pair of shops where the dealers and their customers hung out and dinned them away with clashing dustbin lids and chants. Next day, our front page had a sensational shot of the housewife army in a mad charge, brandishing lids and brooms, re-enacting Bannockburn.

The day after, another call came in, and I leaped down the subway and rattled round to Govan. I was in time to see a band of flat-capped men marching down the high street, tackety boots pounding out a steady rhythm. Each man carried a pickaxe handle and a resolute mien. I followed them as they darted into closes and smashed down doors. They dragged out squealing ruffians and put the boot in. They swung their heavy sticks and bloodied cowering heads until they'd exacted justice on the local gangsters who'd made life miserable with street battles and protection rackets.

It wasn't legal but it was effective; although, as usual, revenge and envy clouded judgements. Old scores got settled under the banner of localised law enforcement. Two young women had their heads shaved and were paraded through the streets of Bellahouston, accused of prostitution. It turned out that the righteous harpy who'd led the moral crusade had lost her man to one of them and was just getting even.

The crime rates were falling like bugs in a vacuum jar but Glasgow was becoming ungovernable. More than usual. And worse was to come. Isaac called the office. He sounded bleak.

'I told you some of my people were of the old persuasion, Douglas. Two of the men used the bagel shop to report on their wives.'

'Their own wives!'

'Suspicions. Jealousies. An old story.'

'What happened?'

'Men in balaclavas visited the women. Both on the same day.'

I could hardly bear to ask. 'And?'

'They made the women kneel. Then they read out a bit of *our* old book to them. *Your* Old Testament. Numbers 5, verses 17 to 27. I have it here. I'll give you the extracts.

'And the priest shall take holy water in an earthen vessel; and of the dust that is in the floor of the tabernacle the priest shall take, and put it into the water . . .

And the priest . . . shall cause the woman to drink the . . . water that causeth the curse . . .

And . . . if she be defiled, and have done trespass against her husband . . . the water . . . shall . . . become bitter, and her belly shall swell and her thigh shall rot: and the woman shall be a curse among her people.'

Isaac switched into his native German and his voice took on the rolling high pitch of his ancestors. He painted such a graphic picture of the scene that it was like watching a movie unfold in front of me . . .

A small hot room, windows wide but no air stirring. Three men standing; one woman on her knees. One of the men is behind the kneeling woman. His ringletted hair tangles with his beard. He wears a long black jacket and black hat. Round his waist is a wide cloth belt. A shawl hangs down across his shoulders and his left hand grips and tugs at the strings that dangle from the corners. From moment to moment he pulls the strings to his mouth and kisses them. He is rocking on his heels, all the time using his right hand to clutch the woman's shoulder to keep her in place.

Her head is scarfed and she is weeping. Her hands are

clenched in front of her. Two men stand facing her, their heads covered by woollen masks except for the eyes and mouth. One of them holds an open bible in his left hand. He has just finished declaiming from it. He holds out a bottle of murky fluid in his right hand.

'Drink! If you're innocent it won't harm you. If you're guilty, it will become bitter. It will eat your vitals. God will see through you. God will judge you.'

The woman shrieks and throws herself forward on to her face.

The masked man says, 'Hold her!'

His colleague and the woman's husband haul her to her knees again and wrench back her head. She is sobbing and flailing. Her husband pulls open her jaw while the man holds her arms by her side. The man with the bottle tips the dirty contents into her gaping mouth. She chokes and coughs and vomits but enough fluid has gone down her throat to matter. The men stand back and the woman falls to the floor. She writhes and her knees jerk up to her chest.

'It's hot. It's burning! I can't breathe,' she gasps.

The man with the bottle waves it in triumph over her head. 'Ha! It is the sign. *Bitter water!* She is defiled!

The husband pulls back, his face red with anger and distress. His wife struggles to her feet.

' God . . .!' Her voice fails her. She chokes and holds her throat. 'Yakob! Not true! Not . . .' Her words stick in her burning mouth. 'Aaah,' she shrieks. She turns her head from side to side until she sees the window. The open window. She takes two long steps, brushes aside the second masked man and dives at the opening. She makes no further sound as her body falls the three storeys to the street below.

Isaac has fallen silent, waiting for me.

I cleared my throat and found my voice. 'Dear God. You said there were two women. What happened to the other?'

'She broke down and admitted adultery. Her husband has

thrown her out. And her children. He refuses to believe they are his.'

'Stupid sod!'

I tried distracting myself from the daily litany of horrors with a swim in the morning and again in the evening. I smelled permanently of chlorine.

Morag was avoiding me – or trying to. It's not easy when you work twenty feet away from each other. I wasn't sure if she'd decided I was cheating on her with Sam or if I should have been trying harder to explain there was nothing in it. Maybe it was the chlorine. Her big blue eyes just looked hurt when I raised my head and caught her looking at me. At the same time, my mother's absence from Sam's house seemed to have disturbed the fabric of the place. Or perhaps just the relationship between Sam and me. We looked forward to sitting reading together in the library or talking and listening to the gramophone in the drawing room. As though we'd been married for twenty years but had somehow skipped all that messy business of sex. It confused the hell out of me.

Saturday evening came and I was standing in my finery in the drawing room waiting for Sam. Dinah Shore was singing softly on the wireless. I still wasn't sure what we'd get out of this evening, other than to put a face on some famous names. We might draw a reaction from anyone with a guilty conscience. At the very least it would apply some pressure, like lobbing some shells on enemy positions to force them keep their heads down and let them know that we were there. When people get nervous they make mistakes.

The stiff collar kept my head up and reminded my back and shoulders of their army training. As did the line of medals in a clanking row on my left breast. It was the first time I'd worn them all together. It felt false and flash, as though I was flaunting them. Or going to an old boys' reunion. But the invite was clear. I'd even given them a polish. I could see from the holes in the cloth that it wasn't the first time this jacket had carried decorations. I needed to ask Sam about her father. In fact there was a great deal I needed to ask her about her father. Such as whether I was some sort of stand-in for him. It was a cheap thought, inspired by a brief examination of Siggie Freud during one term at university. It had all seemed funny at the time. We sophisticates considered that the old boy had some real mental problems of his own to come up with such tosh. And yet . . .

I caught myself in the big mirror. In truth I found myself turning and posing. It had been years since I'd looked this smart. A light touch of Brylcreem kept my dark thatch in place. The grey smudges by my ears looked more distinguished than just plain old. My face glowed with the attention of a new razor blade.

The dinner jacket fitted like a glove. A double-breasted and old-fashioned glove, with slightly shiny trousers, but none the worse for that. It had the look of an outfit worn regularly and nonchalantly at a steady stream of grand occasions throughout the season. My new shoes shone with parade-ground brilliance, and I forgave them their pinching. The black tie – another gift from Sam – sat perfectly in the hard collar; the technique of tying it had come back to me like swimming.

'Show me,' said Sam, standing in the doorway. 'Don't keep it all to yourself.'

I turned round, caught out like a wee boy admiring himself in a shop window. Then my brief embarrassment evaporated. Her floor-length dress was blue silk and fell over her gentle lines like a shimmering river. She had matching arm-length gloves and blue silk shoes. She clasped a glittering bag in one hand and held a cigarette holder high in the other. But it was her head and shoulders that stood out.

'You look lovely, Samantha.'

She'd managed to sweep up her shoulder-length blonde bob into a carefully tangled crown. It was held in place by a small cap of silk and sequins. From her ears dangled long sparkling pendants, and round her slim throat, a matching necklace glittered and drew the eye to the gentle swell of her breasts. Mascara brought out her grey-blue eyes, and her slash of red lipstick accentuated them. My words and my inspection brought a flush to her face. She stepped further into the room and twirled to hide her confusion.

'Now your turn, Douglas. By the way, it's *Douglas* tonight. None of your common Brodie stuff.'

I smiled and pirouetted in a clumsy imitation of her controlled birl.

She walked over and flicked a hair from my shoulder. 'So you weren't just malingering at Edinburgh Castle.' She pointed at the medals. 'What's this?' She fingered the cross.

'A bit of stupidity that came off. Just.'

We were holding a position east of Caen and had taken a pounding for ten solid days. Lying in filthy foxholes, with shrapnel and bullets whistling overhead. I suppose I cracked. Certainly it was a kind of madness. A mind-shaking bout of anger which tore up the rule book that said a man with a machine gun always loses against a tank. I got lucky.

She peered closer. 'It's the Military Cross, Douglas! You're a bloody hero!'

Her eyes were big. On impulse, and to hide my blushes, as the music swept into Perry Como's big hit, I reached out my hand. For a second I thought she'd decline, but then she moved forward, took my fingers and moved into my arms. We smiled at the blatant lyrics:

> 'Surrender, why don't you surrender?
> How long can your lips live without a kiss?
> Surrender, I beg you surrender,
> How long can your heart resist?'

She was light and warm in my arms, and her scent filled my chest. I wanted to lift her up and carry her to bed. We swayed easily together to the gentle rhythms of the music. It wasn't dancing. It was reminding ourselves of our one night of love-making. Then I felt her stiffen.

'Enough, my dear. Enough, Douglas.'

But her eyes betrayed her. I leaned in and kissed her, and felt her mouth tremble and soften on mine. She gave herself up to me and we kissed like lovers reunited after a long break. Then she was pushing me back. She kept me at arm's length, chest heaving, eyes glistening.

'Your medals are cold.'

'I'll take them off.'

'We'll be late.'

'Isn't it fashionable to be late?' In fact as far as I was concerned the soirée could happen without us.

> *'I'll bring you a love you can cling to,*
> *A love that won't be untrue . . .*
> *So please be tender,*
> *And, darling, surrender,*
> *And love me as I love you.'*

She shook her head and her beaded cap glittered in the lamplight. 'If you think I've just spend the last two hours getting *dolled* up just to have it *messed* up, you can think again, *Major* Brodie, MC.'

I noted she didn't deny the temptation, just the waste of effort.

'Perhaps later, Samantha? I mean, I should at least get the second dance.'

'Hmph. We should go.' She glanced at the clock. 'The taxi will be waiting.'

It was. We'd decided to leave her Riley in the garage rather than get our hands dirty with a starting handle. As we stepped outside, I could have wished we were walking. It was a balmy evening, still broad day in this late Northern summer. The park looked tempting. A gentle stroll downhill to the art gallery would have been just the ticket.

Sam must have read my mind. 'It's a pity, Brod . . . Douglas, but these shoes wouldn't make it.'

I handed her into the taxi and we sailed off on the short ride down Clifton Street and along Royal Terrace. As we turned on to Argyle Street and drew near, we could see other cars and taxis disgorging their passengers in front of the Hall. I could see shimmering long dresses and black suits gliding towards the door. I could see . . .

'Stop!' I called to the driver.

'Here, sir?'

'Right here. Just for a second.'

Fifty yards ahead of us was a massive car, a Rolls by its size and shape. A royal car. The doors on either side were being held open by capped and uniformed chauffeurs. On the left-hand side a man was emerging, straightening his jacket and tugging at his cummerbund. On the right, the pavement side, a wheelchair was being set up and a man was being helped into it. He was also in evening dress. But it was the chauffeurs that had caught my attention.

'What is it, Douglas? What's the matter? That's just . . . wait a minute . . . yes, it's Colin Maxwell and his son Charlie. Colin's health's worse than I thought. What's wrong?'

'It's not them. It's their drivers. Look closely. And, Sam, steel yourself.'

THIRTY-FIVE

Sam peered past the taxi driver's head, through the windscreen. She was long-sighted, so I knew she'd be able to see what I saw. The chauffeur on the left closed the door and limped round the car. His black curling hair pushed out from under his cap. On the other side, the sallow face with the flattened nose turned towards us. As recognition dawned, Sam's gloved hand went up to her mouth.

'Oh God!' she yelped. 'It can't be!' She crushed my hand.

'Sam, it is. It's them. But you're safe now. You're with me.'

Under smart grey uniforms and caps were the two ruffians we'd last seen on Arran as bodyguards to Gerrit Slattery. They'd failed in that duty and Gerrit had no further need of them, not now he lay full fathom five undergoing a sea change in the Firth of Clyde.

Curly had earned his limp at my own hand. I'd shot him through the foot back in April as a sort of discouragement to the rest of his gang. The last time I'd seen him and his pugilist-faced pal they were diving into the sea to douse the gobs of flaming petrol that clung to them from my booby-trap. It looked as if their shrapnel burns had healed, though it was hard to tell at this distance.

Their eyes darted about before they got in the car and drove off. Their masters were just entering the building, the tall younger man having bounced his father backwards up the steps in the wheelchair.

'OK, cabbie. Drive on please, and let us out at the entrance.'

Sam clutched my arm. 'No! Wait! We can't go on now! We can't go in! What if they're waiting? What if . . .'

'Sam, Sam, it's OK. They're gone. There's no one to fear inside. Interrogate, yes. Fear, no. The Maxwells have some explaining to do. I have no idea where all this is going, but there are some threads beginning to come together.'

I looked at her. She was breathing hard and clinging to my arm as if it were a lifebelt. Her eyes were wide and her face whiter than usual.

From the front: 'Are we moving, sir, or are we sitting here?'

'Give us five minutes please. The lady needs a cigarette. Keep the clock running.'

We sat back. I lit two and slid one into her holder. She took it in shaking fingers. I wound down the windows and let the soft evening air in. The memory flooded back. I could see it in her own eyes . . .

Wild seas slapping on Arran's rocky shore. The big white house. Setting the pier alight to attract this pair like thuggish moths. The exploding can of petrol shredding their faces with red-hot fragments. My assault on the house to find it empty. Sam carried off into the night by Slattery on his fast ketch. Racing after him in my borrowed power boat. Sam, lying tossed and bruised and hogtied on the deck. My raging attack on the ketch, meting out condign retribution to Slattery. Freeing Sam, terrified, battered and groggy with chloroform . . .

I had soothed her, assuring her that it was all over.

Seems it wasn't.

'Did you hear their names?' I asked her. 'I only know the one with a limp as Curly.' I was thinking that putting a name to a demon would help.

She swallowed. 'Curly's good enough. Gerrit called the other one Fitz.'

'Curly and Fitz. Do you think there's a recruitment agency that specialises in hiring out thugs? Maxwell phoned them and asked them to send round a couple of experienced hood-lums?'

We sat until we'd finished our cigarettes and her breathing had slowed. 'Ready to face this?'

'I'm fine, Douglas. Shall we?'

We had the car drive forward and pull up at the kerb. I got out and handed her out. I gave her my arm and we walked up the broad steps like a charmed couple. A blonde and her beau. Only the turmoil in our heads confounded the image. We were greeted at the door and I waved our invitation. Tall glasses were thrust in our hands and we chinked them together before sipping the bubbles. Rationing? What rationing? We pressed forward into the huge vaulted nave of this baroque cathedral to art.

We followed the noise of a murmuring crowd, guided on our way by liveried staff who smiled and pointed the direction in their chalk-white gloves. The portal ahead showed Glasgow's society at play. A gaggle of colours with black punctuation. They looked as if they belonged here. Belonged together.

I'm an upstart and I know it. My dad was a miner and I only had an education through charity. I'd walked out on my old tribe and never been accepted by a new one. After all this time my instinctive reaction to the upper classes and their privilege is still to knock them down. It was petty and puerile, but for a second I was arriving at my first formal dance at university. My throat thickened and my heart raced. Sam must have sensed it.

'*Courage, mon brave*. Imagine them naked under their fine clothes.'

As we were just passing a particularly plump dowager sporting a pair of fleshy pillboxes on her uncovered chest, I gave Sam a raised brow. 'Thanks for the image.'

She smothered a giggle.

A tall man and woman stood just inside, greeting the couple before us. His head was shiny bald, hers a piled-up highlight of gold and reds. Her diamonds flashed his wealth.

In a smiling and low-voiced aside, Sam explained, 'Kenny Rankin and his wife Moira.'

'The ammunition king.'

'With an art gallery named after him.'

I just had time to look up at the plaque above the door – 'The Rankin Wing' – as we joined the line-up. Then it was our turn to be announced.

'Samantha! It's so good to see you. Haven't seen you in simply ages.' Lady Rankin was gushingly kissing and hugging Sam while I was having my hand pumped by Sir Kenny.

'Saw Samantha was being escorted. Delighted to meet you, Major Brodie. Regiment?'

'Late of the Seaforths, sir. Second Battalion.'

Kenny Rankin was tall, eyes level with mine. In his prime he'd been a big man. He was still vigorous and imposing but his jacket now seemed hollow at the shoulder and bulging round the midriff. He seemed twice the age of his consort, which fitted with Sam being at school with her. Rankin scanned my medals then gazed at me shrewdly.

'MC, eh? A good war, Major. 51st Highland? North Africa?'

'Yes, sir. Then the standard European tour.'

He laughed. 'I was with the Gordons in the Great War. Only ever saw the inside of a bloody trench in France. Not counting a weekend in Paree, eh?'

I felt a hard stare on me, sizing me up. 'Kenny, you're not to start your reminiscing already. Now introduce me to Samantha's young man.' Moira Rankin was smiling as she said it, but not with her eyes. I remembered what Sam had said about her society aspirations and wondered what she and Sam had had in common other than a school uniform.

It would seem from Kenny Rankin's reaction that he hadn't made the connection with Brodie of the Seaforths and Brodie of the *Gazette*. Or if he had, he was too well mannered to mention it. Whereas his wife was now skinning me, analysing my soul and my worth, and finding me wanting on all fronts. Quickly enough her flensing stare flicked beyond me to the next in line, and we were dismissed. As we moved away, in an aside to Sam, I murmured, 'I thought you and Moira were pals?'

Sam looked puzzled. 'We are. I've known her all my days. She knew I was upset at her stealing Kenny from his first wife, but that's all history.'

'Not the way she was looking at you.'

'Just jealous of my handsome escort.' She smiled, took my arm and we plunged into the crowd. We swapped our empty glasses for new ones and the evening began to improve. The gallery was high-ceilinged, the walls freshly painted in soft red. Pictures hung beneath discreet lamps on every wall. No one was pretending to admire them. They were here to inspect each other and compare notes on time's ravages on faces and wallets.

'Well, if it isn't Samantha Campbell. We haven't seen you around for a bit. Been hiding?'

It was a high, clear drawl, without a trace of Scots in it. I felt Sam's hand pinch my arm. She turned us both to greet the voice. It came from a man about my age, with slicked-back waves and an Errol Flynn moustache. Like Flynn, the absence of decorations on his dinner jacket suggested this guy had managed to sit out the war. He stood behind a wheelchair bearing an old man with puzzled eyes and thin grey hair. The eyes were the same brown marbles, but the younger's were unblinking and evaluating. The Maxwells.

Sam cranked her own accent up in retaliation. 'Why, Charlie, I've been busy, you know. Criminals to defend. Juries to convince. You know how it is.' Sam put on her most innocent smile and turned to the seated man.

'Colin, so good to see you.' Sam was bending forward and touching the old man's hand. His eyes focused and a smile touched his face.

'And you, my dear.' It was a breathy, weak voice, struggling to be heard above the babble. 'And is this your husband, Samantha?'

Sam smiled and shook her head. 'No, Colin. Just a friend of mine. My escort for this evening. Major Douglas Brodie. Douglas, this is Sir Colin and Charlie Maxwell.'

We all shook hands and smiled at each other in a stilted fashion, waiting for someone to provide a conversational hook. I took the measure of the younger Maxwell. His eyes had just grazed my medals. The corner of his thin mouth lifted in amusement. Sam had described him as a pompous ass. I was more than prepared to take her word for it. I mistrust anyone who claims to be Scots but sounds like a BBC announcer. The sort of accent that only the best English public schools provide. With one lift of the corner of his mouth, with the languid dismissal of his eyes, I knew him.

Supercilious, certainly; a thin mouth with a built-in sneer as a result of holding the rest of the world in contempt since he learned he had money. He embodied every slight, every disdainful glance, every social cut that put a straitjacket of inhibition on my time at secondary school and then university. I don't normally want to punch someone at introduction, but with Charlie boy I was prepared to make an exception.

It was loathe at first sight.

THIRTY-SIX

Charlie was the first to break. Grudgingly he asked, 'Still serving, Major?'

'Late of the Seaforths.'

'And now?'

'I'm a writer.'

'Really? Novels? *Military* history?'

I smiled. 'Nothing so grand. Newspapers. I'm with the *Gazette.*'

I wish there had been a photographer. Charlie's face seemed to swell.

He asked, 'What was the name again?' He hadn't bothered to listen to Sam's introduction. I hadn't been important enough.

'Brodie. Douglas Brodie.' I watched his brain working it out.

'Is this some kind of bloody trick?' Charlie's face slid from disdain to vicious. His father looked worried and anxious at the raised voice.

Sam interjected. 'Goodness me, Charlie. Is that a bad conscience we've poked? Major Brodie is indeed a reporter, but he's off duty tonight. Aren't you, darling?'

Darling? I patted the flat panels of my dinner jacket. 'No room for my notebook. We can speak freely.' I smiled encouragingly.

There was no answering smile. Instead, Charlie got behind the wheelchair and hustled the old man away.

'I think you've just got me struck me off his dance card, Douglas.'

'But I think he's just added me to his *get-even* card. I wonder how much Curly and Fitz told him about me? And how they got hired?'

I shouldn't have said it. Her face clouded, but then she smiled again. 'Come on, Douglas. Let's get drunk on Rankin's fizz.'

For the rest of the evening we waltzed round the room, greeting and glad-handing Sam's old pals, in a fever of drink-inspired denial. Denial that we'd just seen ghouls from our past in the pay of a man who seemed to threaten our future. Denial that we might have glimpsed the deep vein of corruption predicted on by McAllister. Maxwell junior knew my name. He knew where I worked and that the *Gazette* was picking away at the edges of a tapestry of sleaze. The former Slattery henchmen may well have told them what I'd done to their bosses. The look I'd got from Charlie Maxwell was as close to murderous as makes no difference.

We didn't run into the third member of the crooked cabal, Tom Fowler, but learned he'd scuttled off to his hammock in the Bahamas. A tactical withdrawal, possibly, following Wullie's probing articles.

In our febrile state of mind, Sam and I egged each other on to be sparkling and witty, as though we were trying to impress everyone we met. I found the social gears in my brain being lubricated by the booze, like old machinery coming to life. Or so it seemed. Wit can only be objectively assessed by the recipient. As Burns said:

> *O wad some Pow'r the giftie gie us,*
> *To see oursels as others see us!*

Maybe we just looked drunk.

For Sam, this was a re-engagement with old friends and acquaintances, from school days and university days, from the time of her parents. She was a bright goldfish back in a gilded tank with her kind. Whereas my first thought was that I'd rather be facing the 7th Panzer Division. Then I remembered that I *had*, and none of *this*, none of *them,* had a hold on me any more. The crowns on my shoulder had finally replaced the chips. Beneath their Bearsden accents and their Hyndland airs and graces were a bunch of people with prejudices and opinions, intellects and personalities, no more valid or weighty than any to be found in the Horseshoe Bar on a Saturday night. And a lot less fun.

Burns also summed it up: 'A man's a man for a' that.' I'd fought alongside men from every class for six years, and the only hallmark of worth was how you dealt with being shot at – either literally or figuratively. I thought of Hugh Donovan in his final days: resigned, philosophical almost, concerned more for the woman he was leaving behind. I wasn't there as they pulled the suffocating bag over his head. I didn't stand alongside him as they pulled the lever. But I was pretty sure that Hugh had gone to his maker without lamenting the unfairness of it all. I hoped his maker budged up and gave him a prominent seat on his right.

At some stage in the short ride home Sam and I grew silent. The champagne highs tipped into champagne melancholy. I steered a now wobbly Samantha Campbell up the stairs to her house. We stumbled through the door and I kicked an envelope which had been thrust through the letter box. It skidded down the polished parquet hall. Clutching the handrail, Sam flowed down to the kitchen to put a kettle on. I stooped, picked up the envelope and checked the address. It was for me. I recognised the hand. I opened it.

Brodie,
We need to meet. Be at the McLennan Arch at noon,
Sunday. Come alone. I will.
Ishmael

I stuffed the letter into my breast pocket just as Sam bounced up to the hall from the kitchen and headed for the drawing room. There was no sign of a sobering teapot. She was holding a fresh bottle. I went after her.

I joined her in a glass of Scotch but made sure hers was as well watered as possible. Sam wound up the gramophone. We smiled and she hummed along with Peggy Lee confessing 'I don't know enough about you' as we tried to recapture the mood we'd left behind at the start of the evening.

Sam began to sway and twirl. I caught her on one of the twirls and we danced together as if we meant it. But when I bent to kiss her again and continue where we left off, she pushed me back. Her eyes were full of tears.

'I can't take any more, Douglas. It's too much.'

'Sam, we're fine. Trust me. I won't let them near you.'

The music ground to a halt and I stood holding her as she sobbed in my arms.

'I'm sorry, I'm sorry. I've drunk too much. This is pathetic.'

'Wheesht, Sam, wheesht. It's all right.' I stroked her head and her back like a pony to calm her down. Finally she pushed herself back from me, sniffed, pressed her gloved finger to my lips and wished me a good night.

I stood staring after her, cursing myself for raising my hopes again. I never seemed to learn. I knew I was being unfair. It was one helluva shock for Sam to run into Curly and Fitz. Not to mention charming Charlie. He seemed to hold particularly repellent memories for her. But I was the good guy! Wasn't this when she needed me most? My drunken, maudlin thoughts turned to Morag. *She* wouldn't spurn me. We might have been revelling in bed by now. So why was I here? Why was I making life hard for myself? The choice was surely easy enough: an ageing ice-queen hamstrung by her past, versus the open arms of an eager young woman? Sam would always be hard work. Morag would always be adoring and pliant.

I unpicked my medals one by one and set them down on

the mantelpiece. I hefted the cross. Was this it? The high point of my life stamped in bronze and silver? Downhill from here. Maybe I should have gone back to London. Maybe I still should? I picked up the note from the Marshals. More a summons. Why should I respond? Why was it always me?

I filled my glass and walked round the room touching the soft furnishings. I pulled back the curtains and looked out at the night wondering what or who was out there, and what they were doing. Morag asleep, warm and snug in her wee bed, her red hair curling on her soft cheek. Maxwell and his hoodlums planning what? Against whom? McAllister dreaming of one last set of front-page headlines. And the Marshals, sneaking around bombed-out factories, breaking out from time to time to dispense their arbitrary justice to the sinners of this sleeping city.

I wondered about this meeting Ishmael had called. If he was coming alone to a public park, he'd hardly be wearing a balaclava. What was he up to? And how did it tie into the murders of three homosexuals? And what were we going to do about this new front that had been opened by McAllister against the great and the not-so-good? Defend or attack?

I finished my drink and my sentimental mulling. It was one in the morning. I was tired and drunk. The air had turned muggy and close. There was a storm in the offing, presaging another welcome break in the long sapping drouth.

I started the long climb up to the second floor, pausing on her landing to see that her light was out. I climbed the next flight and pushed into my bedroom hoping stupidly – was there no end to my self-delusion? – to find a warm female body in my bed.

Empty.

But sometime later, as I lay smoking in the dark and listening to the distant rumble of thunder echoing through the deserted streets, my door opened. She came in, dropped her dressing gown, and slid into bed. I stubbed out my fag.

'Can you just hold me, Douglas? Just hold me, please.' She spooned against me and I wrapped her in my arms. She was shivering. I continued where I'd left off in the drawing room, gentling her, until she quietened, and fell asleep.

THIRTY-SEVEN

In the morning I woke alone but to the sound of a melodic humming from down in the kitchen. I checked my watch. It was seven thirty. Outside, the city was quiet on this soft Sunday morning apart from a distant chapel bell summoning the guilty to mass. Still the weather hadn't broken. My sheets were crumpled at the foot of the bed and my body was hot and perspiring. When would it rain?

I turned over and sank my face into her pillow. It smelled sweetly of her. Had we made love? I remembered her body against mine and knew I'd cradled her. But where had we stopped? Dream or reality?

I lay back, wondering if we'd turned a corner last night or if it had just been a champagne interlude. A cry for help in the night? Sister to brother? Or the first stage in a thaw? There was only one way to find out. I shaved, washed and dressed and went downstairs.

She was at the sink, her hands in the water. She wore a favoured blouse and skirt. She turned and dried her soapy hands. Her face was scrubbed and without make-up. Her hair damp and pulled back with Kirby grips. Her eyes were red but bright.

'Good morning, Douglas. I hope I didn't disturb you too much.'

'Any time, Sam. Any time. You're blushing.'

'Of course I am, you big oaf. I made a fool of myself last night.'

'Did you? At which particular point? Telling the Provost's

wife you knew a good hairdresser that would sort out her mad blue rinse?'

She put her hand to her mouth. 'God! Did I say that?'

'She took it well. She'll be there first thing Monday. Or maybe it was telling Justice Bailey that his closing argument in some fraud case last year had missed the point. And then telling him what he should have said.'

She pulled her hand down. 'Well, it's true. Pompous old fart. Anything else?'

'No, my dear. You were funny and bright, and said nothing you should be sorry about. I enjoyed it. So why were you blushing?'

She took a deep breath. 'For crying on your shoulder. For sneaking into your bed like a wee lassie after a bad dream. Sorry.'

'Well, I'm not. Just so's you know. You're welcome to visit any time you like.'

She blushed again and nodded firmly, twice. 'Right. Do you want some porridge?'

While she busied herself over the pot I told her about the letter waiting on the mat when we got in last night.

'You're not going, are you?'

'It's in broad daylight. A public place. What could he do?'

'Shoot you? You said they were bristling with guns at this place they took you to. And it's not as if they're averse to violence.'

I shook my head. 'I don't see the point. I mean, why harm me? Other than not complying with their instructions about what to write? No, I think he's worried. The odd broken limb is one thing, but three murders on the trot is another.'

'He's certainly in the frame.'

'And not relishing getting hanged, whether or not he did it.'

'Right, I'm coming with you.'

'What? Don't be daft. For one thing he said come alone. For another, well . . .'

'Well what? I'm a woman? Some wee *burd* you need to keep out of harm's way?'

'What are you going to do? Hit him with your spirtle?'

Her answer was to stop stirring the porridge and brandish the weapon at me. Persuasive.

'May I remind you that I'm an advocate and this . . . this loonie and his pals just might need a lawyer.'

I gazed at her, surprised as ever by her resilience. 'It's good of you to be above petty revenge.'

There was a gleam in her eye. 'Depends on the result I get.'

We started up the Riley and sailed off down Sauchiehall Street towards the city centre. There were a few Sunday trams and hardly any other cars. I drove.

'Next time we take the car out, let's head west. Cool our feet at Largs. Eat ice cream at Nardini's.'

She smiled. 'Next time.'

We drove down the High Street and along Saltmarket. We parked outside the Justiciary Courts just before the Albert Bridge and walked into the Green. We'd decided to come at the arch through the park rather than head straight towards it from Charlotte Street. It gave us time to spot hooded gangs skulking round the arch. It was also just nice to walk across cool grass on a sunny day.

High noon on a Sunday on Glasgow Green. Great cumulus castles bubbling up but still the sun wouldn't give up its iron grip. The grass was dotted with basking citizens in varying states of sunburn and nakedness. Sam in a pretty sleeveless frock. Me in shirtsleeves.

'We should have brought a picnic,' she said.

'Or a gun.'

'I thought you said there was no danger?'

'I always find a gun's more use in these sort of situations than a pan loaf.'

She laughed. I pressed her hand. We held it for a few steps then disengaged.

'Do you think he'll be mad?'

'Because I didn't come alone? Doubt it. I think as long as I don't gallop up with a posse of mounted police, he'll not mind too much. Besides, he was the one who wanted to talk.'

The McLennan Arch was a kind of cut-down Arc de Triomphe in soiled red sandstone, but no foreign army had ever marched through this one. Unless you were really parochial and counted an invasion by the Busy Bees from the Gorbals. Tackety boots, yes. Jackboots, no.

The McLennan had one grand central arch and two smaller rectangular passageways cut through the wings. It had survived the demolition of the old Assembly Rooms back in the 1890s, then a move to Monteith Row, before coming to its final resting place at the north-west entrance to the Green.

We were walking more slowly now as we got nearer. A couple walked through, then a pack of kids on bogeys hand-made from old pram wheels and vegetable crates. Pigeons smashed into the air in panic as the wee hooligans yipped their way past. There was no sign of vigilantes.

'He could be on the other side,' she said quite reasonably. We walked up to the arch and then through the centre. There was no one on the other side.

'He could have gone round the side just as we—'

'Sam! We'll just walk back through and wait on the other side. It's not quite twelve.'

There were some benches by the road leading up to the arch. We took one and lit up. And watched. And waited.

Exactly on midday a man walked through the arch. Short red hair, bony face, brown jumper, hands in pocket, trying to look as if he was out for a stroll, but instead looking shifty. His eyes flicked back and forth, seeing us and looking beyond us. He would have watched us from the road, sheltering behind the hedges and trees. He walked over. I got up and stood in front of Sam. He took gloved hands out his pockets and raised them as though he was surrendering.

'I said alone, Brodie.'

'Say what you like, pal. You're already spoiling a nice Sunday. Can we get to the point?'

'What's she doing here?'

'Something about you being rude to her. Breaking into her house and holding a gun on her. She's expecting an apology.' I waited.

'It doesn't matter, Douglas,' said Sam.

'It does. If he wants something, he starts with an apology.'

Red looked round me at Sam. He swallowed. 'Sorry. I had to get a message through to your . . .'

'Lodger?'

'Aye, Brodie here.'

'That wasn't the most heartfelt apology, but it's a start. And remember, she's a lawyer too. In case you think you need one.'

We were now close enough that I could see the deepening lines of tiredness round his eyes. It must be hard work performing such a public service. I could also see the scab on the lip I'd split. There was something else in his demeanour this time. Or maybe it was the absence of it. The absence of certainty.

'Do you have a name, or do we go on calling you Ishmael? Or how about Reverend?'

Anger tightened his jaw muscles. 'You don't remember me, do you, *Major* Brodie?'

I shook my head. 'Other than your break-ins and the tour of inspection of your splendid offices the other day. Should I?'

He looked like someone who'd finally made up his mind about something. 'I was in the 51st Highland Division. With Sergeant Alan Johnson.'

I should have guessed. Ishmael and Johnson hadn't just bumped into each other under the arches of Central Station.

'Impossible. I would have met you.'

'You did, Major Brodie. Though it was *Sergeant* Brodie then.'

THIRTY-EIGHT

The cogs meshed and my brain began working again.

'You were taken? With Johnson?' I asked him.

He nodded. 'One of my men. We followed orders. The stupidest thing I've done in my life! I should have made a break for it. Like you! But I had a job to do.'

'What do you mean, "a job to do"? What was your company?'

'Provost Company. I'd joined as a subaltern in December '39.'

'You were an MP! You were ordered to keep us in line. Make the surrender work.'

'I had no choice!'

'Polis or Automobile Association?'

'Inspector. Inverness.'

I nodded. Most of the Provost unit had been ex-policemen or AA scouts. Battlefield traffic police. Essential work when you had a million men and armour on the move.

'The *Marshals*! I should have guessed. The *Provost* Marshals.'

He had the grace to look embarrassed.

'Sorry to interrupt this cosy chat, but could one of you please interpret?' Sam was standing alongside us with her arms crossed and using the look she reserved for hostile witnesses in the stand.

'Look, let's sit down,' I suggested.

We sat awkwardly in a line on the bench, me in the middle, Sam to my right, the ex-MP to my left. It was beginning to add up. Some of it.

'You still haven't given me your real name.'

'Drummond, Fergus Drummond.'

The name rang a bell, a small one. 'There, that wasn't so hard,' I said. I turned to Sam. 'Drummond here was a lieutenant in the Military Police. He and Johnson were in Provost Company of the 51st Highland Division, my old division, at the start of the war. Part of the British Expeditionary Force. Some of the division made it to Dunkirk. Most of the 51st, however, including my battalion of the Seaforths and Drummond's Provost Company, were trapped in Saint-Valery.'

'Trapped with the bloody French!' Drummond cut in.

I nodded. 'We were installed as part of the French army. When they surrendered, we had to.'

'We had orders. Most of us obeyed them.' Drummond said it through gritted teeth.

'He's right,' I sighed. 'I sloped off with a couple of my lads. We got out in a wee boat.'

'While we spent the war in various Stalags.'

'I was commissioned and sent back to fight in a newly constituted 51st Highland. North Africa, then D-Day. I'm not sure who had the worse time of it.'

It was as though I'd lit a firework. Drummond jumped up and stood shaking in front of us, his face blazing with anger.

'You think I had a bloody holiday, Brodie! You think I didn't weep every bloody day I spent behind barbed wire? How do you think I got this?'

He wrenched at his right glove and ripped it off. He thrust out his fist at us. The index and middle finger were missing. He tore off the left with the help of his teeth. The fingertips were all stunted.

I said slowly, 'I don't know, Drummond. My mum used to warn me about biting my nails.'

His anger boiled over. 'It was frostbite!'

I felt Sam's hand grip my thigh. I replied quietly. 'And you've been getting your own back ever since, eh, Drummond? An eye for an eye, a pinkie for a pinkie.'

His arm dropped, then his head. He pulled the glove back on, and I could see now that it was padded out with two false fingers.

'Sit down, man, tell me why you wanted to meet me.'

We listened to his story and I almost began to feel some sympathy for the poor bastard. Until I thought about the sadistic punishments he'd been dishing out. And frightening my mum.

The four men in masks I'd met ten days ago were the remnants of his old platoon. Drummond had kept them going, kept them alive, by cajoling and leading them through five long years of captivity. The 51st had been force-marched from Saint-Valery across France and into occupied Poland. Along the way any laggards were shot out of hand. You risked your life stopping for a pee. It seems Jerry was pissed off at letting so many get away at Dunkirk.

They were incarcerated near Thorn. Anyone below sergeant rank was used as forced labour, as per the skewed articles of the Geneva Convention, written presumably by members of the officer class. Drummond had torn off his pips and joined his men. He'd slaved on roads and farms around the fortress camps of Thorn until the threat of liberation by the advancing Russian army panicked the guards. Drummond and all the other British POWs were driven out of the camp in January 1945, in the middle of a blizzard. They were marched 450 miles westward to another Stalag. Hundreds perished of starvation and frostbite on the way. Drummond got off lightly. Many of them had been my own comrades in the Seaforths.

It's why I hadn't been to a regimental reunion since demob.

He stopped talking and we sat in silence digesting his story.

'You win, Drummond. I prefer my war. Marginally. But how did it get to this? What the hell are you doing this for? You could have come home with honour, got your old job back. Instead you're a renegade. And what's worse – *Lieutenant* – you've led your men astray.'

'You don't understand, Brodie,' he growled.

'Try me. But just remember there's a manhunt on. And recent experience tells me they won't need much evidence – if any – to find you guilty. You and your men are likely to end up on the gallows. Did you know Barlinnie can take three at once? You and your pals can be dispatched in two sittings.'

'Shut up, Brodie! Shut the hell up!'

'Fine. You do the talking,' I said.

He fidgeted with a fag packet until he'd opened it and got one out. I let him struggle. He sat back on the bench.

'We got back in May last year. Bomber Command ferried us home. Back with honour, you say? We were treated like shit. We're the Division that surrendered. We're the ones who went on holiday for five years! While everybody else was earning medals or getting promoted, *Major*, we were stuck in limbo for five – bloody – years!'

I could see how that would rankle. It explained his preoccupation with me and my laurel leaves. If only he knew what a crown of thorns they could be. But it didn't explain the missionary zeal of his punishment squad.

'So your feelings were hurt. So what?'

He bent forward, resting his elbows on his knees. 'It was more than that. I can thole other folk's scorn. But not my own. I had the chance to prove myself on the battlefield. Instead I raised the white flag. And there is not one thing I can do that will change the past. I've missed my chance. Missed the tide.'

I exchanged looks with Sam. I wondered if we were sharing the memory of Hugh Donovan, my boyhood pal, her client. His war too had ended in pain and puzzlement. What for?

'It still doesn't explain your actions, here, in Glasgow. Johnson's sentence and his suicide didn't give you licence to maim.'

He stared at the ground through his knees. Was he hearing me?

'We got back here and rented some digs together. I applied for jobs, first with the police force. Then anybody. This held me back.' He waved his torn hands. 'This and my war record.' His voice sounded exhausted, as though it had been playing the same record for too long.

'The others were struggling too. No jobs. Just enough money for bread and booze. No homes. When the dole ran out we begged and we squatted. Condemned houses and gutted factories. Do you know how many others are doing the same, Brodie? This land fit for heroes? The trouble is, *we* weren't heroes. We survived five years in prisoner-of-war camps and now we were falling apart.'

I lit a fag of my own. Drummond was echoing my own months of wallowing in self-pity and whisky in London. But I'd been jolted out of it. Being summoned back to Glasgow in April to focus on saving Hugh from a hanging had given me a purpose. I'd failed, but I found a new goal: hunting down the men who'd wrought his death. The black dog still bit at my heels from time to time, but I had a new job and some hope. I even had Sam in my life. Sort of. Drummond had bugger all. But it was still no excuse for scaring my mother.

'It's rough for us all, Drummond. But that doesn't let us set up our own law-enforcement agency.'

'You think we're pathetic, don't you, Brodie? Don't you see: Glasgow's a battlefield! Its very soul is at stake.'

'Sodom and Gallowgate?'

'You're taking the piss! This is no different from fighting the Nazis – right here! On the streets! The enemy all round us. The crooks, the spivs, the thieves, the rapists, the razor gangs . . . and no one doing one damned thing about it except us.'

'Bollocks, Drummond! You're not fixing crime. You're adding to it! You're ex-polis. Where's your respect for the law? What makes you think you have the right to impose your will? Quotes from an old Jewish handbook?'

By this time we were both back on our feet, facing each other and jabbing fingers at each other.

'I'll tell you! *I'll tell you!* Five years in a camp does it! Five years of summary justice gives you a proper understanding about how effective it is. And another year of being treated like a leper in my own country, watching gangs roam the street. Women being raped, shops plundered, widows robbed, murderers and pederasts walking the streets with impunity. Drugs being sold on street corners like sweeties. That's what does it!'

'And was this a sign from God?' I needed to watch my sarcasm. It tended to fire folk up.

A sneer shaped his wet mouth. 'Aye, blaspheme if you want to. But where do you think I got the idea from? The papers were full of it. Full of stories about *you*, Brodie. About how you'd shone a light on the corruption in the legal system. The stink and filth at the heart of our useless police service. How could we stand back and let this tidal wave of filth and depravity drown us all?'

'They're not *all* bad. And Barlinnie is full to the brim. You can hardly say people are getting away with – well – murder.'

'You think not? It's broken! The wheels have come off. Sin is triumphing, everywhere you look. We learned how you brought down retribution on the murderers and child-abusers in the Slattery clan.' He paused for effect. 'You make a good role model, Brodie!'

It was a good shot. It drove straight to the heart of my earlier ambivalence about this whole damned vigilante escapade. I flung my hands up in the air.

'I never asked anyone to follow me! I was trying to save the life of my friend. You're just looking for an excuse, Drummond.'

He went still. His voice fell. 'No. An example.'

THIRTY-NINE

I stepped back. I looked past his head to the park beyond, to normal folk going about their Sunday, kids running around wild. We all needed someone to look up to, someone to set the pattern. Finally, calmer, I broke the long silence. 'What are we here for, Drummond? What do you want from us? They have confessionals if you just want it off your chest. A good chapel-going man like you.'

'I'm not! I'm Free Church of Scotland.'

'The Wee Frees? No wonder you're so holy. But what about the quotes from the Apochrypha? They're not in *your* bible.'

Drummond reached behind and under his jumper. He brought out a thin, battered book. It was clearly a bible. He looked uncomfortable.

'It was the only one I could get hold of. From a Catholic chaplain. He died on the long march. It served us well.'

I asked again, softly, 'What do you want?'

'You to believe we didn't kill anyone. Murder was never part of our plan.'

'Not even queers?' I scoffed.

'There's no need for killing. You met one of my men. With God's will, and the man's faith, I brought him back into the fold. It's a choice.'

'Whether he wants it or not, eh? But you left a good man at death's door. Davie Allardyce nearly died. He might never recover properly. A family smashed to bits. It was only chance that you've avoided a murder charge!'

He nodded. 'We might have hit him too hard.' He didn't seem that contrite.

'And what about the two women you *tested* for adultery? Who gave you the moral authority? One of them died and the other is on the streets. *Bitter water* indeed!'

'It is written.' He waved the bible at me.

'In blood! Like so much of the *Good* Book. Which reminds me. What did you do with Jenny MacIntosh?'

He seemed to smirk. 'The abortionist? We prayed with her. We made her join us in prayer and in admitting her sins. She sought pardon from the Lord.'

'You smug bully, you!'

At that moment I didn't know whether I hated this man more for the appalling physical damage he'd done to the Dochertys and Allardyces of this world, or for forcing that poor wee woman to go down on her knees and beg for forgiveness from Drummond's fickle and irascible God.

'Another sinner brought to the light, eh? Anyway, that's not the point. You're on the hook for three murders. How can you prove you didn't do it? Having a poof on your team won't cut ice with a jury. You'll need a good lawyer . . .'

We both turned and looked at Sam, who had been sitting, legs neatly crossed, quietly smoking and watching the two fighting cocks bristle and strut in front of her. She leisurely took a puff and lowered her hand. She blew the smoke out and recrossed her legs. They were nice legs.

'Let me see if I understand this, *Mister* Drummond? You break into my house, hold me and Brodie hostage at gunpoint, threaten us and generally act like a hoodlum. You nearly kill a good friend of mine. And now you'd like me to defend you against a triple murder charge? Is that a fair summary?'

'I'm not asking for your help.' He was every inch the stuck-up Highlander. The sort that would lead his men into battle against English cannon waving his sporran at them.

'Good. Because you can whistle for it as far as I'm concerned.'

I cut in. 'What exactly were you expecting, Drummond? That I'd write a column for the *Gazette* that says, I've met this man. He's a Highland chentleman. He gave me his word. He's no killer. And the polis slap me on the back and say, That's fine, Brodie. We trust you. Someone else clearly did this, and your noble pal is in the clear. Give him our best wishes and tell him to continue with his vigilante work. In fact, more power to his elbow.'

Drummond faced me, his gaze intense and unwavering. 'I don't know why these men were murdered. But it is not our work. I told you before we left certain signs on the guilty. Calling cards, you said. But you've never spelled it out in any of your articles.'

'Because the infirmaries would be full of folk with bandaged fingers and scarred faces. Copycats.'

He exhaled. 'I know. I was police too. But the whole Glasgow force is hunting us! Meantime, the guilty men are sitting there laughing. It's time you went public.'

'And say what? What would convince anyone?'

'In all your reports, you didn't mention *why* we took a finger or left a scar. The people we punished are already followers of Satan. Now they can be recognised.'

He opened his bible near the end. I could see jagged scribbles and underlined passages on the pages. He read aloud:

'Satan . . . causeth all, both small and great, rich and poor, free and bond, to receive a mark in their right hand, or in their foreheads . . . the mark, or the name of the beast, or the number of his name.'

Drummond paused for effect. 'Tell them we are identifying the wicked. We are enforcing God's commandments.'

FORTY

We watched him march back through the arch and out of the park. He kept a good stiff back, as though he assumed I'd be judging his parade-ground manners.

'The Bible's a dangerous book,' I said.

'For a lost soul.'

'Lost marbles.'

'Is it going to help to quote Revelations at your readers?'

'It proves nothing. Except that Drummond is off his head. Have you any idea how many interpretations of that passage there are likely to be?'

'Six hundred and sixty-six?'

'At least. And when you think about the mutilations to the three homosexuals you can easily make the case that the Marshals were complying with the Good Book. But with more enthusiasm. In their twisted minds, punishments fitting the crime. But you're the lawyer. What do you think?

'If these guys are caught, they're for the high jump. Or rather the long drop.'

We were in no hurry now. We walked away from the arch down to the fountain, then followed the riverside path east until we did a full loop of the Green. We didn't say much. The sun was hidden by tumbling clouds. The air felt wet and hot like the steam room at the Western Baths Club. We drove back to the house talking about the big ham salad we felt we'd earned. But we soon lost our appetite.

Sitting on the front step surrounded by a confetti of fag

ends, was McAllister. He rose as we drew up and got out. 'I was beginning to think you'd eloped, Brodie.'

'Without asking your permission, Wullie? Before you say anything else that will get us both into trouble, I'd better make the introductions.'

Hands were duly shaken, and then I said, 'Are you here to find out how we got on last night among Glasgow high society? There's not much to tell. The champagne was too dry. The petits fours too petits.'

'Naw, that'll keep.'

'Just a social call, then?'

'Not very, Brodie. Not very. I assume by your general air of insouciance that you haven't heard.'

'Heard what?'

'About Sheridan. Him and his – pardon my French, Miss Campbell – whore.'

My stomach knotted up. 'Get on with it, Wullie.'

'Dead. Drowned. They were found this morning.'

Sam spoke up. 'You'd better come inside.'

We sat round the kitchen table nursing glasses of lemonade while McAllister talked.

'I got a call from one of my polis contacts this morning. You know the pier at Balloch? Seems an early-morning fisherman found a green Morris Eight lying at the bottom of Loch Lomond. Next to the *Princess May*.'

'Sheridan's?'

Aye, and him in it, apparently. And his floozy. They got a police diver to take a look. The pair of them were floating inside the car, last I heard.'

'Suicide?'

'At first glance.'

'Polis saying the publicity drove them to it?'

'Their first deduction.'

'Except?'

'Jimmie Sheridan's ego. If ever a man could soak up public

humiliation and chastisement and make it into badge of honour, it's Sheridan. This past week he's been charging about, playing the victim of right-wing forces. Man of the people attacked by his detractors etc., etc.'

'And his lady friend from Edinburgh doesn't sound the type to let a bit of mud-slinging get her down,' Sam said. I raised my eyebrow at this lack of feminine empathy. She raised hers back at me.

Wullie said, 'It's all too pat. Sheridan knew too much, and was flaunting it. There will be an autopsy. If there's foul play it should show up.'

Sam was tapping her table. 'I'm just curious why he chose Balloch pier to dive off. The Clyde's closer.'

'The loch's quieter? Deeper? Less likely to be found?'

'I know Balloch well. My folks and I spent summers around there. We were invited to go shooting up by there. On the east bank of the loch.'

'You mean . . .?' I invited her.

'One of the ways of driving to Colin Maxwell's estate is through Balloch. Or for that matter if you were driving round to Helensburgh. Kenny Rankin's mansion.'

We sat for a while smoking round the table and mulling the implications before Wullie rose and headed for the door.

'Well, at least we have Monday's headlines. I'll go and see if Eddie's got it yet.' He turned to Sam and me. 'You've got the car out. Fancy a wee trip up to Loch Lomond? You could phone in any details.'

'It's my day off, Wullie. And it's not my idea of a Sunday jaunt.' I looked at Sam. I assumed she'd had enough dealings with personal tragedies for one day. As so often, she surprised me.

'Why not, Brodie? We've just enough petrol. And I've been saving coupons for a refill in the week. It will be nice to get out of town.'

*

I always forget how close Glasgow is to the real Scotland. Or do I mean the tourist, romantic Scotland? The Scotland that even the most urban of Lowlanders conjures when asked what's Scotland like. The bits with shaved mountains, cowed glens and long troughs of water. In no time, following the Great Western Road – and averting your eyes from the blitz rubble of Clydebank – you're out along the shimmering Clyde and the ragged lumps of rounded rock at Dumbarton. You catch glimpses of the Firth widening out like spilled mercury, and the rumps of the hills and islands beyond. Past Dumbarton, north five miles, through Alexandria and you're on the south end of Loch Lomond. To the north, slicing off the peaks of the great mountains, the skies were a sullen black mass.

We edged into Balloch and along the high street, such as it is. There's little enough of a town. Its focal point is the pier jutting into the loch and the railway station next to it, debouching day trippers who fancied a steam around the water. It was a busy, happy Sunday. Kids clutching sticks of rock, men in shirtsleeves and women in light frocks. Hanging on to the remnants of summer. They knew the weather couldn't last as we slid into autumn.

We parked on the street and walked towards the pier alongside the rail tracks. There was a crowd gathered just short of the start of the wooden jetty. The *Princess May* was stationary alongside. Sheridan had messed up a lot of folks' day out.

Sam said, 'We'll never get near.'

'Let's see who's in charge. This is beyond the local bobby.' We pushed our way through the crowd until we found ourselves out in the open with the pier clear in front of us. Two coppers stood in our way, holding the gawpers back. Beyond them was a huddled group of uniforms and plain clothes. Sangster was standing next to a tarpaulin-covered mound. A man was piling up diving gear on a wheelbarrow. Another was kneeling by the mound with a probably superfluous stethoscope dangling from his neck.

'Sergeant? My name is Brodie. I'm from the *Gazette*. This is Advocate Campbell. She represents Mr Sheridan.'

The sergeant immediately looked worried. 'How did you know it's—?' He pulled himself up. 'Sorry, sir, ma'am, I have strict instructions . . .'

'I know, I know, Sergeant, from Chief Inspector Sangster there. Would you be so kind as to ask your constable to let the chief inspector know we're here and that we may have information that would help.'

The sergeant looked doubtful but he complied. We watched the constable go up to the group and talk to Sangster. It was as though he'd been stabbed. His head shot up and he stared our way. I could see his brain whirring from here. Eventually he said something to the officer who marched back.

'He says, and I quote, sir, *Brodie and the lady can come over, but it had better be bloody good*. Sir.'

FORTY-ONE

Sam and I started walking up the pier. She hissed. 'How could you say I represent Sheridan? And what exactly are you going to tell him that will help?'

'I don't know yet, Sam. Better think fast. And anyway, who's going to argue that you represent Sheridan?'

'You're a menace, Brodie.'

'You love it, Sam.'

And she did. Some people rise to challenges and are rubbish when life is placid. Just as bicycles are only really steady when they're going like the clappers. When folk like Sam have time to dwell on trivial matters they magnify them into full-blown disasters. They're too hard on themselves, unsparing in their self-criticism. Sam's bar was set too high for her comfort. But it made her a good woman to have on your flank. Sam's eyes were bright and her shoulders back as we walked purposefully towards Sangster.

'Are you some kind of understudy for the grim reaper, Brodie? Where there's death, there you are?' He nodded to Sam. 'Miss Campbell, I didn't know you were Jimmie Sheridan's brief.' There was a sceptical tone in his voice.

'I won't comment on that until we find out what's going on. Client privilege, Chief Inspector. As you can tell by the very fact we're here, we know something about this case. Isn't that right, Brodie?' She smiled at me, challenging me.

'First things first, Sangster. What's the initial theory of cause of death?'

'Apart from drowning, you mean?' For a moment he studied us and I thought he was going to call our bluff, but then he turned back to the kneeling figure. 'Doctor, how are you doing? First findings?'

The doctor looked up. I'd known him before the war. 'Jamie Frew, isn't it? Hello, Doctor, I'm . . .'

'I ken you, Brodie. I thought you'd gone to war and never came back?'

'Sorry to disappoint you, Jamie. Here I am.'

'You were always one for finding trouble, Brodie.' Sam nudged me. I ignored her. 'Maybe we could have a wee dram sometime to celebrate your homecoming?'

'I'd enjoy that, Jamie.'

'Could I interrupt this wee social hour and ask you to stick to the job in hand?' said Sangster.

Frew peeled back the corner of the tarpaulin. He stood up and we all looked down on the shocked grey faces of Sheridan and his lover. Water pooled around their heads. The skin of his face lay loose and flabby as though it was coming off in the water. His blue eyes were wide and staring. He couldn't believe where he'd ended up. The woman's face was older and far more lined than the recent press photos of a laughing good-time girl. Her make-up was smeared and washed away. Grey roots showed in her slicked blonde hair. An old mermaid who'd lost the gift.

'Weeell, at first sight, it's a simple straightforward drowning, a terrible accident. A wrong turn? Brakes failed? They've been in the water for at least eight hours, maybe twelve. So sometime last night I'd say.'

'At first sight, Jamie? What about a second?'

Jamie's eyes wandered away. 'I don't want to say anything until we've carried out the post-mortem.'

'But?'

He turned to look at me. 'But when I probed their mouths and massaged the chests, as well as water coming up, there was a distinct sweet smell.'

'Spit it out, man,' said Sangster.

'I'd know it anywhere. Any doctor would. It's chloroform.'

I grabbed Sam as I felt her sway beside me. Even tough ladies have their limits.

Sangster whipped round. 'You know something?'

'We've got some experience of this modus operandi, Sangster. In fact Miss Campbell here has first-hand knowledge. You'll recall that back in April, she was abducted. The man who did it used a chloroform pad.'

Sam cleared her throat. 'It was Gerrit Slattery, Chief Inspector. He used it several times on me over the few days he . . . held me.'

'But they're gone! The Slatterys are gone,' said Sangster, staring at me. Was that accusation in his eyes? Or paranoia in mine?

I said, 'Not all of them. Two of their tough guys showed up last night in chauffeur's uniform. Curly and Fitz.'

'Oh aye. Chauffeurs to who?'

'Whom. They were driving Colin Maxwell and his son, Charlie.'

'Sir Colin Maxwell? That's no' possible. A man like that involved with the Slattery scum?' He shook his head. 'No way. He's a patron to this city. Charity work in the Gorbals.'

'Oh, no doubt he's an angel. But if so, he consorts with the devil.'

'Wait, wait. I just don't get it. Why would Sir Colin be involved in something like this?'

I was thinking fast. Of our two suspects in the area – Rankin and Maxwell – only Maxwell had the vile entourage equipped to dole out death by chloroform. But if I started accusing Maxwell now, where would it get me? Where was the proof that this pillar of society would do anything, including murder, to win the huge contracts for rebuilding Glasgow? Where was the link between these poor drowned creatures and *Sir* Colin Maxwell? The man was in the top rank of Scottish society. Knighted for his efforts in industry.

Fêted for his charitable work. Even I struggled to think of him involved in anything as shoddy. But his son, Charlie . . . now that was something, *someone* else. If I was any judge.

'All I'm saying is that there are some links that you might want to bear in mind, Sangster.' I counted them off on my fingers. 'This is the second councillor who's come to an unhappy end. Morton was the Finance Chairman. And now we've lost Jimmie Sheridan, chairman of Planning. Between them the councillors with key responsibility for Glasgow regeneration. Jimmie suddenly comes into the money and is seen hobnobbing with some big-name developers including Messrs Rankin and Maxwell. Now he's lying at our feet, drowned in very suspicious circumstances. If he's been chloroformed, then dumped in his car and pushed off the pier, we know at least a couple of lads who are handy with the technique. They work for Maxwell, senior or junior.'

'And he lives just over there.' Sam pointed across the bodies, over the loch at the low hills on the east side of the water. Sangster and Jamie Frew turned to look, and then turned back to me.

'But no actual proof of anything, Brodie. Is that right?'

'No proof. But you might just pay Maxwell a visit and see if Sheridan had popped in for tea and scones yesterday before taking a dip in Loch Lomond.'

We drove home, the summer's day darkened by the approaching storm and by what we'd seen and what we thought. Sam was silent beside me gazing out of the window. In twenty-four hours she'd run into her tormentors of the spring and found them working for an old family friend. Now we'd learned that the same pair were up to their old nasty tricks with knockout pads. But this time with deliberate, deadly effect. We'd begun the day with an encounter with the boss of the Marshals and found him a deranged preacher with vengeance in his heart. I was just surprised Sam wasn't punching the dashboard or howling with anguish. It's what I felt like doing.

'You OK, Sam?'

She turned her head. 'No. But what am I supposed to do? Have a fit?'

'It would be understandable.'

'It wouldn't help.'

'You might feel better?'

'The only thing that would make me feel better is to see Curly and Fitz standing on the gallows with ropes round their neck and me with the lever in my hand.'

She said it with such cold certainty that I could find nothing to say for a long mile. 'Let's see what we can do, then. OK?'

'OK.'

When we got back to her house she disappeared to her bedroom. I was sure she had a bottle up there. But how could I stop her? How else could she handle all this? I felt useless, helpless.

I phoned in to the Sunday news desk and briefed Wullie.

'Can we mention the chloroform thing, Brodie?'

'It's not proven yet. I don't want Jamie Frew to get into trouble. He's a good man and I want to keep pals with him. Let's just lead with the drowning and talk about mysterious or suspicious circumstances.'

'Right. We'll get another crack at it with the autopsy.'

'One more thing, Wullie. What about Elsie? Has anyone told her? She might hate his guts but she's still his wife. Or rather widow.'

'I'll give her a wee phone right now. It'll help add colour.'

'That wasn't what I meant.'

'I ken, I ken. See you the morn.'

FORTY-TWO

I woke to the sound of drumming. Rain was pounding the streets and the air was wet and cool. I listened to it in the dark for a long time. My watch said three. It felt like the end of things.

I woke again in the dark. It was 6 a.m. I was alone. Sam hadn't sneaked into my bed for comfort. There would be no unguarded smiles over breakfast. Hardly surprising after the weekend's revelations that her abductors were on the loose and back at their old ways. It should have been a good reason for her seeking warmth and protection in the night. But, then, that was clearly a simple man's view. She preferred solitude and had slid back into her carapace. Or, more prosaically, into a bottle. And I was worried sick for her. Since I'd moved back in, our drinking had moderated. A bit. Suddenly, she'd been thrown back down the greasy slope. I was a poor friend.

I got up and washed and dressed and slipped out of the house. The faint light of dawn smeared the sky. The rain had stopped. The skies were clearing. There was still hope.

I walked through the wet streets and down to the club, savouring the freshness. I'd been speaking to Robert Campbell the Bathsmaster and he'd agreed to let me in for a swim as early as I liked. *A friend of Miss Campbell and a war hero . . .*

The water was icy. Just what I needed. I ploughed up and down until my body was tingling. By seven thirty I was strolling with damp hair and clear head towards the *Gazette*. It was now broad day and I was just in time to sidestep the first of the great lorries roaring out the bowels of the building with their piles of morning papers. I grabbed a free copy from the pile they leave in the entrance hall and studied the headlines above side-by-side photos of a smiling Jimmie Sheridan and the woman. No more smiles from him or her. Both looked ten years younger than the melting faces I'd seen at the pier. The article was good, simple prose, setting out the dark story and hinting at foul deeds and conspiracies without actually saying anything that could be construed as libellous. It took great skill from Wullie's pen and Sandy's blue pencil to tread the fine line between lurid speculation and hand-wringing tragedy. Gossip and pathos. The journalist's nectar and ambrosia.

I hurried past Eddie's office but he hadn't got in yet. Sunday evenings were tough on a family man and he liked to have breakfast with his kids on Monday mornings. I got to my desk and pulled out a sheet of paper and a pencil. I had thinking to do and needed to scribble out my thoughts. It always seemed easier to work through things if I wrote them down.

I had a column to write about the meeting yesterday with Fergus Drummond, former military policeman and now leader of a vigilante gang being hunted by the police for a triple murder. He thought that if the *Gazette* printed an article that mentioned their unique and painful calling card and highlighted the fact that the dead homosexuals had lost a great deal but not their fingers, he'd be in the clear. It was almost certainly a futile throw. The Marshals had solicited naming and shaming slips and that was now seen to be their method of business. The homosexuals died with their 'crimes' on their tongues. Not proof of guilt, but it added more weight to that side of the scales.

I only had Fergus Drummond's word for his army record and what he'd done. I'd better put in some calls to my old regiment's staff unit. See if they could corroborate his claims. They might even have a photo of the former subaltern. If so, we'd have a helluva scoop. Not just a name but 'Face of the vigilante chief'!

Why did that seem like a betrayal?

I picked up today's paper again. For the first time I took in the name of the poor dead woman: Sally Geddies. The name of an ordinary girl. The daughter of some ordinary mum and dad. A rotten ending. I hoped for her sake that she'd been unconscious when they pushed the car into the loch. From Sheridan's expression of horror, he'd been very much awake but unable to do anything about it.

Wullie had also managed to get a phone call in to Elsie Sheridan. She'd been shocked rigid, I imagine, but through the prism of Wullie's reported interview and her moderated language, it was pretty hard to interpret exactly how she'd taken it personally.

'. . . I can't imagine what he was doing up at Balloch. He loved that wee car and to think he died in it is just unbearable. He and I have had our difficulties, but he was still my husband. I will miss him.

'I'm also sorry for his secretary Miss Geddies. She was so helpful to Jimmie. I can't say any more at the moment. I'm too upset.'

Jimmie's *secretary*? Even now, if this was a true transcript, Elsie had to keep face, keep up appearances. Is that all we are, finally? The sum of our lives is other people's perceptions of us? What would that make me? And what should I make of Fergus Drummond? The man was daft as a brush, but how would I have survived five years as a prisoner of war? How would I have coped on my return to this dreary landscape, without a job, without a roof over my

248

head, without honour. And I suspected – for Drummond – it was the loss of honour that cut deepest. Mix in the Wee Free over-zealous interpretation of the Bible and you get a vengeful old prophet: St Fergus the Pain-giver unleashing his own apocalypse on the sinners and evil-doers of Glasgow.

It was clear his men were intensely loyal to him. He'd ripped off his pips and slogged alongside them as a non-commissioned prisoner. No doubt it was his faith that had kept them going, had kept them alive though the soul-racking years, through the long sub-zero march fleeing the advancing Russians. Now they were following him blindly for the lack of anything better to do. Cornered rats. Ignored by the society they'd gone to war for. Jobless, homeless and unloved except by Drummond. Four Sancho Panzas on a righteous quest led by their very own Don Quixote.

I wrote it up as a diatribe against a society that could let this happen to the men who'd suffered for their country. Then I binned it. Sandy's blue pencil would have sliced right through it.

I tried again with the emphasis on the revelation that the Marshals had been leaving a brutal calling card on their victims. That the *Gazette* had deliberately kept quiet about it to avoid encouraging copycat punishments. That in doing so, we'd now uncovered a new seam of wickedness using the Marshals' modus operandi to deceive and mislead. The question was who, and why?

Was it just a vendetta against homosexuals? Did it really madden someone so much that they were prepared to eradicate anyone with that tendency? From what I'd seen of human nature – if we count Nazis in that – the answer was a simple yes. There seemed to be no divergence from the true path that the self-righteous wouldn't punish. They took it as a personal affront that someone thought or acted differently. That it undermined everything the *true* believer stood for. That his or her very soul was at risk if one heresy was allowed to flourish.

Which brought me back to Drummond. He was just as bad. He was the sort they used to burn at the stake, his eyes raised to heaven and rapture on his face as the flames ate his bones. A martyr.

FORTY-THREE

It took three drafts to get the column in a fit state for publishing. Sandy kept sending it back with scrawled admonitions to 'leave out the hearts and flowers'; 'drop the cod philosophy'; and 'we're selling newspapers, not sermons'.

I wasn't happy with the end result, but I understood the need to appeal to our loyal readers' preference for a good story over a lecture about morality.

It went to press for Tuesday's edition but was confined to the inside back page, overshadowed – in truth obliterated – by the ongoing frenzy of salacious gossip over Sheridan's suspicious death. The other papers were in full outrage mode, trying desperately to catch up with Monday's scoop by the *Gazette*. No one wanted to read that the Marshals might be innocent of murder. Readers were just as capable as the vigilantes of jumping to unfounded conclusions.

I was pretty sure the Marshals would be on the phone to the *Gazette* within minutes of the first edition hitting the news stands. I told Morag and the other girls just to take a message. I couldn't face getting my ear bent about failing to write something that fully exonerated them. Twice during the day I got signals that I was wanted on the phone. I waved back to indicate I was out.

Wullie wandered in and out of the newsroom, managing to look quietly smug and serious at the same time. Eddie seemed to be on roller skates, darting in and out of his office every five minutes and revelling in the cacophony of phone calls. In the midst of the hubbub, Wullie stopped at my desk and quietly asked, 'Any chance of corroborating that chloroform thing, Brodie?'

'As it happens, I'm having a drink with Jamie Frew this evening.'

We stood in the Horseshoe between two of the glass and wood swivel panels at the bar. It gave us some privacy. We covered the missing six years in the first five minutes. Jamie was planning an early retirement in a year's time, to allow his passion for fly-fishing on the Spey to consume him. A part of me envied him that certainty, that simple goal. My father and I had stood on many a fast brown burn casting and casting. Some thought it a strange way of passing a day but we found it immensely calming. I learned patience – some, anyway – on the banks of the Afton down by Cumnock.

We finally and reluctantly left the debate about the respective merits of dry and wet flies if a river's in spate.

'I thought this story about Sheridan was yours, Dougie?'

'I'm working it with McAllister. It crosses both our patches.'

'Your lady friend was gie upset when I mentioned the chloroform smell. Was it that bad for her?'

I told him a little of it. He sucked his teeth. 'Bastards,' he said.

'Aye, they were. So you can imagine her delight on finding that some of the old Slattery gang had found new employment but were using their old skills.'

'She knows Sir Colin Maxwell?'

'Old family friend. She was of an age with the son. A total tadger, she says. Likes hurting things. Dogs, horses, humans. According to Sam he doesn't distinguish.'

Jamie was nodding. 'There's a type there. Well, I can confirm that chloroform was used on both Sheridan and his woman. Enough to knock out a horse. Though it seems, from the torn nails and the bruises on his knuckles, Sheridan was awake when the car sank. Tough wee fella. He tried to get out, but with that amount of the drug inside him, and the water pressure, it would have been like fighting in quicksand.'

'Can we use it?'

'Aye, why no'? I'd be happy enough getting my books a year earlier. My pension's no' bad as it is.'

'Thanks, Jamie.' I noticed he was looking into his pint and his mouth was twisting. 'What else?'

'I'm really, really no' supposed to say this.'

'But?'

'You know these poofters? The wans that were murdered at the Winter Gardens ?'

'You're not saying . . .!'

He nodded. 'Same thing. Blood full of chloroform. They must have caught them, dosed them – a pad soaked in the stuff probably; there's indication of slight burning in the nostrils – then stripped them, mutilated them and left them to bleed to death. Poor wee bastards.'

'The first one? Connie at the Monkey Club? Him too?'

Frew shook his head. 'I don't know. I didn't see him. There was no mention in the report. After I found the stuff in Sheridan and the other two I had a look. Nothing.'

'Can you do another post-mortem?'

'We're too late. His pal picked up the body. It would be a struggle to get an exhumation, if he's not already cremated.'

We supped silently for a while, our imagination trying to reject the images swirling through our heads. It took a special depth of depravity to do that to another human being. But I'd seen enough barbarism to know it wasn't rare. Not nearly enough. You just don't expect it on Glasgow Green.

I left Jamie to it and headed back to Sam's house, my mind swirling with the implications. I had no doubt this was the work of the Slattery boys: Curly and Fitz. But why? Just keeping their hand in with a couple of random homosexual slaughters? That didn't make sense. But what the hell was the connection with Maxwell and Sheridan? If any? They'd made the three murders seem like the work of the Marshals, which suggested they didn't want to be linked to them. Apart from the sex angle, there was nothing I knew of that linked the three killings . . . and that's where I'd been going wrong.

If someone had murdered three heterosexuals would I have stopped at that? Hardly. Perhaps the bedroom preferences of the three dead men were incidental? I hadn't done much digging into their backgrounds. I cursed my sloppiness. Just because I was a reporter and not a policeman didn't mean I could get away with shallow investigation. It made me wonder again about the usefulness of this new observer role I'd taken on. I determined to do some real backtracking on each of the victims first thing tomorrow. I wasn't seeing the bigger picture, and that worried the life out of me. What would the killers do next? *Who* would be next?

FORTY-FOUR

The house was quiet when I woke at my now usual time of six. I'd not seen Sam the night before. She was still burrowed in her room. I heard her moving about, so at least she was still alive. Maybe tonight I could coax her out to the pictures.

It was an hour before dawn but already the darkness was edging to grey. I decided to slip in a quick morning swim before Sam rose. I'd take her a cup of tea and some toast, and we'd try to work up some enthusiasm for life.

I set off in the grey light. The skies were clear, making it chilly, but it signalled another perfect day for mid-September. A smell of proper autumn in the air but the promise of a warm day ahead. I knocked on the side door to the club and was let in by Robert. I changed and dived into the green depths, my splash echoing round the vaulted chamber of the pool.

As I swam I planned the set of questions I'd pose to people like Duncan Todd and Wullie about the background of the three murdered boys. Did they know each other? Did the dead pair in the People's Palace frequent the Monkey Club? What about their jobs? Where did they work?

I climbed out of the pool and padded through the quiet corridors to the showers. There was no sign of Robert. Probably brewing up his morning tea or checking the boilers.

My wet skin felt chilled as though there was a draught blowing through. As though someone had left an outside door open. I picked up a towel, rubbed my hair and torso and wrapped it round my waist. I stopped just inside the shower room and listened. I could hear the faint noise of a tram. I couldn't normally. I felt distinctly naked and vulnerable in just my red bathing trunks and towel. I looked around me. There were eight wooden shower cubicles in a big white-tiled room. Wooden slatted benches lined the opposite wall to the cubicles. One side wall was taken up with built-in sinks. Above each hung a mirror. No obvious weapons. No hiding place. No place to get trapped.

I decided to skip a shower and cut through to the changing room. As I altered direction I caught a movement in the mirror. It wasn't Robert Campbell. The movement became two men. Carrying knives. They suddenly saw themselves in the mirror and saw me making a break for it. One hissed and charged after me. My wet feet skidded on the tiles and I bounced off the door frame into the anteroom. I leaped across the cold plunge, fell and lost my towel. I scrambled into the dry room. I had enough time to yank one of the loungers across the doorway before the men piled through.

They crashed over the bed, yelping with the impact on their shins, and clattering in a heap on the floor. A long blade spun away from one of their hands. It looked like a bayonet. For an instant I thought about diving after it and confronting them. But the odds were too much in their favour. I plunged for the door leading back up the stairs to the entrance hall. I tugged the door but at this time of morning it was still locked. I sprinted back and down the other stairs, my feet slapping and sliding at every step. I could hear the men gasping and pounding behind me.

I broke back out into the great pool arena, brain racing and trying to visualise an escape route. There wasn't one. At least not one that I'd reach before the shod hunters caught me up.

I had one stupid thought. There wasn't time for a smarter one. I ran round the pool, past the diving board and over to the far side. I took a clean run and leaped out into the pool. I caught the trapeze bar with one hand, swung and got the other fingers round it. I was spinning and swaying like a drunk, but I pulled myself up and then flung my legs up and backwards over the bar so that I was perched on my stomach. My PE sergeant would have been proud of me. With the last energy of the chase I hauled myself up the ropes until I was standing on the bar. By the time the two knifemen got to my side of the pool the lateral swings had stopped. I was rocking gently backwards and forwards, just out of reach. I was some six feet in the air and a crucial four feet away from the pool's edge.

The knifemen scampered round to my side and stood panting, gazing up at me and clutching their weapons. They looked puzzled, as though I'd set them a hard sum and they couldn't remember their tables.

It was a precarious perch. I was the proverbial sitting duck. If they had guns they'd hardly miss. I could already picture my punctured body floating in a widening circle of red. The Committee would have a fit.

I had time to inspect their blades. They were bayonets but sharpened and honed to thin murderous edges and points. If they'd been *throwing* knives, the men could have two good goes at spearing my bare body and leaving me dead, or wounded enough to drown. Bayonets have all the weight in the handle and if chucked, it was pretty random which end would hit first.

I also hoped they wouldn't want to try the same jump as me. They could leap for the next trapeze along and then do some fancy swings to get within range, but they were muscle men; more circus strong men than acrobats. I was king of the castle and they were the dirty wee rascals that I'd be able to kick into the pool if they tried. It was still two against one but I was counting on human nature. They were fully clothed; I was in trunks. Folk don't like getting wet in their clothes. Nor wrestling with someone in water. Or getting trapped in a pool if someone else arrived.

Hell, they might not even be able to swim.

I didn't recognise them. And they seemed too well built to be members of the Marshal gang. But I'd know their pug faces again. If there was another time. They paced back and forward a couple of times, brandishing their glinting weapons. They seemed to be getting angrier all the time.

'Come on in, boys. The water's lovely.'

I thought I might have overdone it, that one of them was going to take a leap at me. But then the brighter of the two saw the long pole with the hoop on the end for rescuing kids from the deep end. He got hold of it and was swinging it out to hook me and draw me close. I dived from my perch and headed underwater to the centre of the pool, hoping my simple theory about them not wanting to get wet was right. I surfaced to the sound of the fire alarm crashing through the building.

The fisherman flung his pole into the pool in disgust. They sprinted out of the door and were gone. I gave them a count of thirty and began swimming to the side. I was just hauling myself out when old Robert stumbled through, clutching his bloody head. He sat down heavily on a bench when he saw me.

I got towels and cleaned and bandaged his head wound. I supported him to his office and phoned an ambulance. I was just putting the phone down when one of the other early-morning swimmers stuck his head round the door.

'I say, Brodie, what the devil's going on? The front door's wide open and the fire alarm – my God!' He'd just seen Robert.

'Bill, isn't it? We've been robbed. Two men. They beat up Robert and chased me. Can you look after him while I change?'

I gave him no choice with his answer. I darted out of the office and jumped into my trousers and shirt. I took a quick look at Robert as I ran for the front door.

'Sorry, chaps. Must run.'

I left Bill's protestations in my wake and ran out of the door into the soft light of morning. Last night I'd been asking myself who'd be attacked next. Who'd be next to die? The question welled in me. I had the answer. As I pumped up the hill towards the big house at Parkside the panic kept my aching lungs gasping away. I stumbled up the steps with my legs gone. I rammed my key into the door and ran into the hall.

'Sam! Sam! Are you there?'

I dived down into the kitchen. It was dark. I ran back up into the hall again and heard a door open upstairs.

'Brodie! What on earth's the matter?'

I stopped, panting, at the foot of the stairs and gazed up at her. She stood there, hands on hips, in her dressing gown, in all her disapproving glory. I turned and sat down on the bottom steps until the nausea cleared. She walked slowly down to join me. We sat together, like kids banished from the front room. She took my hand.

'Douglas, what is it? You're shaking.'

'A daft notion. That's all. It's OK now.'

'Tell me.'

I didn't want to. I didn't want to bring the fear back. I inspected her face. Her eyes were tired but clear. She was sober. She was coming through this latest setback. This was Samantha Campbell. I told her. She listened, nodding, and then she said, calmly, 'Well then, maybe it's time we took a wee holiday.'

FORTY-FIVE

We made our preparations there and then. I freed the sleek Dixons and the heavy Webley from the gun cupboard and stuffed as many shells into the game bags as I could. We packed two soft leather holdalls with enough clothes to last a week and emptied the whisky cabinet. We stowed away two good pairs of binoculars. We left the fishing rods behind. Reluctantly.

By eight thirty, we were standing, supping tea, crunching cheese on toast, dressed in our rough tweeds: Sam in her own set of well-cut green jacket and matching plus fours, and me in her father's hand-me-downs. We laced up thick brown brogues and donned rough flat caps and I saw a new side of Samantha Campbell, perhaps the Sam side. We smiled at the sight of each other – a pair of ghillies – as though we were off on a great adventure. Though her pale skin was stretched tight over her fine facial bones, she already seemed brighter. Action always helps.

I phoned my mother to let her know I'd be away for a few days. Or at any rate, I phoned her neighbour Mrs Cuthbertson and listened to a lot of shouting up and down the entry before my mum's breathless voice came on.

'What's wrong, Douglas?'

'Nothing, nothing at all. I just wanted to let you know I'm going away for day or two.'

'A holiday? You could do with one.'

'Aye, a wee trip.'

'Just yourself?'

'No. In fact I'm going with Samantha.'

'Oh, Douglas. I'm that pleased. She's a nice lassie.'

'She is. You're all right, Mum? No funny visitors lately?'

'Just every neighbour in Bonnyton to hear about my trip to Glasgow. You ken what they're like.'

I truly did.

'Have the local bobbies been round? Are they keeping an eye?'

'If I've made one pot of tea I've made twenty.'

'Don't give them shortbread or you'll never see the back of them.'

We packed the Riley with our gear, rolled out of the garage and headed west. In half an hour we were passing through Balloch and winding along the bonnie banks of Loch Lomond. We met only one other vehicle: a motorbike and sidecar of the Royal Scottish Automobile Club and got a smart salute for sporting their Saltire badge on our radiator grill.

As we drove I thought with relief about getting Sam away for a few days for safety. She was now sangfroid personified but I felt that at any moment she could break. And disappear back into a bottle. The last few months had been hard enough on her without these new horrors intruding. It might also be a chance for the pair of us to spend quiet time together and see what we had. I had a guilty thought about Morag in all this. Should I tell her I was going off for a few days with another woman? Did I owe her that much? Was there any way she'd understand or believe me if I said I was doing it to avoid getting murdered? I wasn't 100 per cent sure of her answer if I gave her the choice.

Our immediate destination was Tarbet, halfway up the 26-mile loch, along the A82. Sam had stayed there often, as a girl and as a young woman, when she and her parents had gone shooting and fishing by the loch. We reached it in an hour and a half by the old Highland road.

The Tarbet hotel is built on a fork on the road where it branches west to Inverary and Oban, and north to the

Grampians. Its grounds run down to the loch. The bulk of Ben Lomond stands guard on the eastern side of the water.

The baronial pile sat heavy and proud in the weak morning sun. We pulled into the car park and I shut off the engine. We gazed out over the loch, our eyes drawn up the rising mass on the other side, blotched with purple heather.

'We could just go straight on, Sam. Crianlarich is bonny this time of year. So is Fort William,' I suggested.

'"By Tummel and Loch Rannoch and Loch Aber, I will go . . ."?' she sang in perfect key.

Unable to match her voice, I spoke the next line, '"By heather tracks wi' heaven in their wiles . . ." Why not?'

She heard the seriousness in my voice and didn't say anything for a long moment. Then she sighed.

'You know we can't just run away.'

I wound the window down and lit a cigarette. Something bubbled up in me. It had been fermenting for weeks.

'Why not, Sam? Why not? For six years they trained me to be the best killer I could be, and I was. I was one of the best. A natural, maybe. Now I want out. I want to be a journalist. I want to write. Study Eliot again. But they didn't teach me how to get back there. No one gave me a compass back to civvy street when I handed back my uniform. Every time I reach for a pen or a book someone pulls a gun on me. And I react. So what do I do now, Sam? What do I do?'

She put her neat hand on my arm. 'Douglas, my dear, you can't hide from yourself. You're not the type to sit back and let others fight your battles.'

'Really? No choice? I'm tired of taking on the world. Tired of leading from the front. Of fighting. I'm just a reporter, remember? All that pen mightier than sword stuff?'

'If *you* don't, who will? If *we* don't?'

'You're not going to hit me with Burke, are you?'

She laughed. 'All that is necessary for evil to triumph is for good men to do nothing? That one?'

'Define *good*, then. We argued about it for days back in our first year at Glasgow. We thought it was grand stuff. It was simpler then.'

'Oh, it's still simple, Douglas. But we're not.'

I sat and smoked. I hated hearing her arguments. For she was right, of course. It seems there's no escape from your nature. Finally I said: 'You know what really scares me, Sam? I miss it. Some of it. I miss the surge of terror and fierceness in the morning going into battle. Leading two hundred men against an SS division. Testing myself against the best fighting machine the world has seen. Knowing that not all of us will come back. That I might not. But for that moment feeling so alive that death would be a fair bargain. And now the worst thing I face every day is my typewriter keys sticking! I need to find a way of purging those feelings or . . . or I – will – blow – up!' I hit the steering wheel with every word.

She squeezed my arm then asked quietly, 'Purging or accepting?'

I stared through the screen at the great timeless mass of Ben Lomond. Accept I had a duty to use my talent for war? Is that what Sassoon and Owen did when they went back to the Front? Poet *and* soldier. Each with two heads, two hearts? *Was* it that simple? Maybe.

'Besides, Douglas, you're a tidy person. There's unfinished business here.' I flung my fag end out and looked at her. 'Kismet?'

'If you like.'

'Shall we see if we can book lunch? And a room?'

'As in *one* room?'

'Sam, I'll sleep on the floor but I don't want you out of my sight.'

'So this is gallantry, not seduction?' She was smiling, coolly.

'Practicality, Mrs Smith.'

'Oh God, can't we at least have a more interesting name?'

It wasn't much of an objection.

*

The waistcoated porter jangled his keys. 'I'll show you your rooms first, then bring you up a pot of tea, Mr and Mrs Carnegie. No relation . . .?'

'Sadly, no. But it gets us into all his libraries,' I said.

The porter glanced at me queerly as though he wasn't sure I was joking. 'I suppose you've heard that quite a lot, sir?'

'Once or twice.'

Sam raised her eyes.

The summer season was over and we were able to take a suite at half price. It had a small lounge that looked down and across the loch, and an adjoining bedroom and bathroom. We went Dutch; essential, considering my finances. Good sightlines down the road south. Partial views round to the north. I walked over to the window and gazed out. It was too early in the year to have the full autumn colours, but the long hot summer had taken its toll and some of the trees were already edging to russet. The great sweeping bank of Ben Lomond was patched with purple. The haze rose from the loch and blurred the trees on the far bank.

The porter stowed our bags and gun cases and left us alone. 'You do know we're probably closer to Maxwell and his crew than we were in Glasgow?' I nodded through the glass down the loch towards its eastern bank and the hills that rolled up and away from us.

She stood beside me with her arms folded, looking out. 'We've got big Ben between us, but as the crow flies, yes. Or the boat sails. But that's good, isn't it? It's the last thing they'll be expecting.'

'Can I just say this, Sam? You seem very unfazed.'

'You'd prefer to see me teary and quivering? A poor wee damsel in distress? Ready to be saved by her big hulking hero? Or simply drunk?'

I was glad she was smiling as she said it. I laughed. 'It's just a surprise. I saw your reaction to Curly and Fitz, the chloroform kids. As things get worse, you seem to be getting calmer.'

Her face went serious. 'I'm drawing on my reserves of fatalism, Brodie.'

I thought about what had happened to her. Her parents were drowned in this very loch just over a decade ago at the hands of the Slattery gang. Her fiancé David went down with his destroyer on the Murmansk run in '42. Then came her recent abduction and abuse by the same men who were probably out there trying to find us and finish the job. You had choices: you raged against life's calamities until you went mad; you gave up and turned into a jellyfish; or you rolled with the blows and tried to carry on.

'That doesn't mean I don't want to live,' she said, reading my thoughts.

'Good. Then it's not too late to keep on driving north.'

'We've been through that. Besides, Sir Kenny Rankin and his wife, Moira, live just down the road. In case we fancied calling in on them.'

'For a blether about Glasgow regeneration?'

'That sort of thing.'

It made sense. Rather than tackle the Maxwells head on, we could probe the flanks. If Rankin was in cahoots with Maxwell, we might learn something.

'Don't we need an invitation?'

'Moira made it clear her door is always open to me. Let's go chap on it.'

'How near are they?'

'Helensburgh. If we take the back road along Loch Long, it's about twenty miles south of here.'

I nodded. 'That's tomorrow's job.' I looked at my watch. We'd made good time. it was just after eleven. 'I badly need to call in to the paper. Talk to McAllister. He needs a warning. I won't say where I am, but I want to make sure he knows what I found out from Jamie Frew. I can dictate a column about the chloroform connection to Morag. I'll also tell her to hold any messages.'

'Morag?'

'Just one of the girls.' Had my voice changed?

'*Your* girls?'

'*The* girls.'

'She sounds helpful.'

FORTY-SIX

I sat at the small table in the lounge area of the room and scratched out the story that had been rumbling through my head since meeting Frew the night before. It was a delicate balance between fact and supposition. But the bones of it were clear enough: six people, counting Morton, had now died and their deaths were linked. The first murder in the Monkey Club tied in with the second pair in that all three were homosexuals. And they'd had accusatory notes stuffed in their dead mouths. In addition the second pair had been chloroformed. So had Sheridan and his girlfriend. And poor Morton was likely a harbinger for Sheridan's demise.

The brutality of their deaths and the drugging of their victims bore the hallmarks of Curly and Fitz. Both were now working for Maxwell. What I couldn't do was find a motive that connected them all. For the moment, therefore, I couldn't link Maxwell with any of it. Eddie would self-combust at the thought of accusing Sir Colin of skulduggery without photographic proof, a signed confession and an eye-witness statement from the Pope. I'd talk to McAllister and ask for his help on checking out the background of the three dead lads.

I went down to the hallway and found the phone booth. I piled some change on top and dialled the *Gazette*. I pushed the money in and pressed A when I heard one of the secretary's voices.

'It's Brodie. Is that Elaine? Can I speak to Wullie McAllister, please.'

'Hello, Mr Brodie. He's not in yet, but Mr Paton wants a word. He said it was urgent.'

I sighed. 'Elaine, it's always urgent with Eddie. Sure, put me through.'

She giggled. 'Hold on please.'

There was a pause, a ring and then a blast: 'Where the effin' hell are you, Brodie? The world's in flames here! I need you right here, right now!'

'And good morning to you too, Eddie. I'd be there like a shot, but there's a very real chance of getting a chloroform pad in my face followed by a knife in the back. Maxwell's goons are on the rampage and the likelihood is we're next.'

'Whit? Who's *we*? And what the hell do you mean Maxwell's goons? We'll need proof a mile high if you're making accusations like that!'

'One thing at a time, Eddie. The *we* is Samantha Campbell and me. And maybe McAllister as well. We're at risk. I was attacked in the swimming pool this morning. I'm phoning in the story. But I'm not mentioning Maxwell. Not yet.'

'Why didn't you say so! In the mean effin' time, what am I supposed to do with shouty phone calls from these buggers the Marshals? Not to mention visitations by your pal Sangster?'

'No pal of mine. Look, let's start with your news. What exactly are the Marshals shouting about this time?'

'Your effin' Tuesday article, of course. They were phoning all yesterday and again this morning!'

I had a moment's guilt at ducking their calls. 'Why? I was kind. I said the murders didn't look like the work of the Marshals. It didn't have their calling card. What more do they want?'

'Ah suppose it's not so much what you wrote as what the polis said about it.'

'Eddie, we're going round in circles here. Just tell me what happened this morning.'

'It was on the wireless, for God's sake. Did you no' listen? The Chief Constable of Glasgow – the top man, Brodie! – has personally come out and said he was going after the Marshals no matter what – and I quote – *some clever dick local news reporter cares to write* – end of quote. He means you, Brodie. And that means *me*! He went on about returning the streets to the people, upholding the law and a' that bullshit.'

'So why did the Marshals call you?'

'They want *you*. They want to speak to you as soon as you care to drop by, Brodie.'

'What do I do, then? Did they suggest a meeting?'

'They gave a nummer. A Glasgow nummer. But it's only to be used until twelve noon, the day. Then it'll change.'

'Have you tried it?'

'No fear!'

'Tell me.' I pulled my notepad to me and scribbled the four digits after the Glasgow code.

'What about Sangster? What did he want?'

'Your hide, Brodie. Tanned and nailed to his wall. Let me see . . . for having secret assignations with known criminals and murderers. For conspiracy to disrupt a police investigation. For conspiring with police medical practitioners to reveal secret information. And on and on and on.'

'What did you tell him?'

'That the press was independent and free and we were not prepared to reveal our sources. Besides, I had no idea where the fuck you were. Did you, by the by, happen to ascertain anything useful from your medical pal?'

I sighed. 'That's why we're lying low. That's the story I'm going to dictate to one of the girls if you'd just let me. I'm saying that the three murders of the homosexuals are linked to Sheridan and his lady friend's death.'

'Good God! That's terrific! What's the connection?'

'Chloroform. They were all found with high levels of chloroform in their bodies. Sorry, to be precise: the first murder – Connie? – his post-mortem was carried out by somebody else. Jamie's checking, but we can't actually say it was connected with the others. The link there is the homosexual one.'

'But we can run with it?'

'I'm counting on it. Maybe even an evening special? We still don't know why, though we can guess it's something to do with the Glasgow redevelopment project. We're also pretty certain it involves the remnants of the Slattery gang who work for Maxwell. But if Maxwell is involved, we don't have proof. So I'm leaving him and the old Slattery boys out of it for the moment. But the key point is, Eddie, they are ready to get rid of anyone standing in their way. You have to warn Wullie. Is he in yet?'

'No yet. You ken what he's like.'

'Can you get in touch with him? Has he got a phone at home?'

'He stays with his brother, Stewart, out by Govan. I'll get one o' the lassies to get a telegram round to him. Ask him to gi'e us a phone. In the meantime, where are you?'

'Need to know, Eddie. Best not to tell you. I'll phone in from time to time. But now, hand me back to Morag or one of the girls and you'll have a draft column in half an hour. Then I'll call this number you gave me.'

'Where are you?' Morag hissed. She had her mouth pressed against the phone and was shouting quietly at me.

'I'm lying low for a wee while.'

'Alone?'

'No.'

'With that woman, I suppose?'

'Morag, I don't have time for this. I need you to take some dictation. There's a story we need to get out.'

The line went quiet for a bit then a frosty, precise voice responded, 'OK, *Mister* Brodie, I'm ready . . .'

I rubbed my ear after we'd hung up. I'd put things right with Morag when we got back. I dialled the number Eddie gave me. It rang for a while, then: 'Packhorse Inn. We're no' open yet.'

'I want Drummond.'

There was silence, then a distant muttered argument, then: 'Where are you, Brodie?'

'Why does everyone ask that? Having an early pint or two, Drummond? Dutch courage for the next punishment rendezvous?'

'Shut up, Brodie. We're using these premises as a temporary base. Did you hear the wireless this morning?'

'No, but I gather my golden words didn't impress the Chief Constable. I tried, Drummond.'

'Not hard enough, it seems!'

'Cops are simple-minded creatures. Once they get an idea into their heads, it's hard to dislodge.'

'You *know* something, Brodie, don't you? You know who's doing this. It's something to do with Sheridan's death, isn't it?

'I don't know how you make that leap, Drummond. But whatever I have is pure supposition. We don't have the proof.'

'Then what the hell do *we* do?'

'Why the hell should *I* care? You made your bed of thistles. You maun lie in it.'

His voice went quieter, more tense. 'Brodie, this isn't for me. I don't care what happens to me. It's my men. You'll understand that. You have to help us.'

'I really don't. And in truth, even if I did, I wouldn't know how.'

'Brodie, look, we're moving on from here now, so don't try any tricks. I'll leave another number tomorrow morning at the *Gazette*. Just call me. OK?' He didn't, couldn't say please, but it was as near to begging as I think Drummond ever got.

'I'll see.'

FORTY-SEVEN

Sam and I took a stroll through the grounds of the hotel and down along the shoreline. We kept in costume, partly to convince the hotel we were dilettante upper class out for a few days' shooting, partly because it felt comfortable and right among the turning trees and wild scenery. Full tweeds and, over our shoulders, the Dixons, broken open. Our game-keepers' pockets bulging with cartridges.

The last time I'd used these beautiful weapons had been for real, against the Slatterys. This was the chance to enjoy them, savour their weight and perfect balance, bring them up and across to track a flushed pigeon. We took down a couple before deciding that, rather than massacre all the feathered wildlife, we'd get the hotel to set up their clay shoot. We strolled back. A young boy from the kitchen leaped at the chance with glee, and hunkered down behind a dip between the hotel and the shoreline.

We called *pull* and let rip. The loch echoed to the crashing of our guns. Whether it was the excitement of firing or the fresh air and autumn sunshine, I didn't know, but Sam's face glowed. This was what she needed.

Annoyingly, for the first dozen clays she was the better shot. Her gun came up smoothly, tight into her shoulder, her right leg well planted back, her left bent at the knee and braced. Time after time her pellets erupted in deadly accu-racy. She looked like a kid, pink-cheeked and laughing, her eyes bright with the light of competition. I tried to rise to the occasion, but even with fine guns like these it took me a few shots to get my eye in. Eventually the recoil was taking its toll on my shoulder. When we seemed to be honours even, I spoke up.

'Enough. I'm out of practice. You win. Your father taught you well, Sam.'

'I felt him on my shoulder, saying, "Squeeze, don't jerk. Keep it smooth." It still works.'

We cleaned and stowed the guns, and passed the rest of the afternoon walking, interspersed with afternoon tea. We dressed more soberly for dinner. It was then I noticed her hand.

'You're wearing a ring.'

'Mrs Carnegie would, don't you think?'

'Where did you get it?'

'My mother's.'

It was a smart move. Sam must have planned it as we were packing. It left me feeling strange.

Later, in post-prandial satiety, we loitered with whiskies in armchairs in front of the picture window in our room. Outside, the loch lay sullen dark except where the moonlight tore a silver rag from its surface.

Sam's ring picked up the same light. If things had turned out differently she'd have been wearing her own today. And I wouldn't be here.

'What was he like? Your sailor?'

'Lieutenant David Reid, RN? And sometime lawyer?'

'Do you mind? Not if you don't want . . .'

'No, it's fine. We were at university together, same law courses. I loved it. He hated it. David was planning to retrain as a medic before he got called up. Just wasn't cut out for law. Family tradition.' She held up her hand. 'Yes, like mine. But I *wanted* a law career. It wasn't to please my dad. Remind me when all this is over, Brodie. It's time I got properly back to work, instead of all this part-time stuff lately.'

'Good. I will.'

'David was a good man. You're a good man too, Douglas, but different. David hated violence.'

'Meaning I *love* it? I thought you wanted me to fight?'

'No. That's not it. David would turn the other cheek if someone hit him. You'd knock his head off. It doesn't mean David was a coward. He expected to die on convoy duty, but went anyway. He just never thought violence solved anything.'

'Whereas I do?'

'I wish I could have sat and listened to the pair of you arguing your case.'

'Lately, I would have been more on his side than you think.'

'I'm sure that's true. And David would have made an exception for Charlie Maxwell.'

'I'd have liked your man. He had good taste.'

She smiled. 'David could see that Charlie . . .' She waved her hand.

'Could see what?'

'That he was interested in me. For years. I couldn't shake him off. He was used to getting his own way. He couldn't stand it when David came on the scene. He knew David was the better man.' She suddenly got up and walked to the window, and stared out into the night.

'Sorry, Sam. I didn't meant to open old wounds.'

'It's all right. I don't mind talking about David. It's Maxwell.'

'He hit dogs, you said.' I tried to make it light.

She turned and looked hard at me. 'I haven't told anyone this. David was lost in '42. About a year later I was invited out to Inverard. To stay for a couple of days. Shooting and so on. Like we used to. The invitation had Colin's name on it. But only Charlie was there. It was too late to turn round and leave but I decided I'd go home the next day. I came down to dinner and it was like a seduction scene from some B movie. Chandeliers, candles, big fire and Charlie in a kilt.' She stopped and smiled ruefully.

'Bad knees?'

She laughed. 'No, the kilt was fine. But I think he slipped something into the wine. Charlie was always one for cocaine. A habit he picked up in London and Paris. I don't remember much about the evening. But I woke up in my room with him on top of me.'

'The bastard! He raped you?'

A smile drew across her face. 'He tried. But he couldn't.' She raised her pinkie and waggled it, pointing down. 'The spirit was willing, but . . .'

'You must hate him.'

'Not as much as he hates me.'

When dark finally settled across the loch, we separated with a chaste peck on the cheek, Sam to the bedroom, me to the couch with the spare blankets. We exchanged a last rueful smile and closed the door. I sat for a time smoking in the dark, until my eyes adjusted and the dull expanse of water and the treeline took on definition against the black mound of Ben Lomond.

I spent a little time thinking about Sam and me. But it was a track too well worn to walk again. Still, no wonder the girl was wary of men if she kept running into sods like Maxwell. What did that say about me?

I forced my mind to switch tracks, to think what the morn would bring. There were so many threads snapping and tangling in the wind. I found myself worrying about the Marshals, this ragtag platoon of lost souls led by a demented ex-officer with poison in his soul. The months after demob I'd spent in London pickling myself in alcohol had taught me how close the line was between disappointment and despair, melancholy and desolation. There were still moments – when I wasn't engaged with life, when I wasn't in pursuit of something outside myself – that I caught the black dog out of the corner of my eyes. It was never far away.

Lying at three in the morning staring into the dark. Or

waking each morning and thinking about the first drink that night. I knew it had a grip, but I was certain it wasn't a stranglehold. That I could go a day without it. Sam had a problem, but not all the time, and we only really drank to be sociable with each other. Yet I knew that when the morning's nausea cleared and the thudding behind the eyes lifted, the cycle began again, and by evening it was a case of why not? But that was tomorrow's problem. I took another sip and focused on Sir Kenneth Rankin.

We were determined to drive to his house on the hillside above Helensburgh by mid-morning. We'd give no warning, and hope to beard Kenny and Moira in their den and put them to the question.

What could we hope to gain? And why would Rankin play ball? We were gambling on Rankin wanting to disassociate himself from Maxwell's extreme actions. Rankin might have loose morals when it came to making and keeping piles of money, but Sam was certain he'd draw the line at conspiracy to commit murder.

I wasn't so persuaded it would be his moral code that stopped him. No matter how much they had, the rich always wanted more. But I was pretty sure that the risk of a stretched neck would have a penitential influence. Could we get him to admit it publicly? Could we get a confession out of him that would nail Charlie Maxwell? Sam's revelation had convinced me were talking about Maxwell the Younger. He had the right set of standards. She was sure old Colin was being used by his noxious offspring.

I stubbed out my cigarette and made up my bed on the couch. I looked at her door and hoped she at least felt safe from me. I took heart from her sneaking into my bed the other night to shield her from her demons. Some anyway.

FORTY-EIGHT

By 9.30 a.m. Thursday morning we were driving south on the road that wound along Loch Long. The kippers and mountain of toast were healing the damage of the last nightcap or two. We'd dressed in dark suit and cashmere twin-set as befitted calling on a knight and lady of the realm. Even Sam's pearls were getting an outing. I drove while Sam named the peaks rising up from the far bank of the loch. In a gap in her recital, I asked, 'What happens if Rankin just throws us out? If he denies everything, we have no proof and the *Gazette* won't run it.'

She shrugged. 'Then we're in bother.'

We swung through Garelochhead and down towards Helensburgh. I was reminded how pretty a town it was, with the best houses cascading down the steep hillside to the promenade and seafront. We started to wend our way up the switchback rough roads until we were near the top. The houses were solid, light sandstone. They varied from big to huge. This was Bearsden by Sea. We turned right so we were running across the sloping hillside.

The houses on either side of the road sat in their own grounds. High walls or lines of trees and shrubs separated them from the road and their neighbours. Down to our right the tops of the houses staggered down to the town centre. The eye was drawn across the glistening Firth of Clyde away to the west and south, to the nearby Rosneath peninsula, then Gourock on the far bank of the estuary and on down to

Dunoon on the distant hills of the Cowal peninsula. I wished we had time to admire the view. We paused at the entrance to a driveway on our left.

'So this is what money gets you?' I asked.

'And it's why they don't want to lose it.'

We drove in over the crunching gravel and stopped outside a small mansion-house that ought to have its own moat. By the time we'd clambered out, a flunky in tartan trews and waistcoat had materialised and was bidding us welcome in that sort of *I can see you might, just might, be the sort that my lord and lady would know, but no bugger told me you were coming.*

'Good morning, ma'am. Good morning, sir. Is Sir Kenneth expecting you? Whom shall I say?'

'Oh, for goodness' sake, Calumn, do you not remember me?' asked Sam.

Calumn's eyes screwed up – I bet he only wore his glasses to sift the post – before a smile stole across his face.

'Och, Miss Campbell. I'm sorry, it's been a while. It's very good to see you again. Please come in. I'll just tell Sir Kenneth and Lady Rankin you're here. They will be pleased. And the gentleman is . . .?'

'A friend of mine. Major Douglas Brodie. We met Sir Kenny at the gallery opening last week.'

All this while, Calumn was holding open the front door and ushering us into a bright lounge at the front of the house. He left us after summoning a maid to get us tea.

'Nice,' I said, looking around the airy room. There seemed to be more soft furnishings than in Fraser's.

We'd barely sat down when we heard heels clicking fast across the parquet flooring of the hallway, and the door burst open. Moira Rankin sailed in, all swept-up blonde streaks and belted frock, as though she was on her way to high tea at Balmoral.

'Samantha, you should have phoned. Naughty girl. We'd have delayed breakfast and had it all together. Major Brodie, how nice to see you again.' She bustled between us with embraces and handshakes. 'Kenny will be through in a minute. He'll be so pleased.'

I doubted it.

Sir Kenneth Rankin joined us and was gruffly effusive in his welcome. Pleasantries were exchanged, tea and biscuits were brought and we cut to the point.

Kenny asked us, 'Were you just passing?'

Sam shook her head. 'No, Kenny. We needed to speak to you. You'll have heard about Jimmie Sheridan?'

Rankin's face hardly changed. 'A terrible business. I assume his brakes failed or something.'

Moira cut in: 'They said it was suicide. But he just didn't seem the type.'

I edged forward on my chair. 'It wasn't an accident, or suicide, I'm afraid.'

Rankin's eyes had hardened. 'Oh, and how are you so sure? And if it wasn't, what was it, pray?' Suddenly I could hear the deal-maker, the industrial magnate in the rumbling voice.

'Sir Kenneth, it was murder. A double murder. Sheridan and his friend were chloroformed and pushed into the loch.' I let the words sink in to see what effect they had. Moira looked suitably shocked. Rankin looked – well – annoyed. As though something irksome had been said.

'There was no mention of that in the *Herald* this morning.'

'Do you get the *Gazette*?' If Eddie had done his job, the column I'd dictated yesterday to Morag should have been plastered over the front page. Assuming Morag hadn't binned it in pique.

Rankin shook his head as though I'd asked him if he took Iron Brew in his whisky.

'I bet Calum does,' said Sam.

Moira gave us a long look and got up and pulled the bell-rope. Calum appeared as if he'd been standing outside the lounge door. Maybe he had.

'Calumn, do you read the *Gazette*?'

He looked panicked as though he'd been caught flogging the Royal Doulton. 'Why, yes, ma'am.'

'Do you have today's? And if so, might we borrow it?'

Calumn shot a glance at me and disappeared. He was back in a trice, smoothing out a copy of Thursday's edition, clearly wishing he'd had time to iron it. I caught the headlines. It looked like Eddie's lust for a scoop had overcome his fears of upsetting the Chief Constable.

Moira pulled out a pair of specs from the drawer of her side table, glanced at the headlines, skim-read the article and handed it to her husband without a word. She stared at Sam, and then me. Her face was pale. Anger or fear? Did she see what was coming?

Rankin took longer. He read it twice. He folded the paper and laid it down on the table. He gazed at me. 'All a bit tenuous, Brodie. The *Herald* wouldn't print it.'

'It doesn't need to be reported in parliament for it to be news.'

'It might be news or gossip. Call it what you will. But is it true, Brodie?'

'Ask Miss Campbell.' I turned to Sam.

'Kenny, we were there. Douglas and me. We saw the bodies at Balloch. The police doctor in attendance said he could smell the chloroform on them.' She took a breath. 'I know what that's like. Something similar happened to me back in April. It was probably the same men.'

Silence filled the room like a blanket. Moira looked stricken. Then Rankin stirred himself.

'You're keeping strange company these days, Samantha.' Did he mean me? 'All very interesting, I'm sure, but why are you telling me this? A wee round of applause for your detective work, Brodie?'

'The men who did this' – I pointed at the paper – 'are former members of the Slattery gang. They now work for the Maxwells.'

'Maxwell? Do they indeed? I heard Colin had some new staff. He's got a big place to run. Always needing new hands.'

'To carry out murders?' I saw his face darken and his mouth grow thin. I pushed on. 'We think Charlie Maxwell hired them to do some dirty work. We think that the dirty work was to protect his money-making plans for the new Glasgow development programme. There may even be a link to the murder of Councillor Alec Morton.'

'Damned nonsense! Beg pardon, Samantha. But damned nonsense. Colin Maxwell's boy? Never! Known them all my days.'

Moira suddenly sat forward. 'What are you saying, Mr Brodie? What exactly are you saying?'

'I'm saying that there are a number of legitimate opportunities for developers and investors in Glasgow's future. A great big birthday dumpling filled to bursting with silver sixpenny bits. But some folk want more than their share and don't care what crimes they commit to get their hands on a bigger slice. I'm saying that anyone who's linked to these crimes could be facing murder charges.'

Rankin had had enough. He lurched to his feet, face red, shoulders hunched and fists clenched as though he was going to charge me. 'That's enough, Brodie! How dare you! Who the hell do you think you are? Coming into my home and making accusations at me!'

I resisted the urge to stand. I kept my voice calm. 'Is that what you think? I don't recall accusing you of anything, *Sir* Kenneth. But now you raise the matter: what exactly is your relationship with the Maxwells?'

'None of your bloody business, my man!'

'Kenny, Kenny, don't upset yourself! Your heart.' Moira was now on her feet beside him and clutching his arm. 'He's not saying anything. He's not saying *you've* done anything. He's being stupid. Just stupid.'

I really seem to have upset her with my accusations. 'Lady Rankin, I may not be saying anything that points the finger at your husband. But Elsie Sheridan is. You know, Jimmie's widow.' I let that sink in and saw the first signs of retreat on Rankin's florid face.

'Sit down, my dear. Sit down.' Moira coaxed her man back and into his seat. She marched over and rang the bell. Calumn came in. 'Get me a Scotch, please. For Sir Kenneth.' She looked round at Sam and me. 'Och, make that four, Calumn.'

Drinks were brought and set out in front of us in cut-crystal glasses. They were, even by Scottish standards, stoaters, suggesting Calumn was well used to the large appetites of his master and mistress. It also accounted for Rankin's complexion.

Moira took a big gulp and made sure her man did too. She turned to me. 'Now, I'm not as clever as you pair, so you'll have to spell things out slowly for me. Just what exactly are you saying, Mr Brodie?' There was ice all over her words.

I looked at Sam. She nodded. I started.

'I met Jimmie Sheridan's wife Elsie a couple of weeks back. She says Jimmie's been keeping luxurious company of late. Councillor Sheridan is – or rather was – in charge of the regeneration plan. For the last year he's been living beyond his means. New suits, fancy restaurants. Two months ago, after Alec Morton was murdered, Jimmie seemed to have won the pools. Bought himself a new car and a new flat in Hyndland and installed his lady friend.' Moira couldn't help turning her head and looking at her husband with worry frowns across her face.

'Elsie gave us names of the company Sheridan was keeping. Three were prominent. Sir Colin Maxwell, Tom Fowler . . . and Sir Kenneth Rankin.'

'That proves nothing, Brodie! Accusations from some tramp from the Gorbals!' she shot back.

'What does Sir Kenneth have to say?' I asked, looking at him. His glass was empty and he was breathing hard. His eyes were flame-throwers.

'I'll tell you what I have to say, *Major* Douglas Brodie! You'll be looking for a new job by this time tomorrow. I know the chairman of your paper's board. When you leave here, in the next few minutes, I will be calling him and telling him that if his rag prints a single mention of my name in connection with this . . . pack of lies and calumnies . . . I will sue him until I have brought the house down around him. Do I make myself clear?'

We left Rankin fuming like a volcano. His wife showed us the door. As we walked to the car, she slipped out and spoke quietly to Sam as she was about to get into the car.

'You know I have to support him.'

'Of course, Moira. I'm sorry. So sorry.'

'Look, I'll talk to him when he quietens down. How can I get in touch?'

Sam looked at me across the top of the car. I shrugged.

'We're at the Tarbet Hotel for a day or two.'

Moira nodded and we drove off.

We said nothing to each other for the first mile or so.

'He took it well, I thought.'

'Shut up, Brodie.'

I looked across. She was crying. 'Kenny and his first wife were kind to me when I lost my parents. I stayed there for a few days. What a damned mess.'

'It's going to get worse.'

FORTY-NINE

Instead of heading back down to the seafront and round the way we came, we turned up the hill and then cut across the winding roads through Glen Fruin and back down to Loch Lomond. We turned north again with the loch on our right. A wind was whipping up the water, sending waves pulsing against the shore. Dark clouds tumbled overhead, breaking up the shafts of sunlight and turning the loch into a dangerous inland sea.

We got back to the hotel, and I made a phone call to the *Gazette*. Eddie was waiting. In fact Eddie had champed through his bit.

'How the effin' hell am I supposed to run an effin' newspaper when nane of my so-called reporters are gi'ing me any effin' reports?'

'Eddie, relax. You've got a terrific front page this morning. I bet there's wailing and gnashing of teeth at the *Record* and the *Herald*.'

'Aye well, that may be so. But it disnae get you and McAllister off the hook, Brodie! I need you here. Sangster's already been shouting down the phone at me. And his boss has been shouting at *my* boss. They think we're trying to do their job. That we're holding back something. You're not, Brodie, are you?' A plaintiveness crept into his voice; the sound of a man losing his hold on the rope he was dangling from. Over the precipice.

'Am I trying to do *his* job? No thanks. Am I holding anything back? I'm telling you everything as soon as I find it, Eddie. On which point, you'd better know what we've been up to this morning . . .' I told him about the meeting with Sir Kenneth Rankin. I said my impression was that Rankin wasn't a killer and that all signs pointed to the Maxwells. But Rankin had taken the hump and there might be an uncomfortable phone call or two in the offing. There was a short silence when I finished. Then Eddie spoke, quietly and slowly.

'Oh. Christ. We. Are. Fucked.' The rope had just snapped.

'Not necessarily, Eddie. He might be bluffing.'

'Sir Kenny Rankin disnae bluff. He's wan o' the hardest wheeler-dealers in Scotland. And you've chosen to cross him. And he'll tell his pal Maxwell. Ah might as well throw masel' oot the window, right noo.'

'Eddie, before you do, can you pass the phone to McAllister?'

'He's no' here.'

'Did you give him my message yesterday?'

'He didnae show yesterday. No' that it matters any more.' His voice was lead. His career in tatters. His family already on their way to the poorhouse.

'Eddie! Is there any way I can contact Wullie? Have you tried?'

'Aye, well, we sent a telegram round to his brother, Stewart. He phoned back this morning. Says he didnae come home last night. Nor the night afore. Said it wisnae the first time, but even so. You can call him yourself, if you like. There's a call box just outside his house. Somebody will get him.' Not that he cared, now that his life was over.

I wrote down the call-box number, feeling a knot grow in my stomach. 'Anything else, Eddie? Jamie Frew? Duncan Todd? Any of my contacts?'

'What? Oh, aye. They bampots again. The Marshals. A new number. Call afore noon they said. He sounded pissed off too.

In fact you've managed to piss off everybody, Brodie. That's a rare talent you've got.'

I started with McAllister's brother. The phone rang for a while until a kid answered.

'Hello?'

'Can you run into the close and get Mr McAllister to come down?

'Aye. Nae bother, mister. Hing on.'

A few minutes later I heard the box door open and the handset get picked up. Then a man's voice: 'Hello?'

'Stewart McAllister?'

There was a hesitation. 'That's me. Is that Douglas Brodie?'

'That's right, Stewart. I've just spoken to Eddie Paton at the *Gazette*.'

'I was expecting you. Any news from Bill?' It was a smoke-roughened voice, but educated, like a teacher with a sixty-a-day habit. I guessed roll-ups were a family vice.

'Bill? Wullie? No, 'fraid not. We were hoping you'd heard something.'

'I call him Bill. Wullie, then. In the past when he's been hot on the trail of something he's been out all night. But he always tells me. This time, nothing. He's been gone two nights. And there's something else. He left a letter for you.'

'When?'

'Oh, about a week back. It says: "To be given to Douglas Brodie *in extremis*."'

'Is this *extremis*, Stewart?'

'It could be.'

'Can you open it and read it to me?'

'Well, it's up the stair and anyway, it's not something I'd do. This is for you. You need to come and get it.'

'I don't even know where Wullie lives. Where you live.'

'Govan. Summertown Road.'

I thought about it for a moment. It wouldn't take long. We

could be there in an hour. And I owed it to Wullie. Bill? He wasn't a Bill. 'Are you in this afternoon?'

Next I called the number left by the Marshals. There was the now familiar background tussle as the pub or café owner handed over the phone to the occupying force of Drummond and his boys.

'What now, Drummond?'

'You know who it is, don't you, Brodie?'

'Know who?'

'Don't play with me! It's clear from the *Gazette* this morning. You know who killed the queers. You know it wasn't me. Tell me who!'

'I don't *know* anything, Drummond. It's all guesswork at this stage.'

'Don't bloody well hold back on me, Brodie! This is my neck at stake.'

'You should have thought of that before you started your Bible campaign, Drummond. As ye sow, so shall ye reap is how it goes, I believe.'

'For pity's sake, Brodie. Think of my men.'

'So, I give you a couple of names and what do you do? Let me see. Oh yes, there's a pattern. You'd try them – without a defence lawyer, of course – find them wanting, and then punish them. That's how it goes, isn't it, Drummond?'

'I'll get him to confess. Or them. Whoever it is, I'll bring them in. Hand them over to the police.'

'Why would you start doing it legally now? No, I'll keep my suspicions to myself for the time being. Keep your head down.' I hung up.

I sat in the booth and smoked until the air grew too foul. As Sam had said this morning, what a damned mess.

She insisted on coming with me to Govan. We crossed the Clyde by the Erskine Ferry and drove along the south bank past the nodding cranes of the big yards. They said business was booming again, but I don't know where the investment money was coming from. Nor how long it woulld last. Everybody knew the shipyards were using tools handed down from the Victorians. The early Victorians. And many of them were struggling to convert back from their wartime munitions role. The British Government wasn't about to help. Apart from being broke, they were too busy dreaming up plans for the utopian welfare state to worry about Clydeside jobs.

As we turned into Govan we could see that Clydebank on the north side hadn't been the only area hit by the Luftwaffe. Govan had been a prime target. Here and there a stick of bombs had skittled a new alleyway through three or more parallel streets. Factories stood gutted with grass growing through the tumbled mounds of bricks and earth. Packs of weans ran through the bomb sites like plague dogs at the end of time.

Somertown Road scarcely lived up to its name. It was just another row of blackened tenements. We parked by the phone box outside the McAllister residence – the usual dark entry to a three-storey set of six or eight flats – and were immediately surrounded by over-excited kids all wanting to leave their grubby fingerprints on the car.

'Mister, mister, Ah'll watch your car fur ye!' 'Naw, ye'll no'. Ah'll dae it.' 'See you!'

'Why aren't you lot at school?'

A grinning ragamuffin replied, 'We've a' got impetigo, mister. The hale class.'

I looked round them all and now saw the tell-tale red blisters and dried scabs. They all looked mighty pleased with themselves.

'Well, don't you come near me or the car. Understand?'

We left them on the strict understanding that if any harm came to the Riley I would put on gloves and skelp their wee lugs till they rang. And then we'd get hold of their parents who'd no doubt add to their woes. I turned to look back as we entered the close. Four wee boys had taken up sentry duty, one at each corner of the car. They were standing rigidly to attention, ready to repulse enemies intent on nicking our wheels.

FIFTY

The brothers McAllister lived on the top floor, one of two flats sharing a toilet on the stair landing. The door opened promptly on our first knock. Stewart McAllister ushered us in.

I don't know what I'd been expecting, but it wasn't this neat and tidy house. The entrance hall led on through to a back room. We turned left and stepped into the front room and kitchen. A three-piece suite in brown corduroy overwhelmed a strongly patterned carpet, which covered most of the dark linoleum. Antimacassars perched in regimented order over both armchairs and the two segments of couch. Three ducks flew above a tiled mantelpiece and surround. Off to one side of the room ran a small scullery. A kettle rocked on a gas ring. A wireless hummed and glowed on a chest of drawers in the corner, its volume turned down low but sounding faintly of the Home Service. A cigarette smouldered in an ashtray on the coffee table in front of the settee.

Stewart was unexpected too. Stupidly, I'd pictured a more or less twin image of Wullie, a bit younger but still lanky and thin-haired with a fag hanging from his mouth. But Stewart was chunkier and his thick dark hair was Brylcreemed and parted precisely down the middle. His moustache was a thin line of careful grooming. An altogether more dapper version of his brother with worry frowns creasing his forehead.

'No news, Stewart?'

'Nothing. It's no' like him.'

Neither of us could voice the thought.

He shook himself. 'Sit down, please. The kettle's on. While I'm at it, here's the letter he left for you.'

Sam and I sat. I tore open the envelope and recognised Wullie's careful hand.

Brodie,

If you're reading this, it means I've been a stupid old sod. I should have told you everything before. I'd like to say I did it to avoid you getting a pasting too. But if I'm honest with myself I wanted one last front page to myself.

Clearly I'm in bother. Don't rush to arms. Get the polis in and follow the paper trail I've left with Stewart. Ask yourself what the three dead boys had in common besides their 'queer' ways.

Watch your back. Everyone who was getting close has ended up dead. Maybe I am too. If so, nail the bastards for me. And watch out for Stewart for me too.

One last thing. If the story comes out, make sure my name's on it with yours!

Wullie McAllister

I handed the note to Sam just as Stewart brought in a teapot and three cups. I showed it to him while we sat and supped our tea. I was silently cursing myself for my sloppy investigation of the three dead homosexuals. And now it seemed too late. Had I dropped my standards as a reporter? What happened to all my police training? Just rusty or just weary?

Stewart's face was white. 'Do you think something's happened? Something bad?'

'I don't know. He might have gone into hiding. We did, when we realised that someone was playing for keeps. I left messages for Wullie at the *Gazette*. Maybe he got one and is lying low.'

Stewart looked as convinced as I felt. I tapped the letter sitting on the table between us.

'He's right, Stewart. I've been careless. I didn't do any background checking on the three men who were murdered.'

'They were just poofs to you?' said Stewart.

'Aye. Just poofs. Did Wullie – Bill? – say anything about them?'

'Wullie's fine. It's what everybody calls him. As for the poofs, he said it was just that they were other things beside.'

'I don't suppose he said what?'

'They're only queers by night.'

'And by day?' Damn. I could see where this was going

Stewart had lit another cigarette and was hunched forward on his chair. 'Clerks.'

'All three of them?'

'No. He said the first one was, and one of the others. The one called Connie and one of the pair that were found in the People's Palace.'

'Were they, by any chance, *council* clerks?'

He nodded. 'Apparently.'

I could hardly ask it. 'Council clerks in the Planning or Finance Departments?'

'Aye, even so.'

'Bugger.'

'True, but no' just, eh?' Stewart found a half-smile.

'When did Wullie find out?'

'That's what threw him. Seems he'd been getting bits and pieces from them for a wee while, but they'd been sending them anonymously.'

'Did he say *how* he'd found out?'

'Just talk. Round about. Wullie's contacts.'

'These bits and pieces . . .?'

'You'll be wanting them?' At that he got up and walked out of the room.

I looked at Sam and shrugged apologetically.

She asked, 'Wullie never mentioned he'd been getting anonymous papers?'

'He said he'd got some, but not how. But it explains a fair bit.'

'Here you go.' Stewart came back carrying a shoebox. He handed it to me. Inside was a small folded pile of foolscap documents. They seemed to be second or third carbon copies. I flicked through them. Each was marked 'Highly confidential'. Each referred to new or draft contracts being prepared for some aspect of the regeneration project. None was signed but all had signature blocks prepared for James Sheridan and dated from last year through to three weeks ago. By themselves they didn't spell out corruption. But I wondered how many of the signed originals had been minuted in council meetings, far less promulgated in the newspapers and on public notice boards in the council offices. I also guessed the originals might have some scribbles on them. Some added points in the fair hand of Sheridan and the lucky contractor perhaps. Was this what Wullie had hoped to get his hands on through his contacts with the dead men? It would take some thorough back-tracking and research to piece it all together. I handed them to Sam and she began to sift them.

'Why didn't he show me them before, if he thought he was in danger?'

Stewart coloured. 'You ken Wullie. It was *his* scoop. His last hurrah, he said.' He pointed at the box. 'You can keep them.'

I shook my head. 'They're safer here. We're on the move just now.'

We gave him the number of the Tarbet Hotel and he saw us to the landing.

'Listen, do you think they've got him?' he asked. His face couldn't hide the fear.

'I don't know, Stewart. But if they'd harmed him we'd have heard about it by now. We soon knew about the murders. And Wullie is a wily old bird. He can take care of himself.'

It sounded weak even to me. But what else could I say? That I thought the Slattery boys had pounced again?

*

The Riley had all four wheels. We gave the lads a shilling to split between them and set off back up to Loch Lomond. The evening was gathering in as we drove along the waterside.

We couldn't face the echoing dining room and had some soup and cold chicken sent up to the room. We turned in early, Sam to the bedroom, me to the couch facing the picture window.

They came for us in the night.

FIFTY-ONE

It was no more than a movement of air. A half-perception of a presence in the room. I was instantly and fully awake. The couch I slept on faced the window. Its high back kept me hidden from the door. Everything depended on whether the intruder knew the layout of the room and whether he assumed Sam and I were sharing a bed.

There was no light from the door to the hall, which meant he'd killed the hall light. And maybe the hall porter. The thick carpet deadened the footfalls but I could sense him moving away from me towards the bedroom door. Then I heard another sound near the hall door. Two of them. The second man moved faster across the carpet to join his pal by the bedroom door. They were about to rush it. Their backs would be to me. It was my best chance.

If they had guns I was a dead man. If they had knives the odds improved. A little. I gathered myself under the quilt, gripped its heavy folds by the edge and rolled to my feet. Remembering my drill, I charged the dark figures with a banshee screech and saw them jerk and turn just before I hit them.

I drove them back against the door and tried to smother them with the quilt. They staggered and cursed in my heavy embrace but kept their feet. I flailed at where their heads should be and connected with one. He tripped and dragged the quilt with him. It uncovered the other man. He swung at me and I saw the long blade glint in the moonlight. I caught it in the fold of the material. I let it fall, dragging his knife hand downwards. I threw a punch and hit him on the side of his neck.

It drew a gasp and an oath. His hand went up to his throat and I followed up with a left which connected with his cheek-bone. With both hands I grabbed his knife arm at the wrist and pulled him towards me. As I pulled I turned and dragged his arm over my right shoulder. I wrenched downwards and heard something break in the elbow. He screamed and dropped the heavy knife.

The first man was kicking at the quilt and clambering to his feet. He saw his pal go down and lunged at me with his dagger. I threw myself backward and he missed. I fell over the other man who was kneeling, gasping, and holding his damaged arm. I rolled and sprang up. I was near the coffee table in front of the couch. I knew it held two things.

The knife man sprang at me just as I picked up the ashtray and flung its contents at his face. A cloud of ash and fag ends hit him full on. He choked and coughed and lost his bearings long enough for me to smash the bottle of Glen Grant over his head. He staggered back, clutching his face, just as the bedroom door swung open. Light filled the room.

Framed in the doorway stood Sam in her dressing gown. She was holding something in her hand. In both hands. There was an explosion and a flash and the big picture window behind me erupted in a great crescendo of splintering glass.

'Hands up! Hands up!' she shouted over the echoing report of the Webley.

Whether they were brave or stupid, the two injured men chose to ignore her, and simply made a dash for the door. I waited for the next shot and the likely chance of a bullet in the chest. Sam should know that she couldn't be sure of her aim. She was standing with the bedroom light behind her, facing into a shadowed room with three figures flailing about holding a quilt. Any one of them could be me. I hoped she still thought of me fondly. She held fire. The men tumbled out through the door.

'Sam! Give me the gun!' I ran over to her and grabbed it from her firm grip. I ran to the door and out on to the landing. It was pitch dark but I could hear the pair of them tumbling and running down the stairs. I looked over the side and saw them hit the bottom and spring out into the entrance hall, one of them carrying his arm like a wounded bird. I took aim but just then another figure stumbled into view. He was clutching his head and bent double. I pulled the gun back and ran down the stairs. The front door crashed open, then slammed shut again.

The man who'd staggered into the hall fell at my feet. It was the night porter. He was clutching his belly. His hands were leaking blood. He was moaning. The side of his face was bruised and bloody. I stopped to tend to him. I gently pulled his hands away. He'd taken a knife in the side. I couldn't tell if it had sliced anything vital. It's hard to know with a stomach wound. I jumped up and grabbed a cushion from a chair. I pushed it into his side and made him hold it in place. It might not stem it, but it should slow down the flow.

Outside, I heard car doors slam and an engine start up. I ran to the door, opened it and looked out. The car was spinning wheels on the gravel and shooting off down the drive. It had no lights on. I couldn't see number plates or even make out the type of car, but it was big and powerful.

I walked back in, gun in hand, in my pyjamas and bare feet. Sam was kneeling by the injured porter. Lights were coming on. She looked up at me.

'All you had to do was knock, Brodie.'

Rather than wait for an ambulance to drive up from Alexandria, we flung a single mattress into the back of the hotel's delivery van and laid the hall porter out on it. We tucked him in with pillows and sent him off to hospital; the second cook drove and one of the maids held the wounded man's hand. We spent the next half-hour trying to calm down a first hysterical then grovelling hotel manager and the other shocked guests. The manager was all for getting the army out or at least a couple of Black Marias up from Glasgow. We finally convinced them that it was a robbery that went wrong and it would keep till the morning. Sam's legal status and knowhow calmed them down and we retired to our shattered room. Cold air flooded in through the broken window.

'Were you aiming at it?'

'It was the only thing I could see that didn't have someone in front of it.'

'Good shot, Mrs Carnegie.'

'Was it the men who wanted to join you for a dip?'

'Yes. No question.' I bent and picked up the sharpened bayonet using my hankie. As standard Army issue it was a terrible-enough weapon, but this had been ground down on both sides to razor-sharpness. It could open a man up from navel to throat with one upward rip.

'Persistent.'

I laid it on the table and picked up the neck of the broken bottle.

'Shame about this.' A reek of good Scotch rose from an ugly stain of whisky and fag ash in the carpet.

'I hate wild parties. Come on. You can't sleep here.' She led the way into her bedroom. She went into her wardrobe and pulled out another bottle.

'For emergencies.'

'I guess this fits the bill.'

She poured two tooth glasses and we took deep drinks.

'And you can't sleep in those.' She pointed at my pale blue pyjamas, now splattered with the blood of the night porter. 'Here.' She slipped off her dressing gown and flung it to me. Her nightdress swung round her slim body as she climbed into bed. I went into the bathroom, took off my night clothes and dropped them into the bath. I put the plug in and ran cold water on them. I donned the dressing gown as well as I could and went back into the bedroom. Sam was sitting up with the bedclothes pulled round her, smoking a cigarette. Her drink was finished.

'Tight, but suits you,' she said.

I looked down. 'Especially the frills.'

'Come in.' She patted the bed.

I did as I was told and she lit another cigarette for me. We sat there like an old married couple gazing at the wall after a failed attempt at sex.

'Did you mean it?' I asked.

She smiled. 'All you had to do was knock? Och, Brodie, you know I like you. It would be hard to say no. But you know what? You're dangerous. I prefer a quiet life.'

'So says Annie Oakley.'

'And it just never seems quite the right time for us. If there is something between us, I'd like it to be right. Does that make sense?'

'Woman's sense. And I assume this isn't the right time either?'

We glanced at each other. Glanced again and smiled. Then we laughed until Sam's laugh turned to sniffs and she was shaking and sobbing. We stubbed out our fags and turned off the bedside lamps. We were left in strong moonlight. I held her to me and felt her hot tears on my skin. I kissed her eyes until they stopped weeping. Then I kissed her mouth and tasted the erotic warmth of whisky and tobacco. I felt her come alive in my arms. Her face was soft in the pale light. A smile had come back. The mood was promising until she stiffened and held herself back from me. I felt the familiar belly-ache of rejection.

'You look silly in that dressing gown, Douglas.'

I took it off.

FIFTY-TWO

The lounge looked no better in the daylight. And no warmer. The wind was whistling through the great hole in the glass. We smiled a bit more at each other and I put my arms round her once without her pulling away. But we had business to do. The grovelling manager was knocking on our door by eight o'clock. He'd roused the local constabulary at Alexandria and a pair of bobbies had driven up and were keen to inspect us and the scene of the battle. On condition that the coppers were accompanied by a gallon of tea and a mountain of toast, we invited them up.

A grey-haired sergeant and a spotty-faced constable. They were excited by the smashed window and the discarded bayonet. They kept fingering the gun Sam had used. It was a step up from dealing with Saturday-night drunks in Alexandria. We gave them a simplified version of events that fitted with the notion of a failed armed robbery. In the process, we disclosed our real names. This drew some old-fashioned looks between the coppers until Sam told them what her job was. That drew them up. They decided, in the circumstances, that it might be better to use our hotel names in their report. When they'd milked the last drop of interest and drama from the crime scene they reluctantly departed to interview the other witnesses.

Once they'd gone, we had the manager move us into an even bigger set of rooms on the top floor and ordered breakfast proper. Over fried eggs and bacon we discussed the real events of the night. We were both dark-eyed.

'Even though it wasn't Curly and Fitz I'm assuming they were Maxwell's men?' she asked.

'Unless Rankin has some heavier-handed minions than Calumn?'

She shook her head. 'I know Kenny. He might be up to his neck in all sorts of nefarious dealings but he's not a killer. I mean I've known them both – Moira and him – since I was a wee girl.'

'He's not a Henry the Second sort of boss, is he? *Will no one rid me of this turbulent reporter?* And a couple of his minions took him literally?'

'He's never surrounded himself with cutthroats.'

'Sam, if it wasn't Rankin's men, how did Maxwell know we were here? At the very least, Rankin told someone.'

She looked steadily at me. 'Or Moira.' She shook her head. 'Nooo. Too mad for words.'

'Go on thinking the unthinkable. Stewart?' He was the only other person we'd told.

'He wouldn't!'

'He might with a gun against his head. Or against his brother's.'

We let these thoughts simmer in the air for a bit. 'I'd better check in with Eddie.'

It was a bad decision.

'Morag? It's me, Brodie.'

'Oh, Douglas, I cannae talk to you the noo!' Her voice was near hysterical.

There was a clunking of the phone and a tearful half-heard conversation.

Elaine's voice took over. She sounded almost as bad. Tears in it. Had I been such a monster?

'Mr Brodie, you'd better come by.'

'What have I done?'

'It's no' you! They came in and shot at us. They actually shot at us! They made us all lie down. They hit Mr Paton, so they did. It was terrible. And there's the polis. And—'

'Elaine, Elaine! Stop! Calm down. Just tell me what happened. Who shot at you?' But I suddenly knew. The whole thing had just spiralled out of hand.

'Them Marshals. The wans who were hitting a' thae folk. The wan that talks to you. Oh, it was terrible.' I let her have a sob or two.

'Have they gone?'

'Aye. A wee while noo.' She sniffed.

'Are the police still there?'

'The polis are a' ower the place. It's bedlam here, so it is.'

'Elaine, did they hurt you? Did they hurt any of the girls? Is Morag OK?' At that moment any residual pity I'd been feeling for Drummond's lost platoon went out of the broken window in our hotel room. I wanted to break his skinny neck.

'No. No' me. But Mr Paton's been taken away to the infirmary, so he has. A' covered in blood.'

'Did they shoot him?!'

'Naw, naw. Jist hit him with an iron bar. Bad enough, mind! They had balaclavas on, so they did. It was jist like the pictures.' Elaine's voice was losing its fear. Excitement was kicking in.

'But they're gone?'

'Aye, the Marshals left when Eddie telt them what they wanted.'

'Elaine, this is important. What did they make Eddie tell them? What did he say?'

'They wanted to ken wha killed that pair o' wee poofs and Jimmie Sheridan and his girlfriend. That was the silly thing, because we a' thought it was them. The Marshals. They said it wisnae. Course they would, wouldn't they?'

'So what *did* Eddie say, Elaine?'

'Well, it was a' such a commotion, but Ah'm sure Ah heard Eddie say the word Maxwell. And the Slattery gang. But that's daft, is it no'?'

'Damn!'

'Mr Brodie, Elspeth wants a word with you. Can I put her on?'

There was a pause and a call across the desks, then Elspeth's cool voice picked up.

'Brodie? They left another quote.'

I had my pencil poised ready. 'Fire away.'

'They said: "And the priests that bare the ark of the covenant of the Lord stood firm on dry ground in the midst of Jordan, and all the Israelites passed over on dry ground, until all the people were passed clean over Jordan."'

I looked at my scribbled shorthand. 'Can you give me that again, please?'

She did and I corrected my shorthand and read the words back to her.

'What do you think they were saying, Elspeth?'

'This passage is about salvation. It's from Joshua 3, verse 17. The Ark is central to the saving of the whole of the Israeli nation. It provides safe passage.'

'When did they come out with this?'

'They held us up until they got the information they wanted from Eddie. Then their leader spouted this. I know the verse well and just took a note. But how could Eddie's information bring them salvation?'

'I don't know.' But I was beginning to worry.

'Oh, sorry, Brodie, they said one last thing as they were running out. It sounded like, "This time we are the Ark." As though they saw themselves as the saviours. Does that mean anything?'

'Nothing I can think of. Thanks, Elspeth.' And yet, and yet . . . something was nagging at me.

Her voice suddenly dipped and she pressed her mouth to the phone. 'It's the polis. They want a word.'

I heard her handing over the handset, then Duncan Todd's voice came on.

'You've excelled yersel', Brodie.'

'Me? I wasn't even there!'

'You can cause a rammy in an empty hoose, Brodie.'

'Are you with Sangster?'

'Officially on his team. Chief's orders. All hands to the pump.'

'About time, Duncan.'

His voice dropped. 'Except I'm left babysitting Sangster's yes-man, Sergeant Murdoch.'

'Divert him. Tell him to interview a wee lassie called Morag.'

'Brodie, where the hell are you? I'm pretty sure you know what's going on here. Am I right?'

'Duncan, I can't talk just now. I'll call you later. But can you check on someone for me? Wullie McAllister is missing. His brother Stewart is in danger. Can you get a couple of men round to his house to check?'

I gave him the address in Govan and hung up. I went back up to Sam to break the news that the Marshals were on the move.

'There's something about the quote and the last remark that's troubling me. *This time we are the Ark*. Oh hell!'

'What is it?'

'*Ark* Force! 154th Brigade – the Black Watch and the Argylls – was ordered to form a defensive line round Le Havre. The rest of us in the 51st Highland, including the French, were then supposed to withdraw behind Ark Force and get out through the port. But the 7th Panzers cut the line. Ark Force themselves got out through Cherbourg. About four thousand men got home to fight again. But Drummond and the others were trapped in Saint-Valery.'

'So Drummond's saying . . . ?'

'Not this time. He won't be taken again. *He's* Ark Force. Maybe even him personally, the saviour of his men.'

'He's going after Maxwell?'

'With nothing to lose. They see Maxwell as their only hope. To get him to admit to the murders.'

We gazed at each other. 'How long does it take to get to the Maxwell estate from Glasgow?'

Sam pulled out her map and showed me the route. Her finger traced the roads north out of the city to Milngavie and up the A81 to Aberfoyle. It was then B roads past Kinlochard and finally dirt tracks into the dense fastness of Loch Ard Forest itself.

'The road up to Aberfoyle is fine. About an hour and a half, I reckon. Then another half-hour along to Kinlochard on the north side of the loch. From the turn-off it's an hour to Inverard Castle. After this long summer the forest road should still be firm despite the storms on Monday.'

'They'll have stolen a car or a van. It should take them about three hours in total? Four max?'

'That's what it used to do. It's why Charlie got himself a plane to play with.'

'But will they know how to get there?'

'They could find the address at the library.'

I looked at my watch. It was eleven o'clock. 'Let's say they set out an hour ago. Allow an hour to find the route. The earliest they should get there is three o'clock. Maybe four. Then they'll need some reconnoitre time. Drummond isn't the type to just go in guns blazing. MP training. I hope.'

'What are you planning?'

'That depends.'

'On?'

'Whether there's any way we can get there before them.' I was inspecting the map. 'We'd never get round there by car in time, if we have to drive back down to Glasgow. What about these ferries?' I pointed to two marked crossings of Loch Lomond, north of us at Inveruglas and south at Inverbeg.

She shook her head. 'Foot ferries only. Do you fancy a hike?'

'Rowardennan?' I pointed at the crossing south from Inverbeg to Rowardennan. From there it was a stiff climb over the top and into Loch Ard Forest.

'We did it once. My folks and me. Met Colin and his dead

305

wife, Clarinda, for a shoot. I was fourteen. Charlie was there. Being smug. Showing off. Beating his poor horse and his dog.'

'How long did it take?'

'About two hours from Rowardennan. It's a tough climb, mind.'

'Are you saying I'm not up to it?'

'I'm saying I was fourteen the last time. And didn't smoke or drink.'

'What are we waiting for?'

FIFTY-THREE

We dressed in our tweeds and checked the Dixons. We filled the two knapsacks with spare shells, water bottles and binoculars, a slab of Dundee cake and some chocolate. I called the newsroom again. Duncan had left, so I asked Elaine to get hold of him at Central Division and tell him to get some armed coppers to Maxwell's estate. On the double. We piled everything into the Riley and drove south.

The ferry was little more than a wooden raft tethered to a landing at the prominence of Inverbeg. We parked and walked on board with our shotguns over our arm and our knapsacks firm on our backs.

We chugged across under the thoughtful gaze of a monosyllabic ferryman. The loch was mirror calm so that the inverted image of the approaching mountains seemed like a drowned landscape. It took twenty minutes to beach at a similar ramshackle jetty at Rowardennan.

The day was warm and still. By the time we reached the foothills of Ben Uird we'd opened our jackets and stowed our caps. Then the real work began. My legs protested to begin with but soon loosened up. Sam climbed steadily with as little apparent effort as the 14-year-old version. The slope steepened so that we had to work our way diagonally, twenty paces one way then back. We paused at what seemed halfway and gazed back over the shimmering water. The massive mountains rolled to the horizon on all sides, here and there interrupted by flashes and darts of rivers and lochs. We shared some chocolate and gulped from our water bottles, the cool fluid tasting of rubber and reminding me of North Africa.

The going got tough across a huge expanse of purple heather. The deep springy branches clutched at our ankles and slowed us to half-pace. After a hard hour, with the sweat pouring down my back and my thighs shrieking, the top was in sight. But as is the way with Scottish hills, it was a pitiless illusion. Another summit beckoned. Then another. At least it was cooler. A breeze rolled over the rounded top, ruffled Sam's short blonde hair and cooled her flaming cheeks.

We reached the real summit, panting, by one thirty. Behind us the loch stretched north and south, glistening dully like escaped quicksilver in the school science lab. Ben Lomond's mighty shoulders still towered above us to the north but we could turn east and look down over the Forest of Ard.

'There,' she said and pointed to a distant cleared strip by a winding river. We took out our binoculars and focused.

The clearing swam into view. At its centre was a castle, one of the fashionable Victorian fortresses with four or five floors and jutting towers. The sort that was built for vanity rather than protection and would be full of the skulls of slaughtered deer. The heating bill would be enormous.

The castle sat at a horseshoe bend of the river, with clear views up both arms of the horseshoe leading away from the buildings. Good salmon, I'd expect. A road emerged from the forest to the east of the castle and terminated in a flight of steps up to a heavy front portal. I let my glasses follow an imaginary line through the woods until they found another clearing and a glittering stretch of water which I presumed was Loch Ard itself.

To the right of the castle stood a single-storey building studded with windows and half-doors: the stables. Around the castle grounds, at the extremities of the cleared area, were outbuildings and a cottage or two. I lowered the binoculars and took a broader view, then raised them to my eyes again.

On the side closer to us, running east to west, was a long field delineated by parallel lines of markers. A pole with a drooping wind sock stood to one side. Alongside was a building with a wide front door, like a large garage. Inside, with its nose and propeller jutting out, was a small plane.

'How far?' I asked.

'About two miles. If we head down and to the left we'll pick up a path that follows the river.'

We took on more water and set off, making much faster progress on the downward slope. As the ground steepened we again had to switch to diagonal progress rather than straight. Within twenty minutes we were entering the woods, and savouring the tang of hot pine resin. Our going slowed again as we picked our way through the trees, but at least we had shade. Sam brought us out by the river and we walked with its flow towards Inverard.

We lost all sense of time and distance, and any perspective on why we were there and what we were doing. I had no plan. I just assumed something would come to me as the situation became clearer. When in doubt, press forward.

Suddenly we were in a clearing. Dead ahead was a pair of labourer's cottages. Beyond rose the bulk of the castle. We crouched down behind some rhododendrons. I peered through the bush, being careful not to disturb the shrubs.

'Now what, Davy Crockett?' asked Sam. 'I hope there's a plan?'

'That depends.'

'On?'

'Who's here. My first objective is to find McAllister. If he's alive.'

'Why would they bother to bring him here? Why would they treat him differently to Sheridan, for example? Wouldn't they just dump his body somewhere?'

I looked at her. Her pale skin face was freckling up nicely. But it wasn't the hectic flush of a woman about to confront a bunch of sadistic murderers. She looked as if she was out for a Sunday hike, maybe planning to pick a few bluebells on the way back, before sitting down to high tea.

'His body hasn't been found. They might be holding him, trying to find out what else he knows. *Who* else knows.'

As I said it, a giant pang of concern welled up for Wullie. The old rascal was hard work at times, but he was *my* old rascal. The idea had been growing since he went missing. The idea that he was dead. And we would be next if weren't careful.

'Would they bring him here?'

'It's quiet. All they had to do was wait till closing time and pick him up. They probably wouldn't have needed the chloroform. But if he's here he's not likely to be wandering about the grounds taking his ease.'

'We could knock on the front door and ask. Just like at Rankin's.'

'Kenny and Moira had old Calumn. Maxwell has at least two former hit men for a Glasgow razor king, and two thugs who tried to murder us in our beds last night.'

She nodded and her face finally began to take on the gravity of the situation.

'So, what do we do?'

'We need to get closer to find out if old Colin and Charlie boy are here and with how many of their hoodlums. There's no sign yet of the Marshals but I don't expect them to rip up here in a stolen truck shooting from the hip. They're more likely to be parked down the road somewhere and sneaking up on the place, like we are.'

'Assuming this is where they were headed.'

'We're making a lot of assumptions, aren't we?'

'We could wait for the police . . .'

'If they get the message, and if they act on it, they'll still be a couple of hours behind the Marshals.'

She raised her eyebrows, then dug into her pack and pulled out her binoculars. 'Let's see.'

We both peered through our glasses, quartering the castle,

the grounds and the outbuildings. We looked down past the castle towards the road that ran east to Kinlochard. It might as well have been a plague village in the Middle Ages. All we lacked were scavenging dogs. As if in response to my thought, barking started up in the castle.

'Tell me what you know.'

'Inverard was built about eighty years ago. A mad folly by a former Maxwell to ingratiate himself with Victoria. Everybody was doing it. So it's a kind of mock castle. Solid enough, I suppose, but not built to withstand a siege.'

'That's a relief. I've only got half a bar of chocolate left.'

'It's been a few years, but I used to run around the kitchens and cellars. Usually being chased by Charlie and his pals in a game of sadistic hide and seek.'

'Dare I ask?'

'Oh, you know, if you get caught you got Chinese burns or your pigtails pulled.'

'You'd look cute in pigtails.'

'As a matter of fact, I did.'

'So there's a lower ground area. Kitchens and storerooms. Ground floor?'

'Big baronial hall. Lots of shields, claymores, flags . . .'

'Antlers?'

'Dozens. Great sweeping staircase up to umpteen draughty bedrooms and freezing bathrooms. The place is a maze.'

'The buildings alongside the castle?'

'Stables. Cars and a few horses now. Tack room. Smithy. The usual.'

'How many loyal retainers would you guess?'

'Clarinda had a full staff upstairs and down. But since she died, they seemed to let everything and everybody go. Charlie's never around. As I said, he's got his own wee plane. Flies to London or over to France again now the war's over. I imagine Colin still keeps a butler, a housekeeper, a cook, a maid or two. Four at least?'

'At least.'

'And of course when Charlie's in residence, his killing crew.'

I put my glasses away and stood up. 'Come on. We need to get closer. But let's take precautions.'

I dug into my jacket pockets and pulled out two cartridges. Sam did the same. We slid them into the breeches of our shotguns but kept them broken. We didn't want accidents as we manoeuvred. We kept low and followed the riverbank round. As we snaked our way towards the castle, I couldn't help feeling a sense of déjà vu. I was heading towards a rendezvous with a pair of Slattery hoods with a gun in my hands.

FIFTY-FOUR

The riverbank had eroded in the horseshoe bend as the winter's melt had tunnelled away at it. We were able to walk upright or bent over on the shingle without being seen from the castle. I stuck my head up carefully above the grass verge to get my bearings until we arrived opposite the rear of the castle with the stable block to our left. Between us and the buildings was about a hundred yards of open ground. Not the ideal set-up for a daylight attack. The sort of situation I was trained to avoid unless you had surprise or a diversion on your side. At least there was no barbed wire or mines, so far as I could tell.

Sam was at last looking worried. 'What do we do now?' she whispered.

'Wait. We need something to happen.'

'That's it? That's your plan?'

'If nothing happens then we'll make something happen. We've got six hours of daylight.'

'What if someone looks over and finds us?'

'I'll be even more unhappy I didn't bring my rods with me.'

We hunkered down with our backs to the crumbling bank and wished we could smoke. We closed our Dixons but left the safety catches on.

I gazed at the burbling river. It was too exposed to make a good fishing spot. Too open. I'd have chosen downstream about two hundred yards where the forest started and where the water would be dappled and shaded. There would be flies dancing in columns near the trees, whirling in the light, dropping to the surface and tantalising the fish. A chance for Jamie Frew and me to settle which fly worked best.

My daydreams were shattered by the sound of a car. Its engine was racing towards us from the forest road. I took the chance and peeked but was just in time to see it disappear behind the castle. It couldn't have been the Marshals. There were no sounds of shots. It gave us an opening. Was it an adequate diversion? Would there be anyone keeping an eye from the rear windows?

'Quick, give me a leg-up.'

Game girl that she was, Sam never hesitated. She pushed her back against the bank, locked her legs and laced her fingers together in a cup. I took one last peek, then pushed my shotgun on to the bank, clasped her shoulders and put one foot in her cupped hands. I pushed up as best I could without putting too much weight through her slim frame. I scrambled on to the bank, lay down, took her gun, and gave her my hand. I yanked her up, thankful she was such a slight load. She got on her knees, then her feet. We grabbed our guns and ran for the stable blocks to the left of the whitewashed edifice. We crashed against the wall of the stables and crouched there panting, waiting to be discovered.

We could hear a door bang and voices, but then all was still. No running feet. To our left was a stable door, half open at the top. I crept over and keeked in. There was a strong smell of horse and straw and a bit of snuffling and hoof-tapping, but otherwise the stables seemed deserted of humans. I leaned in and opened the bottom half of the door. I signalled to Sam and we slid into the warm dark. We moved through the building and found five horses in their individual stalls. Their tack was polished and neatly hung by each stall. The horses seemed healthy and not nervy, which showed good care and grooming. We steered our way through to the front of the stables and looked out on to the gravel and grass in front of the castle entrance. A car was parked at a cavalier angle as though whoever had driven up in it had abandoned it in a hurry.

Sam gasped, 'That's Kenny Rankin's car!'

She'd barely uttered it when there was more commotion from the main entrance. Then there were running feet. We dipped down below the window just as the running feet sprinted round the corner and headed our way. Did they know we were here? How? There were two or three sets by the sound of it. We could only wait and be ready for them. I undid the safety lock on the Dixon. Sam did the same.

The running feet went past our window and we heard a door thud open and shut at the other end of the building. The car garage end. Things went quiet. I raised my head cautiously and looked out. A small dust cloud was settling in the wake of the runners. I slid down and sat with Sam.

I whispered, 'Rankin has driven up with news. Whatever it was has sent them running. Three men? Yes?' She nodded. '. . . have taken up position in the garage. An ambush? Are they looking for us? Or have they heard about Drummond and his crew? How could they?'

Sam shrugged and mouthed: *What do we do?* I put my finger to my lips and signalled wait.

And then we waited.

I closed my eyes and pictured the layout of the estate. If I were Drummond, how would I mount the attack? Where would I come from? Would I assume I had surprise on my side? The castle sat out in the open with a clear field of fire all round. They could do as we did and get close via the riverbank. Or they could wait till it was dark. Alternatively there was the suicide route: straight up the drive in whatever vehicle they'd stolen, hanging out of the windows or standing on the door sills like G-Men, guns blazing. It seemed unlikely even for a bunch of desperate men. Even for a bunch of military police who'd forgotten all their tactical infantry training.

Sam was tugging at my sleeve. She pointed at a door with a big padlock on it. It was at the end of the stalls. Vertical wood slats with an inch gap. I assumed it was just a storeroom. If so, it had rats. Big rats. Rats that made a groaning sound. I moved over and tried to see in through the slats. Too dark. I pressed my ear to the wood. The sounds stopped. I inspected the lock; a simple big padlock controlling a sliding bolt. I looked around. On the wall above the tack bench was a hook with several keys on it. I tried three before I found the one. I undid the padlock and let it hang from its hasp. I slid the bolt across and eased the heavy door back. The hinges were well oiled and cared for but there was still a creak that seemed to echo all round the stable block.

It was lighter now inside but there was a sour smell. I let my eyes get used to the dim light and finally saw him. A body piled on top of some empty sacks. There was rope round the ankles and wrists. The head lolled away from me, but I'd seen that profile too many times in too many bars not to know it.

'Wullie? Can you hear me?'

There was no answer. I moved closer and clasped his shoulder. He flinched and turned his face to me. It was no wonder he flinched. His face was a mass of congealed blood. The eyes flickered but there was no recognition.

'Wullie. It's Brodie. I've warned you before about mixing your drinks.'

There was no answering smile. No sarcastic retort. Sam was at my shoulder.

'Let's get him out of here,' she said.

We hauled away at him, me carrying his head and shoulders and Sam his feet. We got him into the comparative daylight of the main stable and tenderly laid him on a pile of straw. The full extent of his injuries became clear. His long fine nose was angled cruelly to one side. His set of false top teeth were missing and the bottom ones were bloody. One eye was ballooned and lacerated. As we'd moved him he'd moaned, and I found blue and tender areas on his chest when

I undid his shirt. Some ribs had been caved in. They'd given him a real kicking.

Sam found the tap and a bowl. She tore a bit off his gory shirt and dabbed the blood out of his eyes. I held his battered head while she tried to get him to take some water. The best she could achieve was moistening his cracked and broken lips. For a moment his eyes opened and cleared. There was a puzzled look in them. His tongue licked across his lips and he tried to speak. A gurgle came out, and then he lapsed into unconsciousness.

'Well, isn't this a touching sight.'

Sam and I whirled round and sprang to our feet. Standing framed at the open window, a shotgun pointing squarely at us, was Charlie Maxwell.

FIFTY-FIVE

glanced over at our own guns. They were carefully stood upright about ten feet away, against the storeroom door.

'Have a go, Brodie. I prefer a moving target.' His silky drawl made me tense up, ready to call his bluff. Maxwell nodded to someone outside. The front door was pulled open and Curly walked in with a big grin on his face.

'Aye, huv a go, Brodie. It would be a real pleasure.'

Sam was on her feet. 'Charlie, you're such an idiot! What the hell do you think you're doing?' She'd taken two angry paces forward when Curly hit her with the stock of his shotgun. It took her on the shoulder and she was flung back and into me. We both stumbled back. I put myself between her and Curly.

'Aye, missy. We've got unfinished business, have we no'?'

'Enough!' said Maxwell.

'Get that bloody gorilla out of my sight, Maxwell!' she shouted, rubbing her arm and shoulder. 'He should have a muzzle!'

The gorilla just grinned and stepped forward, raising his gun again like a club.

I pushed her right behind me. 'How's the foot, Hopalong?' I could have asked about his face too. I was pleased to see it still bore the marks of the explosion from our last encounter. Red splotches and white scars.

The grin left him. He swung his shotgun down and aimed at my gut.

Maxwell raised his arm. 'I said, enough! You'll have your chance soon enough.'

The gorilla got the message and pulled back, reluctantly. Revenge postponed.

'How did you and Hopalong meet, Maxwell? Irresistible attraction? Like drawn to like?'

Maxwell's face turned sour. 'We're going to enjoy getting rid of you, Brodie. For my own sake and for Dermot Slattery.'

'Slattery!'

Maxwell grinned. 'I thought you'd like to know what you're going to die for. Dermot and I used to do some business together. Import, export, you might say. You disrupted a nice little income flow.'

Aaah, the pieces were falling into place. 'Your wee plane? Trips to France? Export what? Kippers? Bring back cocaine?'

Sam gasped. 'My God, Charlie. I knew you were rotten, but drug-running!'

'Oh spare me, little Miss Prim and Proper, Miss law-abiding, boring, Samantha Campbell, *LL B*. I don't give a damn what you think. You've been a bloody nuisance all your life and here you are—'

'—being a bloody nuisance again.' The woman's voice came from the window. The light from behind the head obscured the features. But it was a very recognisable voice. I'd heard it only yesterday.

'You cow!' said Sam to one of her oldest friends.

The figure disappeared from the window and then reappeared at the door. Moira Rankin sauntered in, cigarette in hand, dressed like us for the country in tweed skirt and jacket. But she'd added pearls. She took a careful drag on her fag and blew the smoke towards us.

'If you like. But Charlie's right. You have been such a nuisance, Samantha. You never could leave well enough alone, could you?'

'You told this – this scum! – that we were at the Tarbet, didn't you?'

'Silly you. Pity you woke.'

'Have you gone stark, staring, raving mad, Moira? You arranged to have me killed? We grew up together!'

Moira's face contorted. 'And you know something, Samantha Campbell? I always hated you. Charlie's right. Such a little goody two-shoes. All that high moral tone over Kenny Rankin and me. No wonder you don't have a man.'

Maxwell sniggered.

Sam turned to him and deployed her cool lawyer tones. 'It didn't seem to put Charlie here off. Did it, Charles? Always trying to get into my knickers, weren't you? Poor simple Charlie.'

There was a resounding boom and a flash from Maxwell's shotgun. Pellets smashed into the plaster ceiling and showered us all with dust. When the ringing in our ears stopped we could hear Maxwell screaming at Sam: 'Any more from you, bitch, and you'll get the second barrel!'

Even Moira had had the insouciance shocked out of her. 'For God's sake, Charlie! Control yourself. We don't have time for all this.'

'Expecting visitors, Maxwell?' I asked.

'Shut up, Brodie. Just shut the fuck up.'

'You warned him?' I asked Lady Rankin. 'How did you find out?'

She blew a plume at me. 'I rang up your newsroom. So obliging. Morag the name? Very chatty. I said I was Samantha here.'

'You twisted, evil . . . cow!' exclaimed Sam.

I felt my anger rising instantly to boiling point. 'What did you tell the poor girl?' I demanded.

'That you'd been attacked last night. But then I found she already knew. You'd spoken to her this morning. So I told her you'd been very brave and hadn't mentioned your injury. That you'd taken a turn for the worse. That you, my lover, Douglas Brodie, had died. I even managed a little weep.'

'You malicious bitch! Why? What the hell did you say that for? Pure bloody spite?' I shouted.

She pouted prettily. 'A little. Such fun. But no. I wanted to find out what was happening. Stir things up a bit. Like poking an ants' nest. Your common little girlfriend told me – tearfully – that those bloody pests, the Marshals, had been given Charlie's name.' She paused and checked her watch. 'We expect them any time now. One of our chaps down at the Lochard turn-off just phoned.'

'Well, just so you know, the police are on their way too.'

That shook them. They glanced at each other. Charlie stiffened, then relaxed.

'It's not a problem, Moira. They'll get here and find it's all over. These bloody outlaws dead, and this pair caught in the crossfire. Such a tragedy.'

'Everything cleared away, Maxwell. All neat and tidy. Including two councillors. Why did you kill them?'

'One wanted out and was threatening to tell everything. The other got greedy, and careless. Flashing it about.'

'And three young men?'

'They were very naughty boys. Sheridan told me. He got suspicious that they were passing things to him.' He nodded at Wullie's prone body.

As if on cue, Wullie groaned. I moved over to kneel by his side. His face was grey where it wasn't white. A trickle of spit with flecks of blood oozed from his mouth. I'd seen enough battle wounds to know he was in deep shock. There was no saying what internal damage he was suffering from the cracked ribs. But the worst possibility was bleeding in the brain from the blows to his head.

'He's dying. He needs a hospital right now!'

Maxwell spat, 'Fat chance, Brodie. It was his bloody digging around that caused all this. You think I give a shit what happens to this bloody hack now? You three are just loose ends we're about to tidy up.' He'd come through the door and was standing alongside Moira. She turned and tapped his cheek playfully.

'Just ignore them for a bit, darling. We really do need to get ready.'

Sam's mouth was open. 'Darling? Don't tell me? Don't tell me you and Charlie are . . .?'

'Lovers? Why, yes, Samantha. You are slow today. For quite a while now.' She smiled and Charlie looked, well, like a Charlie.

'One title not enough for you, Moira? Or has Kenny run out of money?'

'Something like that. Have you any idea how dreary Helensburgh is?'

'Christ! I don't who I feel sorry for the most,' said Sam.

Moira stepped forward and struck Sam across the mouth. 'I've been wanting to do that for years, you stuck-up little bitch!'

Sam threw herself at her tormentor and bundled her to the floor. Moira screamed as Sam grabbed her finely coiffed mane with her left hand and started slapping her with the other.

'Stuck up, am I, Moira? We'll see how stuck up I am!'

Maxwell moved to hit her with the stock of his shotgun and I kicked out, smashing him against the wall. He bounced back, the gun coming up, aiming for my chest. I dropped on top of the struggling women. I made sure Moira was well tangled up in our embrace. I shouted at Charlie, 'Shoot and you'll hit your lover!'

Maxwell jerked his barrel up in frustration. I held on tight to both women and said in Sam's ear, 'Sam, get up slowly but keep her between you and Charlie.'

I helped her haul up the sobbing, screeching Moira, using her body as a shield. 'Take it easy, Maxwell! We'll let her go!'

Maxwell stood back, chest heaving, as Moira struggled in our embrace. Her smart locks were a tangled knot of hair and straw. Her eyes were wide and shocked. Her cheeks bore Sam's hand prints in red. One by one, her pearls began dropping to the floor.

I couldn't resist. 'Before swine, eh, Maxwell?'

Moira tore herself free. She wrenched the remaining pearls from her neck and flung them at me. She screamed, 'Give me the gun, Charlie. Give me the bloody gun!'

Maxwell looked uncertain and then resolute. He began to hand over the shotgun when a shout went up from outside. Then the rumble of a truck could be heard coming from the forest road.

'That will be the cavalry, I expect,' I said to anyone who was listening. But it didn't sound like a police car.

Charlie whirled. 'Get them in there!' he shouted at Curly and pointed towards the storeroom where Wullie had been held. He ran over and grabbed our Dixons and threw them on the floor by the window. I winced at the sacrilege. Curly ushered us towards the storeroom with a few blows from his shotgun. He shoved us in. Sam fell forward on to her knees and he slammed the door behind us. I heard the bolt go in, and then he fumbled at the padlock and locked it. Maxwell was shouting at him: 'Move, move! Get to the window! Moira, get down!'

I pressed my face against the slats in the door and saw Maxwell kick and bar the outside door. Then he took up a kneeling position at one window, Curly at another. Moira moved back into the room away from the door. With the three other men at the far end of the stables, nearest the road, and with Curly and Maxwell by these windows, they had a killing arc of fire covering the front of the castle.

The sound of the approaching truck grew loud. Against all my predictions, Drummond had hoped for surprise and speed to be his best allies. He had no idea that he'd lost all advantage with one phone call from the lodge at the turn-off to the castle. And speed was no answer to a well-set ambush. Through the window I caught a glimpse of a lorry racing past. It had a cabin, and side panels that could be dropped down. There were figures in the cabin and in the back of the truck. It swept past and I heard it grinding to a halt. There were shouted voices and then the sound of men running on gravel.

Maxwell's voice rang out. 'Fire! Fire!' His own shotgun jerked against his shoulder. Curly's did too. They used both barrels, pausing to reload fast. All that training in the butts against unarmed grouse was paying off. But the noise that shocked me came from further away, from the far end of the building. I'd recognise the British Sten gun anywhere. Two of them. Each with a magazine of 32 rounds firing 9-mm cartridges. The last time I'd heard that metallic clatter was in a charge I'd led on a German dugout on the east bank of the Rhine.

I thought I could make out return fire coming from the truck. But unless they'd secured new weapons since my visit to their den, all the Marshals had were shotguns and revolvers. They were in an ambush and completely outgunned. Their answering volleys were sporadic as they tried to reload. I could hear the short bark of their handguns. They might as well have used pea-shooters against the well-defended machine gunners in the stables. Soon there was only one gun in action outside. The forlorn crack, crack of a revolver. Meanwhile Curly and Maxwell were steadily ejecting their two spent cartridges, reloading, aiming and blasting away.

From the other end of the building, there were pauses as the shooters changed magazines, then the withering fire resumed. There seemed to be no response from the lone pistol. Then suddenly a couple of shots were fired in quick succession. I could imagine the lone gunman hiding behind the truck while the pellets and Sten rounds blasted past him. Then he'd reload, pop up and fire off an aimless round or two in the direction of the stables. It was hopeless. Finally and inevitably there came a time when there was no response. The stables were filled with the reek of cordite.

Through the gloom of the storeroom I looked over at Sam. She understood as well as anyone what had happened. Her hand was at her mouth. She would be thinking what I was thinking: we'd be next. Maxwell and his lover would want no witnesses.

I watched Maxwell peer out of the window, then motion to Curly to open the door. Curly pulled it wide and stepped outside. My ears were still ringing with the sounds of the gunshots in the closed space.

'It's clear, boss.'

Charlie got up and strode to the door. He walked out into the sunshine of the afternoon and I heard gravel crunch as the two men walked forward. There were shouts between Charlie, Curly and his other men. I heard them running and then there was one new shot from a revolver, followed by shouts and expletives. Someone was still alive. I peered out at Moira. She seemed transfixed by what had just happened. She moved tentatively towards the door, fumbled for a cigarette and lit it. I looked at the storeroom hinges round the door. They looked solid enough, but having undone the padlock and the bolt earlier, I knew there were only half a dozen screws holding on the plate.

We had one shot at this.

FIFTY-SIX

motioned Sam back and to one side. I flexed the shoulder muscles I'd built up at swimming. I walked back as far as I could from the door, and took a run. I smashed the lock side of the door with my shoulder. It burst open in a satisfying crash. I followed through with a rolling dive across the room to the two shotguns lying in the dust beneath the window. Moira yelped and ran out of the door. I grabbed a Dixon and put the gun to my shoulder. I peered out of the window down the sights.

She was scampering across the gravel towards the chaotic scenes in front of the castle. I tracked her as she ran, fingering my trigger. It would be just like a taking down a tin duck in a fairground shooting gallery. But I couldn't shoot a woman in the back, even a murderous, faithless bitch like her. Then she was entering the tableau in front of the castle.

Maxwell and Curly were kneeling halfway between the stables and the truck with their shotguns at their shoulders. To their left, their three cronies – Fitz and the two night-time attackers – were scuttling forward, weapons up. One of them had a bandaged head. The other had his arm in a sling and a Sten gun in his left. Accuracy was never the main requirement of a Sten; spraying bullets around was what it did best, even one-handed. Fitz cradled the second Sten. In front of them the truck was slewed across the drive some twenty yards from the wide set of steps leading up to the massive front door. The truck door nearest us hung open. A man lay tumbled at the side. Two others hung over the wooden sides of the truck. Blood dripped from their languid bodies. Their weapons lay in the darkened dust below them. A fourth man sprawled by the rear wheel, still clutching his pistol. None had red hair.

Suddenly Fitz's Sten erupted and a fusillade of bullets sprayed the truck, uselessly whipping the two dangling bodies. There was no answering fire.

'Hold up!' called Maxwell and raised his arm. Cautiously he got to his feet. The five men moved forward in a slow arc. Moira was about ten yards behind them, turning back to see what I was up to but fearful of breaking the concentration of the men in front of her. I saw a flicker from the far side of the cabin of the truck. An arm came up over its roof, then a red head. Drummond let loose a quick shot from his gun. The man with the bandaged head went down with a groan and lay clutching at his side. His shotgun spilled in the dust. Moira screamed and dropped on to her hands and knees. The rest dived flat and began shooting.

It was time to even things up.

In my youth if you'd asked could I ever shoot a man in the back, I'd have vehemently condemned such a notion. It was unthinkable, cowardly. Six years of warfare brings a new perspective. It distils the moral dilemma to the simple matter of kill or be killed. Anyway, the man with the Sten was side on to me. He was also the man who'd come to knife Sam and me in our bed. I took careful aim and squeezed the trigger. It caught him in the right ear and cuffed him over in a spray of blood. His gun stuttered with one last salvo. He dropped like a stone and lay still. That left Maxwell, Curly and Fitz as dangers. The man wounded by Drummond and writhing in the dust had his own priorities.

I trained my gun on Fitz and fired just as he twisted and rolled on the ground. If I hit him, it wasn't enough to stop him. He kept rolling and got behind a dead Marshal. I dropped my empty Dixon and grabbed the loaded one. It gave Maxwell enough time to get to his feet and sprint towards the shelter of the castle steps and stone balustrade. Curly too was up and running. For a moment, Moira got in my line of fire and I held back. Old morals die hard. Curly must have sensed my weakness. He grabbed her and held her in front of him as a shield. He hauled her back towards the steps, with frequent backward glances at the cabin of the truck.

I turned back to Fitz and saw his Sten come up. I ducked just as the bullets blasted through the window. I waited for a second rip but it didn't come. I scuttled over to the door to get a new angle. Fitz was lying on the ground fumbling with a new clip. I had the brief drop on him. I settled my aim, took a slow breath and squeezed. The shot seemed to fall short. Dust blossomed in front of his head. As the cloud settled I could make out Fitz doubled up, holding his bloody face. He choked and spat and got to his knees. His face was a torn mass of blood. I gave him the second barrel full in the chest. He was lifted backwards and down, and stopped moving.

For a long moment there was silence, then two heads appeared over the stone wall. Curly and Maxwell let fly at the stable window and door. Pellets peppered the walls behind me and thudded into the wood of the door. I turned to see Sam crawling towards me, hauling her cartridge bag behind her. She nestled below the window and, with trained fingers, broke open the spent Dixon, ejected the shells and refilled from the plentiful supply in her pack. She held out the gun to me. I dived across and exchanged my empty for it. Quickly, Sam broke open the emptied Dixon and began to slot cartridges into it.

We sat with our backs to the wall, shoulders touching, and got our breath back. All the time I was listening. Then I heard banging and shouting. I took a peek. One of the men was hammering on the castle door with the butt of his shotgun. He was lying low, shielded by the wall. I stood up to aim higher. I let loose. All I achieved was to pepper the wall and door. The door eased open a fraction and Maxwell, Moira and Curly slipped inside, ducking low. The door was slammed shut and silence fell again. I took a chance.

'Drummond! Drummond! It's Brodie! We're in the stables!'

There was no answer for a few seconds. Then I saw a pair of legs running back from the truck cabin towards the tail. A moment later, Drummond's red head peered round the back of the truck. It gave him protection from any shots from the castle window. He waved his pistol at me. He stood up and looked round at the carnage. His four men lay dead and bleeding around him. He clambered into the back of the truck and hauled in the two men hanging over the side. He jumped back down and stooped to check the two lying on the ground. When he stood up, his face was a mask of grief. Then it turned to wrath.

The enemy he'd wounded was still groaning and clutching at his guts. Drummond looked up at the castle windows, then took two swift steps over to the man, gripped his gun in both hands and pointed it downwards. I couldn't have stopped him, even if I'd wanted to. Slowly and deliberately he pulled the trigger. There was a bang and the man twitched once before his limbs unfolded and settled in death's repose. The bullet tore a hole through his face. Blood seeped from under his head. Drummond looked towards me and smiled out of his fleshless skull. The Grim Reaper.

'Come out, Brodie! We've got work to do!' Drummond began darting from body to body, collecting discarded weapons.

I stood up at the window, wary of shots from the castle windows. At my feet, Sam tugged my trousers.

'You're not going out there, are you?'

'We can't just skulk here.'

'Oh yes we bloody can!'

'Sam, this needs finishing.'

'I thought you'd had enough killing?'

'I thought you said I'm not the type to sit back and let others fight my battles? What was it you said? If *I* don't, who will? If *we* don't?' Not that I was rationalising this. I was in a familiar place; gun in hand and enemy to the fore. My head filled with nothing but the combat layout and the options for attack.

She looked up at me for a long speculative second, then scrambled to her feet clutching her shotgun.

'Fine. Come on.' And she headed for the door.

My jaw dropped. She would have put any man in my company to shame. I ran and got ahead of her just before the door. I filled my one empty chamber and stuffed a handful of cartridges in my pocket. I peered out gingerly, trying to see if Maxwell was waiting for us. The curtains had been partially drawn and the reflection obscured what might be going on behind the big glass window.

'Count of three, then run to the back of the truck alongside me. OK?'

She nodded.

'One, two, three.' I sprinted forward, hearing her small feet pattering beside me and making sure I was always between her and the castle windows.

We slammed against the side and edged our way round to the back of the truck. Drummond was checking his loot. He'd got the tailgate down and had laid out the two Stens, three shotguns and two Enfield revolvers on the bare boards. He was clumsily loading the two handguns from a pile of assorted bullets and cartridges. I'd forgotten about his missing fingers. I could see now the revolvers were Enfield No. 2 Mk 1s, fitted for a .38 lead slug. He held each gun under his right armpit and fed the shells in with his better left hand.

'Help yourself, Brodie.' A mad grin split his face.

I hefted the Sten but I'd never liked the damned things. Even barn doors were safe from them. Unless they were kept immaculately clean and serviced they'd jam. One Sten was empty and there was no sign of spare clips. None of the shotguns was a match for my Dixon and I had my own Webley. It fired .455 bullets and had greater stopping power than the Enfields. I took it out from my waistband and checked the chambers. Fully loaded. I slid the cold barrel back down my waistband. Drummond did the same with one Enfield. He picked up the second and squinted down the barrel.

'What's your plan, Drummond? Or were you going to try a full frontal assault again?' It was no time for sarcasm but I couldn't resist.

'I'm just a junior officer, *Major* Brodie. You went to Staff College. What do you suggest?'

'Does this thing still work?' I thumped the wood planks of the truck. 'Do you need to turn a handle?'

He looked at me. 'You're not running away now, are you?'

'No, I'm bloody not. If I got in the cab would I get the engine running or do you need to wind the bugger up?'

'It's fine. One of the boys is – was – a mechanic. Sweet as a pea.'

'OK, here's what we do.'

We lifted Drummond's men down from the truck and laid them gently on the ground. Sam took up position behind the truck holding a Dixon in white knuckles. I took the other Dixon in my left hand and the Webley in my right. I turned to Drummond. 'Ready?'

He nodded.

'Go!'

Drummond and I – armed to the teeth – darted round both sides of the truck, me to the left, him to the right. Both doors hung open and gave us some cover, but as we dived into the cab, I heard a bang and the windscreen exploded. Pellets smashed into my passenger side door. Then both Drummond and I were lying heaving on the bench seat. Drummond began fiddling with the gears and pedals. He tried the key. The truck gave a rumble and stopped. He pulled out the choke.

'Don't flood it!' I hissed.

He shot me a glance and tried again. It coughed and spluttered and stopped. He waited an endless few seconds. He tried again. The engine fired and coughed, died, then picked up again. Drummond got his foot on the accelerator and the engine roared. The whole cabin shook with the vibrations. We looked at each other from our horizontal positions. Ahead of us were the castle steps, a wide flight of about a dozen broad treads, then a flat terrace up to the huge wood portals. It was a ridiculous double gamble. First that the truck would be able to bounce up the steps without simply smashing into them and breaking its front axle. Second that we'd still have enough momentum to crash through the doors. If they were six inches thick and barred, the three-foot length of truck bonnet would end up in our laps.

'Let's go!' I shouted.

I sat up, pistol in hand and started firing at the broken window. Drummond popped up, flung the truck into gear, revved it up to a scream, eased the clutch out until it was straining, then let the brake off. We shot forward, Drummond wrenching the wheel round to line up straight at the steps. I got three shots off without a return of fire, then we were hitting the first step with a bang. The nose came up and we were pounding and bouncing up the flight. We hit the top and the nose dropped. I heard the chassis grind on the top step and then we were flying at the door.

'You bastaaaards!' Drummond shrieked as we hit. The long bonnet hit the doors smack in the centre. They sundered in a spray of wood and metal. The big doors were flung back, flailing on their hinges, and we crashed into the hall of the castle. The noise was deafening and I was flung against the dashboard, losing my pistol in the process. Drummond slammed on the brakes and we skidded across the tiled floor, sweeping aside a magnificent wooden table and its fine porcelain bowl of autumn flowers.

We stopped and the engine stalled. For a long moment we sat there as silence settled around us. Then a shotgun blast raked Drummond's door.

'This side, man. Out this side!' I shouted. I rummaged at my feet, got my Webley, grabbed my Dixon and flung the door open. As I slid out, Drummond was lurching across the seat. I grabbed his arm – it was like grabbing a piston – and drew him across. His face was running red, whether from the collision with the door or the gunshot. 'You're hit!'

'I'm fine.' He wiped the blood off with his sleeve. His face was lacerated down one side, like a rare steak.

Keeping the big wheel in front of me I knelt and peered under the truck. Already a pool of oil was forming. I was in time to see figures scampering away through a far door. I jumped up on the running board and got a shot off. Too late. Sam came charging through the doorway and ran over to us. Her face was flushed.

'The housekeeper's going to be gie upset. Did you run them over?'

'They went that away.' I pointed at the doorway on the far side of the hall.

'It goes down to the kitchens. There's a maze of corridors down there.'

'Damn.' It felt like Caen all over again. An enemy in retreat but fighting dirty and making us pay for every inch. Clearing broken buildings sprinkled with booby traps. Stepping round corners expecting an ambush at every turn. I turned to Drummond. He wasn't there. Next thing, I saw him running towards the doorway where Maxwell had gone.

'Drummond! Wait!'

He didn't.

FIFTY-SEVEN

The hall was a grand affair. Or had been, until we'd added a new centrepiece. We were parked in front of a great sweep of stairs. Above us ran a balcony. The walls were lined with flags and old claymores and heads of slaughtered stags. Portraits of former Maxwells in flamboyant robes and doubtful tartans frowned down at us for sullying their ancestral hall. We'd made a serious dent in the massive square table that had graced the hall and knocked it on to its side. It now sat across one corner: a nice ambush spot with a good sightline of the gaping front door.

'There's your spot, Sam. Shoot anything that looks like a villain.'

'I hope it's Moira,' she said with grim certainty.

There came two shots from the direction taken by Drummond. I gave Sam my Dixon. This was going to be close-quarter work. I reloaded the Webley and left her to man the barrier. I ran round the truck towards the gunfire.

Sam had been right. The door led nowhere except to a stone stairwell going down. I began to spiral my way down. Near the bottom, I could see light. I keeked round the corner and saw Drummond kneeling ahead of me at a junction of two corridors. He fired again, then turned to see me coming towards him. His manic grin turned his bloodied face into a Halloween mask of Auld Nick.

I got to his side. I looked round the corner and was just in time to see the flash of a shotgun. The pellets screamed past me at waist height. They'd been expecting Drummond's head. My quick look told me we were in a main corridor with cross-branches left and right. A dozen ambush spots. I told Drummond what we were about to do. He nodded. For a fleeting second I wondered how far I could trust this lunatic. The previous times I'd done this was with men I'd personally trained and knew I could rely on. But I also knew that we had to attack or we'd lose momentum.

I nodded at Drummond then I charged out from my cover. I hit the far wall and kept running along the right-hand side. Drummond stayed where he was but blasting down the left-hand side to keep the enemy's heads down. The sound of his Webley was like thunder going off in the echoing space. I made it, gasping, to the next crossing and flung myself into cover. We had to keep going, keep attacking. I moved my Webley into my left hand and tried not to worry about the recoil.

'Now!' I leaned out and got off a couple of shots. No chance of hitting anyone but the noise and ricochets were enough to keep Maxwell pinned down. Drummond took his chance and ran forward, screaming his new battle cry – 'Bastards!' – while firing away. The passing shots ripped the air near my head and made me hope he'd been aiming at Maxwell. He slammed into the wall of the cross corridor opposite me. We stood, backs against the wall, panting and staring at each other. I fumbled two shells into my Webley. Drummond swapped guns.

'Again?' I called, conscious of shouting above the ringing in my ears.

He nodded and got to his knees, facing forward, ready to cover me. I steeled myself to make a break – when the lights went out.

'Shit!' I said. 'Wait!' I weighed up the situation. There was one dim light back at the stairwell. In front of us was pitch dark. If I ran forward I'd be perfectly silhouetted. But this side corridor had to lead somewhere. A faint light stole round a distant corner.

'Drummond, this way,' I hissed. There was a brief moment of quiet then a figure dashed across the open corridor. A gun went off up ahead and we heard the ricochet of a bullet whining past. Without another word I darted off down the side corridor. Drummond came panting at my back. We reached the corner and peered round. Ahead, the narrow walls opened up into a room. The kitchen? A light flickered and kept flickering. A fire? I began creeping forward, ready to dive at any moment.

We got to the end of the corridor. I could see into the big kitchen. A pot was boiling on the range. The fire underneath threw its glittering glare round the room leaving shadowy corners and hidden gullies. It seemed deserted but there were too many hiding places to be certain. Drummond came up alongside me and flattened himself against the right-hand wall. Together we stuck our heads round. All was quiet. On the far side a door gaped open. Had they fled through it? We edged forward, guns at the ready.

I saw or heard a movement to my right, behind Drummond. Too late. A huge wooden rack of plates was falling towards us. Drummond went down, buried under it. I took the collateral hit of great china dishes smashing and shattering over and around me in a crescendo of sound. I was knocked flying and lost my grip on my pistol.

I tumbled among the debris with shards cutting into my hands and knees. I couldn't see my gun and expected any moment to get a bullet in my back. I tore myself up from amidst the welter of china and utensils and struggled to my feet. Next thing, I took a huge hammer blow to my shoulder and I went down again. Curly was flailing at me with a shotgun held by the barrel. I rolled before the next strike, wincing as the splintered porcelain and glass sliced my body. I rolled under the kitchen table and staggered to my feet on the far side.

In the glow of the firelight I could see Curly charging round the table towards me, his shotgun held high, still by the barrel, aiming to take my head off. He had to be out of ammo. I looked around and grabbed the first thing that came to hand. I flung a colander filled with steaming greens at his face. He staggered back and I saw the glint on the table. So did Curly. He roared and swung at me, but I moved before he connected. His stock smashed on the table and broke in two. He staggered back and I lunged forward holding the foot-long kitchen knife in my hand. Like a bayonet.

I drove upwards into his stomach and kept going. His eyes widened and his mouth gaped like a fish. I yanked the knife out, feeling his hot blood pulse down my arm. He sank to his knees holding his guts, then keeled over to lie moaning and gasping. Behind me, I heard Drummond cursing as he wrestled his way out from under the rack and the smashed china. There was no sign of Maxwell or his lover. Curly gave a final groan and lost his grip on life. Donne was wrong. This was one man's death that didn't diminish me.

We gathered our weapons and caught our breath. I rinsed my bloody hand in the sink and began reloading. Drummond took his turn at the tap and stuck his head under it. The water again flowed red down the plughole. He rubbed his hair dry with a dish towel and patted his lacerated face. The flesh was weeping and raw. His hands were shaking as the adrenalin ebbed away but his eyes were bright. I'd seen this look many times.

'Is this what it was like, Brodie?'

I shrugged. 'Sometimes. But without the pots and pans.'

Distant shots rang out. From a Dixon. I sprang to the door we'd come through and vaulted over the debris. I skidded down the corridors, heedless of running into Maxwell's guns. I belted up the staircase and ran breathless into the hall.

'Sam! Sam! Are you all right!' I raced across the hall to where I'd left her. I leaned over the table. She was sitting calmly reloading her shotgun. She looked up at me.

'I missed. Sorry.'

I grinned. 'As long as Maxwell did too!'

Then we heard a car start up. Moira's car. Sam jumped to her feet. I grabbed the spare Dixon and sprinted for the door. I got there just as the car shot off in a stir of dust. I lifted my shotgun and fired. I hit the boot. I fired again but it went high over the bouncing roof. The car was revving away from us as fast as it could go. But instead of heading down the drive away from me and back towards the forest, it shot on to the grass and set off across the open field. Towards the hangar.

I turned. Sam and Drummond were skidding across the floor to join me at the torn portals.

'Where are they?' he asked.

'There!' I pointed away across the field at the car, now halfway to the hangar. Sam was clutching her Dixon and inspecting Drummond appraisingly. His face was a mess again, his hair wild, but his eyes held a steadiness that hadn't been present before. It was a pity about his lost years. I could have done something with this man.

'They're not getting away,' he stated as a matter of fact, and started down the steps.

'Come on.' I grabbed Sam's arm and began running after him towards the grass. Drummond paused as he passed the abandoned pile of weapons. He grabbed one of the Stens and kept running. I hoped it was the loaded one.

I was on his heels and, as I ran, I broke open the Dixon and let the spent shells spin away. I grappled in my pocket for cartridges. I slammed in the fresh shells and closed the breech. Far ahead, I saw the car halt and two figures jump out and head into the hangar. A few seconds later came the noise of a stuttering engine. It caught and we heard the propeller chatter up to speed. The nose of the plane emerged and then the rest of the fuselage. Painted red. A Cessna Airmaster. I'd seen them in a display at Prestwick before the war. I couldn't tell what version it was but the engine noise suggested one of the more powerful. A trim little two-seater, it could fly at about 250 miles an hour with a range that would easily get them to France without refuelling. The perfect drug-smuggler's machine. Maxwell was piloting and, alongside him, sat his white-faced lover.

We stumbled and ran over the rough grass towards the fleeing pair. The plane was trundling back past the hangar and then turning round to face into the prevailing westerly. Not that there was much of a breeze. For a moment the small plane sat poised, its wings quivering as the engine vibrations rose. Moira seemed to be shouting at her man to get going. Then he released the brakes. Its speed built up with every bouncing yard.

Like a small flock of starlings we changed tack as one, and started running at right angles to the grass airfield, aiming to intersect with the plane near the end of the runway. The roar of the engine grew. Suddenly the Cessna was in the air and climbing fast. We were about one hundred feet from the last marker on the field. The plane was rising and gathering speed with every yard. It would be past us in ten seconds.

Eight seconds.

Seven.

I halted and lifted the gun to my shoulder. Drummond held his Sten one-handed, above his hip.

Six seconds.

Alongside me, Sam stood already poised, right leg braced behind her, Dixon tucked neatly into her shoulder. Head tilted and aiming along the line of the twin barrels. All three of our bodies were angled to the airfield, our guns slightly aimed to the left, ready for the game birds to be flushed across our sights.

Five seconds.

'Wait for it. Wait!' I called. Our best target would be as the aircraft exposed its entire flank to us.

The plane came into the left corner of our peripheral vision about thirty feet up and climbing, its engine straining for height. Faster than a flushed grouse but a whole lot bigger. I sensed Sam's gun track in unison with mine and pick up the plane. She would do it. I reached over and pushed her arm down.

'No, Sam. Not you.'

She blinked and the trance was broken. I took up my aim again.

Two seconds. The plane came squarely into the left corner of our firing field, reaching higher and higher into the air. I tracked it with a steady swing of my gun.

'Just like a clay shoot, Douglas. *Squeeze, don't jerk. Keep it smooth,*' she said in a calm echo of her father.

Drummond waved his Sten hopefully in the general direction of the plane. We were so close that Maxwell's face was now perfectly visible through the screen. It was contorted with fury. He was screaming and cursing at us. I focused on the cowling and propeller.

'Fire!'

I squeezed and took the recoil. Drummond's Sten joined in with a rapid stutter. I saw my shot blast a fist-sized hole in the engine casing. Amazingly, a line of dots appeared in a rough zigzag alongside. Drummond raked away. The plane kept climbing and was now in the right of my field. Drummond fired again and perforated the tail.

Sam's voice sounded gently in my ear. 'Again. Steady. Squeeze.'

I pulled again. Another hole in the engine casing. Nearer the propeller. A shudder from the nose? Neither Drummond nor I had time to reload. I started regretting being chivalrous with Sam.

We could only watch as the red fuselage sailed above the trees and kept climbing. But the engine noise was different. A black plume flared from the nose. The engine stuttered, picked up, and then continued.

The craft held its height for a while, about two hundred feet above the treetops, aiming for the pass between Ben Uird and Ben Lomond that Sam and I had climbed earlier. The pilot seemed to realise he wasn't going to have enough height, and swung the stick over. The plane dipped its wings to the right and heeled over. The engine coughed, and then cut out completely. The plane had become a glider. But without its power and with no altitude to work with, it couldn't manoeuvre. We watched as it swung further right in silent slow motion.

Sam had her hand to her mouth.

Slowly, inexorably, the small red craft banked and banked and finally dived into the flank of Ben Lomond. It cartwheeled; bits flew off, then the fuel tank burst into flame. A moment later the sound of its passing echoed down the mountain.

I put my arm round Sam and held her close. We watched the wreckage until the flames died out. We looked at each other. Her eyes were glistening. I gave her a big hug. She squeezed my hand.

'That'll annoy the tourist board. Come on. Wullie needs us.'

I released her, broke the Dixon and ejected the spent shells. Drummond fell in alongside us. We trudged back to the castle and the mayhem.

FIFTY-EIGHT

The three of us walked through the carnage, double-checking for signs of life. There was none. But at least there was no barbed wire for the fallen Marshals this time. Drummond was drained, his face old and pained, as he knelt by each of his men. I knew exactly how he was feeling. An experience I'd known too often.

I said quietly, 'The police are on their way, Drummond.'

He looked up at me and nodded. 'Will you help me get my men on the truck?'

'To do what?'

'Bury them, of course. They're my men.'

'Where? In the forest? They deserve better. Leave them with me. I'll see they're taken care of. I'll have a word with Jamie Frew, the police doctor.'

He stared at me with his one open eye, the other clouded with congealed blood. 'And I just slope off?'

'*You* surrender. You face the law.'

'Oh, that's a fine plan! They'll stretch my neck. Either for this' – he swept his hand round the blood-stained forecourt – 'or the homo killings.'

I glanced over at Sam. She shrugged in agreement.

'So what'll you do?'

He looked beyond me at the towering hills. He grinned. 'Take to the heather.' Then his grin shut off. 'Will you tell them?'

'That you're at large?'

He nodded.

'That depends. Is this over? Your search for justice, redemption, whatever it was?'

'You make it sound like I went a bit doolally for a while and now I'm better. It was more than that. It needed doing. It still does. The law stinks.'

'The law's OK. Enforcing it is the problem. But it's not *your* problem.'

'Is it yours, Brodie? It needs to be somebody's.'

'I'm just a reporter.'

He looked around. 'Oh aye?' He shrugged. 'But yes. It's over for me. Enough blood. And you'll take care of them?'

I straightened my back. 'From one brother officer to another.'

He held my gaze, then he walked over to the small pile of arms still lying in the gravel. He swapped his Sten for a shotgun and filled his pockets with cartridges. He loaded both revolvers and tucked them into his waistband. He turned, nodded once to Sam and me, and marched off towards the north, his shotgun at the ready, his shoulders back.

Sam and I climbed the front steps and stepped through the shattered doors. A man was waiting for us, standing tall in a kilt and jacket in front of the intruding truck. He stared at the guns broken across our arms, then beyond us to the bodies lying on the drive. He didn't seem panicked.

'Sir?' he asked.

'What's your name?'

'McGregor, sir. Is that you, Miss Campbell?'

'Yes,' she said. 'Hello, Andrew.'

'Army, McGregor?'

'Gordon Highlanders, sir. Sergeant.'

'Good man. We need a hand. But first, how's Sir Colin? Is he with you?'

'He's fine, thank you, sir. I have him in the library. Away from the noise. He thinks we've had a shooting party. Asking how many were bagged.'

We both looked back at the 'bag' and did our own short sums.

'Look, first thing. Where's the nearest ambulance station?'

'That would be Aberfoyle, sir.'

'Call one. We need it fast. I don't suppose you have a stretcher?'

'Yes, sir. In case of accidents on the estate.'

'Bring it to the stables. Bring any first-aid box you have. Any other staff?'

'A boy, two chambermaids, and the kitchen staff.'

'Is he a good boy? Tough?'

'He's my son.'

'Have him bring out some old sheets. If you think he can face it, have him cover the bodies. I'll leave it to you, McGregor.'

'He's fourteen. He'll be fine.'

We lifted McAllister on to the canvas stretcher and McGregor and I carried him into the house. I had more time to admire the scenery. Sam hadn't understated the baronial trappings. A vast echoing space, walls filled with the bloody detritus of battles and hunts. It seemed fitting. Sam emerged from the library, shaking her head.

'Colin seems to be coming and going. At the moment he doesn't know what day of the week it is, far less what's been happening. Best to leave him alone. His nurse is sitting with him.'

'A nurse? Get her. Wullie has more urgent need of her.'

We carried him into a side room, a pretty lounge, and laid him on cushions dragged from chairs and couches. He moaned as we laid him down. The nurse bustled in and knelt to feel his pulse.

'He's in a bad way,' she said superfluously.

McGregor said, 'An ambulance is on its way. It'll take a good hour, mind.'

'We need to elevate his head. Help me.'

Sam and I stood back and watched her administer first aid. I looked round the room and walked over to the drinks table. I poured two large measures and gave Sam one. She shook her head at first, then accepted. We clinked glasses, nodded at each other and drank. Suddenly I was starving.

'McGregor? Can you get your cook to rustle up a sandwich?'

'Of course, sir, and for you, miss?'

'God, yes, Andrew! I could eat a horse.'

'I think we have some ham, ma'am.'

Then I remembered. 'Oh blast. McGregor, hang on. There was a bit of ding dong in the kitchen, and . . .'

'I saw, sir. What would you like us to do?'

I was thinking fast. I turned to Sam. 'I think we probably ought to minimise our involvement in this business, don't you?' I said.

'How minimum?'

I walked over to where we'd stood the Dixons, picked them up and placed them discreetly in the corner of the room behind a curtain. Sam's eyebrow rose.

'We got here and found the battle was over?' she asked.

'There are two sides out there. Both armed. No witnesses. McGregor?'

He'd had been standing by the shattered window. He turned. 'I kept my head down, sir. Had to watch out for the other staff. I saw nothing.'

'Thank you, McGregor.'

'But between you and me, sir, we'll shed no tears for those thugs of the young master. On which topic, sir, the man in the kitchen?'

'Perhaps he should lie with the others?' I nodded through the broken window.

McGregor caught the drift and we both went down to the kitchen carrying the stretcher. A little later we emerged with Curly between us, a bloodied sheet covering his body. We took him outside and set him down next to one of Drummond's dead men. I picked up the stained kitchen knife resting on

345

Curly's chest, using the cloth I'd found in the kitchen. Holding the blade, I positioned the knife near the empty hand of the nearest prone Marshal and wrapped his dead fingers round the hilt. McGregor and I then tipped Curly out into the dust to lie alongside.

It could have happened just like this.

Sam and I were tucking into thick layers of ham and mustard when we heard the clanking of fast-approaching squad cars. Two of them, by the sound.

Sam turned to me. 'What about Moira and Charlie?'

'As in Charlie, the careless pilot? There isn't much left of the plane. The fuel tank went up. Must have kept it full.'

'Cartridge cases?'

'Place is littered with them. All standard issue. Besides, if you were the police officer in charge of hunting down the Glasgow Marshals and following up murder inquiries involving some of Slattery's old gang, what would be your reaction on finding all that out there?'

'Go down on my knees and say a few thank yous to the great Chief Constable in the sky?'

'Exactly. Shall we say hello?'

Sangster and Duncan Todd got out of the first and second cars respectively and commanded the bells to be stilled. Duncan was in his usual shabby suit, Sangster in full uniform, with Sergeant Murdoch skipping at his side. Behind them and spreading out with drawn pistols were four constables. We were waiting on the steps. They walked towards us and stopped in the midst of the draped bodies and the scattered armaments. They looked round. Then they looked up at the great doors and behind us to the truck parked in the hall. A gust of wind blew a curtain out through the broken window.

Sangster was the first to break the spell. 'Mary Mother of God!'

Duncan was looking at me strangely. 'We got your call,

Brodie. But looks like we were too late. Who's under the sheets? Anyone we know?'

'Four are Maxwell's men including two of the old Slattery gang. The other four are – *were* – the blokes who called themselves the Marshals.'

'Well, that's tidy, isn't it?' said Sangster. 'A shoot-out?'

'Looks like it.'

'You just found them like this?'

'Well, we covered them. It's a warm day.'

'Any of them a Maxwell?' Sangster looked as if he didn't want to hear an affirmative. It was always harder work when one of the landed gentry was murdered.

'No.'

'So, where are the Maxwells themselves?' asked Duncan.

I nodded at the castle. 'Sir Colin is in there. In the library. Charles Maxwell is up there.' I nodded towards Ben Lomond.

'What do you mean, up there? Up where?' asked Sangster.

I pointed. 'On the hillside. Do you see that wee bit of smoke? And the red bits of wreckage around it? That's Charlie Maxwell's plane. An accident. You'll find him in it. Or near it. Along with a friend of his. Moira, Lady Rankin.'

'Oh Christ,' said Duncan softly. Sangster looked as if he was about to choke. I was surprised they were taking this news so badly. Then Duncan explained, softly.

'Brodie? Do ye ken who's in the back o' that car?'

FIFTY-NINE

Oh Christ, indeed. Sam, beside me, said, 'Oh no. Bugger, bugger.' As she spoke, a uniformed officer was opening the rear door of the squad car and helping the long figure of Sir Kenneth Rankin out. He got to his feet and with an effort straightened his back. He pulled his jacket down and smoothed his tie. Once he had his balance, he started to walk over to us. His face was older and greyer than I'd seen it. He tried to march over to us, but his legs were stiff. I watched his face, saw the effort being made, and pitied the man. He stamped over to us and nodded, his face set.

'Samantha, Brodie. This is a fine mess. A fine mess. Seems I owe you an apology, Brodie.'

'There's no need, sir.'

'Yes, there is. Is one of these my girl?' His jaw was muscled tight with tension.

'No, Kenny. Moira isn't lying here.' Sam walked over to him and took the old man's arm. She looked up at him. The tears were rolling unchecked down her flushed face.

Rankin was looking down at her, swallowing hard. 'It's all right, Samantha. Where is she then? Is she with *him*?'

Sam nodded, weeping. 'She's up there, Kenny. Their plane crashed.' She turned to Ben Lomond, pointed out the wreckage. Rankin said nothing, just put his arm round Sam and held her to him, like a father protecting his child.

I said gently, 'Sam? Why don't you take Sir Kenneth inside. See Colin. Get him a drink.'

She nodded and took the big man's arm and led him past us. He didn't look distraught. Just puzzled.

I then squared up to Sangster. Sam had joined us and we were sitting in the drawing room where we'd tended McAllister. Hercule Poirot was pacing up and down. Duncan Todd and Sergeant Murdoch were both taking notes. Duncan had just come back in having phoned for a couple of vans to pick up the bodies.

Sangster stopped his pacing. 'We need statements, Brodie. From you and Miss Campbell. *Detailed* statements.'

'There's nothing we can tell you that any of the staff here can't tell you.'

'You saw *nothing* till you arrived and found – a' this?' Sangster was at his most sceptical. 'Eight bodies! Not counting the two on the top of Ben Lomond? Ten dead bodies.'

'Send for Agatha Christie.'

Sangster glared at me. 'How did you get here?'

'We walked. Up and over from Loch Lomond.'

Sangster was chewing his lip as though he was starving. 'Why? Why did you decide to take a wee walk over that bloody mountain to here, arriving just after a shoot-out worse than anything in Dodge City?'

'Miss Campbell and I are on a walking holiday for a few days. I phoned the *Gazette* this morning – as Sergeant Todd knows. They told me they'd been invaded by the Marshals. I put two and two together and we decided to warn you and our friends the Maxwells.'

'Your friends? You're now pally with Sir Colin Maxwell, Brodie?'

'Miss Campbell is a long-time family friend.'

'You could have phoned.'

'We fancied the walk.'

'But what made you think the Marshals were coming here? And more to the point, why?'

'I told you, Sangster, Charles Maxwell had hired two of Slattery's gang. They're lying outside.'

'Why would he do that?'

'A good question.' We now knew the answer, but if I told Sangster that Maxwell had confessed to being a drug runner for Slattery we'd be here all day. It would also mean that we'd got here before the shooting started, which would be tough to explain. And unless they found some bags of cocaine or heroin in the wreckage on Ben Lomond, there would be no proof of Maxwell's illicit flights.

I shrugged. 'We think Maxwell put out the word that he needed some hard men for hire. Enforcers to cover his machinations on the regeneration contracts. The Slattery boys were looking for a job. A match made in heaven.'

'Hell,' muttered Sam.

'They lived up to their billing. The way Alec Morton was murdered is typical of Slattery-trained sadists. We were pretty certain the pair were also behind the murders of the three homosexuals. We'll never know if they were ordered to commit these murders by Maxwell or whether their natural exuberance went unchecked. But two of the dead men were council clerks dealing with Jimmie Sheridan's dodgy contracts. Which led in turn to the murder of Jimmie and his lady friend. Sheridan had become an embarrassment by flaunting his new-found wealth. We don't know about Morton, but the clear link from Sheridan through the dead homosexuals to the Slattery boys was chloroform. Ask Jamie Frew. Something Miss Campbell has painful, personal experience of.'

'Aye, right. I've already had a wee chat with Dr Frew. Are you getting a' this, you two?'

Murdoch and Duncan nodded. 'Yes, sir. Every word,' they chorused. Duncan had a slightly amazed look about him, as though every word he was taking down seemed like a fairy tale.

Sangster was about to press on when he was interrupted by the sound of a van racing up the drive. We all cocked our ears. I got up and looked out.

'The ambulance. We'll need to see to McAllister.'

I left the room with Sam and walked down the front steps. The two-man crew had got out and were standing frozen, wondering where to start. I walked over.

'These are not for you, boys' – pointing to the sheeted bodies – 'they're beyond your help. But there's a man inside needing you.'

They got Wullie into the back of the ambulance and hooked him up to a saline drip to try to relieve the shock. He was still unconscious. Sam and I debated going with him, but, in the end, decided there was nothing we could do. I phoned the *Gazette* and asked them to send a telegram boy round to his brother Stewart to tell him that at least Wullie was alive, and to expect him at Glasgow Royal Infirmary in two or three hours. I also took the chance to leave a similar message for Morag about me. I ignored pleas to talk to Sandy Logan. Sandy was running things and wanted a report. There would be time enough. We went back in to face Sangster.

'Right, whit aboot McAllister? How did he get here? And how did you know he was here?'

'He was abducted by Maxwell's men. Wullie got too close to the corruption behind the regeneration project. They got hold of him to find out how much he knew. And how much he'd told others. Like me. As to his being here . . . I didn't *know* he was. It's just luck we found him. Let's hope it's not too late.'

'But it's all so bloody *tenuous*, Brodie. All circumstantial. All bloody flim-flam! How the hell am I going to make all this add up without actual solid proof of anything? I mean, whit the hell am Ah going to say to the Chief Constable?'

'Can I suggest something, Sangster?'

'Oh, please do.'

'You and Duncan here – and Murdoch, if his spelling is up to it – can earn yourself a citation or two if you stick to the story I've just given you. You've just solved two cases that have been causing your boss grief. The Marshals are dead and the chloroform-killers of the homosexuals are dead.'

351

There was a dawning look of hope in Sangster's ragged face.

'But what about Sheridan and his burd? Can we *prove* it was murder by Maxwell's men?'

'You don't have to. Your first thoughts were suicide. Maybe you were right all along?'

Sangster was nodding now. He was listening to me as though I was Scheherazade. Duncan was looking on in wonder and trying not to let the corners of his mouth turn up in a smile.

'Aye, aye. Ah suppose you're right. We don't need to try to stitch everything thegither, do we?' Then his brow wrinkled again. 'But what about Maxwell and Lady Rankin?'

'A tragic aircraft accident?

'That's an awfu' lot of mishaps and coincidences, Brodie. What about a' they bodies outside? You can hardly claim there were eight simultaneous shooting accidents. What were the Marshals *doing* here, for God's sake?'

'It's complicated.'

'You think?' asked Duncan, scribbling away.

'Wheesht, Sergeant. Go on, Brodie.'

'The Marshals were in the frame for the homo murders. They attacked the *Gazette* this morning and beat up my boss to find out what he knew. I'd already told Eddie Paton my suspicions about the Maxwells. The Marshals decided to pay a visit to persuade Maxwell and his hoodlums to own up to the killings. A pretty unlikely outcome. It looks like the discussion got a bit heated.'

'You don't say,' said Sangster.

There was the sound of motor vehicles driving up.

'That'll be the wagons for the bodies, sir,' said Duncan. 'Are we finished with the crime scene, sir?'

'Finished? God, we huvnae even started!'

We all sat watching as Sangster's brain sifted through my explanation.

'Do ye really think the Chief will swallow it?' he asked me.

'Your boss is up to his neck in bad publicity. The Marshals running riot but cutting crime rates instead of the police. Chloroform-killers murdering homosexuals. One prominent politician dead in a concrete bucket. Another one and his fancy woman drowned in suspicious circumstances. At a stroke you've solved all his problems.' I shrugged. 'Besides, it's what I'll write in the *Gazette*.'

All four of them – Sam, Sangster, Duncan and Murdoch – stared at me.

'Wait here, Brodie. Just wait here. I need to call the Chief.' He turned to McGregor, who was standing quietly by. 'Where's your phone?'

He was a long time. When he came back he was chewing at his lip. No wonder it was so thin. He looked at me for a while as though wondering whether to arrest me or clasp me to his bosom.

'He wants to speak with you, Brodie.'

The phone was in the small side room on the other side of the crashed truck. I closed the door, lit a fag and lifted the receiver.

'Brodie here.'

'Douglas Brodie?' I recognised the radio voice.

'Chief Constable McCulloch, how can I help you?'

He told me.

SIXTY

While Sangster was rounding up his troops, Sam spent a while with Kenny Rankin in one of the other rooms. She'd be telling him that a team from Glasgow would be sent out in the morning to retrieve the bodies from the burnt-out wreckage on the mountainside. She would also be saying that the paper would refer to a tragic accident and nothing else. A courtesy to Rankin. It was more than Moira and Charlie deserved.

Sam had also found Sir Colin Maxwell having a lucid moment.

'I told him Charlie had gone away for a while. He asked me if he'd gone off with Moira. He knew about them. He was ashamed and was talking about how he'd have to break it to Kenny. I said Kenny knew.'

'Did he mention anything about the regeneration contracts?'

'Just that Charlie had been getting through money like water. Seems Inverard is mortgaged up to its parapets. And Charlie had big plans that Colin didn't understand. I didn't press him, but I'm sure he knew nothing about the drug-running.'

'Does that mean Charlie was acting solo? That Kenny Rankin and Tom Fowler on his Barbados plantation are wee innocent lambs?'

'You should ask the council to review their contract paper-work. That'll show how things were being carved out.'

'It's a start. But we'll probably never be able to pin anything on anyone.'

We came out into the hall. McGregor was enlisting the help of the uniforms to push the truck out through the gaping doors. It bounced off down the steps and settled in the driveway, to continue to puddle away its black life in the gravel. The courtyard had been cleared of bodies. The two black vans with their sad cargoes sat waiting for the off by the stable block. I'd walked among the dead and separated the sheep from the goats. In the first van were the Marshals. I told the ambulance men that when Jamie Frew was finished with their post-mortems, he should give me a call and we'd arrange for a decent burial. I didn't care what they did with the second load.

McGregor came back in, tutting at the mess. He rounded up the household and broke out the mops. His son was already kneeling by the hinges of the big doors with a screwdriver.

Sangster was reluctant to go but his brain had seized as solid as the truck's engine. He had so many more questions to ask me that he didn't know where to start. I compromised with him by agreeing to spend more time at Albany Street in the coming days, if needed. I certainly expected to hear from Duncan, if only to have a pint or three with him and a good laugh, and to find out if his career had been resuscitated or killed off for good.

Finally the unlucky convoy sailed off, leaving a dust pall behind them in the lazy afternoon light. They took with them Kenny Rankin, who had drawn into himself, and was now silent.

Sam and I stood on the steps watching them drive away. We gazed down on the abandoned truck and the several dark patches left on the ground. I looked at my watch.

'It's six thirty. It'll be dark in an hour. Do we have time to get over the hill? Are you up for night manoeuvres?'

Sam looked around. The evening was clear and sharp. A

full moon was already faint against the deepening blue. 'It'll be like daylight up there in these conditions.'

'What about the ferry?'

'There's a lantern kept at Rowardennan by the jetty. He'll come if we signal. We'll have to pay him double, mind.'

'You've done this before, then?'

'Not me. But my parents said they did once. They came over, like us, for a day with Colin and Clarinda. They made it sound magical. Up there under the moon.' Her eyes were shining.

'Well then, let's follow in their footsteps, shall we?'

We brushed aside McGregor's protests about putting us up for the night. Too many new ghosts.

We retrieved our Dixons and knapsacks and set off into the gathering twilight. We ploughed into the semi-darkness and chill of the forest at the foot of the hills. It seemed like a game, a child's adventure. We didn't talk, just grinned at each other as we flushed out pheasants and one lone deer that went crashing through the undergrowth. Then silence fell again. It was like being in a leafy cathedral just before evensong.

We broke out on the lower slopes leading up to Ben Uird. We were suddenly closer, much closer to the plane wreckage. We stopped and looked across at the scattered red fuselage. The cockpit was rammed head-first into the ground, its nose squashed flat against the rocks. There was no sign of life.

'I would have fired, you know.'

'I know you would, Sam.'

'She deserved it.'

'Maybe. But I already own a bad conscience. A few more sins won't weigh me down.'

She reached out and took my hand, and searched my face. 'I'm not so sure, Douglas Brodie. But thank you. Thank you.'

'Do you want to see it?' I asked, meaning *them*. Meaning *her*.

Sam shook her head. 'No, they're dead. There's nothing to be done for them, except try to remember the good bits. Moira had good bits. Or so I thought. She just got greedy. For money, for life. Charlie was rotten from the start.'

We pressed on, our legs beginning to protest at this second tough excursion of the day. The moonlight was much stronger. Like daylight through a grey-tone filter. The giant gilt orb hovered to our left now and was rising strongly. For a while it seemed as though we'd climb to within touching distance of its pitted surface. We stopped near the summit and looked back. The castle was surrounded by tendrils of autumn mists seeping from the river. If we came back in the morning it would surely have been consumed entirely, as if it had never been.

She asked breezily, 'What did the Chief Constable want?'

I laughed. 'Me.'

'Just your hide or the whole thing?'

'A job. Detective inspector.'

'Ha!'

'What does *ha* mean?'

'It means I'm not surprised.'

I stopped and made her turn to me. 'Why, for God's sake? You know what I think about the sleaze and incompetence in the force. What on earth would make me go back? And why would they want me?'

'They want you because they need you. You'd do it because it's what you're good at.' She held my gaze, daring me to contradict her. 'What did you tell him?'

'I said no. He offered me chief inspector.'

'Not bad. Enough?'

'I said it wasn't about the rank, but if it was, I was used to having a crown on my shoulder.'

She whistled. 'Superintendent? But if it's not about the rank, what is it about, Douglas? You know you're wasted as a reporter.'

'You really don't make it easy for a man to live a life of peace.'

'"Blessed are the peacemakers." Depends how you do it.'

'I said I wouldn't fit. That the Sangsters would hate me. Besides, I wasn't a Mason.'

'What did he say?'

'He said he'd find a way round it. Maybe report straight to him.'

'Tempting?'

'Eddie and Wullie are both in hospital. I'm needed at the paper.'

I turned and started up the hillside again. I didn't want to talk about it any more. We suffered two false summits before finally reaching the top. Too symbolic for words.

We stood, chests heaving from the last climb, and gazed around us. It was a different world from the one we left this afternoon. Laid out before us was a palette of lustrous grey and black. We could see clearly right to the distant horizon and the last bars of light like the gateway to a promised land. The folds and bumps rolled away on every side, cut and slashed by pewter rivers and lochs. The great loch itself was riven by moonlight. A shimmering bar of molten silver fled down its length from Balloch in the south on up to the far north. A tantalising highway that beckoned travellers. If only they dared.

Without speaking, we sat on a rock left by the last ice age and I pulled out my cigarettes. I lit two and we watched the light march across the land in hues of grey and silver. We let our eyes be greedy, gobbling up the drama of it all. And I had a sudden clear understanding of our own unimportance.

'It puts it in context, doesn't it?' I suggested.

'A midsummer's night dream.'

'Nightmare.'

'But it's over, Douglas. Isn't it over now?'

'Yes. I think it is.'

'Even Drummond?'

'He was heading north. Maybe he'll get his old job back with the Inverness police. Maybe he'll become the wild man of the glens. I suspect we'll hear one way or the other.'

The evening air floated up around us carrying the latent smells of the day.

'Those tales you gave Sangster. Will they hold?'

'Why not? It's mostly true. And convenient. For everybody.'

'Even Kenny and Colin. Between them, Moira and Charlie would have driven both old men into the poorhouse. Kenny was running out of money. Moira couldn't bear the idea. That and Helensburgh. Charlie promised her London and Paris. Poor Moira. Chose the wrong horse. The Maxwells were in worse straits than Kenny.'

'And ready to kill to get their hands on the contracts.'

'Charlie at least. After you stopped his flow of drug money from the Slatterys!'

'Ripples, eh?'

'Will you write about that?'

I shook my head. 'I don't think we can prove anything. Besides, what's the point? There's no one left to accuse. As you say, just two old men. I've got enough for a column or two. Enough for a whole paper.' It brought our thoughts round to the same thing.

'I hope Wullie's all right,' she said.

'It's not looking good.'

'Poor Stewart.' She said it carefully.

I looked at her. She returned my unspoken question with a raised brow. I turned to look down at the glittering loch.

'You know?' I asked.

'That they're not brothers? Yes. That was obvious.'

I nodded. 'It took me a while to ask myself how Wullie was always first with news about the queer killings.'

'You think he knew them? Personally?'

'It's probably how he got the first inkling of the goings-on in the council planning office. Maybe he met one of the dead clerks at the Monkey Club. Maybe at one of the other haunts.'

'It must be hard.'

'Living a lie? Yes, I expect so. No one should have to.'

We sat for a while longer, unwilling to move, even though the temperature was falling. We drew closer for warmth and shared another cigarette. It was like sitting in a pot pourri. The air rushed up the slopes at us, bringing a mix of smells: dry heather, the bitter tang of deep water, of earth giving up its heat, tobacco, rough tweed and her own scent.

'Sam? Samantha? About us . . .'

'Wheesht, Douglas. Don't break the spell.'

Thanks

Big thanks to: Bill Mann, Honorary Secretary and saviour of the splendid Western Baths Club of Glasgow; John Bell, of the Iona Community, for his eclectic insights and knowledge; Richenda Todd, my all-seeing editor; Nic Cheetham for opening wide this door; Becci Sharpe and Fran Owen in Team Corvus for getting the message out; James Hanley, for reviewing first drafts and for unstinted encouragement; Tina Betts, my agent, for limitless faith. And Sarah Ferris, unpaid marketing director, principal reviewer, chief supporter and helpmeet.